About the Author

After graduating with degrees in history and political science, **Eva Shepherd** worked in journalism and as an advertising copywriter. She began writing historical romances because it combined her love of a happy ending with her passion for history. She lives in Christchurch, New Zealand, but spends her days immersed in the world of Victorian England. Eva loves hearing from readers and can be reached via her website evashepherd.com and her Facebook page Facebook.com/evashepherdromancewriter

Regency Secrets

Regency Secrets:

Breaking the Marriage Rules

EVA SHEPHERD

MILLS & BOON

First Published in Great Britain 2022
By Mills & Boon, an imprint of HarperCollins*Publishers*
1 London Bridge Street, London, SE1 9GF

www.harpercollins.co.uk

HarperCollins*Publishers*
1st Floor, Watermarque Building,
Ringsend Road, Dublin 4, Ireland

REGENCY SECRETS: BREAKING THE MARRIAGE RULES
© 2022 Harlequin Enterprises ULC.

Beguiling the Duke © 2019 Eva Shepherd
Awakening the Duchess © 2020 Eva Shepherd

ISBN: 978-0-263-31797-8

MIX
Paper | Supporting
responsible forestry
FSC™ C007454

This book is produced from independently certified FSC™ paper to ensure responsible forest management.

For more information visit: www.harpercollins.co.uk/green

Printed and Bound in Spain using 100% Renewable electricity at CPI Black Print, Barcelona

BEGUILING
THE DUKE

To Julia Williams, Bryony Green and the editorial team at Mills & Boon, for their support, guidance and encouragement.

Chapter One

London 1893

Rosie Smith raised the delicate bone china cup to her lips, took a sip of the fragrant Darjeeling tea and sighed with contentment.

Despite being a penniless orphan, with no prospects worth mentioning, here she was, dressed in the latest fashion, taking tea at the Ritz, surrounded by Britain's elite.

Her feet, encased in soft kid leather boots, were aching after spending all day walking around the shops and sights of London. She was still tired from the gruelling trip across the Atlantic from New York. And yet she couldn't be happier.

She sighed again and looked across the lace-covered table at her friend, who was smiling with equal contentment.

'What shall we do tomorrow?' Rosie took a cucumber sandwich from the top layer of the three-tiered cake stand and placed it on her rose-patterned plate. 'More shopping? Or shall we take in some art galleries and museums?'

'Art galleries and museums, I think.' Arabella placed a scone on her plate and smothered it with jam and clotted cream. 'After all, I'm sure Father would want us to absorb as much culture as we can while we're in England.'

The two girls giggled conspiratorially.

Rosie lifted a finger and waggled it in Arabella's direction. '"What good is art, my dear? You don't get a decent return on sculptures. Nobody ever got rich from culture."'

Arabella clapped her hands and laughed loudly. 'You do such a brilliant impersonation of Father. It's you who should be on the stage, Rosie, not me.'

Their jubilation drew the attention of the women sitting at the next table, who glared down their imperious noses with looks that might have withered the spring buds on the tree. Rosie was tempted to poke out her tongue. Instead she lifted her head and returned their looks of disapproval. Although she suspected being glared at down a small button nose wouldn't have quite the same impact.

'Humourless old biddies,' she whispered. 'Have they never heard anyone laugh before?' She smiled at Arabella. 'So, tomorrow it's art galleries and museums—perfect.'

The two girls sipped their tea and sighed simultaneously.

A waiter approached the table and bowed low. Arabella smiled her thanks, removed the folded letter from his silver tray and read its contents. Her smile dissolved. Her hand shot to her mouth and her shoulders slumped.

'What is it? What's wrong, Bella?' Rosie reached across the table and touched her friend's arm.

Arabella's hands trembled as she passed her the letter. Rosie quickly scanned the elegant handwriting. It was an invitation from the Dowager Duchess of Knightsbrook, inviting Arabella to a weekend party at her estate in Devon.

'Oh, this is too, *too* terrible, Rosie.' Arabella took a lace handkerchief from her embroidered clutch purse and dabbed at her eyes. 'It's from the mother of that horrid man Father expects me to marry.'

'It's disgusting!' Rosie threw the letter down on the table. 'They think they can buy you. That all they have to do is dangle a title and you'll come running, and then they can get their greedy hands on your father's money. Disgusting!'

'I know… I know. I don't want to go. And I especially don't want to go that weekend. It means I'll miss the opening night of Oscar Wilde's play. I'll miss the opportunity to meet the great man himself.'

'Then don't go.' Rosie thumped the table, making the teacups jump and rattle in their saucers. 'You can't possibly miss the opening of that play. That's one of the main reasons we came to England.'

Her raised voice drew another scowl from the next table. This time Rosie didn't hold back. She screwed up her face, poked out her tongue and let the women know just what she thought of their disapproving looks.

Their gasps and bulging stares would have made Rosie laugh if she had felt like laughing.

Arabella lowered her handkerchief. 'Well, no…the main reason we're here is because Father wants to marry me off after that…' She tilted her head and lightly bit her upper lip. 'After that scandal.'

'Scandal? That was no scandal. Your appearance on the New York stage as Lady Macbeth was a triumph and should be celebrated as such. Your father just doesn't understand your passion for acting.'

Arabella sent her friend a shaky smile. 'Thank you, Rosie. But I'll still have to go, Father will never forgive me otherwise.

'And I'd never forgive myself if you missed that play. There *has* to be a way out of this.'

Rosie drummed her fingers on the table and looked around the room for inspiration. There had to be a way out of this dilemma; there was always a way out of every problem.

'I'll go instead.' She smiled in triumph.

Arabella twisted her handkerchief in her lap. 'You'll what?'

'I'll go in your place. The Dowager and the Duke have never met me. If I tell them I'm Arabella van Haven how will they ever know the difference? We've both got black hair and blue eyes, and everyone always says we look like sisters. They'll see a fashionably dressed young woman, and all they'll be thinking about is getting their hands on your father's money. They'll never suspect I'm not you.'

'Oh, Rosie, you can't... Can you?'

'Of course I can.'

Arabella screwed her handkerchief into a tighter ball. 'But, Rosie, you might get caught.'

'Nonsense. It's a perfect plan. And when has one of my plans ever gone wrong?'

Arabella frowned in concentration. 'Well, there was that time you said Cook wouldn't notice the missing cakes if we moved those remaining around the pantry. And there was the time you said that if we dressed as boys and went to the local fair we'd be able to get work on the sideshows. And then there was that time you were certain that if we told our tutor we knew everything there was to know about—'

Rosie held up her hand to stop the flow of words. 'Those were mere childish pranks. This time it's serious—and, really, what choice do we have? You don't want to go to this party, do you?'

Arabella shook her head.

'You don't want to miss the play's opening, do you? You don't want to marry this Duke, do you? You don't want to end up living out in the countryside, miles away from the nearest theatre, do you?'

Arabella shook her head more emphatically.

'Right, then leave it to me. You said it yourself. I'm almost as good an actress as you.' She stabbed her finger at the abandoned letter. 'This horrid Duke of Knightsbrook will be completely fooled.'

'Well, I suppose you *could* pretend to be me...' Arabella chewed her lip again, as if not wholly convinced.

'Of course I can. And I'll have fun doing it. This stuffy Duke will think he's wooing the wealthy, beautiful Arabella van Haven. Instead he'll be wasting his energies pursuing a penniless, plain, charmless ward. And it will serve him right.'

'You might be penniless, Rosie, but no one could ever describe you as plain or charmless. You're beautiful, kind, funny and the best friend I could ever—'

Rosie held up her hand again, to stop Arabella's praises. 'Whether that's true or not, I can't say—but I certainly won't be appearing charming in front of the Duke. After all, it might be your father's wish that you marry a titled man, but that's not what *you* want, is it?'

Arabella straightened her spine. 'It certainly is not.'

'So I'm going to have to convince this stuffy Duke that

the last thing he wants to do is marry the appallingly behaved and completely unacceptable Arabella van Haven,
despite her father's fortune.'

Arabella smiled and placed her handkerchief back in
her purse. 'You're so clever, Rosie.' She paused, her purse
half closed. 'Except...'

'Except what?'

'I've just thought of a big flaw in your plan. Aunt
Prudence was going to accompany me as my chaperon.'

Rosie rolled her eyes. 'Aunt Prudence is too sick to
go anywhere. Or at least she thinks she is. I suspect she
won't be over her imagined seasickness until it's time to
go back to New York.'

Arabella covered her mouth to stifle a giggle. 'Poor
Aunt Prudence—she *is* a bit of a hypochondriac. But
you can't go without a chaperon. They'd get suspicious
if a young unmarried woman of twenty arrived at their
estate unaccompanied.'

Rosie would not be deterred. 'Then I'll take Nellie.
I'll need a lady's maid anyway, and Nellie enjoys a good
caper as much as we do. When I tell her we're doing it
so we can make sport of a family of greedy aristocrats
there'll be no stopping her. Nellie will be the perfect
chaperon.'

'This is *so* good of you, Rosie. You're always so kind
to me.'

Rosie waved her hand in front of her face to dismiss
the compliment. Arabella's happiness meant everything
to her.

Rosie drew in a deep breath and ran her hand down the
soft pink silk of her stylish gown. Arabella had saved her
from a life of poverty and loneliness. Without her, Rosie
couldn't imagine how hard her life might have been. She

closed her eyes and shuddered. But she was not alone any more. Thanks to Arabella she had not been forced to try and survive on the streets of New York with no money and without a friend.

There was nothing she wouldn't do for the friend who had saved her from such a life. And she hated to see Arabella sad.

Her friend had been so kind to her, had always treated her as an equal, and she had such little happiness in her life. Rosie saw it as her job to keep her friend happy, so she might be distracted from the neglect she felt over her father's constant absences.

Spending the weekend with a stuffy aristocratic family to save her from an unwanted marriage was nothing compared to the enormous debt she owed her friend. And at least poverty had one compensation. While Arabella's father was determined to marry her off to a titled man for his own social advancement, he had no such concerns when it came to Rosie. Nobody, including Rosie herself, expected anyone to want to marry a penniless orphan who didn't even own the clothes she was wearing.

She smiled and pushed away her unpleasant thoughts. What was the point of dwelling on such things? Today was all that mattered. Having fun was all that mattered. Not what had happened in the past, and not what the future might bring.

'Honestly, Bella. I want to do this. I'll get to have fun putting a stuffy duke in his place, and you'll get to see the play. And when I return I'll be able to regale you with tales of my exploits. It's perfect.'

Rosie smiled. She picked up a smoked salmon sandwich and placed it on her plate.

'Oh, yes, the Duke of Knightsbrook is going to regret ever thinking he can buy Arabella van Haven.'

Alexander FitzRoy, Lord Ashton, Eighth Duke of Knightsbrook, stifled a yawn and gazed over at the ormolu clock ticking on the marble mantelpiece. His mother, the Dowager Duchess, was in full voice, enumerating the seemingly exhaustive list of fine qualities that Arabella van Haven allegedly possessed.

'And I hear she's also accomplished on the banjo, and can recite large passages of Shakespeare from memory.'

His mother looked up at him with wide-eyed expectation. It seemed she had finally run out of accomplishments with which to tempt him.

Alexander uncrossed his legs and stretched. 'That's as may be, Mother, but I still have no intention of marrying the girl—no matter how many tunes she's capable of strumming on the banjo, or how many Shakespearean sonnets she can rattle off.'

'Don't be so hasty, Alexander. I know she's American, and that her father's a *banker*, of all things.' The Dowager grimaced. 'But they are minor drawbacks that I'm sure we can overlook. We need to focus on her finer qualities and not think about her background. After all, she is known for her beauty, and I've heard she possesses exquisite taste in—'

'Surely you have forgotten to list her most attractive attribute?' he interrupted, before his mother could start on another interminable list.

She cocked her head and smiled. 'And what would that be?'

'Her money.'

The Dowager spluttered, gripped the black lace at her

neckline and sent him her sternest look. 'Don't be vulgar, Alexander. You're talking like a common tradesman.'

'Vulgar or otherwise, isn't that what this is all about? She has it—we don't. You want me to marry her and give her a title in exchange for her father's money.'

His mother's pursed lips drew into a thin line and her nostrils flared. It was an expression Alexander was familiar with—the one she had when she heard something she didn't like.

'You don't need to put it so crudely, but you can't deny it would solve all our problems.'

That was indeed something Alexander could *not* deny. The American heiress's money would solve their immediate financial needs, but it was a solution he would not demean himself even to consider.

His grandfather and his father had brought the once wealthy Knightsbrook estate to the brink of financial ruin, but their problems ran deeper than the merely financial. He could almost forgive them squandering excessive amounts of money on gambling, partying and women. *Almost.* But what he could not forgive was them bringing the family's once noble name into total disrepute.

He intended to restore the family's fortune by hard work and modernisation. He also intended to restore the family's tarnished name—and that would not be achieved by selling the title Duchess of Knightsbrook to the highest bidder.

'You're right, Mother. Her father's money *would* provide a short-term solution to our money problems.'

The Dowager smiled and rose from her chaise longue.

'But it would be only that. A short-term solution. What is required is a long-term plan of action.'

The Dowager sank back onto her seat and sighed.

'Really, Alexander, sometimes you can be so tedious. Why don't you just marry the girl and be done with it?'

'Because if the estate is to return to its former glory we need to modernise. We're on the brink of the twentieth century and we're still using farming methods from the eighteenth century. That has to change.'

The Dowager flicked open her fan and waved it rapidly in front of her face. 'Not this again. You and your plans to modernise will be the death of me. If you marry the American you won't have to worry about silly steam trains and traction engines. I want to look out on people using scythes to bring in the harvest—not horrible pieces of wheezing and coughing machinery.'

'That's as may be, Mother, but I'm sure the tenants would rather live on a prosperous estate, where their homes and livelihoods are protected, than in poverty in what *you* see as a picturesque setting.'

'Oh, pish-posh.' The Dowager waved her fan more rapidly. 'Anyway, you're twenty-eight now. It's time you married. You shouldn't let that unfortunate incident with Lydia Beaufort put you off marriage for ever.'

Alexander clenched his jaw so tightly it began to ache. *Unfortunate incident.* Was that how his mother described something that had all but devastated him?

He inhaled deeply to release the tension gripping his neck and shoulders. 'Lydia Beaufort has nothing to do with me not wanting to marry the American. And that, Mother, is my final word on the subject.'

It might be his final word, but he knew from experience it would not be his mother's.

She frowned her disapproval and looked around the room, as if seeking further support for her argument.

She spotted Charlotte, sitting quietly in the corner reading a book.

'What about your sister?'

Charlotte looked up. 'What *about* me?'

'Well, you're going to need a husband soon. Heaven only knows no man is going to want to marry a girl who reads as much as you do and is always getting involved in these ridiculous social causes unless she comes with a decent dowry. Your brother wouldn't be so selfish as to deny you the happiness of marriage.'

Charlotte slammed shut her book. 'For your information, I have no intention of—'

Alexander shook his head slightly, giving his younger sister a silent signal that now was not the time to fight that particular battle with their mother.

Charlotte scowled at her mother and forcefully opened her book again, breaking the spine. She frowned at what she had done, and then went back to reading.

'I will make sure Charlotte is well provided for,' Alexander said.

'Yes, and you can make sure she is well provided for by marrying Arabella van Haven.'

Alexander shook his head and sighed audibly.

'Anyway,' the Dowager continued, undeterred. 'It's all arranged. I've invited her to a house party this weekend. You'll be able to discover for yourself just how ideal a bride she will make and how lucky the man will be who marries her.'

Alexander sprang to his feet. 'You've done *what*?'

'Oh, sit down, Alexander, and don't glare at me like that. I've invited her for the weekend. It will give you a chance to get to know her.'

'Mother, haven't I told you often enough that we need to economise? We cannot afford to host lavish parties.'

The Dowager flicked her fan at him. 'It's just a small house party—nothing too elaborate. And you can see it as an investment in the future. Isn't that what you're always going on about? Well, meeting Miss van Haven will be an investment in your future.'

She sent him a victorious smile.

'Putting aside the complete lack of logic in your argument, you've invited her here under false pretences. I won't lie to her. I will make it clear at the first opportunity that I will not be marrying her.'

'Oh, you and that overblown sense of honesty. You were just as bad when you were a boy, but I would have thought you'd have grown out of it by now.'

'Would you prefer it if I told lies, the way Father and Grandfather did?'

The way Lydia Beaufort did.

His mother's lips tightened, but she made no reply.

'Our family has lost just about everything. Surely you don't expect me to lose my belief in the importance of honesty as well? And if Arabella van Haven is as virtuous as you say she is then I'm sure she will also believe in the value of honesty and will want to know the truth.'

'Oh, yes, I've heard she *does* value honesty in all things. I've also heard she's modest, gentle, demure, and temperate in all areas. And they say that she...'

Alexander sat down and sighed as his mother went back to listing the litany of virtues possessed by the apparently saintly Arabella van Haven.

It seemed his mother would not be stopped in her plan to make her the next Duchess of Knightsbrook, and he was going to have to endure the company of the title-seeking heiress for the weekend. But eventually his mother and the American would both realise his mind was made up, and Arabella van Haven would have to pursue some other duke, earl or marquess desperate for American dollars—because the position of his wife was not for sale.

Chapter Two

It was magnificent. Simply magnificent.

Rosie stood just inside the entrance of Knightsbrook House and looked up at the ornate domed window in the ceiling, shedding a soft light over the two-storey entrance hall. She tried to settle her breathing as she took in the opulence and grandeur of it all.

The coach trip through the estate's parklands had been no less spectacular, with its seemingly endless parade of trees festooned with spring foliage. When the trees had cleared and she'd first seen the expansive four-storey house standing proudly beside a large lake, dominating the landscape around it, her resolve had faltered. Arabella's father was a man of immense wealth, but this was something more than just wealth. The house seemed to proclaim that here was the home of one of England's oldest and noblest families—one that was reverently referred to as 'old money'.

Rosie inhaled slowly and deeply. She would not be overawed by her surroundings. Nor would she be daunted by the stern looks of the ancestors staring down at her from the oil paintings that lined the walls of the expansive hall. Arabella's happiness depended on her keeping her nerve.

She just had to remember who these people really were. They were a stuffy aristocratic family who had fallen on hard times. They were people so arrogant that they thought all they had to do was dangle a title in front of a rich American and then they could continue to live in splendour, despite having lost all their own money.

Well, they were about to find out that not all Americans were quite so easily bought. They needed to be taught a lesson, and she was just the woman to do it.

A man and a woman appeared at the top of the grand staircase and began the long descent.

'That must be them, the rascals.' Nellie scowled beside her. 'Go teach them a lesson, Rosie.'

Rosie tried to calm her breathing and stifle her fluttering nerves. She just had to remember that she was no longer poor Rosie Smith. She was Arabella van Haven, daughter of a wealthy and influential banker. And she was a young woman whose tendency to misbehave in polite society made her a decidedly unsuitable bride for a member of the aristocracy.

'Right...' She gave Nellie a pointed look. 'It's time for Arabella to put on a show.'

Rosie spread out her arms wide, smiled and started twirling. Round and round she went, faster and faster, down the length of the entrance hall, her satin skirt spreading out around her in a pale blue circle.

The black and white marble floor tiles merged into one swirling mass. Priceless Chinese urns whooshed past her face. She whirled past statues, past the paintings of the ancestors, all the while emitting a loud *whoo-whee* noise. Dizzier and dizzier, she kept spinning—until she reached the bottom of the staircase.

Stopping abruptly, she looked up to see what impact her entrance had made. The room continued to spin, twirling in front of her eyes as if she were locked inside a child's spinning top.

She reached out, tried to grasp something—anything to stop the room from moving. With both hands she clasped the thin stand of a nearby pedestal, clinging to it as if her life depended on it. The Chinese vase sitting on top of the pedestal wobbled. It tilted. It began to fall.

Rosie let out a loud squeal and dived forward to catch the delicate vase before it crashed to the floor. Her hands gripped the vase. Her feet slid out from beneath her and she tumbled forward.

Before she hit the floor strong hands had surrounded her waist, lifted her up and set her back on her unsteady feet.

Still clasping the vase, Rosie closed her eyes briefly, to try and halt her spinning head and still her pounding heart. She opened them and stared into the eyes of her rescuer. Then closed them again immediately.

It couldn't be.

This astonishingly handsome man could *not* be the stuffy Lord Ashton.

Rosie opened her eyes and blinked a few times, but his appearance became no less stunning.

While he had the haughty, reserved demeanour she had come to expect from the British aristocracy, he had the symmetrical good looks, chiselled cheekbones and full sensual lips she had seen on statues of Greek athletes at the British Museum.

He also had that air of masculine vitality those Greek sculptors had captured so well in their subjects.

Rosie looked down at the floor and gulped, remembering another anatomical feature the sculptures of naked Greek athletes possessed. But she most certainly would not think of that now.

Instead she looked back up and focused on how his dark brown hair brushed the edge of his high collar, and how, unlike most Englishmen she had met, his olive skin was clean-shaven.

And, unlike those Greek statues she wasn't thinking about, he was appropriately attired in a tailored grey three-piece suit, with a silver and grey brocade waistcoat.

Rosie coughed to clear her throat. 'Hello, I'm Arabella van Haven,' she said, hoping she didn't sound as foolish as she felt as she bobbed a curtsey, still clutching the vase to her chest.

He gave a formal bow and reached out his hands. Rosie stared at those long fingers, at the crisp white cuffs of his shirt contrasting with his skin, then looked up into his eyes. Brown eyes...so dark they seemed to absorb all light...eyes that were staring down at her, their accompanying black eyebrows raised in question.

'May I?'

'Oh, yes, of course.' She thrust the tightly clasped vase in his direction.

His fingers lightly touched hers as he removed the vase from her grip, setting off a decidedly unfamiliar reaction in her body. Her hands tingled and burned, as if she had held them too close to the fire. A strange sensation raced up her arm, across her chest, hitting her in the heart, causing it to pound in a wild, untamed manner.

He replaced the vase on its pedestal and turned back

to face her. Her head continued to spin, her heart continued to dance—but surely that had nothing to do with his touch or his stunning good looks. It had to be due entirely to her whirling entrance.

'Miss van Haven, allow me to introduce myself. I'm Alexander FitzRoy, Duke of Knightsbrook, and may I present my mother, the Dowager Duchess of Knightsbrook?'

Rosie bobbed another curtsey, inhaled a quick breath and turned to face his silver-haired mother, who was wearing the strangest expression she had ever seen.

While Lord Ashton was giving every appearance of being unaffected by her unusual entrance, the same could not be said of his mother. Her contorted mouth was presumably meant to be smiling, but a frown kept taking over, causing her lips to twist and turn as if pulled by a puppet master's invisible strings.

It seemed she might have to work a bit harder to shock Lord Ashton, but the Dowager was going to be easy prey.

It was time to have some fun.

'Pleased to meet you, Your Grace.' She reached down, grabbed the Dowager's hand and pumped it in a manly handshake.

Those invisible strings gave her mouth a firm tug. The frown won, and the Dowager's nostrils flared as if she could smell something unpleasant.

Rosie bit the inside of her upper lip to stop herself from laughing as the Dowager finally forced her lips into a smile, her face contorting as if she were undergoing a painful dental procedure.

'I am pleased to make your acquaintance, Miss van Haven,' the Dowager replied, trying discreetly to rub the hand that Rosie had just crushed.

Rosie controlled the giggle bubbling up inside her. 'I'm really sorry about nearly breaking your vase—but it looks like it's a really old one, so perhaps it wouldn't have mattered.'

All three turned and looked at the offending porcelain ornament, now safely restored to its pedestal.

'Yes, it is rather old...' The Dowager sniffed. 'Ming Dynasty, I believe.'

A small giggle escaped Rosie's lips before she had a chance to stop it. 'Oh, as old as that? Well, then, it wouldn't have mattered if I'd broken it. It would have given you a good excuse to replace it with something nice and new.'

The Dowager's eyes grew wide, her tight lips compressed further, and she signalled to a footman to remove the vase, as if concerned that Rosie was about to commit a wanton act of vandalism.

They waited in silence as the footman gently picked up the vase and carried it reverently away in his gloved hands. When he'd safely left the room the Dowager exhaled slowly.

'I'm afraid you've arrived a little earlier than we were expecting, Miss van Haven. We usually greet our guests formally at the entrance,' the Dowager said.

'Oh, I like to take people by surprise. You never know what mischievous acts you'll catch them in.' Rosie winked at the Dowager and received a wide-eyed look of disapproval in response.

'Yes, quite...' she said, flustered.

Rosie looked over at the Duke, hoping to see an equally disapproving look. Instead he stared back at her with unflinching dark eyes, neither smiling nor frowning. Rosie's grin died on her lips and heat rushed to her cheeks.

What was happening? She *never* blushed. And she shouldn't be blushing now. She had to remain in character if she was to convince this man that she was a most unsuitable duchess. Just because he was sublimely handsome it did not mean she should let him unnerve her. She had to remember who he was and what he wanted to do. He wanted to marry Arabella to get his hands on her father's money.

'I imagine there's been a lot of mischief in these halls,' she said, trying to keep her voice light-hearted to disguise the disquiet the Duke was arousing deep inside her. 'I'm sure those ancestors could tell a tale or two.' She threw her arms up in the air and gestured wildly to the paintings lining the wall.

The Dowager took a step back to avoid Rosie's flying arms, while the Duke continued to stare down at her, his face implacable. She lowered her arms. It seemed that bad behaviour wasn't going to upset his demeanour. She would have to try another means of attack.

'Judging by all those portraits, your family has been wealthy for many generations. I suppose you realise that my father was born in poverty? His father was a miner, and his father's father was a mule driver.'

Let's see how the snobby aristocrats react to that!

The Duke nodded slowly. 'Yes, your father's history is well-documented. And he is to be commended for rising so quickly from such humble beginnings to become one of the wealthiest men in America. He's obviously an enterprising man and clearly believes in hard work.'

Rosie fought not to grimace. Was *nothing* going to annoy this man? Surely he couldn't be that rare entity, a member of the British aristocracy who wasn't a snob? Or was he just blinded by the thought of Arabella's substantial dowry?

'You're right. He does believe in hard work—in earning money rather than expecting a hand-out.'

Hopefully this Duke wouldn't be able to miss her thinly veiled disapproval at his plans to marry Arabella for her money.

'Another thoroughly commendable trait.'

Damn. Either he didn't understand that he had just been insulted, or he didn't care.

'It's a shame your father couldn't accompany you this weekend,' the Dowager said. 'I was looking forward to meeting him in person.'

'No, he's too busy back in America.'

Making the money you're so desperate for.

'But meeting me is just like meeting him. I'm a chip off the old block, as they say.'

'Do they? How delightful...' the Dowager said through pinched lips.

Rosie supressed a smile at the Dowager's discomfort. A seed of doubt had definitely been planted in her mind after Rosie's entrance and behaviour. Now all she had to do was water that seed with continued bad behaviour and watch it grow until the FitzRoys realised they couldn't possibly countenance this marriage and sent her on her way.

Alexander almost felt sorry for his mother. This peculiar American woman was most definitely not what she had expected—of that there could be no doubt. But it seemed the thought of Mr van Haven's vast fortune was enough for her to swallow her astonishment and put on a brave face.

With forced politeness his mother led Miss van Haven back down the entrance hall she had just danced up, pausing at each painting and explaining which ancestor it depicted and what great exploit each was famous for.

It was fortunate for his mother that paintings of his father and his grandfather did not adorn the hall. He suspected even *she* would have had trouble finding anything with which to commend those two reprobates, and Miss van Haven's term 'mischievous' was far too tame to describe the damage that those two men had done to the family and to the estate.

Following the two women, Alexander had the opportunity to observe this odd American. His mother had been right about one thing: she certainly was attractive. With her raven-black hair and sparkling blue eyes she was nothing less than radiant. Nor could he deny that her creamy skin with the hint of blush on her cheeks gave her a delicate beauty. And that slightly upturned nose was rather appealing.

His mother was possibly right that she could play the banjo and recite long passages of Shakespeare—although he had no desire to discover whether either of those claims were true or not. But he suspected that nothing else about this young woman was what his mother had hoped for in a future daughter-in-law.

As his mother continued her boastful monologue Miss van Haven nodded furiously, perhaps unaware that her hat had become dislodged as she had flung herself down the hall. It was now sitting at a precarious angle, causing her to look like a very pretty pantomime clown.

Alexander suspected a clown was also not what his mother had had in mind for the next Duchess of Knightsbrook.

Despite her feigned politeness, his mother couldn't stop herself from shooting nervous glances in Miss van Haven's direction. She was no doubt worried that the young lady would suddenly break into a polka, trip over one of the Queen Anne chairs, or send some other priceless antique flying.

There was no question that her performance had certainly been unexpected—but it was quite obviously just that: a performance. While her grandfather might have been a miner, and his father a mule driver, *she* had been raised among America's wealthiest elite. The rules of etiquette and manners were just as strict in New York society as they were in England. And men like her father, who were newly wealthy, tended to follow those rules even more rigidly than those who had been born to wealth.

Miss van Haven had no doubt been given instructions from a very young age on the correct way to behave in every situation—and that wouldn't have involved insulting her hosts by acting in such an outrageous manner.

Why she felt the need to behave in such a way Alexander could not fathom. Perhaps she felt her father's wealth meant she did not have to abide by even the most basic principles of politeness. But, whatever the reason, he had more pressing issues to deal with than the bad behaviour of a frivolous American heiress.

The sooner he could tell Miss van Haven that she would not be the next Duchess of Knightsbrook the sooner they could end this tedious ritual and he could get back to his work of transforming the family estate into a productive, financially viable farm.

She turned and looked in his direction and he realised he had been staring at her. Despite himself, he held her gaze, unable to look away from those stunning blue eyes. The colour was so intense—like a cool lake on a warm afternoon. And, also like a lake, they seemed to contain hidden depths—as if there was a deep, unfathomable sadness behind all her game-playing.

Her excessive grin faltered slightly, and a blush tinged her cheeks before she turned her attention back to his mother and once again resumed her frantic nodding.

They reached the front door, where her maid was still standing, her arms crossed defiantly.

'Now that I've introduced you to our family's history, perhaps Alexander will escort you round the gardens while I attend to my other guests? Your maid can be your chaperon.'

The maid folded her arms more tightly, shot Miss van Haven a questioning look, and received a quick nod in reply. Alexander wondered at the silent exchange, which seemed more like one between equals than maid and mistress.

His mother nodded to Arabella, sent Alexander a stern look—which was no doubt an admonition to do his best to charm the heiress—and then departed.

Alexander suppressed a huff of irritation. Escorting this title-seeking American around the estate was not exactly how he had intended to spend the day, but at least it would give him an opportunity to set her straight. To let her know that she would *not* be the next Duchess of Knightsbrook.

Chapter Three

Alone with the Duke—well, alone apart from Nellie—Rosie knew she had to keep her guard up. She could not let him see how much he unnerved her. She had to keep reminding herself that he was after Arabella's money. That was all that mattered.

She sent him what she hoped was a confident smile and got a familiar stern look in return.

'If I am to escort you round the gardens, can I make one request?'

She shook her head slightly. 'A request?'

'Yes—would you please stop this charade?'

One hand shot to her stomach; the other covered her mouth to stop a gasp from escaping. This was a disaster. He could *see* it was all an act. He *knew* she wasn't Arabella. Her plan was ruined before it had begun.

She looked out through the glass doors to the gardens. Could she escape? No, that was ridiculous. She was in the middle of the Devon countryside, many miles from London. What was she going to do? Walk? All the way back to the train station?

No, she was going to have to bluff her way out of this.

She scanned the entrance hall. Her mind spun with half-formed excuses and explanations.

'Charade?' she squeaked.

'Yes—this play-acting. You may have been able to shock my mother but it won't work on me, Miss van Haven.'

Rosie released the breath she'd been holding and slowly lowered her hand from her mouth. He didn't know she wasn't Arabella. All was not lost.

'Oh, yes. I'm sorry about that…' She gestured around the entrance hall, her hand twirling in imitation of her entrance. 'Just my little joke.'

His dark eyebrows drew together. He frowned slightly. 'Really? Are you in the habit of making fun of your hosts?'

'No, I…' She stopped.

Why make excuses? After all, she didn't *want* Lord Ashton to like her. She had to be completely unlikable if she was to convince him just what a thoroughly unacceptable duchess she would make.

'Well, yes. I do it all the time. I love making fun of people. Don't you?'

His frown deepened. 'No, I don't. Everyone deserves to be treated with respect, no matter who they are.'

Momentarily chastened, Rosie was tempted to agree with him—but she couldn't. The one thing she did not want was to be was agreeable.

'I guess we just see things completely differently. I think everyone is here for my entertainment and I like to have as much fun as possible. If people get offended and think I'm laughing at them—well, that's hardly my fault. Is it?'

He stared at her for a moment longer, as if observing

a strange animal on display at the zoological gardens. 'I'm afraid I can't answer that.'

The response was vague, but Rosie could read his intent in his rigid body language. She had her wish. The Duke disapproved of her.

'Well, don't you worry if you don't know the answer. I'm sometimes not that smart either.'

'I don't doubt that, Miss van Haven.'

Rosie smiled. That almost sounded like an insult.

He offered her his arm. 'Mother would like me to show you the gardens. Shall we…?'

She placed her hand on his forearm and resisted the temptation to give the muscles a little squeeze, just to see how they compared to a marble statue.

They walked out through double French doors, down some sweeping stone stairs and into the gardens, which looked just as magnificent at ground level as it had when she had driven through it in the carriage, with an abundance of trees, lush grasslands and a stunning lake adorned with ornate fountains.

As they strolled along a tree-lined pathway the soft green spring leaves rustled in the light breeze and small birds chirped and flitted between the branches. Rosie breathed in deeply and savoured the fresh country air. She had loved every moment of her time in London, but it was a joy to be in such beautiful, peaceful surroundings.

'I don't know how much you know about Knightsbrook, but this garden was designed for my great-great-grandfather in the mid-eighteenth century, by the famous landscape gardener Capability Brown,' the Duke said, playing the role of dutiful host.

Rosie nodded. When she had first arrived she had

wondered whether the garden was a Capability Brown design, as it had the natural look the landscape gardener was famous for.

She gave a small cough. 'Capable who?'

'Capability Brown—he designed some of the most beautiful and highly regarded gardens in England.'

'Did he always plant so many trees? Trees are quite frightful, don't you think?'

He stopped, turned to face her, and frowned. 'You don't like *trees*?'

'No—awful things. They shed their leaves, making an unsightly mess all over the place. Not to mention all the terrible birds they attract. And as for the mess *those* frightful creatures make—well, the less said about that the better. I think the world would be much better off without so many trees.'

He looked along the path, then back towards the house. 'Then there's probably little point continuing our walk along this path, as it leads to a woodland area that contains some of the most established specimens of English trees to be found in the country.'

'Oh, no. I wouldn't want to see *that*.' Rosie gave a fake shudder. 'Has this estate got anything other than trees to look at?'

He stared at her for a moment, his brow furrowed. 'Perhaps you'd prefer to walk alongside the lake?'

She sighed, as if to say that if a lake was all he had to offer, then a lake it would have to be.

He led her to the gently curving serpentine lake that wound its way around the house. As they strolled slowly along its edge Rosie admired the centrepiece sculpture of Neptune, and the array of carved sea creatures that appeared to be frolicking in the waters. When the fountain sent water cascading high into the air, Rosie was tempted to clap her hands with delight at its playfulness.

'Is the lake more to your taste, Miss van Haven?

She forced her face to remain impassive. 'Lakes are all right, I suppose. But it's a shame it's got all those sculptures in it. Art is so distracting, don't you think?'

'You don't like art either?'

She shook her head vigorously and scowled. 'No—art is so *wasteful*, don't you think? All those galleries, and museums…theatres and whatnot. I'm sure they could all be put to much better use. Don't you agree?'

'Miss van Haven, you're…' He paused and looked around, as if struggling to find the right words.

Rosie smiled and waited for an appropriately disparaging comment that would seal her fate as a completely unacceptable future bride.

'You're quite unusual—aren't you, Miss van Haven?'

Quite unusual. It wasn't nearly as insulting as she would have liked, but it would have to do.

'Unusual? Me? No, I don't think so. I think it's the rest of the world that's unusual. All those people who like culture…plays, books, art, sculptures… They're the unusual ones.' She shuddered, as if the mere thought of art was abhorrent to her.

'In that case I suspect there will be little point showing you the family's collection of Old Masters.'

Rosie abruptly stopped walking and screwed up her face as if in pain. *No.* She had gone too far. Nothing would please her more than to see the FitzRoy art collection. One of the few things she knew about the family was that they had been collecting art for generations and had one of the finest collections outside the national art galleries. And now she had deprived herself of the opportunity to view some of the world's finest masterpieces.

She bit lightly on her tongue, to stop herself from crying out that she would give just about anything to see the collection. Anything, that was, except betray her promise to Arabella to make sure the Duke had no interest in marrying her.

'Yes, I suspect you're right—it would be a complete waste of time to show me *any* pictures,' she said through clenched teeth.

'Perhaps, then, we should sit awhile?'

He led her to a seat on the stone bridge that curved over the lake. While they looked out at the water and the woodland backdrop Rosie tried to think of a scheme that would convince Lord Ashton that, despite her claim to detest art, it would still be a good idea for him to show her the collection.

'Miss van Haven, there is something I must tell you. I hope you won't be offended, but it is essential that I tell you the truth.'

'I'm sure nothing you say will offend me, Your Grace.' After all, Rosie was the one who was trying her hardest to be offensive.

'You were invited here for the weekend under false pretences and I must let you know the true situation.'

She tilted her head. This was intriguing. 'False pretences?

'It was my mother's idea to invite you. I believe she has given you and your father the impression that I am interested in meeting you with the intention of looking towards a possible marriage. That is not the case. You're a very pretty young lady, Miss van Haven, and I'm sure you will one day make some man very happy, but I'm afraid that man won't be me.'

Had she heard him correctly? 'You don't want to marry me?'

'I'm sorry, Miss van Haven. As I said, I mean no offence. I don't wish to marry anyone. I don't know if you are aware that your father and my mother have put this scheme together without my approval, or even my knowledge. So, my apologies for the gross deception, but I don't want to marry you.'

Rosie clapped her hands and laughed with delight. 'That's wonderful news!'

With his eyebrows knitted together, he once again looked at her as if she were a curiosity. 'Wonderful? Am I to assume that you don't wish to marry either?'

She shook her head vigorously, still smiling and clapping. 'No, I most definitely do not. Why else do you think I put on that performance when I first arrived? Why else do you think I said that trees are horrid? Who thinks *trees* are horrid? No one! I was trying to make you dislike me so you wouldn't want to marry me.'

She had expected him to laugh as well, but he continued to frown. It seemed an inability to smile was another thing he had in common with those statues of Greek athletes.

'None of what you said was true?'

'Of course not.' She shook her head at his obvious statement.

'*Why* did you feel the need to put on such an act?'

'So you wouldn't want to marry me, of course.' Rosie was beginning to wonder if the handsome Duke was perhaps a bit dim-witted.

'You've been lying and pretending since the moment you arrived?'

Her smile faltered. 'Um… Well, yes, I guess I have. But I had to.'

The furrow in his brow deepened. 'Would it not have been easier to have told the truth—that you didn't wish to marry?'

'Well, perhaps, but it might have got complicated if you had been determined to marry *me*.'

'And play-acting *isn't* complicated? Lying *isn't* complicated?'

Rosie shrugged, unsure how to answer.

He looked out at the lake and sighed deeply. 'I've always found that lies inevitably cause complications, and often have far-reaching consequences for too many people. Telling lies might benefit the liar, but it almost always causes a great deal of problems for everyone else.'

Rosie wondered at his reaction, which seemed to be about something more than just her deceptive behaviour. His face looked so solemn, even melancholy, almost as if he was recalling some past hurt, some previous act of deception that had wounded him.

Her immediate impulse was to put her hand on his arm—to comfort him the way she often longed for someone to comfort her. She knew what it was like to have suffered in the past, to feel the need to hide your internal wounds from the world. But she did not know this man—would never really know him. So instead she did what she always did. She kept smiling.

He turned his attention back to her. 'Is anything you've said today been the truth?'

'Um…well, I'm definitely American.' She gave an embarrassed laugh.

'Anything else?'

Rosie looked out at the lake, bit the edge of her lip and struggled to find anything to say.

'In that case, shall we try and sort the truth from the lies?'

Rosie shook her head, then nodded, unsure whether telling the truth was a good idea or not.

'Let's start with trees. What do you think of trees?'

She laughed lightly with relief; that was something about which she was happy to tell the truth. 'I *love* trees. And I love the gardens designed by Capability Brown. I've seen many sketches of his work and I was hoping I'd get a chance to see some of his gardens while I was in England. I love the way he combines a natural look with little whimsical features—like the fountains and sculptures. It's quite stunning.'

The furrow in his forehead disappeared and he looked at her as if seeing her for the first time. 'And I take it you don't object to birds either?'

She laughed again. 'Who wouldn't love birds? Of course I love birds—*and* all other animals.'

'And art, sculptures, plays, books, paintings?'

'I'm not a complete philistine. I *love* art, sculptures, books, paintings, plays…all forms of culture.'

'In that case I suspect you *would* enjoy seeing the family's art collection?'

Rosie clapped her hands again. She had got her wish. 'Oh, yes. Yes, please. I'd love to.'

'Then I'd be delighted to show you. But I think there is one thing that I must do first.'

As he moved towards her along the bench Rosie's breath caught in her throat. What was he doing? What was happening?

'Your hat became dislodged when you spun your way down the entrance hall and is now sitting at a somewhat comical angle. Please allow me to set it right.'

Still holding her breath, she forced herself not to gasp when his fingers lightly brushed her temples as he attempted to remove her hatpin.

The whisper of his hands on her cheeks as he gently pulled the hat straight was as light as a feather, but the sensation was all-consuming. Fire erupted within her. Her cheeks burned and her heart pounded so loudly she was sure he must be able to hear its furious drumbeat.

He was so close she could feel the warmth of his body, could sense his physical strength, and she had to fight hard against the invisible force that was tempting her to move even closer towards him.

He gave the hat a final tug and leaned back to observe his handiwork. 'There—that's much better.'

Rosie released her breath and gasped in another, trying to relieve her light-headedness. Instead she breathed in the masculine scent of leather and musk and her heartbeat increased its ferocious tempo.

She swallowed several times and tried to breathe slowly, to regain the composure that his touch had so easily stripped away.

This would not do. This would not do at all. It didn't matter how handsome he was. It didn't matter what effect his touch had on her. The Duke was not for her. He didn't want to marry Arabella. And if he had no interest in Mr van Haven's daughter—a woman from New York's elite society, a woman with a substantial dowry and the prospect of an enormous inheritance—he certainly wouldn't be interested in Mr van Haven's impoverished ward.

It was foolish even to think such things, and any such illusions had to be put out of her head immediately. She was here for one purpose only: to save Arabella from an unwanted marriage. To be bedazzled just because the Duke had touched her would be madness. She had to stay focused on her task.

No, the Duke was certainly not for her. And if she was to stop herself acting inappropriately in any unintended way she had to remember that at all times.

Alexander gazed down at the puzzling Miss van Haven. Her cheeks had once again turned a pretty shade of pink, and her bright blue eyes glistened as she gazed back at him.

Yes, puzzling was the only word he could use to describe her. From her unconventional arrival to her confession that she had no more desire to marry than he did, she presented one big puzzle.

It seemed that telling lies was part of her nature, and that was something he would never countenance. If he had learnt one lesson from Lydia Beaufort it had been about the destructive nature of lies. Lydia had once been a young woman of great promise, but lies had ruined her life and her downfall had all but destroyed him in the process. Miss van Haven's lies might be less destructive than Lydia's, but they were lies all the same.

And Arabella's reason for lying—that it was less complicated than telling the truth—was no excuse. It appeared that Miss van Haven could challenge his mother when it came to a lack of logical thinking.

But there was something about her that he found undeniably attractive. Something he couldn't define. He rubbed his fingers together and could almost feel the touch of her silky-smooth skin, like a soft, creamy magnolia blossom.

But it wasn't that. Nor was it her pretty face or her slim-waisted figure. It wasn't the way she laughed so readily, nor the way she smelled of delicate spring flowers after a rain shower. Nor was it the unfathomable depths of her blue eyes. But there was definitely *something* about her. Why else would he have felt compelled to straighten her hat, when merely informing her that it had become dislodged was all that had been required.

He realised he had been staring at her for longer than propriety would allow, so quickly looked away and out at the lake. What did it matter if she was a beautiful young woman? Lydia had also been pretty and sweet, with a charming laugh...

'So, Miss van Haven,' he said, as soon as he had resumed his usual sense of equanimity. 'We've established that you like nature and art. Am I now seeing the real Arabella van Haven?'

'Oh, yes!' She gave a light, tinkling laugh. 'What you see is what you get.'

'No more lies.'

She coughed slightly, and her cheeks turned a deeper shade of pink. 'No more lies.'

Her assertion did nothing to unravel the puzzle. She claimed to be telling the truth now, but her tightly held smile and rapidly blinking eyes appeared to make a mockery of that claim. She was still holding something back, but what that was Alexander had no idea.

Surely it was of no matter what Miss van Haven might or might not be holding back. She was not Lydia Beaufort. He was not going to marry her. Her lies could not hurt him.

And he had achieved his goal. He had informed her that they would not be marrying, and on that he and Miss van Haven were in complete agreement. That was all that mattered.

It was time to put all speculation about this unusual American heiress to one side. Now that their awkward conversation about marriage was behind them, he could relax and simply play the role of good host.

He stood up and once again offered her his arm. 'If the real Arabella van Haven is interested in seeing the art collection, then I would be delighted to show her.'

She clapped her hands in a genuine show of bubbly excitement. 'Oh, yes, please! I've heard you have a Rembrandt that is reputed to be his best work, and a Vermeer, and several Gainsboroughs that are said to be exquisite.'

She stood up and placed her hand on his arm.

'Then shall we?' he said. 'It will also get you away from these horrid trees.'

Alexander found himself unexpectedly pleased when she playfully patted his arm in response to his teasing.

He looked around for the trailing maid, but she was nowhere in sight. 'We seem to have lost our chaperon,' he said.

'Oh, yes, Nellie. She's probably found something more entertaining to do than watch us. I hope you don't mind?'

He shook his head. Surely it should be *she* who should mind, not him. Yes, she was quite a puzzling young lady...

They retraced their steps along the path. Then he led her through the house to the gallery that contained many of the family's major paintings—including the Rembrandt she had remarked upon.

When she saw the self-portrait she stopped. Her hand went to her neck and he heard a quick intake of breath.

'It's beautiful. It's literally breathtaking,' she whispered, transfixed by the painting.

Alexander nodded. He had seen the self-portrait countless times, but its beauty still affected him deeply. He was inexplicably pleased that it had the same effect on Miss van Haven.

They stood, side by side in silent admiration.

'His sensitivity is superb,' she murmured. 'He's painted himself smiling, but he's still managed to capture a sense of tragedy in his eyes,'

Alexander looked down at Miss van Haven, impressed by her insight. It was exactly what he had thought when he first saw her—that there was a sense of tragedy behind her smiling eyes.

Rembrandt had gone from poverty to wealth and back to poverty, and had suffered deeply as a result. Arabella van Haven had been born into privilege and lived the life of a wealthy daughter of a prominent New York banker. And yet she had the look of one who had quietly suffered. Alexander couldn't help but wonder why.

He led her to a painting on the other side of the gallery, to avoid any further contemplation of what had caused Miss van Haven's sad eyes. 'The Vermeer is slightly more cheerful, but no less powerful.'

She gazed as if enchanted at the portrait of a beautiful young woman playing a lute. 'It's wonderful. He's really captured how a woman looks when she's absorbed in her performance. It reminds me so much of a friend of mine who loves to act.'

'Who might that be?'

She shook her head. 'Just a friend in New York.' She

looked up at him and smiled. 'She often looks like that when she's performing—completely lost in the part, as if the real Ara—as if she no longer exists.'

Alexander led her slowly around the gallery, stopping at the paintings by Gainsborough and at the portraits of his ancestors painted by Sir Joshua Reynolds.

'I think if I lived here I would never leave this room. You're so lucky, Your Grace.' She looked up at him, her eyes sparkling with the pleasure and passion that great art clearly evoked in her.

'Alexander—please call me Alexander. Your Grace sounds so stuffy,' he said, surprising himself with his lack of formality.

She gave another musical laugh. 'In that case you must call me…' She hesitated. 'You must call me Arabella.'

'Arabella.' He savoured the name. 'You're right, Arabella, and it is a room in which I spend a great deal of time. Unfortunately many of these paintings are going to have to be sold to pay my father's debts. We will have to enjoy them while they're still here.'

Her eyes grew wide. 'Surely not? It would be terrible if they were lost to the family—especially the ones that are portraits of your ancestors.'

'Yes, it is unfortunate.' Alexander exhaled to try and drive out his annoyance.

Those paintings would indeed have to be sold to cover his father's debts. Paintings that had been in his family for generations would be sold off because of that man's lying, cheating and irresponsible behaviour.

'It's unfortunate, but I intend to sell them to public art galleries, so they can be enjoyed by as many people as possible.'

'Good.' She nodded her approval. 'The more people

who can see these exquisite artworks and experience the kind of pleasure I have today the better.'

As she stared at the painting she chewed lightly on her lower lip and tipped her head to one side.

'But it would still be better if they could remain in the house—especially the portraits of your ancestors. It's a shame you can't open the house to the public. Then people could pay a small entrance fee and enjoy the gardens and the woodlands, the lake and the art. It would be a lovely day out.'

Alexander stared at her, taken aback by the unusual and progressive suggestion of opening the house to the public. 'Yes, it's a nice idea—but I can't see my mother tolerating anyone except invited guests in the house. Even when I invite engineers and other professional people Mother can barely tolerate their presence. And these are people who are going to help transform the estate and make it profitable—not people just having "a lovely day out".'

She wandered over to the portrait of his great-great-grandmother, painted by Sir Joshua Reynolds. 'Well, she tolerated me and my antics when I first arrived. Perhaps she's more adaptable than you think. And it would mean all these wonderful paintings could stay in the house, where they belong.'

'I suspect Mother would tolerate anything from you if she thought there was a chance we might be married.'

The edges of her lips pulled down in mock concern. 'Oh, dear. She's not going to take kindly to hearing we have agreed that neither of us wants to marry.'

'Unfortunately, Miss van Haven...

She raised her finger in admonishment.

'Sorry—Arabella. Unfortunately, Arabella, my mother

is not one to give up easily. You will have to prepare yourself for some concerted matchmaking from her this weekend. I urge you to be resolute.'

'Oh, I can be resolute, Alexander—believe me.' She smiled at him.

He did not doubt it. Arabella was obviously a woman who knew her own mind. She might have some unusual ways of getting what she wanted, but there was no denying she had admirable determination.

They continued their slow movement around the gallery, admiring each painting in turn, until they halted in front of a pastoral scene of two lovers embracing, their naked bodies entwined under the canopy of a sweeping oak tree.

Alexander had seen the painting many times, but never had it affected him so powerfully. With the memory of Arabella's silky skin still imprinted on his fingers he could all but feel the soft, yielding flesh of a woman's naked body against his own. He could imagine looking down into Arabella's eyes as she looked up at him with the same intensity as the woman in the portrait. Her lips would be parted, waiting for his kiss, her body responding to his caresses.

He coughed to chase away the inappropriate image that had invaded his thoughts. Then coughed again to clear his throat.

'It's stunning, isn't it?' he said, his voice strangled despite his repeated coughs. 'It's by an unknown artist. My great-grandfather bought it while he was on his grand tour of Europe as a gift for his future bride.'

'It's beautiful. She must have felt truly desired,' she murmured, her fingers lightly touching her own lips.

It seemed she too was deeply affected by the passion

in the painting. He noted that her breath was coming in a series of rapid gasps, her face and neck were flushed, and she was gazing at the painting as if enraptured.

Alexander forced himself to lead her away until they reached a much more suitable work to show a young lady—one that would have a less disturbing effect on his own equilibrium too.

But as he stared at an etching of Knightsbrook House made not long after it had been extended, with the west wing added in the early eighteenth century, all he could think of was the previous painting of those lovers entwined, of naked flesh, of parted lips waiting for a kiss…

He drew in a deep breath and exhaled loudly. This was ridiculous. He had no interest in Miss van Haven. No interest at all. He did not want to marry her. He did not want to marry anyone. And he most certainly did not want to marry an American heiress. He would *not* have the world thinking he married purely to restore the family's fortune. And if he did not have any interest in marrying her then, as a gentleman, he had no right to be thinking of her lying naked in his arms.

He coughed again. No, he could not—would not think of her in that way. She was a delightful young woman with whom he was having a pleasant time. That was all.

Perhaps it was simply that it had been such a long time since he had enjoyed the company of a young woman as much as he was enjoying himself now. Perhaps that was why his thoughts had gone off on tangents better reserved for the bawdy houses of London.

Whatever the reason, it would not do.

They moved on to the next painting, which was of the estate's garden, and he saw her smile at the small children depicted playing beside the lake. Seeing her delighted smile, he couldn't help but wonder why it was that such an attractive young woman was so set against marriage. He knew why *he* didn't wish to marry, but she must want marriage, children, a family of her own... For some reason it was a question he wanted answered.

'Arabella, when you said you didn't want to marry, you never told me the reason why.'

She looked up at him, her expression startled, then quickly turned back to look at the painting, her hands pulling at the lace on the cuffs of her sleeves. 'I...well. I... It's because...um...it's because I...um...' She blinked rapidly. Her gaze moved around the room, then settled on the painting of the two lovers. 'It's because I'm in love with another man—we're all but betrothed.'

As if punched in the stomach, Alexander winced. It was not the answer he'd expected but surely it was the most logical one. She was beautiful, sweet and funny. Of *course* she would have numerous men wanting to marry her. And for many men her father's fortune would only add to her appeal.

He drew in a series of quick breaths. What was *wrong* with him? The fact that she was in love with another man was of no matter. In fact it made things easier. There would be no difficulties in convincing his mother what a hopeless cause it was, trying to get them to marry.

He should be happy for Miss van Haven. And he *was* happy for her. Why wouldn't he be?

And, that aside, he had much more important things to think about than the romantic entanglements of an American heiress.

He turned from the painting. 'I believe it is time we joined the other guests.' He placed his hand gently on her back and led her towards the gallery door.

'Yes, I suppose you're right,' she mumbled, still blushing inexplicably, but nevertheless following his lead out through the door and into the corridor.

Why she should be blushing over her admission of being in love with another man he had no idea, but the reasons for Miss van Haven's blushes were of as little consequence to him as her romantic attachments.

He had done his duty as host. Now he had work to do. He had a devastated estate to rescue. It was that which demanded his full attention.

Only a fool would allow himself to get side-tracked by the frivolity of a visit by an American heiress, and one thing Alexander knew about himself: he was no fool.

Chapter Four

Why had she said that? Of all the excuses she could have come up with why had she said she was in love with another man?

Usually she could think much faster than that when put on the spot. Instead she had said the first thing that had come into her head and invented a non-existent lover to explain why an American heiress would not be interested in marrying the eminently suitable Alexander Fitz-Roy, Lord Ashton, the handsome and charming Duke of Knightsbrook.

But she could hardly have told him the truth, could she? She couldn't tell him that the real Arabella van Haven didn't want to marry because her one and only true love was the theatre, and she was determined to dedicate herself to pursuing a career on the stage.

Nor could she tell him that she, Rosie Smith, had long ago resigned herself to remaining unmarried. As the ward of a wealthy man, she knew that none of the men who moved in Mr van Haven's circles would be interested in marrying a woman who had no money of her own and no dowry. How could she tell him that a man like him, who could trace his family back countless generations, was so far out of reach it would be a joke for her even to contemplate marriage to such a man.

And she certainly couldn't tell him that she wasn't Arabella van Haven. She had promised Arabella she would help her and her goal had been easily achieved. But she still couldn't reveal that secret without Arabella's knowledge. It would be a betrayal of her promise to her friend—something she would never do.

Instead she had lied to Alexander. Again.

She should have thought more clearly. She should have come up with a better reason—one that was closer to the truth than her invention of a beau for Arabella. Why had she done that? It must have been because that image of the two entwined lovers was still in her mind. That beautiful painting had made her realise that such passion would be something she would never experience. But it had still been a dim-witted thing to say, and Rosie could kick herself for her lack of clear thinking.

She would have to keep her head and her emotions in check for the rest of the weekend, so she didn't say or do anything so foolhardy again.

She took one last glance over her shoulder at the art works she would never see again as Alexander hurried her out of the gallery. Such a shame. She could have spent the rest of the day and the evening looking at the paintings, but it seemed Alexander had different ideas. It appeared he'd had enough of the gallery. Or he'd had enough of her company.

They rushed down the hall as if they were late for an important appointment, his hand on her back hurrying her forward. It was apparent that now Alexander had done as his mother had commanded—had shown her the gardens and done his duty to his guest—he wanted rid of her.

Rosie tried hard not to be offended. It hardly mattered, really. So he was suddenly tired of her company and wanted to end their time alone together? It mattered not one jot.

And yet previously he had been so attentive to her. Right up till the time she had told him she was in love with another man. But there could be no connection between them; that would be too ridiculous. He had no interest in her. He had said so himself. And yet...

Rosie dismissed such scatter-brained thoughts. Even if his change in demeanour had come about because she had told him about the man she supposedly loved, it was the man American heiress Arabella van Haven loved—a woman from a respectable wealthy family. Not poor orphaned Rosie Smith.

Whatever his reason for such haste, trying to figure it out was pointless speculation.

As they rushed down the corridors towards the drawing room Rosie told herself she would not be offended by his determination to be rid of her. After all, what did it matter? She had got what she'd come for. Arabella was safe from an unwanted marriage. She had seen a beautiful garden, and viewed some exquisite paintings that few people got to see. That was a memory she would treasure always. Her plan had worked—not in the way she had envisaged, but it had still worked. Surely that was a satisfying conclusion?

All she had to do now was relax and enjoy the rest of her weekend in this grand home.

She glanced up at Alexander. His handsome face was set like stone as he focused straight ahead. It was as if he had one purpose and one purpose only: to end his time with Rosie as quickly as possible.

They reached the drawing room and she almost expected him to push her in, slam the doors behind her and make his escape. Instead he stood politely behind her, waited for the footman to open the doors, then followed her in.

The stately room was filled with the murmur of polite conversation as the assembled guests took afternoon tea. Fires crackled in several fireplaces, struggling to warm the expansive room, which held a slight chill despite the mild spring afternoon.

Rosie quickly scanned the room and took in every aspect of its opulence—from the large crystal chandelier suspended from the soaring engraved ceiling down to the intricate silk carpets that adorned the polished oak flooring. More of the family's art collection was on display here. The walls were filled with paintings, and every surface seemed to be decorated with artefacts and antiques—presumably collected by Alexander's many wealthy ancestors.

Rosie could only hope she would have an opportunity during the weekend to admire them more closely.

The Dowager was engrossed in conversation with a group of elderly women. When she saw Rosie and Alexander she instantly excused herself, rose from the chaise longue and with a purposeful swish of her black satin skirt walked over to join them.

Her gaze quickly moved from Rosie to Alexander and back again, giving her every appearance of making an assessment as to just how close her plan of marrying off her son to a wealthy heiress was to completion.

'There you two young people are,' she said. 'You were away so long I thought perhaps you had eloped!'

Alexander's body stiffened beside Rosie. She looked up and could see his lips drawn into a tight grimace.

'No, Mother, you are quite wrong. Yet again.'

'Oh, well, never mind,' the Dowager continued, ignoring the note of censure in Alexander's voice. 'I'm pleased you have had a chance to get better acquainted. Did you enjoy your tour of the grounds, Miss van Haven? I hope Alexander showed you just how beautiful Knightsbrook is—particularly when the trees are in blossom. Although *I* think it's beautiful in every season of the year.'

Rosie smiled politely. Now that the issue of marriage had been settled between her and Alexander there was no need to try and shock the Dowager with her bad behaviour. She could be herself. Well, not quite herself. She still had to be Arabella. But she didn't have to pretend to be a completely unacceptable potential bride who posed a constant threat to priceless heirlooms.

'Oh, yes, he did—and you're right. It is beautiful. I'm sorry we took so long, Your Grace, but Alexander also showed me your family's magnificent collection of paintings in the gallery, and I'm afraid we lost all sense of time.'

The Dowager beamed a delighted smile. 'I see you two have become quite familiar and are on first-name terms already. I'm very happy to hear it.'

Alexander returned his mother's smile with a frown. 'I apologise, Mother, for keeping Miss van Haven from the other guests.' His expressionless voice was a stark contrast to his mother's enthusiasm.

'So, how much of the estate did you get the chance to see, Miss van Haven?' the Dowager asked, drawing Rosie's attention away from the frowning Alexander. 'No doubt Alexander told you we have more than five thousand acres of land and that our gardens are among the finest in England?'

Alexander sighed loudly. 'You're starting to sound like a salesman, Mother.'

'Don't be vulgar, Alexander.' The Dowager's smile faltered slightly, before returning, just as large as before, as she focused her attention back on Rosie. 'I hope he told you that the FitzRoys have lived on this land since the fifteenth century? The house is reputed to be one of the most elegant in the country, with more than two hundred rooms. Not that I've counted them, of course. That includes the summer and winter parlours and two formal dining rooms, as well as the breakfast room, three drawing rooms, the ballroom, and countless bedchambers to accommodate as many guests as you could possibly wish to entertain. Do you like to entertain, Miss van Haven?'

Rosie forced herself not to smile as she watched Alexander roll his eyes. Instead she nodded non-committally.

'And every part of this house is desperately in need of extensive and very expensive renovation work,' he said.

The Dowager's lips drew into a tight line and her nostrils flared. She sent Alexander a quick, narrow-eyed glare then resumed smiling at Rosie. 'And you say that Alexander showed you the gallery? Indeed, it contains many priceless works of art—but it houses only a fraction of the family's collection, which can be found in every room of the house.'

Alexander's frown deepened further. 'And many of those works of art will have to be sold to cover our mounting debts.'

'Oh, Alexander, you can be such a bore sometimes,' the Dowager snapped.

Rosie looked from Alexander to the Dowager and back

again. It was as if she were watching a tennis match, played by two equally determined and equally matched opponents.

The Dowager continued to frown at her son, and then, as if remembering herself, she smiled at Rosie. 'Not that he's a bore, *really*. This is most unlike him. Usually he's not in the least bit serious. Oh, yes, Alexander *loves* to have fun and live life to the full.'

Rosie bit the edge of her top lip to stifle a giggle. The supposedly fun-loving Alexander his mother was describing was as far from the serious, disapproving man standing beside her as it was possible to get.

'Really, Your Grace?' Rosie tried hard not to laugh. 'In that case I look forward to seeing Alexander perform a few party tricks.'

The Dowager flicked a nervous look in Alexander's direction, her smile twitching at the edges. Alexander glared back at her, as if challenging his mother to try and talk her way out of her outrageous claim.

Instead of attempting the impossible, she took Rosie's arm. 'There will be plenty of time for that later, but now our other guests are anxious to meet you.'

They swept their way around the large room and Rosie was introduced to Lord This and Lady That, the Countess of This and the Earl of That. If the assembled guests were anything to go by it seemed the FitzRoys really did mix in exclusive society. There was not a Mr or Mrs among them, with everyone in the room bearing a title from Duke down to Baron.

And each guest, no matter what their title, reacted in exactly the same manner when they were introduced to Rosie—with enthusiastic delight, as if they really were meeting the future Duchess of Knightsbrook. She was greeted with smiles, nods of approval, and even the occasional curtsey from the assembled aristocrats.

It seemed the Dowager was so convinced she was going to marry Alexander that she had all but announced the engagement already.

Alexander was right. The Dowager was a very determined woman. But unfortunately for her she was going to discover that both Rosie and Alexander were equally resolute that they would not be wed.

Their circuit of the large room took them to the last guest, a rather severe elderly woman standing by the fire. The Dowager seemed to hesitate, her smile quivering slightly, before she smiled and made the introductions.

'Lady Beaufort, may I introduce Arabella van Haven? She is our guest from America.'

Lady Beaufort's straight posture grew more rigid and her nose rose higher in the air as she tilted back her head and raked her gaze over Rosie from head to toe, then back again. 'So you're the banker's daughter?'

Rosie's fists clenched at her sides. Since her father had lost all his money through no fault of his own, reducing their family to a state of poverty, Rosie had been forced to endure being snubbed, insulted and belittled by people who had once treated her family with respect.

Through bitter experience she had learnt to let such behaviour wash over her. So she did what she always did in such circumstances: breathed in deeply, forced herself to relax her tensely gripped hands and smiled her sunniest smile.

'That's right. I'm the banker's daughter—Arabella van Haven. How do you do?'

She received the expected glare in return, which only caused Rosie to smile more brightly.

'I hear you're seeking a titled husband?' Lady Beaufort said after a prolonged silence.

Several guests nearby gasped at this blatant breach of the rules of polite conversation, but their shock didn't stop them from leaning forward, eager to hear more of this exchange.

'Oh, come, come, Lady Beaufort,' the Dowager said with a false laugh. 'Miss van Haven is here to enjoy our hospitality. If she and Alexander should happen to fall in love, well…'

'I'm just pleased my dear daughter Lydia is not here to see this shameless behaviour.'

The Dowager's mouth opened and closed as she gasped for something to say.

'And now that I've met the banker's daughter who is trying to buy herself a title I think I'll take my leave.'

Lady Beaufort swept past Rosie, causing her to jump out of her way to avoid getting trampled in her bull-like progress.

But Rosie had failed to notice one of the couples who had moved closer to hear the conversation. She stepped back on to the listening man's foot, causing him to cry out and send his teacup clattering to the ground.

The sound of shattering china brought all conversation to a sudden halt as every head turned in their direction.

'Oh, look what the clumsy little thing has done!' Lady Beaufort said as a young maid scrambled on the floor to retrieve the pieces of broken porcelain. 'It's a shame these Americans don't know how to act in polite society.'

'Lady Beaufort, I think you should leave. Now.'

Rosie heard Alexander's commanding voice behind her.

'Oh, don't worry. I'm leaving. I'm quite particular

about the company I keep. Thank goodness Lydia was saved from seeing this appalling display.'

She gave Rosie another disapproving look and swept out of the room, her exit watched by every one of the assembled guests.

'I think our guests are in need of a drink somewhat stronger than tea,' Alexander announced, and signalled to the servants, who began pouring glasses of port.

Conversation instantly erupted in the room, but it was no longer the murmur of polite chatter. The assembled guests were talking loudly, all at once, and judging from the repeated glances in Rosie's direction they were all speculating on what had just happened.

Alexander leaned down and whispered in her ear. 'Would you like to take some air, Arabella?'

She nodded rapidly. She most certainly did want to escape. The last thing she felt like doing was remaining in the drawing room while a group of gossiping lords and ladies discussed that bizarre outburst.

Rosie had been snubbed by some of New York's finest snobs, and she had smiled through every subtle and not so subtle insult. But she was decidedly shaken by Lady Beaufort's outburst.

Why this woman should hate her was unfathomable. Surely being a banker's daughter was not so shameful? Particularly when that banker was one of America's wealthiest men and therefore, by extension, one of the world's wealthiest men. And why was Lady Beaufort so concerned about her daughter not being exposed to someone like Arabella? And why should she care whether she married Alexander?

This was clearly more than just good old-fashioned snobbery.

Chapter Five

Alexander led Arabella out through the drawing room towards the French doors. Voices fell silent as they passed, and each guest turned and attentively followed their progress as they walked across the room. He'd leave his guests to their gossip and speculation, and he was sure there would be an excessive amount of that. All that was important was to get Arabella away from the wagging tongues.

As he closed the doors behind them every gleeful face turned in their direction, all eyes peering out of the large sash windows with insatiable curiosity.

He exhaled with impatience. No doubt talking about that incident would keep them entertained for many weeks to come. It was a pity they did not have more to occupy their time, but with wealth and a multitude of servants came plenty of free hours to gossip.

For once Alexander was grateful that he had such an enormous task ahead of him in saving the estate.

They walked down some stone stairs and across a gravel pathway to a wooden bench in front of the garden.

Arabella seated herself, then looked back over her shoulder at the house. 'Well, that was certainly strange.'

'Strange' was an understatement. Alexander gazed at her, amazed at her composure. But her lack of distress was neither here nor there. She should not have been exposed to Lady Beaufort's wrath.

Alexander had difficulty understanding why his mother had invited her to an event such as this. It was inevitable that Lady Beaufort would be offended by the possibility of Alexander being betrothed to another woman when he had once been betrothed to Lady Beaufort's daughter.

He could only assume his mother had invited her because Lady Beaufort remained a doyen of society, despite Lydia's fall from grace, and it would be thought a folly to slight her. But whatever his illogical mother had been thinking she had caused upset to Arabella, and that was unacceptable.

The American heiress had done nothing to deserve such treatment. She had been set up for a marriage she didn't want by her father and his mother, and invited into this house under false pretences. And now she had been insulted by one of the guests.

Alexander was unsure why he felt such a strong need to protect her—whether it was just a natural instinct or something stronger. Whatever it was, he did not want her subjected to such outrages again.

'I'm sorry. I hope you are not too distressed by Lady Beaufort's rudeness. Unfortunately she has suffered some major disappointments in her life, and that has turned her into a rather unpleasant woman. But she had no right to take it out on you.'

Arabella shook her head. 'That's usually the way, isn't it? When people are unhappy they tend to lash out. And, no, of course I'm not upset.' She looked over her shoulder at the house. 'I'm a bit confused, but not upset.'

Alexander shook his head, dragged in a long, unsteady breath and tried not to think of what had caused that outburst. He did not want to think of how he had been betrayed by Lydia Beaufort, or of how she had caused him so much pain that he had sworn that he would never allow himself to be hurt like that again.

'Lady Beaufort's daughter Lydia was a lovely young woman and we were betrothed to be married.'

Arabella's eyes grew wide. He obviously had her full attention.

'But you are not any more?' she asked, her voice barely audible.

'No, not any more. Lydia…' He dragged in a deep breath. 'Lydia changed. She did things that caused her to be shunned from society.'

He paused again. Arabella did not need to know the full extent of why Lydia had suffered such a fate. Nor did she need to know how she had almost destroyed him in the process. She merely needed an explanation for Lady Beaufort's outburst.

'Her family is one of the best-connected in England, but even that couldn't save her when she chose to live a life that has shocked many people,' he said, hoping that would suffice.

'And Lady Beaufort blames *you* for this?'

He exhaled a ragged breath and nodded. 'Yes—but she has no right to blame you.'

'I'm sorry, Alexander. Is this something you'd rather not talk about?'

He shook his head. 'It is of no matter,' he said, with as much nonchalance as he could muster. 'I'm used to being on the receiving end of Lady Beaufort's misdirected rage. But you should never have been subjected to it, and I am truly sorry. If I had known she would behave like that towards you I would have insisted my mother not invite her.'

Arabella shrugged. 'You've got nothing to apologise for. And I can't really criticise anyone's bad behaviour— not after my somewhat unconventional arrival. At least your mother was standing right next to me. She could see that it wasn't my fault that the teacup was shattered. I wouldn't want her to think breaking porcelain is my special party trick.' She gave a little laugh and patted him on the arm. 'Let's just forget about that horrible Lady Beaufort and pretend it never happened.'

Alexander could hardly believe it. He should be comforting *her*; instead she was patting his arm in a reassuring manner and making light of the incident. She really was quite remarkable. An experience like that would have had most woman reaching for the smelling salts, but she was completely calm. He wondered what had given this young woman such resilience—something usually lacking in the gently reared women of his class.

'You will not have to worry about her being rude to you again. After that outburst I will make it clear to her that she is not welcome in this house.'

'Oh, you don't have to do that. A few insults aren't going to ruffle me. I'm made of stronger stuff than that and I have learnt to cope with much worse.'

Alexander looked into her deep blue eyes, curious to know why a woman who had lived the pampered and protected life of an heiress would need to be strong. 'And why is that? Why do you need to be strong, Arabella?'

Once again he saw that sadness come into her eyes,

before she shrugged her shoulders and smiled at him. 'Perhaps it just comes naturally to someone whose grandfather was a mule driver,' she said, in her now familiar flippant tone.

It seemed he was not going to get a serious answer to his question. He was not going to find out why that small shadow of sadness seemed to cloud her otherwise sunny disposition.

'Perhaps you are right. Although I suspect there is more to you than you like to reveal to the world.'

Her cheeks burned a brighter shade of red, and she blinked repeatedly before giving a dismissive laugh. 'No, there's nothing more to reveal. I'm just your average young lady with no hidden depths.'

Her words contradicted her look of discomfort. It was obvious to Alexander that Arabella was anything but average. It was also obvious that she was not going to reveal anything to him. And he ought to leave her with her secrets. After all, what business was it of his?

'Well, no doubt that inner strength is going to be called upon soon, when we have to face the guests again. I'm afraid that after Lady Beaufort's outburst you will undoubtedly be the main topic of conversation for quite some time. You will need to prepare yourself for some curious looks at the very least, and no doubt some very impertinent questioning.'

'Oh, that doesn't worry me.' She looked over her shoulder, back at the house. 'It won't be long before someone else makes an inexcusable faux pas—such as using the wrong knife for the fish course—and then they'll be so scandalised that they'll move on from discussing me to some other unfortunate victim.'

It seemed Arabella had the same low opinion of the ridiculous foibles of the gentry as he did himself.

Growing up, he had spent as much time as he could away from this house. His father's riotous gambling parties had often gone on for weeks at a time, and he and Charlotte had taken refuge in the welcoming cottage of Annie, the wife of a tenant farmer, who worked in dairy. It was during his time with Annie and her husband that he had learnt how hard the tenants worked, tilling the soil and making the money which his father and his friends squandered. In contrast to Annie's warm and welcoming ways, the excesses, rituals and snobbery of his own class had seemed absurd, but it was unusual to meet someone who thought the same way as him.

'You must cause quite a stir amongst New York society with that attitude,' he said.

She shrugged her shoulders and shook her head slightly. 'Well, perhaps—but it's an attitude I tend to keep to myself and only share with my closest friends.'

'Your closest friends? Does that include this man you are in love with? Does he share your irreverent attitude to society?'

Damn. He had vowed to ask her nothing about the man, but the questions had come out before Alexander had realised he was asking. Questions that seemed now to hang in the air between them.

Hadn't he told himself he did not want or need to know anything about the man? And yet at the same time he wanted to know everything there was to know about this man Arabella loved. He wanted to know what she felt for him and how he made her feel. And did this man know the reason for the sadness that cast a shroud over her bright blue eyes?

But why should it matter? She was a woman who was in love with another man, and he was unlikely to see her again after this weekend.

And yet it did matter.

His body tensed as he waited for the answers he both did and did not want to hear.

Chapter Six

Rosie squirmed uncomfortably on the wooden bench. How was she supposed to answer such a question? *Did* she share such thoughts with her non-existent lover? *Would* she share such things with him? Probably. Wasn't that what people in love did? But how was Rosie supposed to know? She had never been in love. Never expected to be in love.

She glanced in Alexander's direction. Yes, she could imagine that a woman who was in love would want to tell her man about herself, about her thoughts, her feelings. They would surely want to share their troubles and offer each other comfort and support. A woman in love with a man would also want to hear *his* thoughts, *his* feelings, and to know everything there was to know about him.

If a woman was in love with a man like Alexander she was sure that was how she would be feeling.

She turned to look straight ahead. But she had never been in love—not with this imaginary man, and certainly not with Alexander.

Rosie started. Where had *that* thought come from? Of

course she wasn't in love with Alexander. The mere idea of it was ludicrous.

She gave a little laugh, and took another quick sideways look in Alexander's direction. He was staring at her, waiting for her to answer. An uncomfortable silence stretched out between them. Her cheeks burned hotter. She had to say something. *Anything.*

'Oh, you know…we talk of this and that. And I suppose he's a bit like me when it comes to not taking things too seriously.'

Would that be enough to satisfy his curiosity?

He looked down at her, then stared out at the garden and clasped his hands tightly together. 'What sort of man is he, this man you are in love with?'

Rosie winced. It seemed Alexander wasn't satisfied with her vague answer, and wasn't going to let the subject drop. She cast another quick look in his direction and wondered why he was so curious about her imaginary beloved. He had reacted so strangely when she had first told him, and now seemed to want to know all about him.

But it didn't matter what *he* was thinking. She needed to concentrate. Needed to answer his question. So, what sort of man would he be, this fictional lover of hers? Rosie had no idea, but she had to say something.

'Oh, you know. He's just a man.'

Alexander turned and looked down at her, his eyebrows knitted together. '"Just a man"? He's the man you say you are in love with—the man you're all but betrothed to—and you dismiss him as "just a man"?'

Why was he interrogating her like this? Was he trying to make her feel uncomfortable? If that was his intention then he was succeeding. But it seemed he was uncomfortable too. He was staring down at her, his jaw tense, his hands tightly clasped together as he waited for her answer.

Could he be jealous?

Rosie shook her head slightly. No, she was being ridiculous. He was curious, that was all, and she should be thinking of an answer to his question—not letting her mind drift off to wistful fantasies.

She shrugged as she struggled to find one. What could she say? Especially as the man wasn't even that. He wasn't *just a man*—he wasn't a man at all. He was a figment of her imagination.

'He must at the very least have a name?'

'Of course he's got a name.' Rosie gave a light, dismissive laugh.

He raised his eyebrows.

A name…a name. What on earth would her beloved be called?

She quickly scanned the garden, looking for inspiration. She focused on a statue of Pan, playing his pipes. Pan? Was that a good name? No. Pan might be suitable for a Greek god, but not for a young man in love with the daughter of an influential New York banker.

She spied a ginger cat, curled up and sleeping at Pan's feet.

'Tom—his name is Tom. Thomas, actually, although I call him Tom…sometimes Tommy.' She all but shouted her answer.

'And does Tom, Thomas, sometimes Tommy, have a surname?'

A surname? Yes, he probably would have a surname. But what could it be?

Her gaze shot to the other sculptures. She was desperate for inspiration. Hercules? No. Neptune? No.

She looked at the garden instead, at the sea of daffodils stretched out in front of them, their yellow heads bobbing in the slight breeze. Tom Daffodil? No. She took in the sculpted topiary. Then her frantic gaze shot to the rose garden, laden with multi-coloured buds, ready to burst forth. She looked up to the line of rustling oak trees.

Still no name occurred to her.

An elderly man pushing a squeaking wheelbarrow packed high with weeds and dead branches appeared from behind the line of oak trees and began walking up the path, his boots crunching on the gravel.

'Gardener. His name is Thomas Gardener.'

She slumped back on to the bench in relief. Thank goodness for that. Now he had a name the subject could be dropped and hopefully never mentioned again.

'Thomas Gardener...' Alexander said slowly, as if considering the name. 'And I take it your father does not approve of this Thomas Gardener? Or he would not have sent you across the ocean in pursuit of a husband. What exactly is wrong with him? Why doesn't your father wish you to marry him?'

Rosie sat up straight. Why, indeed? Why would Mr van Haven not want a woman who was not his daughter to marry a non-existent man who was named after a sleeping cat and an elderly man with a wheelbarrow? It was a difficult question to answer.

'Um...he doesn't approve of him because...' Once again she looked around the garden for inspiration. 'Because...' The garden refused to reveal a suitable reason.

She turned to the house and quickly scanned up and down its four-storey exterior. She spotted the balconies on the second floor, and the last play she had seen before sailing for England jumped to mind.

'Because he's the son of my father's sworn enemy, who is the head of a rival New York banking family.'

It was a bit melodramatic, but it would have to do. Normally Rosie prided herself on being able to think under pressure, but the pressure she was feeling now was far greater than any she had felt before. It was as if all Alexander had to do was raise a questioning eyebrow and she lost all ability to think clearly.

'Oh, so you're like Romeo and Juliet? A couple of young star-crossed lovers whose fathers will never countenance the marriage?' His words dripped with derision.

Rosie pulled at her collar, which seemed to be getting tighter and tighter as she dug herself deeper and deeper into a pit of lies.

She stared straight ahead, hoping his disparaging comment hadn't been made because he had seen her staring at the balcony and made the connection with Shakespeare's famous romantic tragedy.

'Well, not really.' She gave a light laugh, which she hoped didn't sound as false to Alexander as it did to her. 'It's not quite so romantic. After all, they're boring bankers and we're not living in Verona.'

'And is it because of your father's disapproval of this Thomas Gardener's family that he sent you to England? Is that why he's trying to marry you off to someone else?'

'That…and because he wants his daughter to have a title; he wants her to be a duchess.'

Rosie smiled. Didn't it feel good to finally be saying something that was true? Well, almost true. Mr van Haven didn't care a fig whether Rosie married or not, but he most certainly wanted *Arabella* married, and married to a man with a title—the higher up the social strata the better. A daughter with a title would place him well above the rest of the New York elite—not just in money, but also in social status.

'So it seems your father is going to be disappointed?'

'Mmm, I suppose he will…'

In more ways than one—especially when he finds out that Arabella has not only refused to give up her aspirations of becoming an actress, but has arrived in England with the intention of pursuing a career on the London stage.

But that was a problem they would deal with at a later date.

'What about you, Alexander? Why don't *you* want to marry?'

Rosie tried to keep her question flippant. After all, she had merely asked the question to save her from telling more lies. Hadn't she?

If Alexander wanted to marry someone else that would mean Arabella was most definitely safe from an unwanted marriage. But the thought of Alexander in love with another woman, wanting to marry another woman, was doing strange things to her nervous system. Her stomach had clenched itself into a tight knot. Her breath was caught in her throat. And an odd light-headedness was making her dizzy.

It was so *wrong* for her to be feeling like this. What was causing her such pain? Could it be jealousy? Ridiculous. How could she feel jealous over a man she couldn't have? Or be jealous of a woman he might or might not be in love with, who might or might not exist?

No, it couldn't be jealousy. That was too ridiculous. But whatever it was she had to stop feeling like this. She had to stop it *now*.

'I have more important things to occupy my time. I

have an estate to save,' he finally answered, his words brusque.

Rosie tilted her head slightly and cast him a sideways glance. His answer was curious. He claimed to abhor lying and yet his words had been so terse. That, along with his clenched jaw and pressed lips, suggested he was not telling the entire truth.

Rosie knew she should just leave it there. What did it matter why he didn't want to marry? The fact that he didn't want to marry Arabella should be enough. But, like an open wound she couldn't stop prodding, she felt incapable of leaving the subject alone.

'Can't you save the estate and be married at the same time? They're not mutually exclusive activities.'

'My father has left substantial debts,' he said, his brow furrowed, his jaw tightly held. 'I would rather wait until I've cleared all those debts and the estate is once again capable of supporting the family. Then I would have something to offer a wife.'

Rosie was tempted to tell him he already had a lot to offer any woman. He was handsome, charming, kind and loyal. In every aspect he was the perfect man, and it was unlikely that she was the only woman to realise that.

'Surely that wouldn't matter if you met the right woman?' she said quietly.

Alexander made no response and Rosie mentally chastised herself. She had to stop asking these questions— especially as every question and every answer was causing that knot in her stomach to tighten another notch.

She took in a few deep breaths to try and loosen its grip and reminded herself that it didn't matter whether Alexander met any woman, the right one or not. It was none of her concern whether he wanted to marry, as long as he didn't want to marry Arabella. If he wanted to wait until he had saved the estate and restored the family's fortune then all the better. That meant it would be a long time before he considered taking a wife, and by then she and Arabella would be gone.

'Not all women think like that, Arabella—and certainly not aristocratic women,' he said finally. 'They and their families want a marriage that not only improves their position in society but also guarantees they will continue to live in the manner to which they are accustomed. My title is attractive on its own merits, but I am a long way from being able to guarantee the second. And I won't consider marriage until I can provide sufficiently for my wife.'

Rosie looked out at the expansive gardens and parklands, then back at the sweeping four-storey house behind her, with, as the Dowager had claimed, at least two hundred rooms, many of which contained priceless art works and treasures.

'And this wouldn't be enough?' she murmured in disbelief.

'No—a bankrupt estate with ever-mounting debts would *not* be enough. A backward estate that has not been managed properly for generations would not be enough. It needs to change. It needs to be modernised. Perhaps when that has been achieved I'll have the luxury of thinking about such things as marriage.'

'The right woman wouldn't care about any of that,' she said quietly. 'The right woman would want to work *with* you to make the estate viable. She would want to make your load lighter, not expect you to do all the work on your own and then hand it to her on a silver platter.'

He looked down at her and gazed deep into her eyes,

as if trying to read her thoughts. 'Not all women are like you, Arabella,' he murmured.

Rosie swallowed away her embarrassment. No, not all women *were* like her. They didn't all lie. They didn't all pretend to be someone else. They didn't all tell tall tales about imaginary men and fake betrothals. And surely most women would be sensible enough to stop talking about something that made them feel so intensely uncomfortable? But then, as he'd said, Rosie was not like most women.

'You deserve to meet the right woman, Alexander. A woman who wants to marry *you*—not your title or your money, but *you*.'

There was so much more to Alexander than his title and his estate, and surely Rosie would not be the only woman to see this?

He gave a small, humourless laugh.

'You should marry a woman who wants to work with you to achieve your dreams,' she went on.

If Rosie had been in love with Alexander, and if he had been in love with her, that was what she would want. Not that there was any possibility of either of those laughable things ever happening.

He continued to gaze down at her, his deep brown eyes burning into hers. 'Thomas Gardener is a lucky man to have a fiancée who believes in supporting her future husband the way you do.'

His words were kind, but his captivating eyes contained an intensity that caused heat to burn through her body.

She swallowed, looked away, and fought to compose herself. *And the woman who eventually becomes the*

Duchess of Knightsbrook is even luckier, she wanted to say, but knew she never would.

They sat in silence for a few moments, seemingly both absorbed in their own thoughts.

Rosie wondered what was going through Alexander's mind. Surely his thoughts couldn't be as confused as hers? *Nobody's* thoughts could be as confused hers.

It wasn't supposed to be like this. The plan had been so simple. But then, when she had come up with this plan over tea at the Ritz, she hadn't expected the Duke to be anything like Alexander. She hadn't expected him to be handsome. Nor had she expected him to be a proud, honest man who was determined to solve his financial problems without resorting to marrying for money.

And she hadn't expected him to make her feel things she should not be feeling—emotions she could hardly understand, even less put names to.

If only he had been a stuffy duke, set on marrying Arabella for her money, then she would have been in her element. She would have had enormous fun at his expense. Instead she was unsure what she was supposed to do, how she was supposed to behave, how she was even supposed to feel.

All she knew was that she shouldn't be feeling the way she was now.

The discreet cough of a footman broke the silence. 'Her Grace wishes to make you aware that it is time you dressed for dinner,' he said, and bowed then left.

'It looks as if we are going to have to face the gossips,' Alexander said, standing and taking Rosie's hand. 'As uncomfortable as this might be, as you are the guest of honour I fear it would be cause more of a stir for you not to appear at tonight's dinner. But of course if you'd rather not then I will tell my mother that you are indisposed.'

Rosie rose from the bench. She doubted his guests could make her feel any more uncomfortable than she did right now. 'No, it's of no mind. They can gossip about me as much as they like. I'm happy to be their source of entertainment.'

They retraced their steps up the path to the stairs.

'At least you won't have to worry about my mother matchmaking. You'll be saved that annoyance. When I tell her about Thomas Gardener even she will have to back down.'

Rosie halted. 'No, please don't do that,' she blurted out, gripping his arm with both hands. She could not have anyone else knowing about Arabella's non-existent beloved. If news of it got back to Mr van Haven it would cause huge problems for Arabella, and Rosie would never allow that to happen.

He raised a questioning eyebrow.

'If it got back to my father…' Rosie said desperately.

Alexander gently patted her hand. 'I understand, Arabella. If you want to keep your Mr Gardener a secret, it will not be revealed by me.'

A mixture of relief and shame swept over Rosie. Relief that she would not be causing any problems for Arabella, and shame that once again she had lied to an honourable man who deserved better.

But what else could she do? It seemed she was trapped inside a complicated story of her own invention—a story she seemed to make more complex every time she spoke.

'Thank you,' she mumbled, releasing her grip on his arm, and hoping she had told her last lie to Alexander.

Chapter Seven

'So, what's the gossip below-stairs?' Rosie sat on the embroidered stool in front of the mirror and looked up at Nellie's reflection.

It was a relief to be in the company of someone who knew who she really was. She could relax, because she didn't have to be constantly on her guard in case she said or did anything that would give her away.

She waited in expectation. Rosie knew that the best way to find out about anything that was happening was through the servants. Their outward appearance remained impassive as they went about their duties, but they saw and heard everything.

Nellie picked up a brush and ran long strokes through Rosie's hair in preparation for curling, braiding and threading it with ribbons, so it would look stylish for tonight's dinner.

More a friend than a servant, Nellie had been with the van Haven family since she'd emigrated to America from Ireland when she was fourteen years old and had been hired as a scullery maid. Intelligent and talented, she'd quickly risen through the ranks to become a lady's maid.

Arabella was very much aware of just how lucky she was to have Nellie, and her abilities as a hairstylist had seen many of the New York society ladies try to lure her away—but to no avail. And Rosie knew that Nellie harboured ambitions that didn't involve spending the rest of her life as a servant.

'Well, the servants are all atwitter about you, so they are.' Nellie frowned as she teased out a knot in Rosie's hair. 'They're all in agreement that you'll make an excellent duchess. Even the ones who thought it wasn't appropriate to have an American have come around.'

'Except I'm Rosie. Remember? And the real Arabella doesn't want to be a duchess. That's why I'm here.'

Nellie shrugged, divided Rosie's hair into several sections and began rolling one of the long tresses. 'Of course I remember. I'm just repeating what the servants said. And they're all in agreement that they're looking forward to having you as their new mistress.'

'Well, it's good that it's not up to the servants to decide who the Duke is to marry, or they'd have me up the aisle in no time at all. Fortunately the Duke himself isn't the slightest bit interested in marrying me.'

Nellie stopped what she was doing and stared at Rosie's reflection. 'That's not what I heard.'

'Why? What did you hear?' Rosie turned on the stool to face Nellie, who frowned, placed her hands firmly on Rosie's shoulders and turned her back towards the mirror.

She picked up the fallen tress of hair and resumed rolling. 'They all think the Duke is completely smitten with you.'

'They *what*?' Rosie started to turn again, then saw Nellie's frown and remained facing forward. 'They think *what*? No, they're wrong. He's not interested in me in any way whatsoever.'

'Well, all the servants who were in the drawing room when you were being introduced to the other guests said he couldn't take his eyes off you. That he was watching you the whole time. And when that horrible Lady Beaufort had her outburst he was at your side immediately, being all protective, like.'

'He was?' Rosie tilted her head, only to have it straightened by Nellie. 'Well, I'm sure it means nothing. He was just being a gentleman.'

'Hmm…' Nellie said, her mouth full of hairpins and her hands occupied with threading silver ribbon through Rosie's hair. She stood back and admired her handiwork. 'And the footman said he hadn't seen His Grace so taken with a young lady since Lydia Beaufort.'

Rosie's gaze shot up to Nellie's reflection. 'What did they say about Lydia Beaufort?

Nellie frowned and put to rights a silver ribbon that Rosie's sudden movement had dislodged. 'I don't know. All I know is when her name was mentioned all the servants looked very serious—as if the footman had mentioned a forbidden topic. But Jennie, the parlour maid, said she thought you were prettier than Lydia anyway, and much nicer. Before she was shushed by the housekeeper.'

'Oh, she did, did she? She said I was prettier?' Rosie patted the side of her hair and tilted her head slightly to admire her reflection. 'Well, that's something, I suppose. So was there any other gossip?'

'No, but Jennie said that she thought you were smitten too. In fact, she said she'd never seen anyone look so dewy-eyed.'

Rosie looked up at Nellie's laughing reflection, then

back at her own blushing face. 'Dewy-eyed? Me? Nonsense.'

'Hmm…'

'There's no "hmm" about it. Stop staring at me like
that and help me into my dress.'

Flustered, Rosie rushed over to the wardrobe, removed
the gown from the hanger and began pulling it over her
head.

'Stop doing that. You'll ruin your hair. And I think
you're going to be needing this first.'

Rosie turned and saw Nellie holding up her corset.
She exhaled loudly, handed the dress to Nellie and waited
while she wrapped the corset around her waist, tied the
laces tight and helped her into her bustle.

'Um…there's something I probably should tell you…'
Rosie said, her cheeks still burning.

Nellie stopped brushing down the cambric fabric of
Rosie's petticoat and waited.

'The Duke believes we're not going to be married because Arabella is in love with another man.'

Nellie's eyes grew wide. 'She's *what*? When did this
happen? Arabella never told me she was in love.'

'She's not really, but I had to make something up to
explain why Arabella wouldn't be marrying the Duke.
So I said that I am—or she is, really—in love with a man
called Thomas Gardener, who is the son of Mr van Haven's arch enemy from a rival banking family.'

'Oh, Rosie, no—you didn't!' Nellie released a frus-
trated sigh. 'You always complicate things. You come
up with a plan which seems to be simple and then you
go and make it complicated. It was just the same when
you and Arabella snuck off to the fair dressed as boys,
so you could get work on the sideshows. You almost got

away with it until you told the sideshow owner you had just returned from the sea, danced that silly jig and your hat fell off—revealing your hair. He nearly hog-tied the pair of you. And then there was that time you tried to trick your tutor by...'

Rosie held up her hands to stop the criticism. 'This is nothing like that. I was put on the spot. I had to come up with *something*.'

'Couldn't you just have said that you want to remain single and have no interest in marrying anyone? Why did you have to invent this Thomas Gardener? And why make him Mr van Haven's arch enemy? Did you *have* to get so overly dramatic?'

Rosie shrugged. 'I was flustered. But what's done is done. Anyway, it's supposed to be a secret. I've asked Alexander not to tell anyone. I just thought I'd tell you in case one of the servants finds out. I didn't want you to be taken by surprise.'

'Hmm...' Nellie frowned in disapproval as she lowered the dress carefully over Rosie's head and began doing up a row of buttons at the back.

'So, what else did the servants say about Lady Beaufort's outburst?' Rosie asked, changing the subject away from her blunder.

'Well, not much. Jennie was annoyed that she had to scramble around her feet to retrieve all those tiny pieces of shattered porcelain, and the housekeeper was worried about the damage the tea had done to the rug, but that was about it.'

Rosie shook her head in disbelief. 'What? No one thought it was odd? No one had any comments or opinions?'

'Apparently she's been a bit odd since Lydia got into

some sort of trouble. The servants all wonder why the Dowager continues to invite her, but she's fabulously wealthy, so I suppose everything else gets forgiven.'

'What sort of trouble did Lydia get into?'

Nellie shrugged, scanned Rosie's appearance, nodded her approval, then turned Rosie around to face the mirror.

When Rosie saw her reflection all questions died on her lips. She could hardly believe what she was seeing. Arabella's evening gown was so flattering on her, with its pinched-in waist, sleeveless top and low-cut neckline. Rosie had never looked more beautiful.

She gave a small twirl and watched the gorgeous silver material spread out around her, its embroidered threads shimmering as they caught the light. She stopped and smiled at her reflection, gently touching the side of her head.

Nellie definitely had a magic touch when it came to hairstyles. She turned her head from side to side and admired the transformation. It was easy to see why so many of the New York society ladies were determined to lure Nellie away from Arabella.

She looked down at the beautiful gown, still smiling, then a shadow of doubt crossed her mind and she frowned slightly.

'Do you think I'm perhaps showing a bit too much flesh?' She pulled up the plunging neck of the gown, only to have her hand swatted away by Nellie.

'Nonsense. It looks wonderful. And it took me hours to iron all that material, so we're not changing now.'

'Has anyone ever told you you're a very impertinent maid.'

'Yes, Arabella has, many times. And I take as much

notice of her as I do of you. Now, m'lady, shall we put on a bit of rouge?'

Rosie batted at Nellie's arm with her gloves. 'Less of the "m'lady", thank you. And, no, I don't want any rouge.'

Rosie had blushed more since she had arrived at Knightsbrook than she had in the rest of her twenty years combined. The last thing she needed was any help to make her cheeks even redder.

'In that case I think you're done. I've been told my services as your chaperon won't be required tonight. So off you go.'

'Mmm…' Rosie replied absentmindedly, still admiring her dress and her exquisite hairstyle. 'So what will you be doing to occupy yourself? Flirting with the footman or flirting with the coachman?'

'There won't be no flirting,' Nellie said, handing Rosie her fan. 'I went exploring the house while you were wandering round the garden, and I discovered the most wonderful library. I wouldn't want all those books to go to waste, would I? Plus, the Duke's valet is a bit of a bookworm himself, so he might be hiding out there tonight.'

Rosie smiled. 'So you'll be indulging in your two favourite pastimes? Flirting and reading.'

Nellie spent all her free hours back in New York in Mr van Haven's library—which was more than Mr van Haven himself did. He had bought the books in a mortgage sale because he had heard that a gentleman always had a library, but he'd never had any intention of actually reading any of them himself. He took as dim a view of reading as he did of all other art forms.

'Well, they're a bit difficult to do at the same time, but I'll try my best. After all, a bit of harmless flirting never hurt anyone,' Nellie said. 'And I imagine you'll be doing a bit of flirting yourself tonight.'

'Of course I won't. I don't flirt. I *never* flirt.'

That was she had never flirted before—had never wanted to. But then she had never met a man like Alexander before. Suddenly she could see the attraction of fluttering the occasional eyelash or doing a bit of pouting.

Soon she'd be seeing him again, and she'd be attired in a dress just made for flirting…

Soon she'd be seeing him again.

The thought hit her like a thunderbolt. Her stomach turned a series of somersaults and her chest constricted as if Nellie had tied her bodice laces too tight.

She wanted to see Alexander again, but felt ridiculously jittery at the prospect. This was not how she should be feeling. She wasn't here to flirt with the Duke. She wasn't supposed to have any feelings whatsoever for the Duke. She was here to make sure he had no interest in marrying Arabella, and she'd already achieved that. Now she just had to get these foolish emotions under control. Emotions she should not be feeling.

But how was she supposed to tell her heart to stop beating so fast? To stop her stomach from jumping every time his name was mentioned?

Rosie breathed deeply, her hand on her stomach in an attempt to calm her riotous body. Her body was refusing to listen to reason.

Alexander FitzRoy, Duke of Knightsbrook, was not for her, she reminded her foolishly pounding heart. He didn't want to marry Arabella, the daughter of a fabulously wealthy man. He didn't want to marry Lydia, who was from a well-connected wealthy family. Under normal circumstances he wouldn't even *look* at someone like Rosie.

So just settle down, she ordered her jittering nerves. A command her nerves chose to ignore.

'Well, stop staring at yourself,' Nellie said. 'Go on, then. Get moving. You're the guest of honour—they'll all be waiting for you.' Nellie gave her a gentle nudge towards the door.

'Oh, well, here goes nothing,' Rosie said, adopting her bravest demeanour.

She took hold of the door handle, then stopped, as if incapable of turning it. This was not like her. She gripped the door handle more tightly. This was ridiculous, she admonished herself. She had no reason to feel nervous. It was all settled. She would not be marrying the Duke. He didn't want to marry her. She didn't want to marry him. There was nothing to worry about. All she had to do was enjoy a lavish dinner at a beautiful country estate. Perfect.

So why was she finding it so hard to actually leave her room?

'Go on—away with you,' Nellie said, removing her hand and turning the handle for Rosie. 'And mind you be careful. Don't complicate things even further by doing something stupid and going and falling in love with the Duke.'

Rosie rolled her eyes. 'As if I would.'

She left the room and headed down the corridor, with Nellie's words still ringing in her ears like an ominous warning bell.

Chapter Eight

'You can stop staring at the door, Alexander,' the Dowager Duchess said, and gave a little laugh. 'Your future fiancée will be here soon.'

Alexander sighed with exasperation. 'I'm not staring at the door, Mother.' He turned from the door and surveyed the other guests having pre-dinner drinks in the drawing room. 'And do I really need to repeat myself? We will not be getting married.'

'You can try and fool yourself, Alexander, but you can't fool your mother.'

'Arabella and I are in complete agreement: I do not want to get married and she does not want to marry me. The only person who wants this match is you, Mother.'

'Me, her father and your heart, Alexander.' She laughed and patted him lightly on the arm with her folded-up fan. 'I've seen the way you look at her. I've seen the way she looks at you. It's as if wedding bells start to chime every time you make eye contact.'

Alexander gave his mother a long, considered look. Such lyrical descriptions were not like her. It seemed the thought of getting hold of Arabella van Haven's generous dowry was making her poetic.

The door opened. Alexander and his mother turned to see who was being announced. A sense of disappointment swept through him as one of his mother's elderly friends entered the room.

Quashing down that ridiculous reaction, he turned to face his mother. 'Despite the noises you're hearing in your fevered imagination, we are *not* getting married, so let that be an end to it.'

'We'll see, Alexander. I'm sure before this weekend is over we will be announcing your engagement.'

'Mother, there will be no such announcement. You can put that idea right out of—'

He was interrupted by the footman announcing Miss van Haven's arrival.

Alexander turned and saw Arabella standing in the doorway. She looked stunning. And stunned was exactly how he felt. Her day dress had covered her from her neck to her toes, but in her evening gown he was treated to the sight of the creamy skin of her neck, her arms and a tempting décolletage. Her hair was no longer covered by a hat, and he could see it was not raven-black as he had first thought, but had copper threads running through it, which glimmered as they caught the light.

He swallowed to try and relieve his suddenly dry throat and could almost hear those bells his mother had alluded to. He shook his head to chase away such fanciful ideas.

Pull yourself together, man.

She looked in his direction and gave him a small, shy smile. At least it appeared to be a shy smile. Alexander wondered if he had been mistaken. A shy smile was not what he would expect from a young woman as confident as Arabella. Nothing about her suggested shyness. And yet she was still standing in the doorway, still looking in his direction from under lowered lashes, still with that small smile on her lips.

Perhaps the events of this afternoon had unnerved her after all. She had disguised her discomfiture at Lady Beaufort's outburst well, but perhaps she had not been unaffected. And now she had to face a room full of strangers—strangers who no doubt had been gossiping about her all afternoon.

No wonder she looked uncomfortable, and he was a fool to think it had anything to do with him.

Alexander stepped towards Arabella, but was stopped by his mother's hand firmly grasping his arm. 'Don't look so anxious, Alexander, or so desperate. I shall look after our guest.'

'I am neither anxious nor desperate, Mother. I merely intend to be polite.'

'Yes, Alexander, I'm sure that's all it is. Well, go and "be polite" to some of our other guests. I want to talk to my future daughter-in-law.'

'She's not—'

His mother walked away and joined Arabella at the doorway, placed her arm through hers and began leading her around the room, so she could exchange a few polite words with each of her fellow guests.

Arabella appeared to be chatting politely, and his fears that she was nervous about how the other guests would receive her following Lady Beaufort's scene abated. She looked completely unfazed as she walked around the room, confidently and majestically.

If things had been different she would indeed have made an excellent duchess and would have done the family name credit.

Shocked by that ridiculous thought Alexander headed for the sideboard, poured himself a brandy and knocked it back.

He looked over at Arabella again. She looked in his direction and once again sent him a small, seemingly shy smile, contradicting her otherwise confident manner. He refused to read anything into those smiles. He was the only person she knew. Of course she would be smiling at him. And if Thomas Gardener was here, no doubt her smiles would all be reserved exclusively for that man.

Alexander knocked back a second brandy and leant against the sideboard, determined not to speculate on what this Thomas Gardener might be like. Arabella had said he was "just a man"—but he was a man with whom she was in love. That made him a lot more than *just a man*.

He poured yet another brandy and swirled the rich brown liquid around the bottom of the glass balloon. No, he would *not* speculate about him. He placed the glass back on the sideboard with a decisive clink. Nor would he think about those shy smiles that Arabella was sending in his direction.

His mother had led Arabella to the corner where Charlotte was standing, her face a blank expression of boredom. She was pretending—not too convincingly—to listen to Lady Richmond, Dowager Duchess of Pemborne, who was no doubt retelling the story of her daughter's success during last year's season. Charlotte found their mother's parties even more dreary than he did, and he felt for his sister, who had fewer opportunities than he to escape the stultifying atmosphere.

The two young women bobbed curtseys and then Arabella took Charlotte's arm, leading her to a seat by the fire. Whatever she was saying to Charlotte, it was eliciting some surprising reactions from his usually serious sister. Charlotte's eyes grew wide. She bit her lip and then smiled slightly, as if she were doing something almost sinful.

As Arabella continued to talk Charlotte's smile grew wider, less guarded, and then she covered her mouth and laughed. Then, much to Alexander's amazement, she began talking animatedly, gesticulating wildly with her arms. When Charlotte finished what she was saying the two women laughed loudly, causing heads to turn in their direction. Remarkable.

'Damn fine woman you've got there.'

Alexander hadn't realised that Lord Darby was standing beside him.

'Yes, indeed,' he answered, before fully taking in what Darby had said. Arabella was *not* his woman.

'And I hear she's an heiress to boot. Capital. You can't go wrong with beauty and money.' The man gave a small chuckle and helped himself to a large brandy.

Alexander felt his nostrils flare as he fought to stifle his rising anger. Wasn't this exactly what he'd expected when his mother had suggested he marry an American heiress? That everyone would assume the marriage was a way for the FitzRoys to save their estate? That they had found an easy and convenient way to get out of debt?

'I have no interest in Arabella van Haven's fortune,' Alexander said through gritted teeth.

'Of course you don't, old boy. Marry for love…that's the ticket.' His Lordship winked as if they were sharing a private joke, slapped him on the back, and, smiling, walked off drinking his brandy.

Alexander looked over at Arabella. That was what everyone would think if he did marry Arabella. That he had married her for her dowry. The proud name Knightsbrook, which had been so tarnished by his father and his grandfather, would be further sullied. And that was something he would not do. He wanted to restore the name— not degrade it further.

It was good that Arabella was not interested in marriage to him. It was good that she was in love with another man—this Thomas Gardener. It made things simple. They would not be marrying. And that meant there was no need for him to get annoyed by comments made by men like Lord Darby.

But Lord Darby was certainly right about one thing. Arabella was most definitely a beautiful woman. She had an enchanting natural grace and ease of manner. And he had never met a woman who enjoyed herself so much. Her joyfulness seemed to infect everyone she met.

When was the last time he had seen Charlotte laugh and look so relaxed? It was hard to remember. And she certainly never laughed at a party hosted by his mother. A scowl or a look of resigned boredom were her more common expressions. Yet here she was, talking and laughing with Arabella as if they were already the best of friends. Yes, she was a beautiful woman, with a rare beauty that went beyond her pretty face.

The gong rang for dinner and Alexander strode over to the fireplace. 'May I accompany the two most attractive women in the room in to dinner?'

Charlotte smiled and stood up, but before she could take his arm Nicholas Sinclair, Lord Richmond, the errant son of his mother's best friend, was at Charlotte's side, bowing and offering his arm.

Nicholas had recently inherited the title Duke of Pemborne and his own vast estate, but the responsibility had done nothing to subdue his intemperate behaviour.

Charlotte stared up at Nicholas and could not suppress her look of disapproval, but good manners prevailed and with a resigned sigh she took his arm. Alexander had no doubt that Charlotte would have no interest in such a man—one whose reputation as an idle rake was as legendary as Charlotte's for being sensible and serious.

Arabella placed her hand lightly on his arm. 'It looks like Charlotte has made a conquest.'

Alexander scowled as Charlotte and Nicholas walked away together. 'I very much doubt if Charlotte would want to conquer a reprobate like him.' He made no attempt to keep his voice low, not caring whether Nicholas heard his low opinion or not.

They joined the procession into the dining room.

'You and Charlotte seemed to be enjoying yourself,' Alexander said, curious to know how she had managed to get Charlotte to laugh so freely.

'Your sister has a delightfully dry sense of humour.'

Alexander looked down at Arabella. He had heard many characteristics attributed to his sister—compassion for the less fortunate, a studious nature and a quick intelligence. But a sense of humour, dry or otherwise...? No, he hadn't heard that before.

'What were you two talking about?'

Arabella gave a tinkling laugh. 'Don't worry—we weren't talking about you.'

They arrived at their assigned places and the footmen pulled out their chairs.

'We were talking about the season and the extremes

mothers go to in finding suitable husbands for their daughters.'

Alexander nodded, surprised that his sister should find anything in that banal tradition to laugh at. 'For Charlotte the season is something to be endured, not enjoyed. Mother has had to drag her kicking and screaming to the few balls she's attended this season, and I doubt if she'll attend any more.'

'Maybe she won't have to. His Grace seems quite taken with her.'

Alexander looked down the table to where Nicholas was sitting next to his sister, whose stern countenance and stiff posture did not support Arabella's assumption. 'I think a snowball has more chance in hell than Nicholas, Lord Richmond, has of wooing my sister. A more unlikely beau I can hardly imagine.'

'Hmm… I guess we'll have to wait and see.'

He looked at Arabella, who was wearing a knowing smile. He had no desire to inform her again that she was completely wrong. He knew his sister well. She most certainly would not be interested in a notorious rake like the new Lord Richmond. They might have been friends once, but that had been a long time ago. They had since grown into adults who could not be more different.

And why should it matter to Arabella anyway?

He took hold of his napkin before the footman could reach it, shook it vigorously and placed it on his lap. In the highly unlikely event that something should develop between Charlotte and Nicholas, Arabella would be long gone. Out of their lives and back to New York—back to Thomas Gardener.

Chapter Nine

Rosie looked down the table at Charlotte and smiled to herself. Alexander's sister was trying hard to act as if she wasn't interested in Nicholas, Lord Richmond, but nothing could disguise the flush on her cheeks or the quick, shy glances she kept flicking in his direction. They were obvious signs that she was interested. More than interested. She was attracted to her dashing companion.

Rosie touched her own warm cheeks. That was due to the heat coming from the many candles in the silver candelabra that adorned the centre of the dining table. It had nothing to do with Alexander. Nothing at all. And it certainly had nothing to do with what Nellie had said about the way she and Alexander had been looking at each other. Dewy-eyed, indeed.

She did not get dewy-eyed. Had never got dewy-eyed over any man. And she was certainly not going to get dewy-eyed over a man she couldn't have.

Rosie blinked several times to make sure her eyes were completely free of all dew.

At least one body part wasn't reacting inappropriately to Alexander sitting beside her. The same could not be said of her skin, her heart, her stomach… And her toes seemed to have curled themselves inside her silk evening slippers. And the least said about the strange tightening that was happening in her lower regions the better.

'You're very quiet, Arabella. That's not like you,' Alexander said as a footman began ladling soup out of silver tureens into porcelain bowls. 'What are you thinking about?'

Rosie blinked again, rapidly, and her mind went blank. She could hardly answer his question truthfully. She couldn't tell him she was taking an inventory of her various body parts, all of which were reacting in such a peculiar and disturbing way to being in such close proximity to him.

'Um…oh, nothing, really. I was just thinking how lovely the table setting is and how beautiful the women look in the candlelight.' Rosie released her breath, pleased that she hadn't blurted out something completely inappropriate.

The table did look wonderful, with an artful centrepiece of delightfully scented flowers, crystal glasses and silverware reflecting the candlelight, and the gilt mirrors adorning the walls shone with light to give a sense of intimacy. And the women seated around the long oval table, dressed in the lastest fashions, added to the sense of opulence. Their wealth was displayed in the diamonds, rubies, emeralds and other precious jewels that adorned their necks, wrists, ears and hands.

'None looks as lovely as you, Arabella. You look beautiful tonight. That colour suits you.'

Rosie's heart seemed to stop beating, and her breath caught in her throat as she took in the implication of what he had just said.

Beautiful...he thinks I'm beautiful.

An explosion of intense heat suddenly rushed to her face. Her stilled heartbeat sprang back to life, hammering furiously within her chest. A tingling pleasure coursed through her body and she smiled with unbridled joy. She did indeed feel beautiful. Nellie had worked magic on her hair, and Arabella's dress, with its cinched waist and plunging neckline, was designed to flatter her figure.

Tonight she felt every inch the society lady—almost as if this was where she belonged.

She had once lived a privileged existence. As a child she'd had expensive clothes, a room full of toys, and had been indulged by a loving mother and father. She had thought her life would always be like that. But then everything had changed. Her father had lost all his money. Her lovely mother had been reduced to working as a governess, and Rosie had become dependent on the reluctant charity of Mr van Haven and the kindness of Arabella.

Arabella did her best to ensure she never felt as if she was anything less than her equal, but her lack of money and security was something Rosie was always aware of.

However, tonight she was like Cinderella at the ball, seated next to her handsome prince, and it felt wonderful.

And, more than that, Alexander had noticed her appearance. He was still noticing—still looking at her—and under his gaze she felt as if she had dressed exclusively for him, so he would look at her, admire her, even desire her.

Alexander looked every bit the dashing Duke, dressed in a black dinner jacket, with a crisp white shirt and tie contrasting with his olive skin. Every man at the table was similarly attired, but Alexander wore it so much better. But then, a Greek athlete would, wouldn't he?

Rosie breathed in deeply, then exhaled slowly through pursed lips. 'Thank you, Alexander,' she murmured, feeling strangely tongue-tied as once again she reminded herself not to think of those naked Greek statues.

When he gazed back at her with those dark brown eyes her cheeks burned even hotter, her heartbeat pounded faster and her breath came in quicker and shallower gasps. Rosie was sure if her cheeks got any hotter she would ignite the table setting. She had to get herself under control.

Stop it...stop it right now, she admonished her traitorous body. A polite compliment should not make her feel this way. It should not cause her face to burn, and her skin to tingle as if it was being lightly caressed, or that disconcerting tightening between her thighs.

She moved slightly on her chair to try and release the tension that was gripping her, then coughed, pulled off her gloves and laid them beside her plate. She picked up a silver spoon and took a tentative sip of her mock turtle soup.

These strange reactions had to stop. Right now. It did not matter whether Alexander thought she looked beautiful or not. She looked the part. That was all that was important. She was fitting in with the elegant women at the table. Whether or not she looked beautiful to Alexander was of no matter.

She paused, her spoon halfway to her mouth. But he *did* think she was beautiful. A man like Alexander Fitz-Roy, Lord Ashton, Duke of Knightsbrook, thought she was beautiful.

No man had ever said that to her. Usually men didn't even look at her. On the odd occasion when she was allowed to appear at one of Mr van Haven's gatherings it was always made obvious that she was just the ward, a woman of no account, and all the men present treated her as such. She had never felt beautiful before.

Rosie sipped her soup although she tasted nothing, her mind awhirl, her body agitated.

She was being ridiculous—she had to get herself under control. So he'd called her beautiful? It meant nothing. In two days she would be back in London and this would all be over. She would not be marrying a handsome duke. The only reason she was seated at this table was because the Dowager Duchess thought she was an heiress and a good catch for her son—which she most decidedly was not.

'So, have you told your mother yet that we will not be getting married?' Rosie asked, reminding herself of her reason for being at this dinner table as much as asking a question.

'Repeatedly. But, as I've said, she's a very determined woman.

'Perhaps I need to start misbehaving again so she realises just how inappropriate a duchess I would make?'

Alexander looked at her over his wine glass and sent her a smile. And, oh, what a smile. It lit up his face and made those dark brown eyes shine with warmth. Warmth that sent shivers of delight coursing through her already agitated body.

Oh, yes, that was a sight Rosie hoped to see much more of.

'What do you plan to do? Throw some of the wine glasses against the wall? Or perhaps you could swipe the table clear and send the dinner service crashing to the ground?'

'Why, Your Grace, I do believe you're teasing me!'

Rosie laughed. 'I am capable of misbehaving in many other ways.'

'That, I believe,' he said, still smiling that heart-stopping smile.

'I thought I might do a dance down the middle of the table. Do you think that would convince the Dowager that I'm not duchess material?'

Alexander nearly choked on his wine. 'I don't think even that would put my mother off. Unfortunately your father's fortune is so vast I suspect there's nothing you could do to offend her. Although I'd love to see you try. Shall I give you a hand up onto the table?'

Rosie swatted his arm lightly with her napkin. 'I'll save my table dance for the dessert course.'

The soup finished, the footmen removed their bowls and served the fish course, and Rosie reluctantly turned to talk to her other neighbour, as etiquette demanded. As he talked to her about the last shoot he had attended, and how many pheasants, ducks and other small creatures he had bagged, Rosie inclined her head in Alexander's direction and tried to hear what he was discussing with his own dinner companion.

To no avail. The murmur of the twenty-four people seated around the long oval dining table blocked out all voices but one—the man sitting beside her, boasting of his prowess with a shotgun.

The fish plates were removed and replaced with the meat course. With relief, Rosie turned back to Alexander. Her heart gave a little flutter when he smiled, suggesting that he too was pleased to be talking to her once again.

A *flutter*? She reminded herself that she was not supposed to be having a flutter, but she was incapable of suppressing it.

Especially when he continued to smile at her. A smile that was made more special because it happened so rarely. A smile that was even more of a treat because it was directed at *her*.

'I hope you're not going to tell me how many things you've killed lately?' She smiled back at him.

He shook his head in question. 'Killed?'

'My other dinner companion has just been telling me about all the ducks and pheasants whose lives he has prematurely snuffed out.'

'I see. No, I don't take part in the shoot. Nor do I ride to hounds.'

'Good. So, what was *your* other dinner companion talking about with such enthusiasm?' Rosie leaned forward and looked at the attractive blonde woman sitting to his left. Her smile faded and her jaw clenched before she forced herself not to be so ridiculous.

Why do I feel jealousy over a man who is not mine— who will never be mine?

'I don't know about enthusiasm, but she knew my father. She was lamenting that he had been missed at Royal Ascot last season and asking if I'll be taking his place this June.'

'Royal Ascot?'

'The race course. My father was very fond of gambling. *Too* fond of gambling.' He stabbed at a green bean, his smile disappearing. 'That's why the estate is in such a sorry mess.'

Rosie looked up from the impaled bean. 'Oh, so I take it you won't be attending Royal Ascot?'

'No, I won't.'

He cut up his roast beef with such vehemence Rosie almost felt sorry for it.

'I certainly will not be squandering what little funds we have left at the races.' He stilled his knife and drew in a deep breath. 'But there's no point getting angry about that. It's all in the past.'

Rosie nodded her agreement. Like him, she tried hard—*very* hard—not to focus on the sorrows of the past, or to worry about what the future might bring.

Sometimes that could be hard. Sometimes memories of her mother and father came crashing in when she least expected it. Sometimes the vulnerability of her situation would overwhelm her. But then she would push that thought away and keep smiling. Even if sometimes that smile was not always as genuine as she would like it to be.

She had decided when she was still quite young that if she couldn't change the past, and the future was uncertain, then the present was the only time worth focusing on. And right now, sitting here, next to this handsome man, the present was rather pleasant.

'What about you, Arabella? Do you or your father like "a flutter"—as gamblers so innocuously describe losing a fortune at the card table, casino or race course?'

Rosie stilled her knife and fork and thought for a moment. Getting involved with Mr van Haven had been a gamble—a gamble her father had lost. He had once been a wealthy man. A successful engineer, he had built up a thriving company, installing modern electrical lighting in more progressive towns and businesses. His life had been comfortable. He had been married to the woman he loved, and living a contented life.

That was until Mr van Haven had encouraged him to borrow more money, to vastly expand his business throughout the country. When a few ventures hadn't worked out, and he hadn't been able to make his loan repayments, like a shark circling its prey, Mr van Haven had moved in. He had taken possession of the business and merged it with his own considerable portfolio.

Rosie's father had died prematurely, a broken man. As a supposed act of charity Mr van Haven had hired Rosie's mother as a governess and allowed Rosie to live in the house as a playmate for his daughter. Then her mother had died, leaving Rosie alone in the world.

She shuddered and blinked away the tears she would not shed. She did not want to dwell on such misfortune. And, anyway, it wasn't *her* father Alexander was asking about. It was Arabella's.

'No, I never gamble—and neither does my father. All he does is work. And when he wants to relax he works even harder. I can't imagine him doing something so frivolous as gambling, and he most certainly would never squander money.'

'It's an example I wish my father had followed.' Alexander lifted his glass to the invisible Mr van Haven and took a sip of red wine. 'But if he's working all the time I doubt you see much of him?'

Rosie nodded at the understatement. Mr van Haven saw virtually nothing of Arabella. She suspected that was one of the reasons Arabella had argued with such passion to have Rosie taken on as his ward after Rosie's mother had died. Otherwise Arabella would have been left alone in that enormous house on Washington Square, with only her new, rather stern governess for company.

Mr van Haven was rarely at home, and when he was he was buried away in his study. He had little idea of what went on in the house. The girls were often left with minimum supervision, and over the years their friendship had grown and intensified, so they were now closer than many sisters.

Arabella's own mother had died not long after Arabella was born, and Rosie's mother had been more like a mother to her than a governess. When Rosie's mother had also died, Arabella had argued with her father, had thrown tantrums and threatened to run away, until Mr van Haven had finally relented and taken the fourteen-year-old Rosie as his ward.

'You're right. I see very little of my father. He's too busy making more and more money—as if no amount of money can ever be enough,' Rosie answered, as she imagined Arabella would.

'That must be very hard for you?'

She shrugged. 'Perhaps. But there are worse things in life than living in luxury with your every need catered for.'

That was something Rosie was well aware of. Thanks to Arabella, she did live in luxury, and did have her every need catered for. Without Arabella it might have been so different. She might have learnt first-hand what it was like to live in abject poverty, to be cold, to go hungry, to be vulnerable and alone.

Alexander took another sip of his red wine and gave her a considering gaze. 'That's true, but I suspect it is only your material needs that are catered for,' he said softly.

Rosie held his gaze, unable to look away. It was as if he were looking into her very soul and seeing the pain that she tried hard to bury, the past hurts she tried to forget, the vulnerability she hid behind a sunny smile.

'Oh, Arabella, I didn't mean to upset you,' he murmured.

His hand moved across the table and gently covered

hers. It was a feather-light touch on her naked skin, but it sent a burst of fire coursing up her arm, consuming her in its blaze. She looked down at her small hand, covered by his strong, elegant fingers. That tender gesture had ignited a tempest within her—a tempest she felt incapable of quashing. She looked back at him. His dark eyes burned into hers and she gasped in a quivering breath as her body pulsated to the rapid beat of her heart.

The voices of the assembled guests seem to fade away. It was as if they were alone, no longer under the scrutinising gaze of society, and she longed for him to do more than just touch her hand—longed for him to take her in his arms so she could feel the strength of his body against her own. She ached to be held in those powerful arms, to give herself to his strong body, to have him complete her.

They held each other's gaze. Rosie hadn't noticed till now, but his dark brown eyes contained small gold flecks, like the last rays of sun on a summer's day. When she'd first seen him she had thought his eyes had a dark intensity, as if they absorbed all light. But she had been wrong. They contained warm lights. And now those lights were drawing her in, making her feel safe and protected.

She could gaze at those lovely warm eyes for ever… drown in them…forget everything else…

As if emerging from a trance she blinked several times and slowly slid her hand from underneath his. With shaking hands she took a sip of her wine, clutching the delicate stem of her glass as if it provided a lifeline back to reality, away from such fanciful thoughts.

She gave a light laugh that sounded false even to her own ears. 'No, you didn't upset me. As I've said before, I'm much stronger than I look.'

* * *

Her smile was false. There could be no doubt about that. And Alexander could hear sadness in her attempt at cheerfulness. He wanted to comfort her, to drive away that sadness behind her happy smile and her sunny disposition, to take her in his arms and make her safe.

'So what has made you so strong, Arabella?' he asked quietly.

'Oh, you know… I guess it comes from having a father who grew up in poverty. It puts iron in the soul.'

She took another sip of her wine and he could see her hand was shaking slightly, making a lie of her flippant response. He resisted the almost overwhelming urge to take hold of those trembling fingers. But she was not his to comfort—would never be his.

'I can tell you are a strong woman, Arabella. But even the strong need people to care for them and support them.'

She lowered her wine glass and looked up at him, her deep blue eyes capturing his gaze, capturing *him*. He couldn't have looked away even if he'd wanted to, and he didn't want to.

He had only known Arabella for one short day, but it was as if they had connected on a level he had not thought possible. He didn't know what it was that drew him to her. Was it her laughter, or the sadness in her eyes? Was it her vulnerability, or her resilience? Whatever it was, there was something infinitely attractive about this complex young woman—something that was drawing him to her.

'And is it the same for you, Alexander? Do you need someone to care for you and support you?' she asked, her voice barely a whisper.

Alexander shook his head, dismissing the idea. He

had never expected support. After all, it was he who supported other people.

He had provided seemingly endless support for Lydia. She was a woman who knew only how to take, not to give. She had taken money to fund her gambling habit and taken from him emotionally, leaving him drained, with nothing left to give. He had thought he loved Lydia, but look where love had led him. And when she had finally left he'd known the only way to protect himself from such emotional demands was never to allow himself to get into such a position again.

So, yes, he had to be strong. He had his family to support, plus the tenants who all depended on him.

But in Arabella's eyes he could see such compassion, such warmth, such tenderness. He could imagine what it would be like to have such a woman by his side. A woman who would not only support him, but was also beautiful, delightful and captivating.

He shook his head again to drive away that fanciful idea. It didn't matter how beautiful Arabella van Haven was—she was in love with another man.

He gave a false laugh of his own. 'And is that what you offer Thomas Gardener? Your support?' Alexander could hear the bitterness in his voice and mentally chastised himself for such pettiness.

Arabella blushed a deeper shade of pink and took another sip of her wine, seemingly reluctant to discuss it.

'I should like to think that the man I love would always know he could rely on me to be by his side.'

She continued to toy with the stem of her wine glass. Once again her words seemed a contradiction of the emotion she was expressing. It was such a loving, positive statement, and yet she looked so sad—as if it was something she would like but knew would not happen.

Slowly she raised her gaze and looked into his eyes. For a moment he could almost believe she had been talking about *him*. The softness in those blue eyes spoke of a depth of emotion that almost left Alexander breathless.

He gripped his own wine glass tightly, to stop his hand from reaching out and caressing her soft cheek. His gaze moved from her eyes to her lips—full pink lips which parted slightly under his gaze. Like him, she was taking in quick breaths, and she leaned in towards him as if mesmerised.

If only they were alone... Then he could do more than just gaze at that beautiful face.

The discreet cough of a footman drew him out of his trance and he saw the dessert course being placed on the table. Alexander waved the plate away and with the greatest reluctance turned towards his other dinner companion.

He hardly heard a word Lady Aubrey said. All he could think of was how Arabella had looked at him. Desire had sparked in her crystal blue eyes. Her lips had parted invitingly, as if waiting for his kiss. Like him, she seemed to have lost herself, forgotten who she was...

He had claimed he was strong and he was going to have to be. He could not succumb to temptation. She belonged to another man. *That* was what he had to think about when he looked at her—not how her raven hair caught the light, nor how plump her full lips were, nor how beautiful she looked when she sent him those shy smiles from under lowered lashes.

Quaffing a long draught of his wine, he reminded himself yet again. *She belongs to someone else.*

* * *

The dessert plates were removed and cheese and fruit platters were laid out on the table. Rosie turned back to Alexander, her heart beating fast, hoping he would look at her again with such intensity, with such longing.

Instead he gave a small, polite nod. It seemed the sensitive man she'd glimpsed had once again disappeared beneath a stern, aristocratic exterior.

'So, what were we discussing?' Rosie asked, not really caring about words, just hoping he would once again look at her with affection and warmth.

'You mentioned that your strength comes from having a father who was born in poverty.'

'Oh, yes, so I did. But what about you, Alexander? Did you get your strength from your father or your mother?'

Alexander gave a sudden humourless laugh. 'I don't know if I'd describe either of them as *strong*. My father and grandfather thought only of their own pleasure. They thought the family coffers were bottomless and they could spend and spend without a thought to the future, or the future of the tenants who depend on the success of the estate for their livelihoods. My mother is much the same. She brought a sizable dowry with her when she married my father, but he soon managed to squander that. There was no love between them, which perhaps made it easier for her to live with such a man. Having had a loveless marriage herself, she has no reservations about trying to get me to marry a wealthy heiress. All she can see is a way to save the estate. Hence your presence here this weekend. And no doubt when she finally accepts that we are not going to wed she will be in pursuit of some other heiress to throw in front of me.'

Rosie's heart lurched, and the bubble of exhilaration inflated by that look finally burst.

Another heiress.

Maybe the next heiress his mother threw in front of him would be a real one—one who actually wanted to marry Alexander. Maybe she'd be someone Alexander was interested in. Maybe she'd be someone he *wanted* to marry.

She stabbed her cheese knife into a piece of Stilton. There was no 'maybe' about it. Eventually Alexander was going to meet someone he wanted to marry. Someone who wasn't just pretending to be an heiress. Her prodding reduced the wedge of Stilton to a pile of mush and she moved on to massacre a slice of Wensleydale.

But surely it would be a *good* thing if he met and married a real heiress. Surely she should want him to be happy. After all, she didn't want him to remain single, did she? He should find himself a wife—someone he could love and who would love him in return.

'Are you planning on eating that cheese, Arabella? Or are you just going to cut it into smaller and smaller portions?'

Rosie gave a small fake laugh. 'I think I've had enough.' She placed her knife down. Yes, she'd had enough food. And, more than that, she'd had enough of this play-acting and enough of being caught up in the moment and thinking she could mean something to Alexander.

She had felt like Cinderella at the ball, wearing her beautiful gown and sitting next to her handsome prince. But this was just another fairy tale—one she had foolishly allowed herself to think was reality. But in the real world the pauper didn't get the prince.

What did it matter how he gazed at her? What did it matter how often he touched her hand? What did it matter if he said she looked beautiful?

It didn't. And she was a fool to think otherwise.

A crushing heaviness suddenly descended on her, sweeping away the sense of lightness and excitement that came from talking and laughing with Alexander.

She had been trying to fool Alexander and his mother by pretending to be Arabella and she had succeeded, but in the process she had managed to fool herself. Fool herself that she could be part of this world, could have a man like Alexander really wanting her, little Rosie Smith, a no-account orphaned ward, with no money, no position—nothing. She didn't even own the beautiful gown she was wearing.

Yes, she had been a fool—a deluded fool.

All she wanted now was for this evening to end, so she could drop this pointless pretence and get back to reality. A reality that did not contain handsome but unattainable dukes or dreams that were far above her expectations.

Chapter Ten

'Ladies, shall we adjourn and leave the men to their port and cigars?' The Dowager stood up before anyone dared to answer her rhetorical question.

Footmen rushed forward to pull out the chairs of the assembled female guests and the women immediately fell into line, as if under orders from a commanding officer.

Rosie joined the brightly coloured trail of well-dressed woman exiting the room to the accompaniment of rustling silk and satin. Mixed emotions coursed through her as she left the dining room…left Alexander's side.

She wanted to spend more time with him, but knew she had to get away. Her behaviour during dinner had been inappropriate—and not in the inappropriate manner she had intended when she had concocted her plan over tea at the Ritz.

Instead of presenting herself as a thoroughly unacceptable future bride she had been giving him long, lingering looks. Instead of making absurd and discourteous statements to prove what an unacceptable duchess she would make she had been sharing an intimate conversation with him. Instead of acting unimpressed and dismissive she had been getting all dewy-eyed, just as Nellie had said.

She had been acting like a woman who was being courted by a man she adored—a woman who was loving every minute of it. And, worst of all, it had not been an act. She had thoroughly enjoyed being in Alexander's company. Had loved the way he looked at her. Had loved him touching her…had wanted more, much more.

What was *wrong* with her? Her friend was depending on her. Her best friend. The friend who had saved her from a life of penury. The friend to whom she owed so much and for whom she claimed she would do anything. Was she such a terrible person that she would allow her head to be turned by a handsome man and forget her promise to her friend? It would seem so. There was only one reason for her visit to Knightsbrook House: to save Arabella from an unwanted marriage. Nothing else.

Rosie wanted to hang her head in shame. Instead she turned before she left the room, for one last look at Alexander. He smiled at her and her foolish heart did a somersault.

The door closed behind the train of women and Rosie shook her head slowly from side to side.

No, this would not do at all. She could not go on behaving like this. She was sending out all the wrong messages. It was time she stopped acting like an infatuated debutante at her first ball of the season. And if she couldn't trust herself with Alexander then it was best if she spent no more time in his company.

The women entered the drawing room, where coffee was being served. Rosie took a delicate white china cup from the parlour maid, sat beside the fire and sipped the rich, nutty drink. Charlotte soon joined her, flopping down in the adjoining wing chair and exhaling loudly.

'Thank goodness that's finally over. These dinner parties are always such a bore,' Charlotte said, and took a decisive bite of her Florentine biscuit.

'Really? You seemed to be enjoying His Grace's attention.' Rosie couldn't help herself. She had to tease the girl.

'No, I was not.' The quick and vehement reply made a lie of Charlotte's answer.

Rosie raised her eyebrows and Charlotte shrugged. There was obviously more to this story than Charlotte was telling.

'Nicholas and I were friends once, but he's changed so much,' Charlotte said. 'All he cares about now is enjoying himself and chasing after—' Her cheeks reddened slightly and her lips pinched with disapproval. 'Chasing after women. He really is quite frightful—and he had so much promise when he was young.'

'But you still find him attractive?'

Charlotte shrugged and stared into the fire. 'Only his appearance is attractive. The things he does and the way he lives his life are anything but attractive.' She sat up straighter in her chair and turned to face Rosie. 'But what about you, Arabella? You and Alexander seemed to be completely absorbed in each other, talking quietly with your heads so close together they were almost touching.'

Rosie took another sip of her coffee while she composed her response. 'Your brother is an interesting conversationalist,' she said, in her most nonchalant manner.

Charlotte's eyes grew wide. 'Really? Alexander? Most of the ladies who attend Mother's dinner parties describe him as taciturn and complain that they can hardly get a word out of him. Not that I blame him. Who wants to spend an evening making small talk about the weather, the last ball they attended or the next ball they plan to attend? Certainly not me, and certainly not Alexander.'

She took another bite of her biscuit and chewed it thoughtfully while watching Rosie.

'So, if you weren't talking about the weather or this season's balls, what *were* you talking about?'

'Oh, I can't really remember. This and that.'

'It must have been a very interesting "this and that". I've never seen Alexander so engrossed in a conversation with a woman. Not since…' Charlotte took a sip of her coffee and looked into the fire, then back at Rosie. 'Not for a long time. And I can hardly remember the last time I saw him laughing. But when he's with you he seems to laugh and smile a lot. I think you're really good for him, Arabella.'

Rosie cringed at the sound of her friend's name. She was *not* Arabella. Whether Rosie made Alexander laugh or not was of no importance. In a few days she would be gone and would never see the FitzRoys again.

'So?' Charlotte said, looking down at her coffee cup and turning it round in the saucer. 'Were you and Alexander discussing your wedding plans?'

Rosie almost spluttered on her coffee. 'No, we weren't discussing *any* wedding plans. I'm afraid Alexander and I will not be getting married. We've discussed it, and neither of us wants it. It was a plan concocted by my father and your mother, without the approval of either of us.'

Charlotte's lips drooped into a pouting frown. 'But you seem to be getting on so well. You seem so right for each other. You were looking at each other as if…' She shook her head slightly and sighed. 'Can't you at least get to know each other a bit better before you decide? You might change your minds. My mother might, for once in her life, be right.'

Rosie shook her head. 'I'm sorry, Charlotte. It's not

possible.' She could not tell this lovely young woman that it was impossible because she wasn't really Arabella.

Charlotte gave another heavy sigh and stared into the fire, her shoulders slumped.

Rosie doubted it was possible to feel any worse. This was not how her plan was supposed to work out. She was not supposed to actually *like* the FitzRoys. They were supposed to be a stuffy, snobby family, grasping after Mr van Haven's money. They were supposed to be people she would not have any qualms about making fun of. Instead the Duke was handsome and charming and his sister was a lovely young woman who was honest, trusting and extremely likeable.

The only person who was despicable was Rosie herself. Despicable for playing this trick on such good people, despicable for lying to Alexander, and despicable for not sticking to the plan she had agreed with the real Arabella over tea at the Ritz. No, she couldn't feel much worse than she did right now.

Charlotte turned from the fire and gave Rosie a sad smile. 'But *we* can still be friends, can't we? Even if you don't marry Alexander?'

Rosie slumped in her chair. She had been wrong. It *was* possible to feel worse. Now she was going to have to lie to Charlotte.

She nodded her head and cringed inwardly. 'Of course we can.'

Another lie, to add to the long list of lies she had already told. Obviously she could not be friends with Charlotte after she left Knightsbrook, as they would never see each other again. And it was unlikely Charlotte would want to be friends with Rosie if she discovered the truth and found out that she had been so shamefully deceived.

'Good. And who knows? Maybe eventually you and Alexander will realise it's not such an impossible match after all and we'll be more than just friends. We'll be sisters!'

Rosie's inward cringe became an outward wince as she gritted her teeth and tried to smile through her embarrassment.

Smiling with satisfaction, Charlotte picked up her coffee cup, lifted it to her lips, then put it back in the saucer. 'I'm sorry, Arabella. I've just realised I'm behaving exactly like my mother. She wants you and Alexander to marry and she cares little for what you two want. And I'm doing exactly the same. I would love it if you got married, but obviously you have to make your own decisions and nobody should force you to do anything you don't want to do.'

'Thank you, Charlotte. But you have nothing to apologise for.'

And that was definitely the truth. If anyone should be apologising it was Rosie.

'But you don't need me putting on the pressure. You're going to have enough of that from Mother—and, believe me, she is a master at putting on the pressure.'

'Is she pressuring you to marry as well?' Rosie was curious to know, but also desperate to change the subject, away from herself and Alexander, or at least form Arabella and Alexander.

'Yes, it's already started.'

Rosie listened while Charlotte detailed the plans and schemes her mother was putting in place to try and get Charlotte married off to Nicholas, Lord Richmond. While Rosie commiserated, a small part of her was grateful that

Charlotte was passionately diverted from discussing any future plans of Arabella and Alexander.

The drawing room door opened. Several men carrying brandy glasses entered along with the waft of cigar smoke. Full of bonhomie, they joined the ladies and the volume of conversation in the room rose markedly. Servants began arranging card tables and the lid of the grand piano was lifted. It seemed the party was not about to end any time soon, and a range of entertainments had been organised for the evening.

Rosie's stomach tightened as if the coffee had been far too strong. It seemed she would be expected to spend more time with Alexander, and to continue pretending for a while longer yet.

Her confusion mounted. What was it she was actually pretending to be? Was she pretending to be interested in Alexander, or not interested in him? Was she not interested, but pretending she was, or interested but pretending she wasn't?

Another smiling man entered the room and Rosie quickly looked up, her stomach clenching. It was not Alexander, and Rosie was both pleased and disappointed. She wanted to see him again, but knew it was wisest not to. And if she was going to avoid seeing Alexander now was the time to take action—because once he entered the room she was unsure whether she would have the willpower to walk away from him.

'I'm starting to get a slight headache,' Rosie told Charlotte—something which did have a kernel of truth to it. All this confusion over what she did and didn't want was starting to make her head spin. 'I'm also a little tired after such an eventful day.'

'Oh, of course—you must retire for the evening if you

aren't well. But Mother will be disappointed. She was expecting you to give us a performance on the banjo tonight. She purchased one especially for the occasion.'

The banjo? Why on earth would the Dowager expect her to play the banjo? Rosie played the piano, not the banjo.

Then suddenly she remembered, and gave a small laugh.

'You *do* play the banjo, don't you, Arabella? You're looking somewhat surprised, but we were told you had been playing since you were a child and are quite brilliant.'

Both Rosie and Arabella had learnt the banjo briefly, when they were in their early teens, when they'd harboured dreams of running off and joining a group of travelling performers. But that dream had died a sudden death, as had so many of their outlandish youthful plans for travel and adventure, and the banjos had been consigned to the attic to gather dust.

Mr van Haven paid such little attention to his only child that he presumably thought Arabella had continued with her banjo lessons and had claimed it as one of her accomplishments.

'I afraid that is one talent I suspect has been greatly exaggerated. So I think it might be best if I do retire early, if I'm to avoid ruining the evening and subjecting the guests to that particular torture.'

She bade Charlotte goodnight, then approached the Dowager, her brow furrowed with fictitious pain.

'I'm sorry, Your Grace, but all the excitement of the day and the journey has left me quite fatigued, and I can feel a terrible headache coming on.' She placed the back of her hand on her forehead to emphasise the point. 'My apologies, but I fear I must retire for the evening.'

It might be another lie, but it was in a good cause. She would be saving the guests from her lack of finesse on the banjo, not to mention saving herself from having to cope with the strange, tumultuous emotions that Alexander elicited in her.

The Dowager smiled and patted her arm. 'Of course, my dear. You must rest. Then you'll be fresh tomorrow. I know Alexander is very keen to show you the rest of the estate; he was talking about it earlier and quite bubbling with enthusiasm.'

Alexander? Bubbling?

It seemed Rosie wasn't the only one capable of stretching the truth.

'I'm sure no one bubbles quite like Alexander,' she couldn't stop herself from saying, before giving a tired smile, bobbing a quick curtsey and retreating as quickly as she could without looking too energetic.

The door closed behind her with a decisive click and she walked as quickly as decorum allowed down the tiled entranceway towards the staircase.

The dining room door opened, releasing a group of smiling men, all talking loudly. She nodded greetings as she passed, determined to escape before she saw Alexander again.

Reaching the staircase, she fought the temptation to run up the stairs. That would hardly fit in with her claim to be tired and have a headache coming on.

'Arabella, are you retiring early?'

His deep, velvety voice was behind her. She froze, then slowly turned to face him, her hand tightly gripping the bottom of the carved banister. He was standing at the dining room doorway, a brandy balloon in his hand, and Arabella's breath left her chest. He looked even more magnificent than when she had first seen him.

Was that even possible?

A shiver ran through her. Her hand clasped her stomach, to still the riotous storm of nerves that had erupted deep within her, and her gaze wandered over the sublimely handsome man staring back at her.

Yes, it seemed it was possible.

With his strong body filling the doorframe, he was a picture of masculine strength and virility. Rosie gasped in a quick breath and slowly exhaled as her gaze moved down his body to those long, lean legs, and the muscles delineated through the black fabric of his trousers. Oh, yes, her original assessment had been right. He was the very image of a Greek statue.

Her gaze moved back up to his face, to his dark brown eyes. Eyes that were sparkling with the reflected candlelight of the large chandelier. Eyes that were drawing her in and holding her tight with the intensity of his gaze. Part of her was frightened by the power of that gaze, but most of her wanted to surrender herself to the strong tidal pull that was sweeping her towards him.

She coughed lightly. 'Yes, I'm feeling a little tired, so I thought I'd retire.'

And I need to escape from you before I make even more of a fool of myself than I already have, she added truthfully to herself.

He placed the brandy glass on a nearby table, the amber liquid swirling in the balloon-shaped glass, and crossed the entranceway. 'Yes, you look pale, Arabella. Is there anything I can do?'

You can stop being so handsome. You can stop being so charming. You can stop making my heart skip every time I see you. Then I wouldn't be looking so pale. Then I wouldn't be feeling so shocked at seeing you again.

'No, nothing. I think I just need an early night.'

'Then allow me to accompany you up to your room. Shall I call my sister to act as a chaperon?'

Rosie shook her head. 'No, don't disturb her. And there's no need to accompany me. Nellie will be waiting for me. She can see to my needs.'

Another lie. Only Alexander would be able to see to the need that was surging up within Rosie. A need to be taken in his arms. A need to be held by him. A need to feel those full, sculpted lips pressed against hers.

Rosie closed her eyes and blinked several times to try and clear that image from her mind. But when she opened her eyes she was staring straight at those sculpted lips…lips that were saying something…something that the pounding of her heart prevented her from hearing.

'I beg your pardon? What did you say?'

'I was offering you my arm so I can help you up the stairs.'

'Oh, yes. Of course.'

Rosie was sure that touching him right now was the worst thing she could do, but what could she say? *No, I don't want to take your arm? If I take your arm I don't think I'll be able to trust myself not to do something so inappropriate that even I'll be shocked by it?*

He held out his arm and Rosie drew in a series of steadying breaths. She commanded her fingers to un-clench themselves from the banister and lightly placed her hand on his forearm.

She briefly closed her eyes, registering the touch of

her skin on his muscular arm, and tried to ignore the tingling sensation burning its way up her arm to her chest and taking over her body.

As they ascended the stairs she could hear him making polite conversation, but what he said she had no idea. All she could do was react to the closeness of his warm body and the wonderful scent of him…pure, heady masculinity.

Rosie followed where he led, sure that if she had been trying to find her way down the maze of corridors with their array of paintings and sculptures adorning the walls she would have got completely lost, her mind was so befuddled.

They'd reached her door.

He paused, removed her hand from his arm and took it in both of his. He smiled gently down at her. 'It seems you are starting to feel a bit better, Arabella. Colour has returned to your face,' he said, his voice concerned.

Rosie didn't doubt that she was blushing—the heat radiating from her burning cheeks was making that very clear. And it was not just her cheeks that were burning. Rosie was sure her entire body must be blushing. It was pulsating fiercely as her heart thumped within her chest, as if she'd just undertaken some kind of furious exercise.

'Th-thank you,' she stammered, unsure what she was thanking him for.

'Well, I will leave you to your rest.'

But he remained staring down at her, once again capturing Rosie with the intensity of his brown eyes.

'Goodnight, then,' Rosie murmured, unable to move herself.

He lifted her hand and lightly kissed the back of it, his eyes still burning into hers. Rosie closed her eyes, loving the feeling of the touch of his lips on her skin. But she wanted more.

As if her hand had a mind of its own it turned over and lightly stroked his strong jawline. Her gaze moved to his lips. Those full, sensual lips. And she imagined what it would be like to be kissed by him.

Tingling erupted on her lips and she gave a small moan. She caught her bottom lip with her teeth, slowly raking them across the skin to stop any more tell-tale reactions.

Alexander's hand gently clasped her wrist. Their eyes locked. Heat surged through her as she registered the hunger in his dark eyes…a hunger both exciting and un-nerving.

Time froze. Every inch of her body tensed as she waited for him to act. Her breath caught in her throat. She stared up at him, waiting to see what he would do next. Would he kiss her? Oh, how she wanted him to kiss her.

In answer to her silent plea his lips met hers, his kiss crashing over her like turbulent water escaping from a ruptured dam. As his skin rasped against her cheek she inhaled the lemon scent of his shaving soap. Then a stronger, underlying masculine scent and taste filled her senses like a powerful narcotic, taking her over, intoxi-cating her, leaving her incapable of thought.

But now was definitely not the time for thinking.

Her lips parted wider, to savour more of that musky masculine taste and the delicious hint of brandy. To her surprise his tongue entered her mouth. Was this how men and women kissed? It was her first time, so how could she be sure—but, oh, how good it felt.

His tongue continued to lick and probe, tasting her until she was sure she would collapse from the heady pleasure of having it so intimately inside her mouth. But she couldn't collapse—not with his arms holding her close, so close she could feel the muscular imprint of his strong chest against her breasts, feel his long, lean thighs against hers, feel his hard arousal against her stomach.

Rosie gasped, realising what was pressing against her, his unmistakable need for her.

What would happen now?

Rosie had no idea. She had often wondered whether a man would ever kiss her and, if so, if she would know what to do. But it seemed all she had to do was surrender herself to Alexander and he would guide her. With him to lead her she was free to give herself over to the wild, primitive need building up inside her. The insatiable need for *him*.

Tendrils of hair became dislodged from her carefully constructed coiffure, tumbling around her naked shoulders, intensifying that glorious sense of abandon.

Her tongue took a few tentative licks at his lips, then entered his mouth. Their tongues engaged in an erotic dual, causing him to release a soft moan of pleasure. Exhilaration surged through her. She had made him moan—moan for *her*. Oh, yes, this felt so right. She wanted more of this. Wanted to explore his strong masculine body... wanted to discover just how much pleasure she could experience and how much pleasure he could give her.

Encircling his neck, she ran her hands up through his thick brown hair. She growled with pleasure as his kiss deepened. Her body moved to its own rhythm as his hands ran down her spine, cupping her buttocks and pulling her firmly against his body.

Oh, yes, she definitely wanted more of this. She wanted him never to stop kissing her, never to let her go.

Without thinking, just reacting to the needs of her body, she rubbed her swollen breasts against his hard chest, her tight nipples pressing through the soft fabric of her gown and aching to be touched. To be touched by *him*.

His lips left hers, but her disappointment was quashed when he kissed a line slowly down her neck. Rosie tilted back her head, loving the touch of his lips on her exposed skin as every kiss sent waves of pleasure rippling through her body.

When he reached the base of her neck she mentally urged him to go further. His lips obeyed.

He slid the neckline of her dress off one shoulder, then the other, his lips kissing a tantalising line across her skin. Rosie's breath came in faster and faster gasps, her heart pounded loudly in her chest, and a throbbing pleasure erupted deep within her core.

'Oh, Arabella, you're so beautiful,' he murmured, then kissed her neck, his husky voice almost unrecognisable.

Rosie froze.

Arabella. He had called her Arabella.

She was not Arabella. She was Rosie Smith. And what was she doing? Kissing a man who thought she was Arabella. She was tarnishing Arabella's good reputation. How could she *do* that? What sort of woman *was* she?

She closed her eyes and took a few deep breaths to bring herself back to reality. When she opened her eyes he too had changed. His posture had become rigid, his face stern. Her hesitation seemed to have broken the spell that had captured them both. He appeared to be emerging from a trance, as if he were suddenly registering just what they were doing.

'I beg your pardon, Arabella. Please forgive me.'

She shook her head. He had nothing to be sorry for. It

was she who should be sorry. She was the one who had forgotten who she was—the one who had betrayed her best friend's good name.

He coughed, inhaled deeply, then released his breath slowly. 'I took advantage of you. I'm so sorry.'

She stared at him as if he were talking an unknown foreign language. What did he mean? Took advantage of her? How?

In a daze, she watched as he pulled up her dislodged neckline and retrieved her abandoned hairclips from the floor.

'Kissing you was unpardonable, but I hope you can one day forgive me?'

'No. I mean yes. I mean, you've done nothing that needs my forgiveness.'

Rosie touched her lips. That kiss had been the most wonderful thing that had ever happened to her. How could he say it was unforgivable?

He looked down at his hands, now clenched into fists around her hairclips. 'I have. I took advantage of you and I am sorry.'

Rosie shook her head again. He was so wrong. She had wanted him to kiss her. She still wanted him to kiss her. To hold her. To caress her. Even now that she knew it was wrong and could never happen again.

'My behaviour would be unforgivable under any circumstances, but it is especially reprehensible that I took advantage of a woman who is all but betrothed to another.'

What was he talking about? *All but betrothed?* Then with a sinking feeling she remembered Thomas Gardener. The non-existent Thomas Gardener. He thought he was betraying a non-existent man, when it was Rosie who was betraying a real person—her best friend, the friend who had saved her from poverty, the friend who had always treated her like a sister.

'Please, I implore you, do not feel you have in any way wronged me.'

'You are an admirable young woman, Arabella. It seems that is another virtue to add to the long list.' He handed her the retrieved hairclips.

She took them from his outstretched hands and stared down at them as if unsure what they were, once again shamed by her actions. Admirable? Nothing about her was admirable. And if she actually did possess any virtues she couldn't think of a single one right now.

No, there was nothing admirable about the lies she had told him—was still telling him. Nothing admirable about what she had just done. To satisfy her own longings she had put her friend's reputation at risk. The only admirable person was the man standing before her, begging for her forgiveness.

And there was certainly nothing admirable about her wish that he would kiss her again. Even now—now that she realised just how wrong it had been—she still wanted it. How could she want something that was so wrong so badly? No, there was nothing admirable about Rosie Smith.

'Perhaps we should put it down to the heat of the moment,' she said, as much to excuse her own bad behaviour as to make him feel less remorseful. 'We must put it behind us and pretend it never happened.'

Although she knew that was yet another lie. There was no way she would ever forget the touch of Alexander's lips on hers, nor how it had felt to be encased in his arms. That feeling would stay with her for ever.

He bowed. 'You are very gracious. I wish you good-night, Arabella.'

Graciousness—that was another virtue she doubted she actually possessed.

'Goodnight, Alexander,' she murmured.

She remained rooted to the spot, watching his back as he retreated down the corridor. When he disappeared around the corner she inhaled deeply and placed a steadying hand on her rapidly beating heart. She entered her bedroom, leaned against the closed door and slid to the floor, her body suddenly too heavy for her to remain standing.

With her head in her hands she vowed that it would never happen again. If she could not trust herself in the Duke's company she must never allow herself to be alone with him. *Ever*.

Chapter Eleven

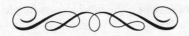

That should not have happened. That most definitely should not have happened. What had he been *thinking*? That was the problem. He hadn't been thinking—just reacting.

He had felt so close to her over dinner. They had laughed together, talked together, shared a closeness that he had not felt for a long time, and it had affected his ability to reason clearly. And then, when he had seen her looking up at him, desire sparking in those big blue eyes, the last vestige of reason he'd possessed had been trampled under his need to take her in his arms.

He had ignored the small voice in his mind that had warned him it was wrong because he'd wanted her so much.

Alexander slammed shut the door and paced his bedroom floor. With his blood pumping, his body tense and his throbbing lust for Arabella straining his breeches, he desperately needed release from this pent-up desire. He had to free himself of this demanding need for her, for the feel of her, the taste and smell of her.

And that wasn't going to happen if he continued to

think about what she'd looked like with her hair tumbling loose around her naked shoulders, her red lips wet and plump, her full breasts arching towards him invitingly and with that look in her eyes—a look that had mirrored his own insatiable desire.

No, it should never have happened. He should never have taken her in his arms. The moment he'd given in to that temptation he had been incapable of stopping, incapable of resisting the need to kiss her, to caress her warm, silky skin.

Balling his hands into tight fists at his sides, he tried to erase the feel of her, tried to chase away the fresh scent of spring flowers that still filled his senses, tried to drive out the image of her gazing up at him with hooded eyes, her lips parted, the mounds of her breasts rising and falling in her tight bodice as she waited for his kiss.

That he was falling for the beautiful Arabella van Haven there could be no denying. He slammed his fist against the wall. He was a fool—a damn fool. After Lydia's betrayal, the next woman he'd fallen for was someone betrothed to another. Was he a glutton for punishment? Had Lydia not hurt him enough with her lies, her tricks?

Because of Lydia he had vowed never to let a woman affect him ever again. But he had let his guard down because Arabella was not like Lydia. She didn't lie. She didn't deceive others for her own ends. She was an innocent young woman. And that only made his behaviour worse.

Lydia had been betrothed to him and had been seduced away by another. Now he had almost done to Arabella what that rake had done to Lydia. He had tried to have his way with a woman who was in love with someone else, who planned to marry someone else. At the time he had despised the man who had seduced Lydia, and yet now he had shown himself to be no better—to be just as much a reprobate as that man had been, a man driven only by his lust for a beautiful woman.

He paced backwards and forwards, rubbing his now bloodied hand, his breath coming in a series of rapid gasps.

Lydia had given herself to that man and followed him into a life of debauchery. Her position in society had been ruined for ever. And now *he* was set on ruining the reputation of a lovely young woman all because he'd wanted her so badly he had forgotten himself—had forgotten all sense of propriety, all sense of decency.

He could only be grateful that she had come to her senses and stopped him. Her sudden withdrawal from his touch had allowed the memory of her telling him that she was in love with another man to invade his fevered brain.

If she hadn't come to her senses he would have been incapable of stopping at just a kiss. He would have taken her to his bedroom and torn off her restricting clothing. He would have freed those enticing breasts, released the tight, sensitive nipples so he could take them in his mouth, kiss them, nuzzle them, lick them until she was senseless with lust for him.

She would now be lying beneath him, writhing under his touch as he kissed every inch of her body. Her legs would be wrapped tightly around his waist as she gave herself to him, opened herself up for him so he could enter her. She would be calling out his name, desperate for the pleasure he would give her, the pleasure she would give *him*.

He slammed his bloodied fist against the wall, leaving a red smear on the cream paper. Yes, he was a fool.

A damn fool. He should not even be *thinking* such things. She belonged to another man. She was in love with another man. Yes, she had kissed him back. Yes, she had responded to his touch. But she was an innocent. It was he who should have known better than to take her into his arms. It was unforgivable.

He had been so desperate to satisfy his own consuming lust for her that all he had cared about was satisfying his own needs. But it wasn't just her body that was driving him mad with desire. He could not remember the last time he had enjoyed a woman's company more. Talking to her had made his mother's unbearable dinner party more than just bearable—it had been entertaining.

It was wrong—and yet for one moment it had felt so right. It had felt as if she was his. When she had been in his arms it had felt as if she belonged there, belonged to *him*. But it was not where she belonged. She was not his. She was in love with another man—all but betrothed to another man.

Explosive energy continued to pump through his veins. He would go mad if he remained in this room, pacing like a caged tiger.

With unnecessary force he pulled open his bedroom door and slammed it shut behind him. He had to get out of the house, out into the open. He needed to feel the cold night air on his face.

He ran down the stairs and out through the front door, ignoring the startled looks of the servants. He crossed the lawn, bathed in the soft light spilling out through the house's large windows, ripping off his jacket, his waistcoat and his shirt. When he reached the lake he pulled off his boots and his trousers and tossed them to the ground. Naked, he dived in.

The cold water hit him like a punch—the punch he needed...the punch he deserved.

But the cold water was not enough to douse his burning lust for Arabella. He swam the length of the lake, his arms rapidly slicing through the water. When he reached the opposite edge he turned and swam back, again and again.

The lights from the house did not reach the lake, and the dark moonless sky made it almost impossible to see his way as he raced up and down in the inky black water. But he had swum this lake many times. He knew it so thoroughly he could navigate his way without sight, without thought. And that was what he needed. Not to think. To exhaust himself.

His body finally began to tire, but he pushed himself on, forcing himself to continue despite his fatigue. Finally, his energy completely spent, he came to a halt. He flicked the water out of his hair and held on to the stone paving at the edge of the lake, his breath coming fast, his heart thumping with the exertion.

He looked up at the house, now in complete darkness. While he'd been swimming the guests, his family and even the servants had all retired for the night. Arabella was no doubt now asleep.

An image of Arabella in her four-poster bed invaded his mind, with her long black hair spread out across a white pillow, her lithe body lying in repose. Her delicious curves would be visible through a linen nightdress...

He slapped at the water. Why did he have to think of that? Why did he have to torture himself? All that strenuous exercise had been for nought if it hadn't driven thoughts of Arabella from his mind.

He forced himself to swim one more length of the lake.

Slowly he ploughed through the cold water, his muscles screaming out for him to stop. He reached the end, but his mind still reeled with images of Arabella.

This was insufferable. His fatigue was so intense that if he swum another length surely he would drown. It seemed if he was ever to be free he was going to have to exercise strenuous control over his mind, not just his body.

Summoning up every last ounce of strength, he dragged himself out of the lake, grabbed his trousers and pulled them over his wet body. He picked up his boots and crossed the lawn to retrieve his discarded shirt, waistcoat and jacket, now damp from the night-time dew. Slowly he retraced his steps up the path to the dark house, returned to his room and fell onto his bed in complete exhaustion.

He stared up at the ceiling and made a solemn vow. Even if the opportunity arose, and even if the temptation was overwhelming, he would not succumb to his feelings for Arabella van Haven. He would never again take her in his arms. Never again would he kiss her. He would exercise stringent self-control.

He just had to keep reminding himself that she would never be his. Her heart belonged to another. Whatever he might feel for her, she was not his. He had to be strong and never touch her again, never kiss her again. *Ever.*

Chapter Twelve

Drawing in a deep, steadying breath, Alexander paused outside the breakfast room. He nodded to the footman to indicate that he wasn't yet ready to enter, and spent some time composing himself.

It was time to put his resolve into action—to stay true to the promises he had made to himself last night. His muscles ached slightly, reminding him of his new determination. Arabella van Haven was simply a guest in his home. A guest who would be leaving tomorrow. A guest from whom he would keep his distance. He would not get too close to her, either physically or emotionally. Getting close contained too many dangers. That was all he had to remember.

Forcefully he turned the door handle and strode into the room. The three people sitting at the breakfast table looked up at him and smiled simultaneously: his mother, Charlotte and Miss van Haven.

Seated with her back to the large sash windows, Arabella was bathed in morning sunlight. Alexander almost suspected his mother of placing her where her beauty would be displayed at its most advantageous. The sunlight glinted off the copper strands in her otherwise black hair, her skin appeared luminescent and a golden glow surrounded her—as if she were a maiden in a Renaissance painting.

He nodded a greeting to the three women and turned his back—ostensibly to serve himself from the silver tureens arranged along the sideboard, but in reality to regain his equilibrium and remind himself once again of his resolve. It didn't matter how beautiful she looked in the morning sunlight—not in the slightest. He would not let that or anything else undermine his determination.

Standing straighter, he walked to the table without looking at Arabella, sat down, whipped open his napkin, placed it on his lap and stared down at his food. Why had he served himself a full breakfast when he didn't feel like eating?

He coughed lightly to clear his throat. 'I trust you slept well, Miss van Haven?' he asked, for politeness' sake. From now onwards it would be formality only. She would be Miss van Haven. No more of this calling each other by their first names. After all, look where adopting the more informal American ways had got them. No, he did not wish to go there again.

'I slept very well, thank you, Your Grace.'

Good. She too had the sense to see the necessity of formality. On that it seemed they were in complete agreement.

His mother, however, had raised her eyebrows and was looking from one to the other of them with curiosity. But what his mother thought hardly mattered. It was his mother who had created this problem in the first place, inviting the American heiress into his home without his knowledge or his permission.

'And you, Your Grace? I hope you also slept well.'

Alexander nodded once, quickly, in response to Arabella's enquiry. Yes, he had indeed been able to sleep—but only because he had exercised so furiously he had been in a state of complete physical exhaustion. Without that rigorous swim he doubted he would have been able to chase away thoughts of kissing her, of her soft lips on his, of her pliant body crushed against his, her soft breasts and tight nipples pushing into his chest…

He coughed again as heat flooded his body, then shook his napkin vigorously to drive out those treacherous thoughts and set about carving up his breakfast.

'Well, now that we've established you both slept well, perhaps we can discuss what activities you have planned for the day,' his mother said. 'Alexander, I think it would be a splendid idea if you showed Miss van Haven more of the estate. That is, once you've finished decimating that defenceless kipper.'

Alexander stopped and looked down at the mash of white flesh spread across his plate, then pushed away his uneaten breakfast. 'I'm not sure what Miss van Haven has planned for today, but I intend to inspect the marshlands at the bottom of the estate. The engineers are coming next week, to begin draining the area so it can be turned into viable farmland. I'm sure that would be of no interest to our guest.'

'Oh, I'm sure Miss van Haven would be delighted to accompany you.'

Alexander inhaled a deep, exasperated breath. Would his mother's infernal meddling never cease? He knew the answer to that. No, of course it would not. Not until Miss van Haven was in her carriage, heading for the railway station and moving out of his life.

'I very much doubt if the marshland would be of any interest to a lady—it's swampy underfoot, and hardly suitable for a leisurely stroll,' he said, hoping that would be the end of the matter.

'Well, if—'

'Nonsense,' his mother answered, cutting off Arabella before she could express her opinion. 'It will give you a chance to show Miss van Haven the parts of the estate she hasn't yet seen—and who knows? She might be interested in your plans for modernisation.'

His mother's lips turned down and her nostrils flared, as if the very idea of anyone being interested in such a subject was extremely unlikely.

'Well, if His Grace would rather—'

'Or you could stay inside all day, Miss van Haven,' his mother interrupted again, a mischievous look sparking in her eyes. 'Our parish priest, the Reverend Truebridge, is an amateur historian, and he has volunteered to give us a talk on the history of Devon—starting with the Bronze Age and working forward to the present day, covering each period in the minutest detail. He can be a little tedious at times, I must admit, and he does tend to go on and on, but he is certainly enthusiastic about his topic. Do you think you might prefer that?'

Arabella's polite smile started to falter, while his mother's smile grew more gleeful.

'After that, some of the older ladies in the party and I are planning on playing cards. Poor Lady Cathridge is having such problems with her lumbago, so we're hoping to discuss that—and many of the other ailments the ladies have suffered with so much over the winter. Aged bodies can be such a trial... The card game will be a good chance for us to catch up and discuss our aches and pains. You're most welcome to join us for that as well, Arabella.'

She smiled with mock innocence at Arabella and waited for her reply. Arabella stared at the Dowager, her brow now deeply furrowed and her lips pinched— like a prisoner watching the iron gates being slammed shut behind her.

Alexander knew he had to offer a reprieve. 'Or if you prefer you can, of course, accompany me. The marsh-lands may be a bit unsightly, but the walk there will take us through the woodlands and across the farm areas, which are very pleasant at this time of year.'

'Oh, yes, thank you!' she gasped, in obvious gratitude. Recovering, she smiled at his mother. 'And thank *you*, also, Your Grace, for your kind invitation, but I would like to get some fresh air.'

The Dowager smiled in triumph. 'Think nothing of it, my dear. You young people go off and enjoy yourselves.'

'But we must take a chaperon with us.' Alexander stated emphatically.

'Oh, yes—most definitely.'

Arabella's quick response cut Alexander to the quick. She obviously feared being alone with him.

'Nellie will accompany us,' she said.

'That's all settled, then.' His mother smiled. 'And don't feel the need to hurry back—unless, of course, you want to catch some of Reverend Truebridge's talk.'

Alexander glared at his mother. It seemed she had won. Yet again.

Alexander paced backwards and forwards, his boots scrunching on the gravel path, as he waited at the bottom of the stairs for Arabella. A quick walk around the farmlands and back to the house would suffice. That way there would be no danger of them being alone together. They would be in the presence of the tenant farmers through much of the walk, and he was hardly likely to act inappropriately with an audience.

And there would also be Nellie. That should solve both their problems. It would save Arabella from his mother's threat of a torturous death by boredom without the risk of him being alone in her company. Then he could get back to what he'd originally intended for the day: a survey of the marshlands. There was nothing to worry about.

So why did he feel so agitated? He pulled in a few quick breaths to quash the gnawing feeling in the pit of his stomach. This was ridiculous. He did *not* get anxious. And certainly not because of a pretty face.

'Hello, there. I'm ready.'

He turned to see the owner of the pretty face that was causing all this perturbation standing at the top of the stairs, accompanied by her maid. The pretty face was wearing an attractive blue hat that made her crystal-blue eyes even more enchanting.

He coughed to drive away such nonsense. She had a blue hat on which happened to match her eyes. That was all. There was no need to make more of it than that and become absurdly poetical.

'Miss van Haven.' He nodded a terse greeting as she skipped down the stairs.

'Your Grace.' She bobbed a curtsey.

For politeness' sake he offered her his arm, and refused to allow himself to react when he felt the pressure of her gloved hand.

They walked along in silence and Alexander knew that he should make conversation. But what should he say to the woman whom he had taken in his arms and kissed with an intensity as if his very life depended on it? Should he ask about her health? Should he mention how warm it was for this time of year?

No words came, and once again he coughed lightly. This was not like him. He *never* felt awkward. But he was feeling increasingly awkward in her company. Like an adolescent boy unused to the company of the opposite sex. Ridiculous.

'I hope you're not feeling at all worried about what happened last night,' she said, finally breaking the prolonged silence.

About to say he was not worried in the least, he pulled himself up. That would be an outright lie. Of course he was worried by his behaviour. How else should he feel when he had taken advantage of a vulnerable woman for his own lustful purposes?

'I'm very sorry it happened. I can assure you it will never happen again.'

She stopped walking and looked up at him. 'I said last night that you had nothing to be sorry for and I meant it. I would hate what happened to come between us.'

Beseeching eyes stared up at him. Alexander's stern countenance slipped as he stared down at her and he almost forgot his resolve.

He forced himself to look away from those blue eyes and into the distance. 'It is perhaps a bit too late for that.'

'It doesn't have to be, Alexander.' She gripped his arm with both hands, forcing him to look at her. 'You did nothing wrong. I am not offended. The only thing that upsets me is that it has caused a rift between us. I wish we could go back to how we were before the kiss.

Then we could be friends again and comfortable in each other's company.'

'But it *did* happen.'

'Well, I can pretend it never happened if you can.'

Was that possible? Alexander doubted he would ever forget what it had been like to take her in his arms, but he nodded his agreement.

'If that is what you wish, Miss van Haven.'

'It is. And I also wish that you would stop being so formal. Call me Arabella again.'

Not for the first time he realised what a remarkable woman she was. She had every right to be offended, to be upset, to be angry, but she was none of those things. Thomas Gardener was most definitely a very lucky man.

He clenched his jaw at the thought of that man—the man who would have what he could not. He dragged in a deep prolonged breath to drive away the ridiculous thought. Jealousy was something else he did not experience, and he wasn't about to start experiencing it now.

'As you wish, Arabella,' he said, through clenched teeth.

Strolling with him arm and arm, Rosie could almost convince herself that things were just the same between her and Alexander. Almost. But she could sense the tension in his body, feel the unease in her own.

While she might not be able to forget that kiss, she knew she had to pretend it had never happened. They had one more day to spend together and she wanted them once again to be relaxed in each other's company. And that wouldn't happen unless they did indeed try and pretend nothing had changed…that they had not experienced that moment of passionate intimacy.

But she most certainly had no intention of trying to forget that kiss. It was the most wonderful thing that had ever happened to her. Yes, it had been wrong—so wrong—but it was something she would always treasure…something she would savour when she was alone.

Kissing him was so completely outside her original plan as to be almost unbelievable. After all, she had arrived with the intention of making the Duke dislike her. She had intended to behave in a manner that would make her a thoroughly unacceptable bride. Instead she had caused this sublimely handsome, imminently eligible man to desire her.

A thrill of excitement ran through Rosie's body. Who would ever have thought it possible that poor little Rosie Smith, an impoverished ward whom nobody ever noticed, would be kissed with such intensity by such a man? But she *had* been.

She ran her tongue along her bottom lip, where his lips had touched, and shivered at the delicious thrill of it all.

'Are you all right, Arabella?' His look was solicitous. 'You're not too cold?'

'Not in the slightest. It's a beautiful day.'

And so it was. The sun was shining in a bright blue sky dotted with puffy white clouds. She was walking through lush green pastures filled with bleating sheep and sweet baby lambs accompanied by a sublimely handsome man. It was indeed a most beautiful day. And her shiver had nothing to do with the temperature, which was delightfully warm.

Rosie gave a contented smile. As long as they remained in public, surely there was no harm in indulging in a little fantasy that she was taking a lovely stroll on the arm of the man who was courting her? It was a fantasy that would come to an end when she left Knightsbrook, and as long as Rosie did nothing to act on it no one would get hurt.

And with Nellie as her chaperon she was safe.

She looked over her shoulder and saw Nellie lagging behind in the distance. It seemed she had already become distracted and oblivious to her duties.

'Do keep up, Nellie!' she called out.

Nellie stopped staring at the farmhands and rolled her eyes at Rosie in a most un-servant-like manner, but she walked a little faster to catch up.

They resumed their walk, which now took them along the side of a furrowed field, where a line of men and boys were casting seeds from sacks on their backs. As they passed by the men all lifted their cloth caps to Alexander and he shouted out hellos, addressing many by name.

'You seem to know everyone well,' Rosie said, surprised at their informality.

Alexander smiled. 'Yes, I suppose so—but I grew up with them. I almost spent more time with the farmhands as a child than I did with my own family.'

His smile died and he looked out at the tenants, his face solemn.

'Those times were among the happiest of my childhood. My father saw our tenants as a mass of people who worked the land and brought in the revenue that he spent. But I learnt to see each and every one of them as an individual. I could see that they were hard-working people who deserved to be treated with respect.'

He sent her a melancholy smile and she gave his arm a small squeeze.

'Well, it's certainly a beautiful estate to have grown

up on. It's so picturesque. Watching the men work is like seeing a painting by Constable come to life,' Rosie said, breathing in the earthy smell of freshly turned soil.

'Yes, my mother would certainly agree with you on that.'

Rosie tilted her head. 'You don't approve?'

'The tenants aren't here to be "picturesque". They want to make a good living—they want the land to be productive. They should be using machinery to plant out the crops and machinery to bring them in. Not doing it by such intense physical labour. If my father had spent as much money updating the estate as he did at the card table these people would not still be involved in such back-breaking toil. And that is something I intend to change.'

Rosie looked at the men labouring over their work and had to agree. She would hate to have to work that hard—especially when there was machinery that could do the work more quickly.

'Oh, yes. You should. If you used steam engines for ploughing the land and bringing in the harvest, it would free up men and you could farm more intensively and diversify your crops.'

He had stopped walking and was now staring down at her, that wonderful smile once again lighting up his face.

'Exactly. That's *exactly* the sort of modern equipment I want to buy. It will transform the estate.'

Rosie smiled back at him. 'If you brought electricity to the estate then the dairy and the shearing sheds could be made much more productive. And if the train came as far as the estate you'd be able to sell produce in London. And once it reaches London, who knows? With refrigeration you could export to Europe and even farther

afield. Oh, the possibilities are endless for making this
estate really modern and efficient!'

He was still staring down at her, no longer smiling,
but looking at her with wide eyes, his eyebrows raised.
Rosie suspected she had been babbling.

'I'm sorry. My father was—' She halted as she remembered who she was supposed to be. 'My father has worked
with electrical engineers and I think it has instilled in me
a love of all technological advances.'

Rosie had only been a young girl of eight when her
father had died, but she could still remember the passion in his voice when he'd talked of the progress being
made in America, and how electricity was transforming
the lives of so many people. Alexander's enthusiasm reminded her of those happy times.

He shook his head and sent her another of those lovely
smiles. 'You truly are a remarkable woman, Arabella,
and I applaud the fact that you are so enthusiastic about
modernisation. Most people of my class are content to
continue living as they have for centuries, just sitting
back and letting the money roll in from their land. They
don't realise that times are changing—that we're being
overtaken by the more progressive farming techniques
used in America and the Antipodes. But I, for one, am
determined not to be left behind. I want to be ready for
the twentieth century and all the modern advances it
has to offer.'

Arabella smiled, feeling warm inside.

'But unfortunately it will take money—which, thanks
to my father, I don't have.'

The tone of his voice had dropped from excitement to
pain and anger, and a stab of guilt pierced Rosie's heart. If
she hadn't come up with her plan to trick Alexander…if

the real Arabella were here instead of her, and if they had actually fallen in love…maybe Arabella's dowry could have been used to settle those debts and modernise the estate. Then the tenants would have had security and Knightsbrook would have been saved.

'So Ara—so my father's money would have gone to good use?' Rosie asked, feeling guilty bile rise up in her throat.

Alexander shook his head. 'It might have been a short-term solution, but it was never something I was prepared to consider. I intend to raise the money through bank loans and make the necessary changes to ensure the estate becomes profitable once more. I want it to be a place where both my family and the tenants feel proud to live. I want the name of Knightsbrook to be an honourable one once again—a name associated with industry, innovation and enterprise. And that won't happen by taking a hand-out from your father.'

Rosie could hear the passion and determination in his voice and she swelled with admiration. He was most definitely a proud man, and she was honoured to be in his company—even if it *was* under false pretences.

The path had reached a stone fence with a wooden stile. Alexander quickly climbed over, then offered his hand to her. She didn't really need his help—she was used to fending for herself—but it was nice to feel his hand in hers once again, even if it was through her linen glove.

She stepped over, and was about to jump down when he placed his hands on her waist and lifted her gently off the wooden step. Her feet touched the ground lightly and his hands remained on her hips, his body close to hers. He stared down into her eyes. She looked up at him expectantly. A gasp escaped her lips and for a hopeful moment she thought he was going to kiss her again.

What she wouldn't give for another kiss…what she wouldn't sacrifice to feel his lips on hers!

His lips drew into a tight line and he removed his hands from her hips. It wasn't to be.

Disappointment, guilt and shame waged a war inside her as they continued their walk in silence, with Nellie trailing along behind. How could she want him to kiss her so much when she knew the harm it would cause? How could she feel so disappointed when she knew they must not kiss? How could she be such a shameful, terrible person?

She cared for Arabella more than she cared for anyone in the world—even more than herself. She would do nothing to hurt her, to tarnish her good name. And yet she still wanted Alexander to take her in his arms, to kiss her. It was beyond reprehensible.

Their walk took them towards a group of thatched cottages nestled together beside a small stream, smoke rising from their chimneys.

'I hope you don't mind,' said Alexander, 'but I can't pass by this way without visiting Annie.'

'Annie?'

Alexander smiled. 'You'll love Annie. She was like a second mother to me and to Charlotte when we were children. More than a second mother.'

A group of women were sitting in a circle outside the cottages, chatting and laughing while they darned socks and mended clothing. When they saw Alexander and Rosie approaching they stopped what they were doing and stood up.

One woman started walking towards them, her arms

outstretched. Although her lined, weathered face suggested she was elderly, the woman still had a youthful agility to her movements and a healthy glow on her round cheeks. Her welcoming smile caused Rosie to warm to her immediately, as if she too was being welcomed home by a loving grandmother.

'This is Annie,' Alexander said, his smile growing as wide as the older woman's.

'Alexander!' Annie said, reaching up and embracing him. 'Or should I say Your Grace? I keep forgetting you're all grown-up now. It's so good to see you again.'

'To you, Annie, I will always be Alexander. And it is very good to see *you*—you're looking younger than ever.'

Annie waved her hand at him, as if refusing to take any flattery, but her smile showed how much she enjoyed it. 'And who's this lovely young lady?'

'This is Arabella van Haven—a visitor from America. I'm showing her around the estate.'

'Oh, indeed? So *you're* the young lady from America. Well, well... I'm pleased to meet you, m'lady.'

Annie made a low curtsey, causing Rosie to laugh.

'Please—there's no need for formality with me. I don't have a title.'

Annie's eyebrows rose and she looked sideways at Alexander. 'Not yet, perhaps—but if what the servants up at the big house are saying is right you'll have a title soon enough.'

Rosie waited for Alexander to counter her claim but he merely shrugged, as if to apologise, indicating that even if he didn't agree he wasn't going to contradict Annie.

'So, tell me what's been happening on the estate, Annie?'

'I'll let you know all the gossip—but, please, come inside. I'm sure you'd like tea.'

'Nothing escapes Annie's notice,' Alexander said, still smiling as they followed her inside. 'She knows everyone who works on the estate, and all the people in the village, and everyone knows her.'

Rosie looked around to see where Nellie had got to but she was nowhere in sight. It seemed the call of the library had been too great and she had deliberately hung back once again.

They entered Annie's tidy cottage and were greeted by the welcoming aroma of freshly baked bread. The cottage was simply but pleasantly decorated, with handwoven rugs on the wooden floor, spring flowers in pottery vases and old but comfortable-looking furniture.

Alexander breathed in deeply and smiled. 'That's the smell of my childhood—bread fresh out of the oven.'

They sat down at a scrubbed pine table while Annie put the kettle on the stove and poked some wood into the firebox.

'Charlotte and I spent many hours here at this cottage, gorging ourselves on Annie's cooking and playing in her garden. We probably spent more time here than we did in our own home.'

Rosie could see why any child would want to visit Annie's cottage. It was much more welcoming than the opulence and formality of Knightsbrook House, and there was a caring warmth to Annie that no child would be able to resist.

'Poor Lady Charlotte,' Annie said as she poured hot water into a brown teapot. 'She's such a lovely girl, but so serious. She needs a good man in her life.'

Alexander gave a mock frown. 'Don't let Charlotte hear you say that. She's determined to remain single.'

'Oh, don't worry—I've already told her. She gave me that look she always gives when she hears something she don't like—just like your mam.' Annie pinched her lips together and flared her nostrils, causing Alexander to laugh. 'But I'm very happy *you've* found someone special, Alexander—and such a pretty girl as well.'

Again, Rosie expected Alexander to disabuse Annie, but still he said nothing.

Annie took a golden loaf of bread out of the oven, and Rosie stood and offered to help. But she was shooed away with a smile and the wave of a tea towel.

'I can already tell she's a good influence on you, Alexander. The last time I saw you, you seemed to be carrying the weight of world on your shoulders and I could barely get a smile out of you.'

She placed the bread on the table, along with the teapot and three teacups. Rosie inhaled the mouth-watering, yeasty aroma. Was there anything more irresistible than freshly baked bread? Rosie doubted it.

'Oh, yes,' Annie continued. 'You need a good woman who'll not only share your burdens but will make you laugh, make you see the joy and wonder in the world. And by look of this pretty young thing she's just the one to do it.'

Annie turned to face Alexander, as if daring him to disagree, but it was a dare that Alexander was apparently reluctant to accept.

When the tea was deemed sufficiently brewed Annie poured. 'You'll be wanting some cheese to go with your bread, won't you, Alexander? Well, you know where it's kept.'

Alexander crossed the small cottage in three steps and

took some cheese out of the cupboard while Annie cut doorstop-sized slices of bread.

'As a child I think Alexander lived on my bread and cheese,' Annie said to Rosie. 'I sometimes wondered whether they ever fed him up at the big house.'

'That's because the cook there could never make bread as good as yours, and there's no better cheese anywhere in the country than the cheese made in your dairy, Annie,' he said as he placed the cheese dish on the table. 'One day soon, when the railway comes through here, I'm hoping that people throughout England will be able to taste the wonderful cheese made in the Knightsbrook dairy under the watchful eye of Annie.'

Annie smiled proudly, cut some generous slices of cheese, and handed plates to Alexander and Rosie.

Rosie took a bite of the still warm bread and murmured her agreement. The cheese had a nutty flavour that was simply delicious. 'I think you're right. This will be very popular. I'm sure it will fetch high prices in London and the other main cities. It's wonderful!'

Alexander took another bite of his own bread and cheese and nodded. He seemed to be enjoying the simple fare much more than the lavish feast that had been served last night in the ornate dining room.

'So, what's been happening on the estate?' Alexander asked again as he served them both another slice of bread and cheese.

Rosie listened as Annie told him all the gossip about the other tenants—about couples who had married, others who were having difficulties, what their children had been up to and who had fallen out with whom.

All the while Annie was talking Rosie watched Alexander. He was smiling, laughing and commiserating about these people he obviously knew well and cared for deeply. The man she was watching was a different man from the one she had first met. He was so much more relaxed sitting in this plain cottage than he was in Knightsbrook House.

Rosie could imagine him as a young boy, running around the fields, playing with the other children on the estate and then, when he was tired and hungry, retreating to Annie's warm, comfortable cottage and the arms of this loving woman.

When she had first met him it would have been impossible for her to imagine that such a commanding man could ever have been a child. He had exuded such authority and been so aloof as he'd glared down at her while she acted the fool.

When Annie finally ran out of gossip Alexander cleared the table, took the plates and cups to the bench and placed the kettle back on the stove to heat up some water for the dishes.

'Oh, be gone with you,' Annie said, flicking a tea towel in his direction. 'I'm not so infirm that I can't wash a few dishes. You take this young lady on that walk you promised her and leave me to my chores.'

Alexander smiled, then bent down and kissed Annie on the cheek. 'Thank you, Annie. It's been lovely to see you. I'll see you again soon.'

'Mind you do. And tell Charlotte she's due for another visit.'

'I will—I will!'

Annie escorted them to the door and took Rosie's hands in hers. 'I hope to see much more of you too. You'll always be welcome at my cottage.'

Rosie smiled her thank you, even though she knew she would never see this warm, wonderful woman again...

Chapter Thirteen

The world always seemed like a better place after a visit to Annie's cottage. But his conversation with her had also reinforced in Alexander's mind his duty to the tenants. All those people she had talked about depended on Alexander. He had their livelihoods to protect. He needed the estate to survive and prosper as much for their sake as for the sake of his own family.

Annie had said he was like a man with the weight of the world on his shoulders. It wasn't quite the weight of the world he carried, but it was the weight of so many people's futures—futures that his feckless father had put in jeopardy. It was a weight that he had no option but to bear.

Annie had also said that Arabella was the woman who could share his burden, lighten his load and make him laugh. During her short time at Knightsbrook Arabella had most definitely made him laugh. Before her arrival he could hardly remember the last time he had laughed, but in the last two days he had laughed often. She was a woman full of fun, who shared her joy of life with everyone she met. It was a rare and valuable quality that he seemed to be lacking.

He suspected she was also a woman who would gladly share the burdens of the man she loved. Most women of his class expected to live a life of cossetted privilege after they married, in which their burdens were no more exacting than keeping up with the latest fashions and admonishing the servants.

He certainly could not see that in Arabella's future. He imagined that her marriage would be a partnership—that she would ease her husband's burdens, not contribute to them. But whether he was right on that count or not, he was destined never to discover.

Annie had also been right in saying that Arabella was a very pretty young woman. That was something he had been aware of from the moment he had seen her spinning down the entrance hall of Knightsbrook House, and every time he looked at her she seemed to grow more beautiful.

Sitting in Annie's cottage, he had been struck once again by how enchanting she was. It had nothing to do with her fine clothes or her stylish hair; she would be just as beautiful in a simple dress with no adornments. Nor was it her bright blue eyes and creamy skin, fetching though they might be. It was an indefinable inner quality that made her quite radiant.

He smiled at her now and she returned it.

Yes, quite radiant.

They retraced their steps back through the fields. The men all tipped their caps as they passed, and one even called out a greeting to Miss van Haven. Alexander shook his head in disbelief—although he really had no reason to be surprised. Gossip spread faster than wildfire on the estate. No doubt one of the women seated outside Annie's cottage had told the men of their visit, and had informed them about the young woman Alexander was escorting.

They had also, no doubt, been told that Arabella was the likely future Duchess of Knightsbrook.

Well, on that, they were going to have to accept disappointment.

Despite her radiant good looks, despite her ready laugh and despite the way she made him feel, she was not for him. She had all the qualities that would make his perfect duchess, but it was not going to happen.

Annie had said he needed a woman who would lighten his burdens, but his burdens seemed even heavier now that he had met Arabella. Yes, it had been a long time since he had laughed—and he suspected that when Arabella left, when she returned to Thomas Gardener, she would take the laughter with her.

They walked on along the tree-lined path down to the river, then halted together to take in the tranquil scene. This had always been his favourite spot on the estate when he was a child, and it looked particularly beautiful at this time of year. Weeping willows bearing their bright green spring foliage dipped in the gently running water, and multi-coloured wildflowers dotted the long grass.

'It's lovely—and so peaceful,' she murmured

It was indeed. All they could hear was the gentle babbling of the river running over mossy rocks and the sound of birds chirping in the foliage.

He led her along the edge of the river until they reached a stone seat beside the old, now abandoned mill.

'I spent hours here as a child,' Alexander said almost to himself as he took a seat beside Arabella. 'It was a place to play but also my sanctuary—somewhere to escape from "the big house", as Annie insists on calling it.'

'A place for a child to get dirty and have adventures?' she said with a laugh.

'Indeed.'

'I can just imagine you as a small boy, your knees muddy, trying to catch fish and skimming stones across the river.'

Alexander smiled as memories came back to him. When he'd got away from the house and played on the estate with the tenants' children his childhood days had been almost carefree.

'My record was eight bounces.'

She gave a little laugh. 'Really? Prove it.'

Alexander turned to face her. 'What? You don't believe me?'

Smiling, she shook her head.

'Well, then…' Alexander stood, took off his jacket, rolled up his shirtsleeves and looked around for a suitable stone. 'It's been a long time, and I'm somewhat out of practice…'

'Oh, excuses, excuses.'

To his surprise she stood up, picked up her own stone and stood beside him.

'I challenge you to a duel!' she said.

'You're on.'

Side by side, they bent their knees, leant back and flicked their stones across the river's surface. Alexander had no idea how many times his own stone skipped because he was watching Arabella's stone fly across the river, bouncing once, twice, three times.

'Well done!' he exclaimed in amazement. It was obviously not the first time she had skimmed stones.

'But not good enough. You beat me by one.'

'Well, I do have the home advantage.'

She let out a delightful tinkling laugh. 'Ever the gentleman. So, are you ready for a rematch? Then I'll be able to find out if you're as much of a gentleman in defeat as you are in victory.'

'I accept your challenge,' he said, and immediately began searching for appropriate stones.

Caught up in the game, he lost count of the number of stones they threw, or who was winning—he just knew it was a long time since he'd enjoyed such childlike pleasure

Having skimmed all the flat stones they could find, they collapsed, laughing, onto the stone bench.

'I think we should declare it a draw,' Alexander said.

Arabella nodded her agreement. 'That was fun. Do you come down here often?'

'This is where I first met Annie. Charlotte and I had escaped from the house because Father was hosting another one of his week-long gambling parties and Mother had taken to her rooms, supposedly with one of her headaches. Charlotte was crying and I was trying to comfort her. Annie found us, took us back to her cottage, fed us and let us stay the night. After that, every time there was a house party the two of us would immediately escape and spend time at Annie's. She saved us from what would have been a miserable childhood.'

'She's a lovely woman,' said Arabella quietly. 'You were lucky to have someone so warm to comfort you as a child.'

Alexander nodded. 'But I haven't been back here for years. Not since…'

He paused and began thinking back to when he had last sat here by the river. He certainly hadn't been since his father had died and he had taken control of the near-bankrupt estate. The moment the lawyers had informed him of the state of the accounts had heralded the end of all frivolity. It must have been some time before that.

Whenever it had been, it was a considerable time ago, but exactly when he could not recall.

'Not since Lydia?'

Her voice was quiet but her words hit him like a cannon ball, knocking the wind out of his lungs.

'I'm sorry, Alexander.' She placed her hand gently on his arm. 'I shouldn't have mentioned her name—not if it pains you.'

Alexander shook his head. 'No, it doesn't pain me.' And he realised that it was true. Not so long ago his grief over Lydia had been so intense he'd preferred to try and forget she had ever existed, had ever been part of his life. Now he had no objection to talking about her.

'Lydia was the love of my life. She was the woman I intended to marry.'

Arabella nodded but said nothing.

'She was a cheerful and loving young woman.' Alexander sighed, remembering what Lydia had been like when they were young. 'But she changed. And that, too, was my father's fault. He ran regular card evenings at the house. They were not sociable events, like the ones my mother hosts, where gossip is more important than winning or losing. These were serious gambling events, where fortunes could easily be lost. And reputations.'

He stopped talking for a moment and looked out into the distance.

'Usually I was able to protect Lydia from the excesses of those weekends, but she visited one weekend when I was away and met one of my father's gambling companions…'

He paused again, and considered how much he should reveal about that debauched man to a woman as innocent as Arabella. He was a notorious rake—a man who loved corrupting innocent young women. And that was exactly what he had done to Lydia.

'She thought she was in love with him and that he was in love with her. She fell in with his lifestyle—the parties, the gambling… Gambling and that man became all she lived for. Then she started to lose. A lot. That was when the real change happened. She borrowed money. She lied to everyone she knew—including me—to get more. She even started to steal from people to pay her gambling debts. I tried to help her…to encourage her to stop… But nothing I did worked. *Nothing.*'

They sat in silence for a moment, both staring into the gently burbling river.

'Where is she now?' Arabella asked, her voice almost a whisper.

'Her debts grew so big she eventually fled to the Continent. I believe the wastrel left her and moved on to his next conquest. The last I heard she was working as a—'

But Arabella did not need to know the extent of Lydia's downfall. She didn't need to know that Lydia had attached herself to a series of wealthy but increasingly disreputable men in order to support her gambling habit, until she'd been reduced to selling herself in order to fund her desperate lifestyle.

'The last I heard she was working at a gambling establishment in Italy.'

An establishment where the women dealt more than just cards.

'It must have been painful for you,' said Arabella.

Alexander nodded. 'It was very painful to watch someone I cared about change and be powerless to do anything about it. It was painful to hear her constant lies. Eventually it was as if every word that came out of her mouth was a lie. She lied about the extent of her debts. She lied about how much money she had lost. And she lied about how she had managed to repay those debts.' Alexander shook his head. 'I sometimes wonder if she was so lost that she no longer knew when she was telling the truth and when she was lying.'

He sighed deeply. It was the first time he had told anyone about Lydia's downfall. It had always been too painful to remember it before, and certainly too painful to talk about it. At the time he had done everything he could to help her. Tried endless ways to keep her away from that man, from the card table and the gaming houses, and in the process of trying to save Lydia he had lost part of himself. He had lost his trust in people, and lost his ability to relax and enjoy himself.

He shook his head, picked up another stone and tossed it into the river. The reality was that there was nothing more he could have done for Lydia. For years he had tortured himself with guilt. Had believed that if only he had been at home that weekend Lydia might never have met that terrible man. Had thought that perhaps there were things he could have done to turn her away from her downward spiral.

But Lydia's path was one she had chosen for herself. Continuing to torture himself about what he might have done, what he might have said to stop her would help no one—not him, and not Lydia.

He sighed again, then smiled at Arabella. 'In answer to your question, I don't remember the last time I visited this spot on the river, but I'm pleased I brought you here today.'

She smiled sadly and nodded. 'So am I.'

It seemed Annie was right again: talking to Arabella

had lifted the weight of the guilt and remorse over Lydia that he had been carrying for many years, and he felt much lighter for it.

Thomas Gardener was a lucky man to have a woman like Arabella in his life. She was indeed a woman who could lighten a man's burdens and take away his worries. He could only hope the man appreciated what a treasure he had. A woman who was not only beautiful, but also clever, funny and supportive.

But this would not do. He had originally decided to take a quick stroll around the estate to save Arabella from the ordeal of a dreary talk by the Reverend Truebridge and the horror of playing cards with his mother and her cronies. Instead he had lost all sense of time.

He looked up at the sky. The sun was heading towards the horizon and there was a slight chill in the air. It must be late-afternoon. He picked up his jacket and pulled his fob watch out of the pocket. Yes, he was right. Time had got away from them, and instead of a quick stroll they had been away all day. It seemed that in Arabella's company he even forgot the passage of time.

His mother would certainly be pleased, and would no doubt read much more into their absence than it warranted.

He stood up, took her hand and helped her to her feet. It had been a delightful day but it was time to bring it to an end.

'I suspect my mother and her friends will have finished their card game, and that every ache and pain will have been discussed in exhaustive detail, so it should be safe to return to the house.'

She gave a light laugh and rolled her eyes. 'Oh, yes—I

haven't thanked you for saving me from that ordeal, have I? It's been a lovely day, Alexander.'

He draped his jacket over one shoulder, dangling it from his thumb, and took Arabella's arm in his. Slowly they walked back along the river, as if neither was in any hurry to return to the house. White swans sailed majestically past them, ducks dived in the water and birds flitted between the trees, fully occupied with finding food for their offspring and oblivious to the couple walking in companionable silence beneath them.

For the first time in many years Alexander enjoyed the simple pleasure that nature brought and the soothing effect it could have on the soul.

They followed the path from the river and walked under the canopy of the tree-lined path that led back to the house. A light, rustling breeze shook the trees, and Arabella lifted her hands and laughed as a cascade of spring blossoms showered them, falling like pink confetti.

She took hold of her skirts and gave them a shake, sending tiny flowers skittering in all directions, while Alexander brushed the blossoms off his shoulders.

'Leave them,' she said, laughing. 'Pink really suits you.'

'I'm not sure about that, but the blossoms adorning your hair are certainly fetching.' He laughed too, and picked a few of the flowers off her hat.

Leaning over her, he could feel the warmth of her body, could almost feel her soft curves, almost taste her silky skin. He closed his eyes and breathed in deeply, inhaling the remembered scent of fresh flowers.

This could not be happening. He had to resist temptation. He could not take her in his arms again. He could not kiss her again. Even if her feminine scent was overwhelming his senses…even if every inch of his body longed to take her in his arms. Even if his throbbing desire was telling him how much he wanted her. This could not happen.

He had to remember his vow. He had to remember his aching muscles, remember his plunge into cold water, how hard he'd had to exercise last night to try and free himself from his desire for her.

Opening his eyes, he discovered his hand was suspended in mid-air above her head, clasping a pink blossom. Despite his self-admonition on the dangers of touching her, he ran his hand down her soft cheek.

Her breath caught in her throat as she stared up at him, her pink lips parted tantalisingly. Even while words of warning rang in his head, he took hold of her chin, tilted it towards him and leant in closer.

How could he not kiss her again? How could he deny himself such temptation? How could he not do what his body was commanding him to do?

But his mind knew better than his body. She was not his. She would never be his.

He released her chin, stood up straight and looked off into the distance.

'We can't do this.' He heard the formality in his voice, so at odds with how he was feeling. 'Don't you agree?'

He looked down and saw her blink a few times, as if unsure she had heard him correctly.

'Don't you agree?' he repeated. Surely she, even more than he, could see the folly of their actions.

'I agree,' she said, in a barely audible whisper.

Once again they walked in silence, although now that sense of companionship had evaporated, to be replaced with a tense uneasiness.

Alexander knew he deserved to feel uncomfortable. He had allowed his desires to overcome his good sense. Wasn't that exactly why he had wanted to avoid being alone with Arabella? And hadn't he been proved correct?

They entered the house and he bowed to her formally, as if their encounter had never happened...as if he hadn't almost kissed her...as if he hadn't unburdened his soul and shared with her intimate details of his relationship with Lydia.

'It is nearly time to change for dinner. I'll bid you farewell till then.'

He bowed again, and then, like the coward he knew himself to be, retreated to his rooms.

Chapter Fourteen

'Ooh, lovely—a bath. Thank you, Nellie, that's exactly what I need.'

Rosie stripped off her dress and undergarments and lowered herself into the warm water of the freshly drawn bath. She slid down until only her head was above the water and rested her head on the soft towel Nellie had kindly draped on the edge of the bath for that purpose. Perhaps Nellie was feeling guilty for abandoning her duties as chaperon, but this bath more than made up for it.

A small fire flickered in the tiled fireplace of the chamber adjoining her bedroom, making the room warm and cosy, and Rosie issued a small sigh of complete contentment.

This was perfection itself. A chance to lie back and have a long, leisurely soak. She picked up the soft sponge and the rose-scented soap, worked up a lather and gently ran the sponge over her body while her mind wandered to the day's events.

And what a day it had been.

It was possibly the happiest day she had ever experienced, and even Alexander's formal parting could not detract from her joy. A few days ago Rosie would not have thought it possible that she could spend such a wonderful day with a man as charming as Alexander Fitzroy, Duke of Knightsbrook.

After her treatment by every man who had ever entered the van Haven home, being snubbed was all Rosie had known. It was a role she had accepted—the poor ward who had no prospects and was of no interest to any man. But not any more.

A man who was head and shoulders above all those men—literally and figuratively—had spent the day with her, had laughed with her, played games with her, unburdened his troubles to her. He had treated her as an equal—more than an equal—and as someone whose views he respected and admired. And, what was more, he had almost kissed her. *Again.*

Rosie wiggled her toes above the warm water and closed her eyes as images of everything that had happened ran past her mind's eye—from Alexander's stiff greeting in the breakfast room through to their enjoyable lunch at Annie's, from their playful encounter by the river to his revelations about Lydia, and then to that almost-kiss under the blossoms.

She squeezed the sponge and released a stream of scented soap bubbles into the water. Oh, yes. It had been quite a day. Within the space of a few hours she had seen so many sides to Alexander. The stern man at the breakfast table. The loving man in Annie's cottage. The childlike man who had skimmed stones on the river. The serious, almost melancholy man who had talked of Lydia. And the passionate man whose hungry eyes had burned into hers when he had nearly kissed her again.

So many men—and she adored them all. Even the

stern Alexander. She knew where *that* man came from. As Annie had said, he carried the weight of the world on his shoulders—the responsibility for his family, for his tenants, and his need to undo the damage his father had done to the family name.

And he also carried the weight of wanting to do the right thing when he was with her. She was sure it was only the non-existent Thomas Gardener that had stopped him from taking her in his arms this afternoon and kissing her.

Rosie squeezed the sponge again and let soapy water run over her shoulders and down her chest as she contemplated how she could get rid of pesky Thomas Gardener. Perhaps she could tell Alexander that she had just had news that the unfortunate man had suddenly dropped dead, or had decided to become a monk instead of marrying her, or had set off for an expedition to deepest Africa and was unlikely to be seen again.

She sighed and rubbed the sponge slowly across her shoulder and down her arm. None of those stories had the slightest chance of being believed. It seemed the imaginary Thomas Gardener was going to have to stay healthy, alive and working at his family's bank for a few days more.

And at least he did serve one valuable purpose. If Thomas Gardener hadn't stopped Alexander from kissing her, Rosie doubted if anything else would have—certainly not her. She sighed again. She was a terrible friend. She knew she had to protect Arabella's reputation, and yet she seemed to forget all about that whenever there was a chance that Alexander might kiss her.

It was as if she was powerless to stop the way she felt about him.

Rosie stopped rubbing her arm and dropped the sponge, then sat up straighter in the bath and gasped.

The way she felt about him?

It was obvious how she felt about him. She had fallen in love with him.

Her hand covered her mouth, as if she must stop herself from blurting out this shocking revelation. But it was true. She had to face the facts. She had fallen in love with Alexander, Lord Ashton, the Eighth Duke of Knightsbrook.

She lowered her hand, picked up the floating sponge and clasped it to her chest. This had most certainly not been part of the plan she had devised over tea and scones at The Ritz just a few days ago. No, falling in love had been the last thing on her mind. Less than the last thing. It had been so unlikely that she had never even considered it.

But that was before she had met Alexander. She sighed loudly and shook her head. How could she *not* fall in love with a man like Alexander?

'There's an awful lot of sighing going on in there,' Nellie said, poking her head around the corner, a clothes brush in her hand. 'Are you all right? Is the water too hot? Too cold?'

'No, it's perfect.'

'So what's all this sighing about?'

'It's just been rather a confusing day, that's all.'

'Don't worry,' Nellie said, heading back into the bedroom. 'Only one more evening and we'll be back in London. This will all be over.'

Rosie couldn't stop herself from sighing once again. This time in frustration. One more evening. That was all. After that she would never see Alexander again. She would have to live without him in her life.

How was she going to be able to bear that?

And it was obvious that Alexander felt something for her as well. That look on his face when he had almost kissed her... He felt it too. Could it be that the Eighth Duke of Knightsbrook *would* consider marrying someone like plain Rosie Smith?

She squeezed hard on the sponge. Oh, what would it be like to be married to Alexander? Bliss. That was what it would be. Pure bliss.

She sighed again and sank down into the water.

But he didn't even know Rosie Smith.

She shot back up.

He thought she was Arabella van Haven. How would he react when he realised she wasn't the daughter of a wealthy banker but an orphan without a penny to her name?

She dragged herself out of the bath and wrapped herself in the soft white towel. Alexander wasn't a snob. He didn't want Arabella's money. Didn't want to marry an heiress. Wasn't it possible he *might* want to marry her, the real Rosie Smith, a woman with no money? Was she being unrealistic to think that he would consider someone of her background as a potential bride? Was that just too ridiculous?

Well, there was only one way to find out.

Rosie padded on bare feet through to her bedroom, where Nellie had laid out her undergarments and the pale blue gown she was to wear that evening.

She would just have to tell him who she really was and see how he reacted. Only then would she know how he felt about the real her, Rosie Smith. That was exactly what she would do.

She sat down at her dressing table, nodded at her reflection, then frowned. But she would have to tell Arabella first. After all, Arabella had agreed to a plan in which Rosie behaved so abominably that the Duke would not *want* to marry her. She had not agreed to a plan in which Rosie pretended to be Arabella and then, when it suited her, let the cat out of the bag and announced to everyone that she wasn't Arabella after all.

No, she owed it to Arabella to let her know first. And then she would tell Alexander.

Yes, that was a much better plan. It was all settled.

With a light step she skipped down the stairs and entered the dining room, to find the family already seated.

Alexander stood up and a footman ushered her to her seat.

'What happened to the other guests?' Rosie asked as she took her seat.

The footman shook out her napkin with a practised flourish and placed it on her lap, and Rosie smiled her thanks.

'The other guests were invited only for yesterday evening so they could meet you,' the Dowager said, signalling to the footman to begin serving the soup. 'Tonight it's family only.'

'Family and one guest,' Alexander added.

It seemed formal Alexander was back again. Rosie smiled at him. She loved even formal Alexander, the honourable man who was so determined to do the right thing.

'Quite right, Alexander.' The Dowager raised her wine

glass. 'To our honoured guest, Arabella van Haven, who already feels like part of the family.'

Alexander glared at his mother and received an equally reproving glare in return, before she turned her attention back to Rosie. 'So, Miss van Haven, did Alexander show you the rest of the estate. It's magnificent, isn't it?'

'Oh, yes. We met some of the tenants and had a lovely walk along the river. It really is quite beautiful.'

The Dowager smiled her approval. 'Indeed it is. And it's so lovely to see the tenants working on the land in the same way they have for generations. So much nicer than horrid steam engines. Steam is diabolical, don't you think?'

Rosie bit her lip to stop her smile as Alexander continued to glare at his mother. 'Well, a "diabolical" steam train brought me here from London. And an even more diabolical steam ship meant I could cross the Atlantic in seven days in considerably more comfort than I would have had I travelled by sailing ship. So, if it weren't for steam I doubt I'd be here this evening.'

'Well, there's that, I suppose…' the Dowager conceded reluctantly. 'But there should be limits to all this modernisation.'

Alexander shook his head and exhaled loudly.

'Did you have a chance to meet Annie?' Charlotte asked, interrupting what Rosie suspected was a familiar argument between the Dowager and Alexander.

'Oh, yes—she made us tea and served us some freshly baked bread and the most delicious cheese I've ever tasted.'

Charlotte smiled and nodded. 'I must go down and visit her tomorrow. Perhaps we could go together in the morning? It would be lovely if we had a chance to spend some time together before you return to London.'

Rosie smiled at the young woman, touched by her offer of friendship. 'I'd enjoy that very much.'

Polite conversation continued throughout all the courses, with just the occasional black look from Alexander when his mother alluded to the topic of marriage or the horrors of the modern world.

'I hear you're an accomplished banjo player, Miss van Haven,' the Dowager said when the meal was almost over. 'Perhaps you can entertain us after dinner? I bought a banjo especially for this weekend.'

Rosie almost choked on her chocolate mousse, and took a sip of water while she recovered herself. 'I suspect my abilities on the banjo have been greatly exaggerated. Unless you enjoy the sound of cats being strangled it might be best to keep me away from that particular instrument.'

The Dowager's lips pinched slightly. 'Then perhaps you would care to recite some verses for us from Shakespeare?'

Oh, dear. She had helped Arabella learn her lines for various Shakespeare plays, but unfortunately had retained none of them.

'I'm afraid in that area too my talents may have been exaggerated.'

The Dowager's already pinched lips tightened further. 'What *are* your accomplishments, my dear?'

'Well, I have some talent on the piano, and I have taken singing lessons.'

'Wonderful.' The pinched lips turned into a smile. 'The piano is so much more cultivated than the banjo, anyway. After dinner you can play for us.'

'I'd be delighted.'

Rosie smiled. There were so many accomplishments Mr van Haven could have attributed to his daughter—but the *banjo*? What had he been thinking? Well, he hadn't been thinking… It seemed he rarely thought of his daughter and didn't know anything about her.

Their meal finished, they rose from the table and all followed the Dowager into her private drawing room, where a grand piano took pride of place.

Rosie sat at the piano and shuffled through the sheets of music until she found one of her favourite pieces, while the family seated themselves and turned towards her with expectant faces.

The piano had been a means of escape for her ever since she was a little girl, and she soon lost herself in the music, forgetting about her game-playing, forgetting about the way she was deceiving the friend she loved, even for a moment forgetting about Alexander.

When she came to the end of Beethoven's 'Moonlight Sonata' she turned to face the family. The room remained silent. Had she done something wrong?

Then Charlotte, the Dowager and Alexander stood as one and applauded enthusiastically.

'It seems you have been hiding the truth,' Alexander said as he continued to clap his hands.

Heat rushed to Rosie's cheeks. He had finally found her out. But how? And which of the many lies she had told was he referring to?

'You have more than *"some talent"*. You're a virtuoso,' he continued. 'I don't think I've ever heard that piece played with more beauty and more warmth.'

Her cheeks grew hotter—but from pleasure, not discomfort. 'Thank you,' she murmured, and turned back to the piano.

His praise had touched her deeply. It seemed there was another Alexander she was also in love with. The one who looked at her with tender admiration.

Chapter Fifteen

She was continually amazing him. Beautiful, funny—
and now it seemed she was also talented. He watched
her shuffle through the music sheets, looking for another piece to play, her pretty forehead furrowed in concentration.

She was not the way his mother had described her
when she had first been trying to convince him that he
should marry an American heiress. And it seemed her
claim that she played the banjo was wrong—thank goodness. But his mother was right in that the man she married would be very lucky indeed.

It was just a shame it wouldn't be him.

If it wasn't for Thomas Gardener he would have no reservations about courting her, despite her father's fortune.

Yes, he'd always had objections to marrying anyone—
and an American heiress in particular—but whether that
was due to pride, his worry that people would assume he
had married for money, or because Lydia had put him off
love and marriage for ever, he couldn't say. Whatever it
was, all those reasons were losing their hold.

When it came to her father's fortune there would be

options. An astute businessman like Mr van Haven would surely prefer to invest his money in the estate and be paid a healthy return rather than merely hand over money in the form of a dowry. And if people thought he had married Arabella for her father's money, so what? He couldn't possibly be so shallow that he would let what others thought of him dictate his actions.

He did care about restoring the nobility and prestige of the family name, but that was in order to honour his ancestors' hard work and the sacrifices they had made. And a respected name was something he wished to pass on to future generations of FitzRoys. It wasn't because he cared what others thought of him personally.

And as for the pain that Lydia had caused him—well, that was fading into a distant memory. It was no longer an obstacle when it came to thoughts of marriage. And Arabella was nothing like Lydia, with all her lies and complications.

But all that was neither here nor there. Arabella was in love with Thomas Gardener. She wanted to marry Thomas Gardener—not him.

He was sick to death of Thomas Gardener.

Arabella replaced the sheets of music on the piano stand, turned around on the piano bench and smiled. 'If you'll indulge me, I think I'll play a tune that I've learnt just recently. When I was in New York I bought a book of contemporary English songs and fell in love with them. I'm playing from memory, so please excuse any mistakes.'

'Oh, I'm sure it will be wonderful,' his mother said, beaming with pleasure. 'Play on…play on.'

Arabella gave a cheeky grin and began playing the opening bars of the music hall song 'Champagne Charlie'.

Alexander suppressed a smile as he watched his mother to see how she would react to such a low-class form of entertainment being performed in her private drawing room?

When Arabella sang the first few lines in a false Cockney accent his mother's smile quivered, but then it returned even wider and she started clapping along to the tune.

Unbelievable. Arabella had got the wife of the Seventh Duke of Knightsbrook clapping along to a music hall song. Simply amazing.

When she repeated the chorus—*Champagne Charlie is me name, Champagne drinking is me game*—the Dowager and Charlotte even joined in, leaving Alexander so stunned his mouth literally fell open.

'Oh, that was so funny!' his mother said when Arabella had finished, wiping away a tear. '*"Champagne Charlie is me name..."* Oh, yes, very funny.'

Arabella smiled. 'What would you like next? More Beethoven or more music hall?'

'Music hall! Music hall,' his mother and Charlotte chanted together.

Alexander shook his head in surprise and admiration. Anyone who could get Charlotte to laugh so easily and his mother and sister to enjoy each other's company really was special. He was beginning to wonder whether he should let Thomas Gardener have things all his own way.

After all, wasn't all fair in love and war? And he was most certainly falling in love with Arabella van Haven...

She began a round of music hall songs, many of which Alexander had heard before, and he noticed she skipped the bawdier verses. A wise decision. It was surprising enough to see his mother enjoying something she would normally dismiss as common; if she knew the true lyrics Alexander suspected it would be a step too far.

Arabella finished and turned to her appreciative audience.

Clapping enthusiastically, his mother stood up and approached the piano. 'That was marvellous, Arabella. Just marvellous. Thank you so much. I can't remember the last time I enjoyed myself this much. But I'm getting tired, so I think I'll retire.' She gave Charlotte a pointed look. 'And I believe *you* were hoping to get an early night as well—weren't you, Charlotte?'

'No.' Charlotte shook her head, then noticed her mother angling her head in Alexander's direction. 'Oh, yes... I was.' Charlotte gave a fake yawn. 'I'm rather tired also, so I think I'll retire early as well.'

Charlotte joined her mother at the piano and kissed Arabella's cheek. 'Thank you so much. For once Mother and I are in total agreement. That was the most fun this family has had for a long time.'

'Yes, yes, it was wonderful,' his mother said, leaning over to kiss Arabella's cheek, and jutting out her elbow in the strangest manner as she did so. Her arm caught the edge of the pile of sheet music and sent the pages scattering to the floor. 'Oh, dear, I beg your pardon. Alexander, help Arabella pick up that music—and come on, Charlotte. It's time we retired.'

She grabbed Charlotte's arm and hurried her out of the room. When the door had closed he could hear the two women giggling and humming the last tune as they headed up the stairs.

Alexander shook his head, still looking at the door. It was an unsubtle move on his mother's part to leave them alone together, but then subtlety had never been his mother's strong suit.

He turned to face Arabella. The room suddenly seemed very quiet. He remained standing in the middle of the room, staring down at Arabella, feeling uncharacteristically awkward. Then he bent down and picked up the scattered sheets and handed them to her.

She shuffled them into an orderly pile, placed them on the music stand, then picked them up again and gripped them in tight hands. It seemed she too was nervous now that they were alone.

And perhaps she was right to be nervous. If she knew what he was about to do…

He sat down beside her on the piano bench and heard the breath catch in her throat. Had he deliberately sat so close that his leg was touching hers? Perhaps. Or had he wanted to be close so he could surround himself in that beautiful floral scent? Whatever it was, being so close to her was intoxicating his senses and making him forget what he wanted to say.

'Thank you for that, Arabella,' he said finally. 'Charlotte was right. That was the most fun our family has had in a long time. You have certainly brought laughter into this house. And I've never seen Charlotte and my mother leave a room together singing. I would never have thought such a thing possible. You really are a remarkable woman.'

'Oh, I'm pleased they enjoyed it.'

She shuffled the music sheets again, put them on the stand, then picked them up once more.

'You really *are* a remarkable woman, Arabella,' he repeated.

She sent him a small smile. 'Well, I love to play the piano and I enjoy singing.'

'It's more than that.' He took the sheets of music from her hands, placed them on the music stand, then took her hands in his.

She looked down at her small hands, encased in his larger ones, then back up at him, her blue eyes sparkling in the candlelight.

'You are truly exceptional, Arabella. You're funny, clever, kind, sweet…and now it seems you're talented as well. You're the most wonderful woman I have ever met.'

'Oh!' she gasped.

'And, what's more, I think I've fallen in love with you.'

Her eyes momentarily grew larger, then she blinked rapidly. 'You think you've…?' She closed her eyes, as if trying to absorb this surprising admission.

'No, I'm wrong. I don't *think* I've fallen in love with you.'

Her eyes sprang open.

'I *know* I've fallen in love with you.' He smiled, feeling buoyant, as if his declaration had cut loose the weights that were tying him down. 'Nothing would give me more pleasure than to court you, one day to marry you.'

'But I…' She swallowed, her breath coming in gasps. 'I…um…'

'I know. I know,' he interrupted, desperate to put her at her ease. 'I've put you in an impossible position. You're already in love with another man—all but betrothed to Thomas Gardener. But I could not let you leave this house without telling you how I feel.'

Her blinking became more rapid. 'Oh, Thomas Gardener… Yes. Him.' She chewed lightly on her lower lip.

Not for the first time Alexander cursed the man's existence, and ungraciously wished that some accident might befall him and take him out of Arabella's life. Or, better still, that Arabella would decide she no longer loved him, making the path easier for Alexander.

But what was the chance of that happening?

Alexander had to know whether he was chasing an impossible dream.

'And I could not let you leave without finding out how you felt about me. I know you said you were in love with him, but do I stand any chance of winning your affections?'

Alexander held his breath and waited for her answer. She was looking down at their hands. He followed her gaze and saw her small hands were clenched into fists inside his larger ones.

She hadn't spoken, but that gesture had given him an answer. It was not one he wanted, but it was one he would abide by.

'Forgive me, Arabella.' He released her hands. 'I've spoken out of turn. I've embarrassed you and made you feel uncomfortable.'

'No, no—not at all.' She took hold of one of his hands in both of hers, clasping it tightly. 'It's just complicated. I need to return to London. There are people I need to talk to before I can tell you how I feel. All I can say is that you have done nothing for which you need to beg my forgiveness. You have not embarrassed me nor made me feel uncomfortable. Quite the contrary.'

He brushed a stray curl back from her face. 'Thank you, Arabella. Thank you for giving me hope,' he murmured.

She angled her head as he ran his hand along her soft cheek. Closing her eyes, she parted her lips slightly, her breath turning to a quick gasp.

His gaze lingered on those soft lips, parted so invitingly. She had given him hope—hope that she would one day be his. Surely that was enough? But those lips...those beautiful, full pink lips...how could he resist?

Perhaps just one small kiss?

He leant forward, unable to fight the fierce urge building up inside him. His lips lightly touched hers. A sound escaped her mouth. Was it a gasp or a moan? Whatever it was, it caused her lips to part further, and they remained parted, seemingly asking him to intensify the kiss.

If that was what she was asking, then it was a request he was more than happy to grant.

He pulled her into his arms and kissed her harder, more deeply. Her sigh of pleasure as he used his tongue to open her mouth told him he had not misread her actions. And when her hands encircled his neck he had definitive proof.

She wanted this as much as he did. And he most certainly wanted this kiss—desperately wanted it, and much more.

A powerful need was driving him on, and he licked those sweet lips, desperate to devour her feminine taste, to devour *her*. Her need matched his own, and she ran her hands through his hair, clasping him close, seemingly urging him on. Then, to his immense pleasure, her tongue entered his mouth, tasting, probing, teasing.

She was just as lost as he was. He would make her forget Thomas Gardener...make her surrender herself to the pleasure he was giving her...make her think only of him.

He clasped her slim waist and pulled her in, closer towards him, impatient to feel those soft breasts against his chest. Even through the silk of her gown her nipples pushed hard, and he could feel the fast beating of her heart.

Her arousal was driving him almost insane with desire, and he kissed her neck, savouring the taste of her soft, warm skin. He heard her purr with pleasure as his lips trailed a line across the naked skin of her chest and along the soft mounds of her breasts, which were rising and falling with each rapid breath.

His hunger for her was rising to an almost insatiable level, and he was tempted to tear open the delicate fabric of her gown, to feast himself on her beautiful body. But he would not compromise the woman he loved.

He withdrew from her and bit down hard on his lip, hoping the pain would distract his mind and his body. He would do nothing to harm her or compromise her. Instead he would lovingly recall every erotic detail of their encounter when he was alone in his room—the touch and taste of her skin, her intoxicating feminine scent, and that look of sensual abandonment on her face.

She remained in his arms, her eyes closed, her lips parted, her face flushed. His erection was almost unbearable now, but that was a price he had to pay.

'So, can I take it from your reaction that I have a chance against Thomas Gardener?'

She slowly opened her eyes and blinked a few times. 'Oh, you most certainly do,' she said, her voice husky. 'After a kiss like that I'm beginning to think that Thomas Gardener is just a figment of my imagination. It's as if he doesn't exist at all.'

That was exactly the response Alexander wanted.

With final victory now close at hand, he took her in his arms and kissed her again.

Chapter Sixteen

Was there ever a more wonderful day? Rosie stretched luxuriously in the four-poster bed. It was as if her entire body was smiling with contentment. Today she would return to London. She would recount to Arabella every delightful, delicious detail of what had happened over the weekend. Then, with Arabella's blessing, she would pen a letter to Alexander and confess all.

In her letter she would tell him that she loved him, loved everything about him, and most of all loved the way he made her feel. All would be revealed—who she really was, what her silly scheme had been about, and the reasons why she had been pretending to be Arabella— and then everything would be put to rights.

She stretched again, her smile turning into a sigh of pure pleasure. It was a perfect plan and one she could hardly wait to put into action. It certainly wasn't her original plan, but this new plan was so much better.

Everything had turned out perfectly. Arabella was saved from an unwanted marriage and could now pursue her real love—the theatre. And Rosie had met a man who had swept her off her feet and changed her life for ever.

She had received a declaration of love and had been given a delightful taste of what it would be like to be loved by a man like Alexander FitzRoy. It was all perfect.

Sweeping back the covers just as Nellie arrived to help her dress for the morning, Rosie all but danced across the room, threw open the curtains and looked out at the grey cloudy sky, edged with threatening black rain clouds lining the horizon.

'Have you ever seen a more beautiful day, Nellie?' She beamed a smile at Arabella's lady's maid.

'Well, *you're* certainly in a good mood,' Nellie said, giving her a sideways glance.

Rosie did a twirl in front of Nellie. 'Indeed I am. Oh, Nellie. It's all too exciting. Last night Alexander declared his love for me. Well, at least he declared his love for the woman he knows who goes by the name of Arabella. But as soon as I let Arabella know what's happened he'll be declaring his love to a woman who goes by the name of Rosie,' She pointed to her chest. 'Me!'

Nellie stared at her, her face closed. It was not the reaction Rosie had expected. Surely Nellie should be more excited and happy for her?

'Yes, I know who you are. I just hope the woman called Rosie knows what she's doing. The Duke may have fallen for you—I don't doubt that—but here you're Arabella: an heiress, the daughter of one of America's wealthiest men. Not a woman with no family and not a farthing to her name.'

Rosie frowned at Nellie, then shook her head, her smile returning. 'No, Nellie, you're wrong. Alexander's not like that. I *know* him. You don't. He didn't want to marry Arabella precisely *because* she's an heiress. He's too proud to take her father's money. He's a proud, honourable man.'

He was also handsome and could turn her to jelly with his kisses, she wanted to add as a shiver of remembered pleasure rippled through her body.

'Oh, Rosie, just don't get your hopes up too high—otherwise when you come crashing down to reality the fall might be more than you can cope with. Men like the Duke do *not* marry women like Rosie Smith.'

Rosie shook her head vehemently. 'No, you're wrong. He loves me. *Me*.' She pointed to her chest again. 'And that's all that matters.'

Nellie was wrong. Rosie knew it. She had seen how Alexander had looked at her last night. That had been the look of a man in love. In love with *her*. It hadn't been just passion she'd seen in his eyes, and it hadn't been just lust. It had been love. Real love.

Nellie sighed and shook her head slowly. 'Well, that's as may be, but hold still now while I get you dressed. Stop spinning round like a top.'

Rosie tried to remain still while Nellie helped her out of her nightdress and into her clothes, but it was too hard—she just wanted to dance and sing in celebration of the night before and the day that was to come.

Her desire to see Alexander again was overwhelming. She desperately wanted the day to begin so she could see his handsome face. But she also wanted the day to be over, so she could return to London as soon as possible and be set free from pretending to be Arabella, return to being Rosie Smith. Then Alexander could get to know the *real* Rosie—the Rosie that he had fallen in love with, the Rosie he had kissed, the Rosie he had caused to writhe in pleasure under his touch.

Then it really would be perfect.

There was no sign of Alexander in the hushed dining room. Only the Dowager and Charlotte were sitting at the highly polished walnut table, with matching grim expressions on their faces. It seemed last night's good grace between them had come to an end and they were once again adversaries.

Never mind. Rosie would talk to Charlotte when they spent time together this morning, and try and make things better between them. After all, wasn't she the breath of fresh air the servants said the family needed?

'Good morning…good morning,' she trilled, and headed towards the sideboard.

It seemed it was self-service this morning, as none of the usual bevy of servants were in attendance.

She lifted the lids of the silver tureens and was greeted by the delicious aromas of crisply fried bacon, scrambled eggs, fried mushrooms and tomatoes. The food looked delicious, and she had never been so hungry. It must be the excitement. Or perhaps being in love stimulated the appetite. Whatever it was, she needed food. Lots of it. Instead of her usual toast and marmalade, this morning she would treat herself to a full English breakfast.

Her plate piled high, she joined her future family at the table. Smiling, she removed her napkin from the engraved silver napkin ring and placed it on her lap. 'Isn't it a beautiful day?'

No greeting came from either woman. Instead the Dowager picked up the newspaper and gripped it tightly, as if frightened that it would fly out of her hands, and Charlotte stared down at her half-eaten plate of food, her shoulders slumped.

Rosie's smile faded. What was wrong? This was

more than their usual ill humour towards each other. Had something happened to Alexander?

Rosie waited, looking from Charlotte to the Dowager and back again, but it seemed neither women felt compelled to enlighten her.

'A beautiful day, is it? I don't think so.' The Dowager finally snapped, her long bejewelled fingers twisting at the paper. 'Perhaps you'd like to explain *this*.'

The Dowager sent the newspaper skidding across the table in Rosie's direction. Rosie's hand shot out to stop it before it fell off the edge, and she looked down at the headline: *New Oscar Wilde Play a Resounding Success.*

'Is that not good news?' she asked, but got a scowl from the Dowager in response.

Perhaps the Dowager didn't approve of Oscar Wilde. Rosie had heard that some people objected to his somewhat flamboyant lifestyle, and the Dowager was hardly likely to be familiar with the ways of theatrical people.

'You have no shame, have you?' the Dowager shot back through clenched teeth.

Rosie sent the Dowager a questioning look, then continued reading the article, which discussed the intricacies of the storyline, the wonderful performances of the cast, and mentioned the series of standing ovations the play had received.

When she got to the bottom of the page she read a paragraph about the notable people who had attended the opening, including American heiress Arabella van Haven, who had dined with the playwright.

So Arabella had got her wish. She had attended the opening night of an Oscar Wilde play and had not only got to meet the great man himself but had actually dined with him. Wonderful.

Smiling, she looked up at the scowling Dowager and the frowning Charlotte—then looked back down at the newspaper.

'Oh,' she squeaked. 'I see…'

'Oh, indeed,' the Dowager said, standing and glaring down at Rosie.

'I can explain…'

Rosie bit the edge of her bottom lip. But what was she going to say? She could hardly tell them she was here taking her friend's place because Arabella would rather go to an Oscar Wilde play than attend their weekend house party, even if it *had* been hosted in her honour.

'Who are you? You're obviously not Arabella van Haven,' the Dowager thundered.

'Um… I'm…'

Where should Rosie begin? What could she possibly say to explain herself?

The Dowager Duchess held up her hands and turned her face away, as if repelled by even looking at Rosie. 'No, I don't want to know. You've lied to us already— as if I would believe anything you would say now. You come into my house…make a fool of me and my guests…insinuate your way into my son's affections… And now you think you can talk your way out of it. You're shameless.'

Rosie stood up, still clutching the newspaper. 'No— no, I didn't…'

She gripped the edge of the table, her mind spinning, her body feeling weak. She wanted to entreat the Dowager, to convince her that she'd meant no harm, but what could she say without betraying Arabella?

'The servants are packing your bags. I would not be so uncivil as to throw you out without your breakfast, but once you have finished eating *our* food—' she scowled at Rosie's laden plate '—the carriage will be ready to take you to the railway station. And that will be the end of it.'

'But Alexander? Where's Alexander? I need to speak to him.'

'As if my son would want to talk to a woman like *you*.'

'But I need to tell him—'

'You will tell him *nothing*. And if you have the slightest shred of decency you will tell no one about the way you have made complete fools of this family.'

The Dowager turned and walked towards the door.

'I didn't mean any harm!' Rosie called out to the retreating ramrod-straight back. 'It's just that I... The plan wasn't going to cause any harm... It was just to... I didn't mean to...'

Her hand on the doorknob, the Dowager stopped and turned back to Rosie. 'Stop talking, you thoughtless girl. I don't want to hear any more of your lies. Be thankful that I care about the good name of FitzRoy and want to avoid a scandal. If I didn't I would have you arrested for your fraudulent behaviour. Instead of catching the train home you would be spending the night in jail. And instead of eating that hearty breakfast you'd be dining on bread and water.'

'But I need to talk to Alexander—'

'Don't push me, girl. I can still change my mind and call for the constabulary. My son does not want to talk to you. *No one* wants to talk to you. Now, come, Charlotte, let's leave this criminal to fill her belly with *our* food.'

With that she left the room, followed by an obviously distressed Charlotte.

'But… But…' Rosie called out to the now closed door. 'But I didn't mean any harm,' she said quietly, and then slumped down on to a dining chair, the crumpled newspaper still clutched in her hand.

Chapter Seventeen

It was all over. How could Alexander not hate her now? The Dowager had said he didn't want to talk to her. This was as bad as it could get.

How had everything gone so horribly wrong? Her plan had been simple enough: save Arabella from an unwanted marriage and have some fun at the same time by making fools of a greedy duke and his snobbish family. Then she would return to London with a funny story to tell Arabella—something that would amuse her just as so many of Rosie's antics had amused Arabella in the past.

But instead of making a fool of a stuffy duke, it was she who was the fool. Instead of having a joke at their expense, *she* was the joke.

She gripped both sides of her lowered head and released a deep sob. And now she would go home in disgrace. It was all too, too terrible. And, worse than that, she had caused the man she loved to despise her—had caused his family to think she was a fraudster instead of merely a silly, foolish girl who thought it was amusing to play tricks on people.

'Damn, damn, *damn*,' she cursed under her breath.

And the worst thing of all: her behaviour had hurt Alexander. His lasting memory of her would be as a liar, a woman up to no good, not a woman who loved him, a woman he had held in his arms and who had surrendered herself to his touch, to his kisses.

No, that could not happen.

Rosie stood up quickly, nearly toppling over the chair. She had to do something. She could not just sit there, wallowing in despair. There was no time to waste in self-indulgence. The carriage would be taking her away soon—taking her away from Alexander. Despite the Dowager's threats, she had to find him. She had to try and explain herself.

Even if it resulted in her being thrown in jail, she couldn't leave without talking to Alexander.

She ran out of the dining room, down the corridor, out through the entrance hall, and then halted at the top of the stairs, looking in every direction. Over the vast estate, at the gardens, the woodlands, the green pastures dotted with sheep.

Where would he be?

The door opened quietly behind her and she turned expectantly. But instead of Alexander it was Charlotte, her mouth turned down in a frown, her shoulders slumped.

Intense shame swept over Rosie. Charlotte was hurt too. It had never been her intention to hurt anyone. But she had.

'Oh, Charlotte, I'm so sorry.' She reached her hands out towards the distressed young woman who had shown her nothing but friendship.

Charlotte took a step backwards, as if shocked by the gesture. 'It is unforgivable that you betrayed Alexander. He did not deserve to be betrayed again…to be lied to again.'

Tears filled Rosie's eyes: 'I know. I *know*. I want to

apologise to him. I want to try and explain to him what I did and why I did it. Please, Charlotte, can you tell me where he is?'

Charlotte released a long sigh. 'I don't know who you are, or why you are here, but I do know my brother has fallen in love with you, and I do believe you have fallen in love with him. So if you want to talk to him you'll find him down by the river. There's a favourite place of his he used to go when he was a child. It's—'

'I know where it is!' Rosie called out, running down the stairs. 'And I'm sorry for everything I've done,' she shouted over her shoulder, while running along the pathway, her shoes crunching on the gravel.

Her mind spinning with half-formed explanations and excuses, she ran as fast as she could down the tree-lined path towards the river. How could she explain her behaviour? What could she say to him without betraying Arabella?

No answers came, but she had to think of something— had to say something. Had to make him see that she had meant no harm.

Surely when he saw her he would forgive her? After all, he had said he loved her, wanted to court her, even to marry her. And she was still the same woman he had declared his love for. That hadn't changed. Nothing had changed. Not really. It was just that she was not called Arabella and didn't really have a fortune, a rich father or a dowry.

Reaching the river, she came to an abrupt halt and stopped, giving herself time to catch her breath. As she approached the spot where yesterday they had skimmed stones with such child-like joy, she saw him sitting on the stone bench, staring into space.

In profile, his handsome face looked morose, and his body was rigid. Rosie's stomach clenched tightly with guilt. It was her fault he was in such pain. She had to put it right.

It had to be possible to change his mood. Wasn't that what she was good at? Making people laugh? Making them happy? She had spent most of her life entertaining Arabella, making her laugh when she was sad, lightening the mood in Mr van Haven's otherwise gloomy home. It was what she was best at.

But how?

For once she had no plan.

He turned his head slowly and stared up at her. His expression changed from sadness to impassiveness, as if he was shutting down all emotions. It was the same look she had seen the day they'd first met. Gone was the warmth in his brown eyes…gone was the loving look, the friendly smile.

Slowly, she walked towards him, her steps tentative, as if entering an ice-cold stream. When she was close to the bench he stood and faced her, his body tense, his face as harsh and bleak as a winter's storm.

'Oh, Alexander, I can explain…' She reached out to him.

He looked down at her hands, which remained suspended in mid-air between them, then back at her face, his eyes granite-hard. 'I'm sure you can, Miss van Haven—or whatever your real name is. I'm sure you have a very good explanation for why you deceived me, my family and our guests. You no doubt have a very plausible reason for your lies. Unfortunately for you I have been taken in by your lies once and I will not do it again.'

She slowly lowered her hands to her sides. 'Rosie—my name is Rosie.'

A sneer of contempt curled his lips. 'Rosie, Arabella—it makes no difference. Whoever you are, you are no longer welcome here. It is fortunate that your lies were exposed before the full extent of whatever crime you had planned was carried out.'

A gasp escaped Rosie's lips. 'No—*no!* There was no crime. You must believe that. Yes, I lied about who I am, but I meant no harm, and I was certainly never intending to commit a crime.'

Alexander glared down at her through narrowed eyes. 'How can you possibly think you would cause no harm? How could you possibly think that telling such lies, acting in such a manner, would not cause harm? Are you insane as well as deceitful?

Cringing at the insult, she reminded herself that he had every right to be angry with her. She would be angry if she thought he had lied to *her*. But she had to make him see that there had never been any ill intent behind her actions—quite the opposite. Perhaps her plan had been flawed, but how was she to have known that the stuffy, greedy Duke would be someone she would fall desperately in love with? If she had known that she would never have lied to him.

'I'm sorry. So very sorry. I know it was stupid of me. And I'm very, very sorry. I intended telling you the truth—just not yet.'

He shook his head and laughed—a harsh, mirthless laugh. 'Oh, I *see*. Well, that makes everything all right, doesn't it? How could I possibly object if you were planning on telling the truth one day. So, when would that have been? When would you have told the truth? After we had married? When our first child was born? Or were you planning a deathbed confession?'

His sarcasm stung and she grew smaller under his withering stare. He could not think that of her. This had to be put right. But how?

Silently she asked for Arabella's forgiveness. There was no choice now but to tell Alexander who she really was. He already knew she wasn't Arabella, so it was time to tell the whole truth.

'I had intended to write to you after I got back to London, but I will tell you who I am now.'

He shook his head and gave a snort of sarcastic laughter. 'I can hardly wait…'

She forced herself to ignore the barb. 'My name is Rosie Smith. I'm Mr van Haven's ward and Arabella's friend. I'm not an heiress. In fact, I have no fortune of my own. I'm all but penniless.'

He stared at her for a moment, his disdain obvious. 'Yes, that I *do* believe.'

Rosie exhaled in relief and smiled slightly. He believed her. Thank goodness for that. Perhaps now they could put all this unpleasantness and these accusations behind them and return to the way they had been.

'An impoverished ward with ambitions to become a duchess? Yes, that makes perfect sense,' he sneered.

Her smile dissolved. 'No, I never had ambitions to—'

'It explains everything. Unfortunately, Rosie Smith, I have no interest in marrying an impoverished ward who uses such chicanery to advance her position in society. And I certainly have no respect for a woman who would use her *obvious* charms…' his dark eyes raked up and down her body '…to catch herself a titled husband.'

Rosie recoiled as if struck, blood rushing to her face,

her heart pounding violently against the wall of her chest. 'How dare you?' she seethed through clenched teeth. 'How dare you accuse me of—?'

'I dare quite easily, Miss Smith. You have used the oldest tricks known to woman in order to ensnare a man. And I must say you are particularly adept at it.'

Rosie stared at him, uncharacteristically speechless, hardly able to believe what he was accusing her of. This was worse than his mother calling her a criminal. This was too bad.

How could he think that of her? He had ruined everything—tainted what had happened between them and reduced their affection, their passion and their love, to something sordid.

'No! *No!* It wasn't like that,' Rosie cried, barely able to hear her own voice above the sound of blood pounding in her ears. '*I'm* not like that,' she said, her voice rising. 'I wasn't trying to—'

Alexander glared down at her, his merciless eyes burning into hers, his lips a thin, disgusted line. 'That's exactly what it was like, Miss Smith. That's exactly what you were trying to do, and that's exactly the sort of woman you are. But this time you failed. Perhaps you'll have better luck next time and you'll be able to get some other hapless aristocrat to drag you out of the gutter and give you a title.'

Rosie felt her eyes grow wide and her mouth drop open. It seemed Nellie was right. Now that he knew who she really was he thought he was too good for her. As Nellie had said, men like him did not marry women like her. But that did not mean he had the right to insult her.

She closed her mouth, tilted her chin and glared back at him. 'You are an appalling man. You might be a duke but you are most certainly not a gentleman if you think you can speak to a lady like that. How I ever could have thought you were honourable and kind, I don't know.'

'Honourable? Kind?' He gave another humourless laugh. 'I don't think *those* were the attributes you were after. A title and a position in society? Weren't those the qualities you were looking for in a man?'

'I couldn't care less about your title,' Rosie fired back. 'I couldn't care less if you can trace your family back to the Stone Age. But it seems you do care. You think that because you've got a title, all this land and your fancy house, that you're better than me and you can talk to me any way you want.'

'I'm afraid, Miss Smith, your behaviour this weekend has shown that I *am* better than you. You're a liar and a charlatan who isn't above using her body for financial gain. And there are some *very* unpleasant names to describe a woman like that.'

'You—! You—!' Pain surged through Rosie as she clenched her hands so tightly her nails dug into her palms. She stared up at him, attempting to catch her breath as she tried to think of a way to wipe that arrogant sneer off his face.

Forcing herself to unclench her hands, she looked down at the ground and took a few steadying breaths. Slowly she raised her head, pulled herself up to her full height and stared him straight in the eye.

'Perhaps I have told a lie or two, but you're rude, insulting and a snob,' she hissed.

She had hoped her insult would affect him, but he stared back at her with eyes as cold and dark as a winter sky.

'And *you*, Miss Smith, are a liar and a wh—'

'I am no such thing!' Rosie interjected, even though

it meant lying again. Of course she had lied—but that wasn't the point, was it? It didn't mean he could talk to her in such a disrespectful manner or question her morality.

'All right—all right, I lied. And I've said I'm sorry about that. But you have no right to accuse me of…to accuse me of…'

'To accuse you of being a tart? A strumpet? A hussy? What word is it that you're searching for, Miss Smith? There are so many words available to describe a woman who uses her body to get what she wants.'

Her jaw and hands clenching tightly, Rosie glared up at his arrogant face. 'You contemptible man. To think I actually thought that I was in love with you. How could I have been so stupid as to think I loved a man as detestable as you? If I never see you again it will be far too soon.'

'Well, it seems there is one thing on which we are in complete agreement. I suggest you leave immediately and stop wasting my time.'

Rosie stared at him, her face burning, every muscle in her body clenched. There was so much more she wanted to say to him—so many more insults she wanted to fling in his direction. But what was the point? His arrogance was impenetrable. Nothing she could say would make any difference to his low opinion of her.

Summoning up as much dignity as possible, she turned abruptly and strode up the path, her skirts whipping around her ankles. As she walked quickly towards the carriage waiting outside the house a light rain started to fall, the raindrops merging with the tears of anger, shame and remorse running down her cheeks…

Chapter Eighteen

Pebble-sized circles formed on the river as raindrops hit the water, but Alexander was oblivious to the change in the weather. Nor did he hear the burbling river as it raced over the mossy rocks. With his mind shrouded in a fog of anger everything around him was all but silent and invisible.

Yes, he was angry. Angry with Miss Rosie Smith, or whoever she was, but he was even more angry with himself.

Angry that he could be so gullible. He had fallen for her lies, for her beauty, for her play-acting. Hadn't he learnt his lesson with Lydia? It would appear not. The next pretty liar who had come his way had bewitched him and he had fallen again—fallen even harder this time.

He picked up a willow stick and whipped it against the nearest tree, trying to beat out the pain that had overtaken him. His pain over Lydia's betrayal had been intense, but it had been nothing like this. It had not been so all-consuming.

He had trusted her, this Miss Rosie Smith. He had believed her. Believed her lies. He had let down his guard—

the guard that Lydia had taught him was essential if he was to avoid being betrayed again. And this was how his trust had been repaid.

Pain and anger continued to wage a war inside him as he walked up and down the edge of the river, determined to quash down all emotion. Anger he could cope with. Almost. But the pain—that was unbearable.

And he had a right to be angry. Everything about her had been a lie. She had even had the audacity to attempt to explain her actions. As if *anything* could explain her lies, her betrayal. And he had almost been taken in by them. For one fateful moment when he had seen her standing beside the river looking so forlorn he had wanted to *comfort* her.

He was a fool—a complete fool.

He hit the stick against the tree—harder. He knew what it was to be lied to repeatedly. Hadn't Lydia used exactly the same tricks? Hadn't Lydia said anything, done anything, to try and free herself from the web of lies she had woven around her? And he had believed her again and again, until it had been impossible to believe one more lie.

Well, not this time. Miss Rosie Smith had lied. She was a liar. That was all he needed to know. He did not need to know why she had lied or what her intentions had been. She was a liar. And he had been betrayed. *Again.*

Lydia's betrayal had been a mere bee-sting compared to the knife in the heart inflicted by Miss Smith. With Lydia he had never felt such all-consuming passion—a passion he could have drowned in, that could have taken him over and swept him away, so all he could think about was her, a woman he didn't even really know.

Yes, he was a fool. He had fallen in love with a chimera—a woman who didn't really exist. A woman who had been created as a device to ensnare him.

And she had almost succeeded.

Who she really was, what she was really like, he would never know. Never wanted to know.

An image of her laughing face and sad eyes entered his mind and his anger subsided slightly. He had never learnt why there was such sadness behind her laughter. Perhaps it was simply because she was poor and wanted a position in society.

He grabbed both ends of the willow stick and broke it in two. No, he did not need to know about her sadness. Did not need to know anything about her. She was gone and he had been saved from making even more of a fool of himself than he already had.

And yet here he was, standing by the river like some love-struck youth. He just had to remember that the woman he'd thought he loved did not exist.

Alexander tossed the sticks into the stream, watched them float away with the current, then turned and walked back towards the house. It was time to put this entire unfortunate incident behind him. He had work to do, and he had allowed himself to become distracted for far too long.

He should not be wasting time wallowing in self-pity. He should not be thinking about that woman—should not be remembering how she'd looked in the candlelight, or how her lips had felt on his, or what it had felt like to hold her in his arms. No, he should not think of such things. And he wouldn't ever again. Nor would he remember the sweet taste of her soft pink lips, the way she smelt of spring flowers, or how she looked when she lost herself in the passion of their embrace.

Instead he would write to the engineers tomorrow.

They would begin draining the marshlands and that neglected area would be converted to farmland. He would
arrange a loan with the bank to buy a steam-driven har-
vester, so the next harvest could be brought in more effi-
ciently. He would contact the owners of the local railway
company and begin discussions on bringing the line
through his land. He would even investigate the possibility of introducing electricity to the dairy and woolsheds.

He stopped walking. Hadn't electrification been *her*
suggestion?

Dragging in a deep breath, he strode off towards the
house. It was of no matter where the idea had come from.
He had much more important things to occupy his mind
than thinking about that woman, or dwelling on such
fripperies as her beauty, or how she played the piano
with such passion, or how lovely her singing voice was.

He increased his walking pace. No, he would not think
of such frivolous things—not when he had so much work
to do.

As he neared the house Charlotte raced out to meet
him, clutching a large black umbrella, her face contorted
with worry.

She handed the umbrella to Alexander and he gripped
the curved cane handle in a tight fist, sheltering his sister
from the increasing downpour.

'Oh, Alexander, I'm so sorry. I know she meant so
much to you.'

Anger continued to simmer inside him. That woman
had also caused pain to his sister—a woman who had
never hurt anyone.

He took her arm and patted her hand gently. 'It's all
right, Charlotte. I'm all right. Please, I think it best if we
just try and pretend none of this ever happened.'

'But what did she *say*? Why did she pass herself off as an American heiress? What was it all about?'

Charlotte clutched his arm, her questions coming in a rush, her eyes pleading with him.

'I have no idea, Charlotte. I'm just pleased that she has gone,' he said, his words more clipped than he intended.

'But didn't you ask her? Didn't you want to know? Didn't you *need* to know?'

Alexander released a sigh and looked over Charlotte's head into the distance. 'No, I didn't ask her. I neither needed nor wanted to know why she tried to trick me into marrying her. She's gone. There's no more to be said about it.'

Charlotte inhaled deeply, then slowly released her breath. 'You asked her to marry you? You really were in love with her, weren't you, Alexander? Oh, Alexander, surely you need to know why she did it?'

Alexander gripped the umbrella more tightly, his teeth clenched so firmly his jaw ached.

'If only you had asked, Alexander—asked her why she lied. Perhaps there was a good reason,' Charlotte said, her voice softening.

He looked down at his sister, her face pinched with concern. But it was misdirected concern. Like him, Charlotte needed to forget all about Miss Rosie Smith.

'There can be no good reason to excuse her lies, her deception,' he said, keeping his voice even so his anger would not upset her.

Charlotte shook her head. 'I can't accept that, Alexander. She was here for only two days, and in those two short days she changed you. Because of her you opened up your heart—a heart that had been closed since Lydia left. Please, Alexander, don't just dismiss her...don't close down your heart again. You deserve to be happy—and Arabella, or whoever she is, made you happy.'

Alexander shook his head and exhaled loudly. His ever-perceptive sister was right. Thanks to Miss Rosie Smith he had opened his heart—and look what had happened. For that, he would never forgive her. He had felt so many emotions over the last two days—emotions he'd thought he had forgotten how to feel. And now all he was left with was anger and pain.

Charlotte released her grip on his arm and lightly patted it. 'Perhaps when you calm down you should contact her and find out why she lied to us.'

'No, Charlotte,' he said through gritted teeth, to stop himself from shouting. 'I will *not* be contacting her, and I forbid you from having anything to do with her.'

Charlotte tilted her head and raised her eyebrows.

Alexander knew he had made a mistake. The best way to get Charlotte to want to do something was to forbid it.

'I'm sorry, Charlotte,' he said, his voice softening. 'I did not mean to lose my temper with you. But I entreat you to leave this alone. Nothing good will come of contacting that woman.'

Before she could formulate any other arguments he took her arm and walked her towards the house. He knew he would have to speak to Charlotte again on the subject at a later date because, like his mother, once her mind was made up it could be a monumental challenge to get her to change it.

And the last thing he wanted was for her to have any contact with Miss Rosie Smith.

Chapter Nineteen

Being a strong and resourceful woman was something Rosie had always prided herself on. She'd had to be strong when her father had died. She'd had to be even stronger when her mother had died and she'd been left all alone in the world. She'd had to be strong to endure being poor in a world of extreme wealth, and she'd had to be strong to cope with being completely dependent on Mr van Haven's reluctant charity.

Now she had to be even stronger. She had to be brave and to appear unaffected by the reality that she had fallen in love with a man who now despised her…who thought she was an immoral, gold-digging con woman.

When she'd returned to London she had resolved to keep what had happened a secret from Arabella. All her friend needed to know was that she was safe and did not have to marry the Duke. Arabella did not need to be upset by the painful details.

All her life Rosie had tried to repay her debt to Arabella by entertaining her, keeping her happy, distracting her from the sense of neglect she felt as a result of her father's constant absences. And that was what she intended to do now.

Arabella was trying to establish her career on the stage and that was all that mattered. Rosie would force herself to be happy, to smile, to laugh. After all, wasn't that what she always did? Kept smiling no matter what. Even if her heart was breaking.

Her tea whirled round and round in her cup as she continued to stir long after the sugar had dissolved, the spoon clinking against the fine bone china. Yes, she had to be strong for herself and also for Arabella.

Things were going so well for Arabella. While Rosie took afternoon tea Arabella was attending an audition for a play being staged by a small, newly formed London theatre. She was so close to achieving her dream of becoming an actress, and Rosie would not burden her with her own problems.

She was happy for her friend—very happy. And once that vicarious happiness would have been enough. Not long ago all she had ever wanted was for her best friend to achieve her dreams. She owed so much to the kind and generous young woman who had saved her from a life of poverty and vulnerability on the streets of New York. Just a few short days ago she had been prepared to dedicate the rest of her life to being Arabella's companion, and that ambition had been more than enough for her.

That was until she had met Alexander FitzRoy, Lord Ashton, the Eighth Duke of Knightsbrook. He had turned her world upside down and had changed everything.

Now she had to fight so hard to keep smiling that her cheeks often ached with the strain. It was becoming increasingly difficult to stop the edges of her lips from trembling, to stop her misery breaking through the veneer of joy she was determined to maintain.

Rosie released a quiet sigh. She lifted the teacup to her lips, then lowered it again, un-tasted, and tried to take comfort in the fact that her plan had actually succeeded. At least she had achieved her goal, she thought with sardonic humour.

She had arrived at Knightsbrook with the intention of behaving so badly that Alexander and the FitzRoys would eventually drive her out of the house, never wanting to see her again. And she had succeeded.

She lifted the cup once more to her lips, took a sip, but tasted nothing of the now cold tea. Yes, she deserved the pain she was feeling. Her actions had been appalling. She had lied to Alexander, betrayed his trust and the trust of his family. Charlotte had been right. Alexander did not deserve to be treated in such a manner. Another deep blush of shame swept over her. He deserved someone so much better than her.

Arabella entered the Palm Court at The Ritz, her charming demeanour and pretty face causing every head in the room to turn in her direction. She made her way between the tables, her face a beaming smile, her eyes sparkling.

Rosie forced herself to sit up straighter and to adopt her sunniest smile.

'I got the part! I can't believe it, but I did it—I got the part. I'm going to appear on the London stage!' Arabella nodded her thanks to the waiter who was pulling out her chair and sat down, still smiling. 'It's just a small part, but it's mine, and I appear in virtually every scene.'

'Oh, Bella, that's wonderful news,' Rosie said, clapping her hands together. 'Congratulations! You deserve it. You really are very talented.'

Arabella signalled to the waiter for afternoon tea, pulled off her gloves, clasped her hands together and placed them on the table. 'So… I think I've given you enough time,' she said, her face becoming serious. 'If you're not going to volunteer to tell me, then I'm just going to have to ask you. What's wrong, Rosie? Why are you so unhappy?'

Rosie shook her head and forced her smile to grow even larger. 'Nothing's wrong. I—'

'Don't tell me that nothing's wrong, Rosie. You've been miserable since you came back from Knightsbrook. I know you think it's your role to be the happy one, to entertain me. You've always been like that since we were young girls. But I don't want any more of your fake smiles and pretend joyfulness. What happened? Were they really mean to you?'

Rosie's mouth turned down and she shook her head. 'No, they were lovely.'

'Oh… Was the Duke stuffy and unbearable?'

'No, no… He was actually rather nice. Handsome, kind, honourable—not stuffy at all.'

Arabella gave her an assessing stare and Rosie's cheeks burned more fiercely.

'Oh, Rosie. Is that what the problem is? Was he *very* nice, *very* handsome, *very* kind and honourable?

Rosie nodded.

'And has he captured your heart?'

She nodded again.

'And was he uninterested because you have no money of your own?'

Rosie shook her head, then remembered what Nellie

had said about aristocratic men not marrying out of their class and nodded. But she was sure Nellie was wrong, so she shook her head again.

'I don't think such things matter to Alexander.'

'Then what went wrong? Why was he uninterested? Is the man a simpleton? You're beautiful, funny, charming. If you set your mind to it no man could resist you.'

'Oh, Bella. You're so kind.' Tears welled up in Rosie's eyes. 'But it's not that straightforward. He *was* interested. In fact he said he loved me, said he wanted to marry me—but that was when he thought I was *you*.'

Arabella tilted her chin and narrowed her eyes. 'So it *was* money he was after. Well, you're better off without him.'

'No, no, Arabella. You don't understand. He never wanted to marry you—well, at least he never wanted your money…never wanted to marry for money. He's a fiercely proud man, and even though the FitzRoys have lost their wealth he wants to restore the family fortune and their good name through hard work—not by marrying an heiress.'

'Well, there's no problem, then.' Arabella gave a little laugh. 'You have no money of your own. You're exactly what he's after.'

Rosie shrugged and sighed. 'Except he's also an honourable man. When he found out I'd lied to him by pretending to be someone else he was furious. He saw what I'd done as unforgivable.'

'But surely when you told him *why* you were lying he must have understood? Surely an honourable man would know that if you're lying to save someone else then it's not an unforgivable action.'

Rosie looked down at her teacup and then back up at

Arabella. 'I didn't tell him why I was pretending to be you. At first it was because I didn't want to betray you. And then I got so angry… I said some terrible things to him that just confirmed all the bad things he thought about me. And then he got angry with me and said some awful things back. And then we both said we never wanted to see each other again. And then I left.'

'Oh.'

'Yes. *Oh.*'

The waiter served Arabella's tea. She spooned several sugars into her cup and began stirring. 'So what's your plan? How are you going to win him back?'

Rosie stared wide-eyed at her friend. 'What? I have no "plan". Well, the only plan I have is to forget all about it eventually. I'm sure when enough time has passed I won't even remember what he looked like.'

Rosie gave a tentative smile and placed a smoked salmon sandwich on her plate, although eating was the last thing she felt like doing.

Arabella stopped stirring and placed her teaspoon on her saucer, her pretty mouth turned down. 'Hmm… You really are in a bad state, aren't you? When have you ever *not* had a plan? You're a fighter, Rosie. You don't give up easily. You never have before and this is not the time to start.'

Rosie shrugged again. 'You can't *make* someone love you, Bella. All I seem to have done is a very good job of making Alexander hate me.'

'I'm sure that's not true,' Arabella said, shaking her head. 'If he said he loved you once then I'm sure you can make him see that he still loves you—even if you're not who you said you were, and even if you did tell him a few innocent fibs.'

Rosie held up her hands. It was time to end this uncomfortable conversation. 'I know you mean well, Bella, but there's nothing to be done. Alexander is in the past, and I think it would be best if that's where he stays.' She forced another smile. 'So, tell me about this play—what part did you get? Let's start reading lines together after tea, so you're word-perfect for the first rehearsal.'

As long as she kept her mind occupied Rosie was certain that eventually, in time, Alexander would stop monopolising her daytime thoughts and her night-time dreams.

Arabella stared at her for a moment, her brows drawn together in question. 'Right…and once we've done that we'll get down to formulating a plan to recapture the Duke's heart.'

Rosie stifled a sigh. Arabella had the best of intentions, but this time there would be no plan. It was time to admit defeat. It was time to forget Alexander. It was time to move on.

Alexander looked out at the marshlands. After many days' work alongside the engineers and workmen the trenches had been dug and draining the area would soon commence, so that it could be turned into productive farmland. It should be a satisfying sight. He had secured good terms with the bank to pay for the work and had finally started on his plans to transform and modernise the estate.

And yet he was far from satisfied. Discontent racked his mind, and despite his tired muscles his body continued to be in a state of agitation.

He had laboured hard beside his tenants, digging from sun-up to sun-down, trying to exhaust his body so he would fall into a dreamless sleep at night. But still thoughts of a raven-haired beauty had invaded his dreams. And she was constantly on his waking mind, no matter how many distractions he placed in his own way.

He walked along the edge of the marshland, his boots squelching through thick mud. Their final encounter played over in his head once again. How he regretted his cruel words. He should never have flung those insulting names at her. He had no real evidence that she was an immoral woman.

He stopped and stared out at the boggy land. If he could take those harsh words back he would—in a second. But he couldn't undo what had been done. He'd thought of sending her an apology, but he had vowed to himself that he would have no contact with her, and he doubted she'd want any contact with him.

Anyway, what would be gained by an apology?

What would be gained by making contact?

And if he did apologise what would he say?

How could he explain that he had lashed out like an injured animal, thrashing about without thought, only aware that he was in pain and that he would do anything, say anything, to make the pain stop?

He picked up a stick and poked it into the damp earth.

But there had been one good outcome of her visit. She had been right about those plans to diversify. It had been that which had convinced the bank to lend him a substantial amount of money. They had been able to see the good business sense in producing a diversity of crops that could be transported by rail around the country and even abroad. And it had been her suggestion of electrification that had sealed the deal.

He had hoped that the whole unfortunate incident

would put his mother off her quest to find a future duchess with a substantial dowry, but it had not been the case.

His mother was wasting her time. Alexander could not see himself taking an interest in any other woman— not when he found it impossible to get Rosie Smith out of his mind. He would always compare all others to her, and he could not imagine meeting another woman who was as funny, as pretty and such a delight.

Although how much of her charm had been real and how much of it pretence he had no way of gauging. But the woman she had pretended to be—the one who had made him laugh, who had made him forget himself and his troubles—was one he had so easily fallen in love with.

It seemed Rosie Smith had ruined his chances with any other woman. He had fallen in love with a charade, and no real woman would ever be able to match her.

He pulled the stick out of the sucking mud and threw it into the marshland. It was time to be true to his commitment and force himself to excise her from his mind. It might take a while to get her out of his thoughts, but that was what he must do. And hopefully one day, some time in the distant future, he would have forgotten what she even looked like, forgotten her voice and the pretty laughter that came so easily, forgotten those disconcertingly sad blue eyes.

He had plenty of other things to occupy his thoughts. His negotiations with the railway were going well, and preparation of the land where the tracks would be laid would soon start. Once again he planned to join in with the men and help in the clearance of the land. He enjoyed the easy camaraderie of his tenants, and the feeling of pushing himself with hard physical labour.

He turned and headed back to the house. His muscles

ached from the hard day's work, and that at least gave him some satisfaction. Tomorrow would be another day of constant activity, and tonight he would bury himself in plans for the railway. As long as he was making plans for the estate and throwing himself into hard physical toil he could hopefully keep all invading thoughts of a pretty, tormenting, deceitful American at bay.

At least, that was the plan.

Chapter Twenty

Rosie needed time—that much she knew. But how much time?

That was a question she couldn't begin to answer. How long did it actually take for a broken heart to mend? Perhaps she should consult a doctor, because no one else seemed to know. And while that elusive amount of time was passing what was she supposed to do to ease her pain? How was she supposed to remove the constant memory of her last encounter with Alexander from her mind? How was she supposed to stop recalling all those other bittersweet memories of how he looked, how he talked, how his face changed when he laughed and, most painful of all, how his lips felt on hers?

She wandered aimlessly around the hotel suite, picked up a pen from the writing desk, twirled it in her fingers, then put it down again. She moved to the floor-to-ceiling windows. Outside there was a bustling city, just waiting for her to explore.

She pulled back the chintz drapes and looked down at the smartly dressed men and women walking along the pavement below, at the roads congested with horses and carts delivering goods to the many stores, and the carriages and omnibuses ferrying busy people to their destinations. Strains of music from the organ grinder at the street corner reached her.

There was so much activity just outside the front door of her hotel and she should be a part of it—not merely staring down at it from on high, like some miserable princess trapped in a tower.

Yes, she had to move on. Like the organ grinder's handle, the world kept on turning—so she should get out, leave the hotel and join in with that world.

She released the curtains, the mere thought of it draining her of energy.

The door burst open and Arabella swept in, waving tickets above her head. 'Right, you've been moping too long. It's time we went out and enjoyed ourselves. I've got tickets to the Gaiety Theatre on Saturday night. Rumour has it that Lillie Langtry is going to be putting in a guest appearance, so that is one performance we cannot miss. Nellie's going to make us both look beautiful, and Aunt Prudence says she's recovered and can accompany us—so no excuses. You're going to have some *fun*.'

Rosie forced her lips to smile. 'That's wonderful, Bella, how exciting,' she said, with more enthusiasm than she felt.

Just a few short weeks ago the idea of going to the Gaiety Theatre would have filled her with genuine excitement. And actually seeing the famous actress and socialite Lillie Langtry on stage would have been a dream come true. But now she was having to force herself to summon up even a modicum of enthusiasm.

She looked at her smiling friend and realised Arabella was right. She had to shake off this wretched misery, if for no other reason than she didn't want her sadness to make Arabella unhappy as well.

'In the meantime there's shopping to be done,' Arabella continued. 'We'll both need new gowns, new shoes, new hats, new evening bags—new everything if we're to attend the theatre. Plus, we've been very remiss in our exploration of London. We haven't yet visited any of the department stores. I've been dying to see inside the new Harrods. They say it's been rebuilt in spectacular fashion since the fire. It's the largest store in Europe, so it should have everything we could possibly need, and more, all under one roof. We can spend the day there, buy everything we need, and then when we're exhausted with shopping we can take afternoon tea to replenish ourselves for more shopping!'

Rosie smiled her first genuine smile for many days. It was usually her job to make Arabella feel happy, to entertain her friend—not the other way around. But her dear friend was doing everything she could to divert Rosie from her sorrows. Arabella truly was a good friend. The best friend a woman could ever have.

'Thank you, Bella, that sounds wonderful.'

'Oh, don't thank me. Just get ready and join me down in the foyer as quickly as possible. We're on a mission. There's much to do, many items to buy, and no time to waste.'

The two girls stepped down from their hansom cab, stood in front of Harrods and stared up at its seven-storey exterior. It was indeed spectacular, combining the modern American concept of a department store with a British sense of elegance. Adorned with cherubs and its new modern Art Nouveau windows, it seemed to draw them in with the promise of luxury and indulgence.

Inside it was no less spectacular, and the two girls were instantly absorbed into the hubbub of excited shoppers. As they rushed from counter to counter, trying on hats, gloves and scarves, sampling perfumes and watching elegant models display the latest fashions, Rosie was almost able to forget her sadness. *Almost.*

It was just unfortunate that she kept seeing Alexander among the bustling crowd, and then realising she was wrong. The breadth of one man's shoulders reminded her of Alexander's strong physique, but when he turned round it wasn't his handsome face she saw but that of a complete stranger. Another man held his head erect in just the same manner as Alexander, but when he looked her way she was again disappointed.

This was silly, she reminded herself. Alexander was in Devon. She would never see him again and she had to put him out of her mind.

Which was an equally silly idea. Rosie knew she would *never* be able to put Alexander out of her mind.

But at least she could keep trying. Even if she failed again and again and again.

After a whirl of shopping—broken only by a stop for afternoon tea—a hansom cab was summoned to take them back to the hotel, along with their many carefully wrapped packages.

Rosie had expected to return to the hotel suite to have a much-needed rest. But Arabella had other ideas. It seemed she had prepared a full itinerary of activities to keep every minute of Rosie's day and evening occupied.

Her friend knew her so well. Without these activities Rosie knew she would sink back into her morose state. So

Arabella had deemed that there would not be a minute left for Rosie to sit staring out of the window of her London hotel, dwelling on what had happened with Alexander.

'Look what I've got.'

Alexander raised his head, tearing his eyes away from the sorry tale told by the estate's financial ledgers, and gazed at his smiling sister. She was standing at the door of his office, holding a torn envelope and waving two pieces of paper.

'I've got tickets to the Gaiety Theatre on Saturday night.'

'I'm very pleased for you,' he said absentmindedly, placing his hands on the desk and returning his attention to the dilemma of how to save costs on the estate's expenditure without losing any workers.

'They're for us. We need to get out of this dismal house for a few days. We need to go up to London for the weekend. We need to have some fun for a change.'

Frowning, Alexander scrutinised his sister. *Fun?* This was not like Charlotte. The only time she went up to London was when she was visiting one of her charities, or attending a political meeting. When had she ever wanted to do something frivolous like seeing a play? Next thing she would be saying she actually *enjoyed* going to balls.

'I'm far too busy, Charlotte. And we can't spend money on plays and trips to London. We need to cut back on expenses—not waste money.'

Charlotte entered the room, slammed the tickets down on the desk and furrowed her brow.

Startled by this uncharacteristic display of anger, Alexander looked up at her.

'You're not too busy, and it won't cost us much. We

can stay at our London townhouse. It will be good to make use of it one last time before you sell it. And you'll only be away for a few days. You deserve a break after all your hard work and everything you've been through.'

'No, Charlotte.'

'*Yes, Charlotte*. That's the response you're meant to give. If you won't do it for yourself then do it for me. You've been such a misery to live with these past few weeks. You might enjoy being miserable, but I don't like being subjected to all this gloom and doom. I need cheering up as well, you know. So do it for me.'

He stared at his sister. What was happening to her? Was she having a kind of personality change? Insisting on having fun one moment and admonishing him the next. Perhaps his miserable countenance *had* been adversely affecting her, causing her to behave strangely. And she did deserve to have some fun after Miss Smith's betrayal and the uncertainty of their financial woes.

'All right,' he said slowly. 'I suppose one weekend won't hurt. And if you're prepared to waste your allowance on tickets to the theatre, then I suppose I can waste a bit of money on train tickets to London.'

'Good—that's settled.' Charlotte walked away, humming the chorus of 'Champagne Charlie'.

Alexander shuddered at the sound of the tune Miss Smith had entertained them with. He did not need reminding of her. He did not need reminding of all the damage she had caused. He did not need reminding of the pain he had felt—the pain he had been forced to crush down inside him until it sat in his stomach like a lead weight.

He turned back to his ledger, found the figures swirling before his eyes. He had to concentrate. He could not let her invade his mind again and distract him from the important work he had to do. She had taken up too much of his time and his thoughts already.

He would not think of her. He would drive all memories of her from his head. He closed his eyes, took in a deep breath, then stared back at the accounts, forcing himself to concentrate. He could not be distracted—especially if he was going to waste an entire weekend on a visit to London…

Arabella was bubbling with eager anticipation as they headed towards the Gaiety Theatre, and Rosie couldn't help but get caught up in her excitement. Even Aunt Prudence seemed to have brightened up a bit. After spending several weeks in bed, recovering from her imagined sea sickness and then a bout of hay fever, followed by an unidentified malaise, she had finally dragged herself out of her sickbed to fulfil her role as chaperon.

Rosie watched the busy London streets pass them by as the carriage clip-clopped along the cobbled road. Lit up by the gas lamps and the soft white light of a full moon, London looked spectacular.

When they arrived at the Gaiety Theatre their driver jostled with other coach drivers, all dropping off their cargo of excited theatregoers. With careful manoeuvring he managed to find a spot right outside the covered front entrance, so the ladies could disembark comfortably.

'Oh, dear. It's very noisy, isn't it?' Aunt Prudence complained as they entered the foyer. 'I hope it doesn't bring on one of my headaches.'

Rosie and Arabella looked at each other and giggled. *Everything* tended to bring on one of Aunt Prudence's imagined headaches.

But she was right about one thing. The crowded foyer presented a wall of sound, with a mass of bejewelled women and men in formal evening wear talking loudly, laughing and greeting their friends. There was a palpable buzz of excitement, and the rumour that Lillie Langtry might be making a guest appearance had obviously spread, because every group they passed seemed to be talking of her.

The girls made their way up the wide, richly carpeted stairs, along the corridors, and found their box. When they entered their own exclusive little room the noise of the crowd dimmed slightly.

Rosie seated herself and looked out on the assembled audience. The patrons in the stalls below bustled and jostled as they found their seats. In the rows of boxes across from them wealthy patrons entered at a more leisurely pace and settled themselves in for the night's entertainment.

'If Lillie Langtry is going to be on stage, then perhaps the Prince of Wales will attend as well,' Arabella said, scanning her programme. 'They say that she's his mistress, and he *is* rather partial to actresses. Perhaps when I become a famous actress I should become his mistress. I wonder what Father would prefer? Me being the future King's mistress or the wife of an aristocrat.'

Rosie looked at her giggling friend. It wasn't like Arabella to make fun of the way her father was using her to advance his own social status. She was obviously in a very good mood tonight.

The door to their box opened.

Rosie and Arabella turned as a smiling Charlotte Fitz-Roy entered. Rosie shook her head in bewilderment, as if an apparition had suddenly appeared, and then her heart plummeted to her stomach when she heard a familiar deep voice.

'Charlotte, what are you up to? I don't believe your meagre allowance could possibly stretch to taking a box. Are you sure our tickets aren't for the stalls?' said Alexander as he followed his sister into the box, looking down at the tickets and scowling.

When he looked up and saw Rosie staring at him he halted, his face wary, like a man suddenly aware he was entering an ambush. And that was exactly what this was.

Rosie looked from Charlotte to Arabella, then back again. They were wearing identical smiles. This encounter was obviously not a bizarre coincidence. It was something Arabella and Charlotte had concocted.

'Hello, I'm Arabella van Haven—the real Arabella van Haven,' her friend said, standing and smiling like Alice's Cheshire Cat. 'Rosie you already know, and may I present my aunt? Miss Prudence van Haven.'

Alexander stared at them for a moment, as if too stunned to talk, then his well-conditioned manners took over and he bowed to all three women. 'And may I present my sister? Lady Charlotte.'

'It's a pleasure to meet you, Lady Charlotte,' Arabella said, taking Charlotte's arm and leading her to a seat beside her.

The two women commenced chattering enthusiastically, as if oblivious to the tense atmosphere that had now descended on the box.

Rosie remained frozen in her seat, staring up at an equally stunned Alexander. For several painful seconds they remained motionless, like prey caught in a snare and unable to make any move to get free without fear of ensnaring themselves further.

'I'm sorry about this, Alexander,' she said finally, her voice a small croak. 'I didn't know a thing about it. I know you think I'm a liar, but you have to believe me. This is not my doing.'

'Oh, I do believe you. I can see the hand of my sister at work here.'

Rosie nodded. 'And my friend Arabella. The real Arabella. But you're here now. You might as well enjoy the play.'

He cast an annoyed glance at his sister and entered the box.

Rosie had almost forgotten how very handsome he was. Tall, and with such wide shoulders and dark good looks that he was nothing short of stunning. And seeing him again had certainly left *her* stunned.

But as he approached she became aware of a change in his appearance. There were dark rings under his eyes, and a sallowness to his olive skin that hadn't been there when she had visited Knightsbrook. He gave every appearance of a man who had not been sleeping properly.

Had he been working too hard? Worrying about the estate? Whatever had caused this change in him Rosie wanted to help, to soothe away his worries, to brush back the dark brown hair from his furrowed forehead. But caring for the Duke was not her role. It never had been and never would be.

He hesitated, then walked towards the one remaining seat—the seat beside Rosie.

Time seemed to slow down. The tension between them grew. The very air seemed heavy, and Rosie struggled to breathe. The noisy crowd fell silent. It was as if every member of the audience was aware of Rosie's embarrassment and discomfort, and were waiting with bated breath to see what happened next.

Arabella patted her arm. 'Rosie, stand up. The Prince of Wales is here.'

Rosie turned in her seat and as if through a haze of confusion saw a portly gentleman with a full beard enter the royal box. She gathered herself and stood up as Alexander reached his seat and stood beside her.

Someone in the crowd shouted out, 'Three cheers for His Royal Highness,' and they all joined in on three hearty 'hip-hip-hoorays'. All except Rosie and Alexander, whose somewhat muted responses were fortunately drowned out by the happy crowd.

How could Rosie be expected to cheer when she was in a state of shock? When her skin was tingling with nerves and her throat was so constricted she suspected she was incapable of speech?

The band struck up a lively tune and the audience took their seats again. Rosie closed her eyes to try and regain some composure. But how was she supposed to do that in this impossible situation? The man she had thought she would never see again was now sitting close beside her. The man she had treated so badly, the man she had lied to and insulted, the man she had fallen in love with, was now just a few inches away from her.

Rosie wriggled slightly in her seat to try and move away from Alexander, but the arrangement of the chairs allowed no room. A chill ran through her, as if the temperature had suddenly plummeted in the warm theatre. The naked skin of her arms and shoulders tingled, and she was aware that she was all but brushing up against his arm and shoulder. Her leg was so close to his they were almost touching.

She looked down at his legs and could see the muscles under the fabric. Then she quickly looked up again. She must not look at his legs. She must not even think about his legs, nor any other body part. Not the arms that had held her, not the chest that she had pressed herself against, and not his lips. Definitely not his lips. She did not want to think of them most of all.

But how was she supposed to stop her mind from thinking of such things when they were so close it would be easy to reach out and take hold of his hands? Hands that were clenched together between his knees—clenched so tightly that the whiteness of his knuckles was showing.

Oh, yes, it would be easy to touch him. Easy and yet an impossibility.

Throughout the performance Rosie hardly heard a word the actors said, and nor could she follow the plot—which seemed far too complex for a simple musical comedy. Even when Lillie Langtry came on stage, to the accompaniment of rapturous applause and cheers, it seemed to pass her by in a blur. All she could think about was the silent man sitting beside her.

Like her, he sat ramrod-straight in his chair, as if attending a solemn funeral service, not a light-hearted comedy. When the audience laughed, he remained rigid. When they clapped enthusiastically at the end of each scene he gave a brief token applause.

To say he was not enjoying the play would be an understatement. He was obviously hating every minute of the performance. And she knew that was not the fault of the actors, the band, the writer or the director. There was only one person responsible for Alexander's bad mood. And that was her.

After an interminably long time the intermission arrived. At least this ordeal was halfway over. But that was of small comfort. With the lights now raised Rosie could no longer hide behind the darkness of the blackened auditorium. No longer could she pretend to be distracted by the performance.

She might have to make conversation with Alexander.

The prospect caused her already thumping heart to increase its tempo, and her skin to burn as if the theatre had suddenly turned into an inferno.

Charlotte and Arabella stood up and rushed out, saying something about getting refreshments.

Rosie sent a pleading look towards the door they had so hastily departed through, silently begging them to return and save her from this intolerable situation. But the door remained firmly shut. The girls did not return.

She turned to stare straight ahead. They were now alone. All alone except for Aunt Prudence, who seemed to have dozed off at some time during the performance.

Alexander also stared ahead, his body still rigid, his face implacable.

With her heart beating to a frantic rhythm and her breath coming in short, shallow gasps, Rosie scrambled for something to say. Anything to break this uncomfortable silence. But nothing came to her befuddled mind.

'Are you enjoying the play, Your Grace?' she finally asked, her voice barely audible.

'Yes,' was his terse reply.

They slipped back into silence.

'And did you have a good trip up from London?'

He exhaled loudly. 'Oh, for goodness' sake, Miss Smith. After all that has happened between us are we *really* going to indulge in meaningless polite conversation?'

Rosie bit her lip. Even thinking of polite conversation

had required the concerted effort of all her mental capabilities. How was she supposed to think of anything more interesting to say when her mind was completely distracted by the close proximity of the man sitting beside her? A man who had once kissed her, had once told her he loved her, had even said that he wanted to marry her.

Rosie swallowed to ease her dry throat and tried not to think such things. She was supposed to make interesting conversation, not polite chatter. She most certainly did not want to say anything that would allude to what had happened between them at Knightsbrook. But what could she say?

She took a quick glance at Alexander, who was staring straight ahead. He wasn't much help. It was obvious he had no intention of making any conversation at all. At least she was trying—and all she had got for her trouble was a reprimand.

'Well, if you prefer we can sit here in embarrassed silence, staring at the walls and pretending we're somewhere else.'

He breathed in deeply and exhaled slowly. 'Forgive me—that was rude of me.'

Rosie shook her head. She did not want to argue with him. 'No, you have no need to apologise. This is awkward for both of us. I'm sure Arabella and Charlotte meant well, but I more than anyone should know that sometimes you should not interfere with people's lives.'

'Hmm...' came his monosyllabic reply.

Once again they sank into silence.

Alexander crossed his legs, uncrossed them, then crossed them again. Arabella wondered if he too was struggling to think of something to say. She wished that in his agitation he would remain still. All his crossing and uncrossing was once again drawing her attention to his legs—and all the other parts of that magnificent body she was not going to think about.

Rosie swallowed again, her throat still stubbornly dry, and joined him in staring straight ahead.

'So Miss van Haven knew what you had done, I take it? She was in complete agreement with you pretending to be her?' he finally asked, breaking the protracted silence.

'Oh, yes,' Rosie nodded. 'It was a silly plan, I know. But Arabella—the real Arabella—didn't want to go to Knightsbrook because she didn't want to marry you, and she especially didn't want to go that weekend. She wanted to see the opening of Oscar Wilde's new play. So I came up with the plan, which she agreed to. If I pretended to be her and misbehaved terribly then you wouldn't want to marry her—or me, I mean.'

'You're right. It *was* a silly plan. But it looks like you succeeded.'

Rosie closed her eyes, his words like a stab to her heart. Yes, she had succeeded. Succeeded in saving Arabella from an unwanted marriage and succeeded in destroying her own chance of happiness with the man with whom she had fallen in love. But then, had Rosie Smith—the real Rosie Smith—ever had a chance of marrying the Duke or had she deluded herself?

'Well, that's something, I suppose,' she murmured, before they sank back into a tense silence.

Charlotte and Arabella bustled back in, their cheeks pink with excitement, matching smiles on their lips, and the curtain was raised for the second act.

Rosie could not be angry with her friend, nor with Charlotte. The two women had meant well, but they were trying to achieve a hopeless goal. Alexander despised her. That was undeniably evident to her, if not to them. He had made his feelings about her perfectly clear before she'd left Knightsbrook, and he was making them clear now. And even if he didn't despise her, the best she could hope for from Alexander was indifference. He was a duke and she was a nobody—a nobody he could now hardly bear even to speak to.

Once again she returned to staring at the stage, seeing nothing and hearing nothing of the performance, and waited anxiously for the whole embarrassing episode to be over.

Alexander had never felt like a victim before. But, sitting in The Gaiety Theatre, it seemed to him that was exactly what he was. The unwitting victim of a female conspiracy.

He had no doubt that this ridiculous situation was all down to Charlotte and Miss van Haven's scheming. While they had both looked as pleased as Punch when he and Charlotte had entered the box, Miss Smith had looked as shocked as he had felt. Her stilted conversation and awkward demeanour had made it abundantly clear that she would rather be anywhere than confined in this small theatre box watching this seemingly endless play.

He had never expected to see Rosie again. Had hoped he would never see her again. Now, with her sitting next to him, so close he could easily take her in his arms, everything about their weekend together came crashing over him, like a furious wave smashing against a rocky coastline.

The scent of spring flowers filled the air and the soft skin of her naked arms and shoulders seem to offer an all but irresistible temptation. An image of folding down the delicate straps of her gown and kissing a line along the skin of those slim shoulders invaded his mind.

He coughed discreetly and crossed his legs.

Yes, he really was a victim. A victim of Charlotte and Arabella's scheming and a victim of his own foolish desires. And he was going to have to fight those desires with the full might of his strength if he was to maintain his resistance and stop this woman from once again tearing out his heart.

She had hurt him. There was no denying that. And only a masochist would subject himself to continued pain. He was no masochist. As soon as this play was over he would leave, and then he would never have to experience the turmoil of such unwanted emotions ever again.

Finally the play finished, and the sound of hundreds of gloved hands applauding erupted in the theatre. Charlotte and Arabella instantly started chatting enthusiastically about everything they had just seen, while Rosie and Alexander maintained their now familiar uncomfortable silence.

'Right,' said Miss van Haven, standing up and picking up her shawl. 'We're staying at the Savoy and I've booked a table in the restaurant for supper. It will be my treat. It's the least I can do for you, Your Grace and Lady Charlotte, after the appalling trick I played on you.'

Alexander quickly stood up too. 'Not at all, Miss van Haven. You owe us nothing, and Charlotte and I would not dream of imposing.'

'Oh, please, Alexander,' Charlotte entreated him. 'I've never been to the Savoy and I'd love to see it. I'm sure you would as well. It's got electric lighting, you know, and a wonderfully modern contraption called a lift car that carries you up from one floor to another and then back down again.'

She stared at him, wide-eyed, as if the thought of seeing modern innovations should be enough to counter his severe reluctance to spend any more time in the company of Rosie Smith.

'That's as may be, Charlotte, but—'

'Oh, please, Alexander,' Charlotte said again, her eyes pleading. 'We don't get up to London often, and who knows when we'll come again? I would enjoy it so much.'

'Oh, all right, Charlotte. Fine,' he agreed through clenched teeth, sending her a silent message that they would not be staying long.

Charlotte clapped her hands together and beamed at him. It was obvious that it wasn't the thought of supper at the Savoy or of being able to travel by an electric lift from floor to floor that was causing so much excitement, but the fact that she had succeeded in forcing him to endure even more time with Miss Smith.

He escorted the ladies out through the noisy milling crowd and hailed a cab to take them to the Savoy.

As they travelled towards the well-known London landmark Alexander had to admit that Charlotte was right to be enthusiastic about the way the Savoy had embraced modernity. Like a beacon, it shone out in the London night sky, with electric lighting illuminating every room. The carriage pulled up into the courtyard and he helped the ladies down.

Rosie waited till last, and seemed to take a moment to compose herself before she took his offered hand. She placed one foot on the carriage steps and their eyes met.

Despite his attempted resistance to her charms, he had to admit he had never seen her look more beautiful.

Her blue eyes sparkled with reflected light, capturing his gaze, and he stood in front of her as if transfixed.

It wasn't until she lowered her eyes and a blush came to her creamy cheeks that he remembered himself. He took her hand in his and forced himself to recall who she was and what she had done. Even with her gloved hand in his he would not lose his composure—he would not react to the light touch of her fingers that was burning into his hand.

Her touch brought memories flooding back…of taking her in his arms and kissing her with such passionate intensity it had seemed to shake his world off its axis.

Do not think of that—and for goodness' sake, man, pull yourself together.

But even this admonition couldn't stop him from noticing that one tendril of black hair had become dislodged from her coiffure and now curled temptingly around her neck, across her shoulders and down to her beautiful cleavage…

They entered the restaurant and the head waiter ushered them to a table by the French doors, overlooking the balcony and garden.

'Would you like to see the electric lift?' Arabella said to Charlotte, ignoring the waiters who were holding out their chairs.

Before anyone else could respond the two girls had rushed off, leaving Alexander, Rosie and their elderly chaperon standing at the table.

They seated themselves in the plush red leather chairs and a bottle of champagne arrived, unordered. It seemed Miss van Haven's arrangements extended beyond merely getting Alexander and Rosie together. She wanted to make this a celebration as well. But this evening had more in common with a wake than it did a festive occasion.

Alexander made polite conversation with Miss van Haven's elderly aunt, who suddenly announced that all the excitement of the evening had brought on one of her headaches and decided to retire for the evening.

It was a complaint Alexander could have made himself. The tension of the evening was starting to leave its mark on him, in the form of tight shoulders and a stiff neck.

He offered to escort the aunt to her suite, but she waved him away with her fan and bustled off towards the stairs. It seemed that the elderly aunt, like his mother, abhorred modern apparatus such as electric lifts and would prefer to walk up to her room.

He lifted the champagne out of the ice bucket and poured it into two glasses.

'Champagne? Although I'm not entirely sure what we're meant to be celebrating. Perhaps we're supposed to offer up a toast to my sister for discovering the devious side of her personality?'

He handed a champagne flute to Rosie.

'I'm equally surprised by Arabella putting this plan into action,' she said, taking the champagne glass from his hand but carefully avoiding touching his fingers. 'I knew she had received a lot of letters lately that had made her very happy. I'd assumed they were from the theatre she's about to perform with, but they must have been from Charlotte.'

'Hmm... So you and Miss van Haven in the habit of concocting devious plans?'

She screwed up her pretty face and her shoulders rose

up to her ears. 'Yes, I'm afraid we are. But I've learnt my lesson—even if Arabella hasn't.'

'She thought she'd be helping you by getting us together, and you thought you'd be helping her by passing yourself off as a badly behaved American heiress?'

She shrugged again. 'I suppose so…yes.'

He considered her for a moment as she blushed under his gaze. 'So the only reason you did it was to help your friend?'

'Well, no, that wasn't the only reason.' She bit her bottom lip. 'I also wanted to have some fun at the expense of a group of stuffy aristocrats. I thought you were just greedy people who didn't want to work for your money… I thought you deserved to be made sport of. I was wrong and I'm sorry. I know now that I shouldn't have. I shouldn't really make fun of anyone.'

Alexander looked down into his glass at the bubbles rising up through the straw-coloured liquid and bursting when they hit the surface as he absorbed this piece of information.

'Perhaps… But your main reason was to help your friend. You had honourable intentions, even if you were misguided,' he said.

He looked over at her. Despite his conciliatory words her blush had not subsided.

'You're very kind to say that,' she mumbled. 'But I still shouldn't have done it and I beg your pardon.'

He shook his head. 'No, it seems you have nothing to apologise for. You were helping a friend. I jumped to the conclusion that you were up to no good—that you were playing games with me or performing some sort of confidence trick on my family. I judged you unfairly. I should have known there would be a reason for your behaviour and I didn't give you a chance to explain. For that I am sorry.'

Alexander suspected his reaction had also been influenced by his history with Lydia Beaufort. He had been lied to before, cheated before, tricked before, and that had coloured his assessment of Rosie Smith. But Rosie was not like Lydia. Lydia had lied to achieve her own disreputable ends—not to help a friend.

'No, no, no.' Rosie shook her head emphatically. 'You most definitely have nothing to apologise for. My behaviour was terrible—and not in the way it was meant to be terrible. When I came up with my plan I didn't think about the people I would be deceiving. I just wanted to save Arabella and have some fun in the process. It really was quite appalling.'

'No, Miss Smith. I should be the one to apologise. I said some awful things to you. I was rude and offensive, and you did not deserve that.'

Alexander cringed as memory came flooding back—all those accusations he had made, all those harsh words he had said. It really had been unforgivable—especially now that he knew she had not been lying to him for her own sake, but to help her friend.

She held up her hands to stop his words. 'You were angry. And you had every right to be after the way I acted. I came into your home, I was rude to your mother, I tricked you and Charlotte. It was disrespectful. You said when we first met that everyone deserves to be treated with respect. You most certainly do—as does Charlotte, and even your mother...' She gave a little laugh. 'Well, perhaps your mother deserves to have tricks played on her...' She pulled her face into a more serious expression. 'No, even dowager duchesses deserve to be treated with respect.'

It was lovely to see that smile again—that beautiful, radiant smile—even if it was only for a fleeting moment. Alexander took a moment to bask in its remembered glow before asking a question that had been tormenting him since he had found out she was not really Arabella van Haven.

'And what of Thomas Gardener. Was he in on this game?'

She bit the edge of her bottom lip again. 'Oh, him. Yes, about him… I…um… I sort of…well, I made him up.'

He stared at her as she sent him a tentative smile. 'So there is no Thomas Gardener?'

She shook her head.

'Why on earth did you invent him? What did *he* have to do with your plan?'

Her flushed cheeks coloured a darker shade of pink. 'Well, you put me on the spot when you asked why I didn't want to marry. I couldn't think of any reason why I wouldn't want to marry a man like—' She bit that poor lip again. 'I couldn't think of any reason why I wouldn't want to get married, so I invented a beau. I named him Thomas after a sleeping ginger tomcat, and Gardener after an elderly man pushing a wheelbarrow.'

He stared at her in disbelief as she smiled through her embarrassment, and then laughter exploded within him. He had tormented himself with jealousy over a cat and his aging gardener.

'Oh, Rosie, you really are—' He stopped suddenly, his laughter dying. 'I'm sorry. Miss Smith.'

Her smile grew wider. 'Oh, no, call me Rosie, please.

It is my real name, after all. And I'm so sorry I lied about having a beau.'

'As I've said, you have nothing to apologise for. Now that I know the full story it seems it is only I who needs to apologise. I should have given you a chance to explain. I should not have jumped to conclusions. You say you have behaved terribly, but you were doing so for honourable reasons. I have no such excuse for my own unreasonable behaviour.'

She sent him a small smile. 'Oh, well…perhaps we should just agree that we're both really terrible people?'

Alexander laughed again. 'Yes, we're terrible people who deserve each other!'

He placed his hand over hers, and then, suddenly realising the easy level of informality he had slipped into, removed it, picked up his champagne and drained the glass.

'So, perhaps you'd like to tell me about the real Rosie Smith.' He placed the now empty glass back on the table. 'I know she plays the piano exquisitely, that she loves nature and that art enraptures her. I know she's funny, and that she is a good and loyal friend to Miss van Haven. But what else can you tell me about the real Rosie Smith?

She shrugged. 'There's not much to tell, really. As I already told you, I'm Mr van Haven's ward. I have been since I was fourteen.'

That familiar sadness washed over her deep blue eyes. It had intrigued him from the first time he had seen her. A sadness so at odds with her ready smile and easy laughter.

'But I once did have my own family.' She smiled as if lost in her memories. 'My father was an electrical engineer, and he ran a successful company installing electricity in towns and businesses throughout New York State. Mr van Haven convinced him to expand, but unfortunately it didn't work out. He lost money on bad debts and other misfortunes. He couldn't repay the money he owed to Mr van Haven's bank, so the bank took over his company. Not long after that he died. I think he died of a broken heart. He was certainly a broken man. Mr van Haven then employed my mother as a governess for Arabella. I don't know if that was an act of charity, guilt because of what he had done to my father, or because he knew my talented and accomplished mother would make the perfect governess and substitute mother for Arabella. And, being a cunning businessman, he knew she was desperate to find work and a place to live—somewhere she could keep her child with her. That meant she wouldn't object to the low wages he paid. My mother died when I was fourteen, but thanks to Arabella Mr van Haven took me on as his ward. That's why I owe so much to Arabella; she's the best friend a girl could ever have.'

Alexander could now see why such sadness clouded her otherwise sunny disposition. She had lost her father and her mother at an early age—had gone from a secure family life to one of insecurity, dependent on a man who seemed to have little regard for other people. He could also see why she was such a resilient young woman. She'd had to be, if she was to survive under such conditions.

He had been right in his original assessment: she really was a remarkable young woman.

'I'm sorry, Rosie. That must have been very hard for you,' he said, gently patting her hand.

She sent him a sad smile. 'It was. But I always had Bella.'

'I can see you two are very close.'

She nodded and they slipped into silence, both staring into their glasses.

Her life had been so hard, he thought, and yet she continued to smile and laugh, even through her sorrow. She was clever, witty, loyal and so beautiful it could take his breath away. How could he ever have doubted her? And why had he wasted so much time and so much energy feeling pain and anger towards her? It had to be due to what had happened between him and Lydia Beaufort.

But Lydia was in his past. Rosie was here, now, and very much part of his present. And the two women couldn't be more different.

He looked up at her and smiled. 'Your father was an electrical engineer?'

Rosie beamed a smile back at him. 'Yes, I'm sure you two would have got on well. He would have loved your plans for modernisation and would have had many ideas to contribute.'

'And he also produced a rather lovely, rather clever and innovative daughter as well,' he said, causing that delightful blush to tinge her creamy cheeks once again. 'I would have been honoured to meet him. It's men like your father who will transform this country. Not the old aristocracy who are still clinging on to their old ways, desperate to preserve a class system that is rapidly becoming outdated.'

She looked at him sideways, no longer smiling. 'Don't let your mother hear you say that. She thinks a title means everything, and that finding you a woman from a wealthy family who thinks the same way will save Knightsbrook.'

Alexander exhaled loudly. 'My mother knows exactly what I think of that. I've told her often enough. I don't care about my title and I care even less about other people's titles. The estate I have inherited means more than the title. What I have inherited is the responsibility of running it well, and improving it—not just for my family, but for everyone who depends on the estate for their livelihood. My mother and many like her think a title gives you privileges, but the title of Duke and Duchess should go to people who take their responsibility seriously.'

'Really?' Rosie gave him another sideways glance. 'You don't care about titles, class, background…? All that sort of thing?'

'There are more important things—like character, personality, resilience.'

He was about to add other frivolous attributes, such as beauty, a ready laugh and a lovely smile, when he was interrupted by the two co-conspirators, returning arm in arm.

Alexander suspected they had been hiding just out of sight and watching all that had unfolded between him and Rosie, waiting until their differences had been resolved before they made their reappearance.

Over the meal they discussed the play—although Alexander could contribute little, having seen virtually nothing of it, his mind having been occupied elsewhere. They also talked of what the girls had seen in London, and Arabella's ambitions as an actress. Uncharacteristically, Rosie did not say much, but she smiled a lot, particularly when she looked at Alexander, and that warmed his heart.

The crowd at the Savoy Restaurant began to thin, until they were the only people remaining at their table. Alexander had so thoroughly enjoyed the company of these young women, and the pleasure of once again being comfortable in Rosie's company, he had failed to notice how late it was getting.

He looked over at the waiters, who were not too successfully stifling yawns, and reluctantly decided it was time to call it a night. But he knew it would not be the last time he would see Rosie Smith. They had a lot of time to make up—time they had wasted in foolish misunderstandings and unnecessary pain and anguish.

Arabella was the first to stand, and she asked Charlotte to accompany her to her suite. 'It will give you one more chance to play on the electric lift,' she said. And the two girls rushed off together, leaving Alexander and Rosie alone to say their goodbyes.

Alexander stood and held out his hand to Rosie. With a shy smile she placed her hand lightly on his and stood. They gazed at each other for a moment.

'It has been lovely to see you again,' he said, knowing his words were inadequate to express what he was feeling.

'And you too, Alexander.'

Charlotte was suddenly at his side, still beaming the smile that had not left her lips all evening. Rosie kissed Charlotte on the cheek and thanked her for everything she had done, before sending Alexander another smile and departing.

As Charlotte and Alexander waited for their hansom cab to take them back to their townhouse, curiosity got the better of him.

'I have to ask you,' he said. 'How did you manage to organise all this?'

Charlotte gave a little laugh. 'Oh, it was surprisingly easy. I wrote to the newspaper that reviewed the Oscar Wilde play—the one that mentioned Arabella van Haven. I asked them to forward a letter on to her. They did. She wrote back and explained what Rosie had done, and why.

I knew there was no point just telling you—you'd never listen…'

Alexander had to nod his agreement. He was so stubborn he had refused to listen to Rosie when she had tried to explain herself by the river, and he would no doubt have refused to listen to Charlotte. He had been so caught up in his own anguish he had become completely unreasonable.

'Arabella and I decided the best thing to do was to get you two together so you could talk it out yourselves. So we did. And it seems we were right.'

Alexander smiled at his sister. Normally he would be annoyed with anyone trying to interfere in his life—after all, didn't he get enough of that from his mother? But this time, he had to admit, a little interference had been a great success.

Chapter Twenty-One

Alexander stared at his reflection as his valet brushed down his jacket, removing every last speck of dust so it was immaculately clean. Although such meticulous attention to detail was wasted. He would be returning by train to Knightsbrook this morning, and no doubt when he arrived he would be speckled with the smuts emitted from the steam train's funnel.

He hadn't wanted to come to London—had not wanted to waste time on such frivolity. It was only Charlotte's insistence that had dragged him away from his work. He had been annoyed by the interruption, but now he couldn't be more grateful to Charlotte for insisting he accompany her to the theatre.

She had also been right that he'd needed to find out why Rosie had deceived him. He had tried to convince himself that it didn't matter, but in reality he had been tormenting himself with unanswered questions. Possible reasons to explain why someone who had seemed so lovely could behave so treacherously had been spinning round and round in his head.

And now he knew the answer. She was not treacherous, and she was not deceitful. She was an honourable, lovely and lively young woman.

He smiled to himself at the memory of how she had looked as they'd dined at the Savoy. Then further images entered his mind. Her twirling her way down the entrance hall at Knightsbrook…her talking and laughing with Annie…her playing the piano with such passion and virtuosity.

Yes, he owed a debt of gratitude to Charlotte for tricking him and overcoming his stubborn resistance to meeting Rosie again.

He thanked his valet, picked up his hat and gloves and headed downstairs. Charlotte was waiting for him, her trunk and hat box stacked by the front door, ready for their departure.

They were going home—back to Knightsbrook. Away from London…away from Rosie. Alexander knew he must pen a letter to her immediately, before they left town. He had to inform her of how much he had enjoyed their reunion and how much he was looking forward to seeing them again.

He called for some pen and paper.

Or, better than a quick farewell note, perhaps he should extend an invitation to Rosie, Arabella and Aunt Prudence to spend some time at Knightsbrook. That would provide an opportunity to re-do their time together—this time with no pretence, no artifice, and no barriers put in place by him.

The pen and paper arrived and he dipped the pen in the ink, watched over by a very interested Charlotte. He put the pen to the paper, then hesitated.

'What's wrong, Alexander?' Charlotte asked, her brow furrowed.

'I've changed my mind.'

The furrow grew deeper.

'I believe we deserve a longer break in London. Perhaps we should invite Miss Smith and Miss van Haven to accompany us on a drive around Hyde Park? I'm sure the air would do us all some good.'

Charlotte's furrowed brow smoothed. She clapped her hands together and smiled. 'That's a marvellous idea, Alexander.' Then her smile disappeared and she placed the back of her hand theatrically on her brow. 'Oh, but I think you might have to go by yourself... I can feel a terrible headache coming on.'

Alexander shook his head and smiled at his sister. 'If that's your best performance, then I don't think you should consider a career on the stage. And you don't need to feign a headache. I'm sure Miss Smith and Miss van Haven would be delighted to see you again.'

'Well, perhaps—but I can see them another time. I hope there will be many more times we will all spend together. So, off you go.'

Alexander grabbed his hat and gloves and hailed a hansom cab to take him to the Savoy. There, standing at the reception desk, he penned a note to the Misses Smith and van Haven, inviting them and their chaperon for a drive in Hyde Park.

As he waited for their reply he paced up and down the foyer, feeling ridiculously nervous, like a young man waiting for his beau.

He heard the clanking of the electric lift behind him, turned and saw Rosie emerging. Dressed in a dark blue skirt, with a blue and white striped blouse, she looked a vision. Could she have become even more beautiful overnight? Was that even possible? He could have sworn it was a fact. And she was smiling at him—that radiant smile that seemed to light up the room.

'Alexander,' she said when she reached him, still beaming that smile.

He nodded a greeting, unable to stop himself from smiling his own foolish smile.

She looked back at the stairs. 'I'm afraid we're going to have to wait for Aunt Prudence. She refuses to take the electric lift as she says it is a new-fangled contraption.' Rosie bit the top of her lip, as if suppressing a giggle. 'And Arabella says she can't join us because she has a headache.'

Alexander laughed. 'There seems to be a lot of that going around. Charlotte, too, seems to have been struck down suddenly by a mysterious headache.'

Aunt Prudence joined them, and Alexander took both ladies' arms and led them to a waiting carriage.

The carriage took them through the grand entrance to Hyde Park, where they joined the parade of locals exercising their horses and riding in carriages along the path, under the canopy of lightly rustling trees.

'Oh, let's walk, Alexander!' Rosie said, patting his arm. 'You know how much I love trees and nature.'

Alexander laughed, but told the driver to stop. 'From memory, I think you said trees were horrid and those terrible birds were even worse.'

Smiling, Rosie patted him on the arm again. 'I never said that. That was Arabella.'

He helped the two ladies down from the carriage and took each one by the arm. They walked in silence for a few moments, before Aunt Prudence released his arm and headed for the nearest bench.

'You two young people go ahead. I can feel another one of my headaches coming on.'

Alexander rushed to the older woman's side. 'Shall I summon the carriage?'

'No, no. I'll just sit here under the trees until I start to feel better. You two young people carry on with your walk.'

Rosie sent him a small wink.

'Did you know that would happen?' Alexander asked.

'You can almost set your clock by Aunt Prudence's headaches, so I knew if we decided to walk it wouldn't be long before she claimed another imaginary headache and then we'd be able to spend some time together.'

He laughed as she raised her eyebrows and tried to look innocent. 'You really are quite devious, aren't you?'

'I thought you would have realised that by now, Alexander,' she said, and laughed as she took his arm.

They strolled along the path together. Alexander was suddenly strangely tongue-tied—unsure what to say now that all barriers between them had been lowered.

'I hope you enjoyed last night's play,' he said, to break the silence.

'Oh, yes, it was marvellous,' she responded, and then gave one of her now familiar tinkling laughs. 'No, I'm sorry, Alexander. That's not true. I can hardly remember any of the play. I wasn't concentrating. I was so distracted by seeing you again.'

He had to smile at her response, which was so unguarded. 'I was the same, I'm afraid. But apparently it has had good reviews, so it seems we missed an excellent play.'

'Well, we might have missed an excellent play, but I for one think it was still a great night.'

He squeezed her arm lightly in agreement.

Their walk took them past a pond, where groups of young boys were playing with boats on the water. The miniature flotilla included vessels of all sizes, from simple boats of sticks and cloth to elaborately carved sailing vessels.

'Shall we stop and watch for a while?' Rosie asked.

'I'm so pleased we talked last night,' he said as he led her to a nearby park bench. 'I feel we now have a chance to start all over again, and for me to get to know the real Rosie Smith.'

'Oh, I'm afraid the person you've already met is mostly Rosie Smith. I might have been lying about my name, but almost everything else about the person you met at Knightsbrook was the real me.'

She tucked her skirt underneath her and sat down.

'Sadly, the person who twirled down the entrance hall at Knightsbrook, and the person who sang inappropriate songs in the Dowager's drawing room, is the real Rosie Smith.'

Alexander smiled as he remembered her unusual entrance and the look of horror on his mother's face. 'I'm pleased to hear that.' He sat down beside her on the bench and looked out at the busy children. 'And I wouldn't have it any other way. Your twirling entrance was priceless.'

She patted his arm again and smiled. 'That wasn't my intention. I was supposed to be shocking you, not impressing you. You were supposed to conclude that I was entirely unacceptable.'

'I don't think it would be possible for me to think that the real Rosie Smith is unacceptable.'

She sent him a shy smile and a delightful blush tinged her cheeks.

'And I was the one whose behaviour was unacceptable. You said you expected to meet a stuffy aristocratic family, and after my reaction that must have been exactly what you thought of me. A delightful young woman had come into my home, bringing laughter and joy, and I reacted by being disapproving and stern.'

'Oh, no—no.' She turned to him, shaking her head, with a deep furrow in her brow. 'You are most definitely not stuffy, and you were nothing but polite. I mean, the first time we met you saved me from falling to the ground.'

Alexander smiled again at the memory of Rosie, diving across the room to save the Ming vase. It was strange, but even then he had been more concerned for her welfare than for an irreplaceable valuable vase.

'And if you were sombre at times—well, you had reason to be,' she said in a quieter voice. 'You've had all those problems with your father, with the estate, and then there's Lydia…'

Lydia. The name caused no reaction in Alexander whatsoever. It was as if some kind of an exorcism had been performed and her spirit no longer haunted him. 'The only problem with Lydia is that she caused me to judge you more harshly than you deserved.'

Memories of what Charlotte had said came back to him—that because of Lydia he had hardened his heart, had shut down emotionally. And yet when he had met Rosie she had managed to find a chink in his armour and he'd begun to open himself up to her. That was why her perceived betrayal had hurt him so much. But now he knew she had not betrayed him. He had been given a second chance.

He smiled at her, and got a beautiful smile in return.

'As for the estate—I've secured sufficient advances from the bank to begin a modernisation programme, and what convinced the bank manager the most was my telling him of your suggestion to diversify and bring electrification to the dairy and the woolshed. He was most impressed with my progressive thinking.'

'*Whose* progressive thinking?' she said, raising her finger and waggling it in front of his face.

'*Your* progressive thinking!' He laughed, taking her finger and giving it a light kiss. 'And for that I thank you—on behalf of my family and all the tenants of Knightsbrook.'

He continued holding her soft hand for a moment, before reluctantly releasing it.

'I'm so pleased, Alexander,' she said quietly. 'I know how much Annie and the tenants mean to you. They're more than just people who work on your land, aren't they? They're family.'

He nodded. 'They are indeed. As a child I often used to pretend to myself that Annie was my real mother, her husband my real father, and the tenant children my brothers and sisters.'

She placed her hand gently on his arm and he smiled at her.

'At least that is something for me to be grateful to my father for,' he said, with a laugh that contained no humour. 'He taught me a valuable lesson: that there are good and bad people in all classes. It doesn't matter what your background is, who your family is, or how much money you have, it's what's in your heart that matters.'

She nodded her agreement.

'And that's something I admire in *you*, as well, Rosie.'

'Me?' she said, pointing to herself.

'You've risen above your circumstances. You might have become bitter or angry, but instead you smile more than some people who have had a good life handed to them on a silver platter.'

She shook her head in disagreement. 'In many ways I think my life has been much easier than a lot of people's. Before things changed I had a very happy childhood, and I have warm, lovely memories from that time. I had a mother and father who loved me, and a home that was full of laughter, joy and music. I think it was that start in life that gave me such resilience and allowed me to rise above misfortune. When my father lost all his money, and then died, it was heartbreaking. But I still had my lovely mother, who was a very strong woman. She tried to protect me as much as possible from what was happening. And when she became Arabella's governess she continued to be a loving mother to me and became a substitute mother for Arabella as well.'

She paused and took in a deep breath.

'When she died…yes, I was devastated, and I felt very frightened and alone. But I had my friend Arabella. We were united in our grief and we supported each other. That's why we're such good friends now.' She sent him a sad smile. 'So, yes, I've had a lot of sadness in my life—but there's also been a lot of happiness and a lot of kindness.'

Alexander's admiration for this remarkable young woman continued to grow. She had been through so much, and yet there wasn't a hint of self-pity, a hint of anger against how unfairly the world had treated her.

'I've said it before but I'll say it again: you really are an impressive young woman.'

She raised her hands in protest. 'Well, perhaps it's as

you said. Life teaches you lessons. Your father's behaviour taught you to value your tenants, and my misfortune taught me to appreciate my friendship with Arabella and all the good things in my life.' She tilted her head and gave another sad smile. 'And my time with you taught me the folly of playing silly games—they can backfire spectacularly.'

'Oh, no, Rosie, don't change a thing about yourself.'

They smiled at each other, then went back to watching the young boys at their carefree play.

'Oh, Aunt Prudence!' Rosie said suddenly, standing up. 'If my timings are correct she should be starting to feel slightly better and will by now feel that she is capable of the arduous journey home. That is as long as the driver doesn't go over any bumps and set off her imagined lumbago.'

They made their way back to the bench where they had left Aunt Prudence, but as they approached Alexander could see they had no need to worry. She had engaged an elderly gentleman sitting at her bench in conversation.

'Well, well, well!' Rosie laughed. 'It looks like Aunt Prudence has found the cure for a headache. Perhaps we should patent it.'

Alexander bowed to the elderly gentleman and they made a round of introductions. While Rosie smiled on, Aunt Prudence blushed and simpered, almost like a young girl. And then the three of them made their way back to the park's entrance, where Alexander hailed a carriage to take them back to the Savoy.

He escorted them into the foyer and Aunt Prudence departed up the stairs. Alexander knew he had to say goodbye to Rosie, but he was reluctant for his time with her to come to an end.

'Lady Jennings is having a ball tonight, and Charlotte and I have been invited. I would be honoured if you, Miss van Haven and Aunt Prudence would join us.'

In fact Alexander had already declined the invitation, as had Charlotte, but he was sure Lady Jennings would have no objection. He rarely attended balls, and had no real interest in attending this one, but he did not want to leave London without seeing Rosie at least one more time. Having to dance and make small talk would be a very small price to pay for one more evening in her company.

She smiled her delightful smile and bobbed a little curtsey. 'Why, Your Grace, I would be honoured,' she said, with mock formality.

Chapter Twenty-Two

The ballroom glittered with reflected candlelight and couples glided round the highly polished parquet dance floor, the women in an array of colourful gowns, and the sound of music filling the air.

Rosie and Arabella paused at the entrance and Rosie took a moment to compose herself. Her heart was beating so hard it was almost drowning out the sound of the music, and her nerves were tingling at the thought of meeting Alexander again.

Their day together in the park had been so special. And now she was going to spend the evening dancing with that wonderful man.

She took in a deep breath and looked around the room. Then she she saw him, standing on the far side of the room, staring straight at her. She gasped in another breath as once again the image of a Greek statue entered her mind. She swallowed. And this Greek statue was walking straight towards her, his dark eyes fixed firmly on hers.

He reached the group and bowed his greetings to Arabella and Aunt Prudence, and then, taking Rosie's hand he formally asked her to dance.

Her heart hammering in her chest, Rosie could only nod her agreement and hope she wouldn't betray her nerves by tripping over the hem of her pink gauze gown or trampling his leather-booted feet.

He took her in his arms and they joined the couples circling the room in a waltz. It was the first time she had been in Alexander's arms since he had kissed her. And now he was dancing with Rosie Smith, a poor orphan, not with the woman he assumed was an American heiress. And he was doing it in front of everyone.

Rosie doubted it was possible to feel happier.

His hand held her waist firmly as he led her round the floor. She suspected the gap that was supposed to be maintained between dancing couples at all times was narrowing scandalously. But Rosie cared not a bit whether anyone was scandalised. All she wanted was to be even closer to this magnificent man. For his arms to be encircling her, for his lips to be kissing hers.

She sighed deeply and moved in even closer, tempted to place her head on his broad shoulder.

The dance ended and he led her off the dance floor. Rosie could see outraged faces looking in their direction, and hear muttered voices. Everyone was wondering who this nobody was that she had captured the attentions of His Grace the Duke of Knightsbrook.

Usually such a reaction would have got Rosie's hackles up—would have caused her to poke out her tongue or do something else outrageous to shock them further. But tonight she was too happy to care how they looked at her or what they were saying about her.

Removing two glasses from the tray of a passing footman, Alexander handed one to Rosie. She was sure her face must be burning red—something she knew young ladies should avoid at all cost. But how could she stop her excitement from being reflected on her cheeks?

Alexander smiled at her—that wonderful smile that had once been so rare, but which she was now starting to see more often—and her cheeks burnt brighter.

'May I write my name on your dance card for the next dance?'

She handed him the card and the tiny pencil, then laughed as he wrote his name in bold letters diagonally across the card, claiming her for himself for the entire evening.

'Why, Your Grace, I don't believe that is entirely appropriate.'

His smile turned to a laugh. 'Why, Miss Smith, being in your company makes me want to behave entirely *inappropriately*.'

Rosie didn't think she could smile more brightly, but she did. 'I'm very pleased to hear it.'

'Shall we?' He offered her his arm to escort her back on to the dance floor for the quadrille.

They danced together throughout the night, only breaking apart when supper was announced, but Rosie knew she was far too excited to eat.

'Would you like to take some air?' Alexander asked, and Rosie nodded gratefully. 'With the doors open Aunt Prudence will be able to see us, so we won't further scandalise the guests.'

They looked over to where Aunt Prudence was seated, talking to the elderly gentleman she had met in the park. It was unlikely that the distracted chaperon would be keeping an eye on her charge, and that suited Rosie just fine.

With as much discretion as possible they left the ballroom for the balcony. She looked out over the dark garden, where the nearby flowering shrubs were lit up by the light cascading out of the ballroom.

Now that they were outside she was hoping the night air would cool her burning cheeks, but there was little chance of that. Not with Alexander standing so close she could feel the warmth of his body and smell that wonderful masculine scent of his.

He gently took hold of her hands and Rosie made a small step closer to him.

'Rosie, thank you so much for coming tonight. It's as if we've been given a chance to start again.'

Rosie sent him a quivering smile. Wild horses wouldn't have stopped her from coming to tonight's ball and the chance of seeing him again.

She nodded her head slightly. 'It's been magical, Alexander,' she murmured.

He pulled her closer, into the shadows, and Rosie eagerly moved with him. He leant down and his lips lightly touched Rosie's. It was the lightest of touches, but it set off a burning on her lips that sparked through her body.

She reached up and put her hands around his neck, wishing he would kiss her the way he had when they were at Knightsbrook.

Her wish came true. He swept her into his arms, holding her tightly. As if a dam had been ruptured his kiss burst over her, swamping her in its passionate embrace. She moulded herself against his strong body as his kiss deepened. It was as if he could not get enough of her, and she knew she could not get enough of him.

Closing her eyes, she surrendered herself to the sensation of his lips on hers, his arms surrounding her, his body pressed up against her. Her lips parted wider as the hunger of his kiss intensified. She moaned with pleasure as his tongue entered her mouth, probing and tasting, filling her up, causing her to lose all sense of where she was. All she could do was give herself over to the powerful sensations rippling through her.

His hot, hungry lips kissed a line down her neck before returning once again to her demanding lips. She ran her hands through his thick hair, holding him closer, kissing him harder, loving the feel of his rough skin against her own soft cheeks, loving his masculine scent, loving the strength of his body. Loving *him*.

Music filled the air, as if in celebration of their kiss. And then Rosie realised she was being fanciful. The music signalled that the dancing had recommenced.

Slowly, Alexander broke from their kiss. 'Oh, Rosie. You are the most beautiful woman I have ever met,' he said, his voice cracking. He drew in a deep breath and looked towards the open doors. 'The dancing has recommenced. I believe we should return to the ballroom. We've already set tongues wagging, and our absence will be noted. If nothing else I wouldn't want to embarrass Aunt Prudence with our behaviour.'

Reluctantly, Rosie had to agree, and they re-entered the ballroom.

For Rosie the rest of the evening went by in a magical whirl of dancing and laughing. It really was a fairy tale come true, and she was the beautiful Cinderella on the arm of her handsome prince.

But when the evening came to an end she did not have to flee at midnight. Instead Alexander escorted her to the waiting carriage, which most definitely had not turned into a pumpkin.

He bowed formally, before helping her into the carriage. 'I'm afraid commitments are forcing me to return home tomorrow, but I would love you to visit Knightsbrook again soon.'

Rosie could hardly speak—could only nod, repeatedly.

'I will send a note with the arrangements. And of course Miss van Haven and Aunt Prudence are invited as well.'

Rosie raised her eyebrows. 'You aren't worried that your mother will try and matchmake you with Arabella?'

'In that case we will just have to invite Thomas Gardener as well,' he said, then laughed and kissed her hand.

Rosie's heart was singing as she rode home with Arabella and Aunt Prudence. He had invited the real Rosie Smith to Knightsbrook. He would be introducing her to his mother. Rosie knew this could only mean one thing: Alexander was officially courting her—Rosie Smith, a penniless orphan. It really was like a dream come true.

He had not yet declared his love for her, the way he had at Knightsbrook, and nor had he made any suggestion of marriage. But surely that was only a matter of time.

Oh, yes, it was almost too wonderful to believe.

But there was one thing Rosie did believe. Her excitement was so great she would not be sleeping that night.

Chapter Twenty-Three

Rosie was waiting anxiously for his letter to arrive. That had been her main occupation for the past week. With Arabella away at rehearsals she had little else to occupy her time. So she waited. And waited.

Apart from the wonderful affectionate note he had sent before he'd returned to Knightsbrook the day after the ball nothing had arrived from him, and it had been a whole week. A whole week of waiting.

The happiness that had filled her heart was ebbing away, to be replaced by increasing anxiety.

She paced backwards and forwards, up and down her hotel suite. Should she contact him? Would that be too forward? But what if something had happened to him? What if he was ill? Wouldn't he be expecting to hear from her? But if he wasn't ill, what would he think then? Should she just be content to wait until he contacted her? After all it had only been a week.

One whole week.

Once again she went down to the foyer, to ask the receptionist if there was any mail for her. This time surely there would be something waiting for her.

Making enquiries at Reception was something she

did several times a day, even though she knew that if any letters did arrive they would be immediately sent up to her room.

As she approached the desk the receptionist shook his head sadly before she even had a chance to ask. She returned to her room, that fleeting bubble of optimism once again bursting, and leaving her deflated.

After being so loving and attentive, there had to be a good reason why he hadn't contacted her.

Rosie sat down at the desk and took out a piece of stationery. She was being silly. She should just write to him. A casual letter of enquiry about his health.

She wouldn't ask why he hadn't contacted her. She wouldn't ask why he hadn't written to her. And she would not mention that she was still waiting for her invitation to Knightsbrook. No, she wouldn't mention that. She would make sure her anxiety did not come through in any of the words she wrote.

And she most certainly would not accuse him of being remiss, of letting her down, causing her to go over and over their conversations, looking for something she might have said or not said that had given him offence. Something that might have caused him to change his mind and decide not to contact her again, as he had promised.

She dipped her pen in the ink pot and put it to the paper. Yes, she would write a casual, friendly letter, just enquiring after his health.

She stared at the blank page, her mind equally blank. Instead of writing she stood up and paced the room some more, wondering if any mail had arrived and whether she should take another trip down to the reception desk

A knock on the door sent her rushing across the room. It had arrived. The much-awaited letter had finally arrived.

She pulled open the door and clapped her hands together with glee when she saw a porter, bearing a silver tray containing the most valuable treasure Rosie could ever want. A crisp white envelope embossed with the Knightsbrook crest.

Rosie held it to her chest and sighed loudly. *Finally.* Finally he had contacted her. She savoured the moment and forced herself not to rip it apart to get to its contents. Instead she walked to the desk and picked up the silver letter opener, and with trembling hands slipped it under the edge of the envelope.

It was then that she saw the address. It wasn't for her. It was addressed to Arabella van Haven.

She stared at it. It had to be a mistake. Or was it a joke? Was Alexander playing a joke on her? Calling her Arabella instead of Rosie. That had to be it.

But until Arabella came home she would just have to wait and find out.

She placed the envelope on the desk, leaning it against the shelves, and stared at it.

She walked to the window and turned back to stare at the letter from across the room.

She looked over at the clock, ticking on the mantel. It would be another hour before Arabella was back from rehearsals. Could she hold out that long? Or would she succumb—do the unthinkable and open her friend's mail.

She walked over to the desk, picked up the letter, scanned both sides of it, then placed it down again. Picking up a book, she slumped down in an armchair, determined to divert herself as she waited for Arabella.

But her eyes kept leaving the book she wasn't reading and staring across the room at that letter.

After what seemed like the longest hour in Rosie's life Arabella returned. Before she had time to remove her hat and gloves—before she even had time to say hello—Rosie rushed across the room and grabbed the letter.

'There's some mail for you,' she said, thrusting the letter and the letter opener in Arabella's direction.

Arabella looked at Rosie's reflection in the mirror, one hand on her hat, the other removing a hatpin. She took off her hat and placed it on the sideboard, then took the letter from Rosie's outstretched hand and slit open the envelope while Rosie watched on anxiously.

Rosie waited, her anticipation mounting, as Arabella read the contents. Arabella placed her hand across her mouth. Not a good sign. She looked up at Rosie, her eyebrows pinched together, her mouth turned down in a frown, then back at the letter. Definitely not a good sign.

'What is it? Is Alexander ill? Is it worse?' *Oh, please God, do not let it be worse.*

'He's... He's...' Arabella handed her the card. 'I'm sorry, Rosie. I think you had better read it yourself.'

Rosie took the thick cream card and scanned the contents.

*The Dowager Duchess of Knightsbrook
has pleasure in inviting
Miss Arabella van Haven
to Knightsbrook on May the fifteenth, 1893,
to celebrate the engagement of her son,
Alexander FitzRoy, Lord Ashton,
Eighth Duke of Knightsbrook,
to Elizabeth Barclay-Fortescue,
daughter of the Earl and Countess of Suffolk*

Time seemed to stop. All sound seemed to evaporate except the pounding of Rosie's heart and the gasping of her breath.

There had to be a mistake.

She read the card again, then turned it over to see if there was anything on the back that would explain this absurdity. Nothing. She turned it over and read it one more time. There was no mistake. Alexander was engaged.

The card dropped from her hand and fluttered to the floor as her legs gave out from beneath her. She dropped to the floor, her voluminous skirts crumpling around her.

'Why would he do this? *Why?*' She looked up, appealing to Arabella, who looked down at her with an ashen white face.

'I am so sorry, Rosie. So very sorry.'

Rosie retrieved the card from the floor. 'Perhaps it was all a cruel game—a trick…a way of getting revenge on me? Perhaps that's what this has been all along. He wanted to hurt me the way I hurt him. He made me think that all was well between us so the shock would be even greater.' She looked questioningly at Arabella. 'Could he be that cruel?'

She looked back down at the card. Rosie had not thought he would be capable of such a thing, but after everything that had happened she no longer knew what to believe.

'Or perhaps he's just succumbed to the reality of his financial situation. He needs money to save the estate, to protect everyone's livelihood. Perhaps he has decided that marrying an heiress is the most sensible, most responsible thing to do after all. And courting a penniless ward was never going to save Knightsbrook. But why didn't he tell me himself instead of letting me find out this way?'

She threw the card onto the floor.

'Oh, Rosie, I'm so sorry,' Arabella repeated, sitting down beside her and taking her in her arms. 'I should not have interfered. Now all I've done is made things worse for you, caused you even more heartache.'

The two friends sat together, holding each other, taking comfort in their friendship in a world that could sometimes be unfair.

Rosie rested her head on her friend's shoulder. 'No, Bella. This is not your fault. It's nobody's fault but mine—setting my sights on a duke, of all things. What was I *thinking*? Men like the Duke of Knightsbrook do not marry poor little orphans like Rosie Smith. They marry women like Elizabeth Barclay-Fortescue, daughter of the Earl and Countess of Suffolk.

'But Alexander did not seem like that to me,' Arabella said quietly.

'Nor to me either, Bella, but that is just the way of the world. I foolishly thought that after I'd explained everything to Alexander and he'd forgiven me we'd have some sort of future together. I'd forgotten one important fact. He's a duke and I'm a nobody. Well, I've remembered it now and I won't make that mistake again.'

'You're not a nobody, Rosie, and if he can't see how special you are then he's a fool.'

Rosie stood up and straightened her crumpled skirts. What was done was done and there was nothing she could do to change it. She knew she just had to get on with her life.

'Oh, well,' she said, with as much good humour as she could summon. 'I've already had practice in putting Alexander out of my thoughts. Now I have even more reason to forget him. He'll be more than out of my reach once he's married—he'll be completely unattainable. So the sooner I start not thinking about him the better.'

Arabella stood, picked up the discarded card, ripped it in two and sent Rosie a tentative smile. 'Yes. Just remember you're a survivor, Rosie. You've survived a lot in the past and you'll survive this as well.'

Rosie smiled at her friend and blinked away her tears. She hoped Arabella was right, but at that moment she felt completely lost, and survival seemed far out of her grasp.

Chapter Twenty-Four

Alexander could hardly believe his mother's treachery. She had sunk to new depths in order to get her way. If he hadn't received a bill for one embossed invitation he would never have known what she was up to.

That she would have the audacity to send out a fake invitation to Arabella van Haven was beyond reprehensible. And then, when he confronted her, it had been to discover that she had been intercepting the mail and removing his letters to Rosie before the servants had had a chance to deliver them. That had left him speechless.

He had to put things right. Taking the train up to London and telling Rosie the truth was the only way. A letter would get there no faster, and he had to ensure that she understood the true situation.

Arriving at Paddington Station, he immediately jumped into a hansom cab and instructed the driver to get him to the Savoy as quickly as possible. He jumped from the cab almost before it had stopped, threw the fare in the driver's direction and ran into the foyer.

'I need to speak to Miss Rosie Smith,' he demanded of the receptionist.

The receptionist looked up from his ledger and shook his head. 'I'm afraid Miss Smith is not here. She left for the docks this morning. I ordered the carriage myself.'

The news hit Alexander like a punch to the stomach. She was leaving. She was going home. He was too late. His mother's plan had worked.

He turned and ran out of the foyer, hearing the receptionist calling out that he had left his hat behind. Running down the road towards the docks, he waved his arm wildly in the air to hail a cab.

Jumping in as soon as one stopped, he ordered the man to drive to the docks as fast as he could.

Unlike him, the driver knew which dock the steam ships departed from for America, and as they approached the Royal Albert Dock he could see a forest of sailing ships' masts and steamer chimneys.

A cacophony of sound hit him as he disembarked from the cab. Sailors of all nations were talking in a babble of foreign tongues, dock workers were yelling at each other as they loaded and unloaded cargo for the waiting vessels, chains clanked as large loads were hauled high in the air, wooden sailing ships creaked and the water lapped against the wooden beams of the docks.

Alexander looked in every direction, trying to see Rosie among the multitude of workers, passengers and merchants milling round the docks. Then he saw her, along with Aunt Prudence, standing beside a mound of trunks and suitcases. Her pretty face looked sad and she stared down at the ground, her usually upright posture slightly stooped.

He started running again. He had to stop her before she boarded the vessel that would take her away from him. He had to explain. He had to stop her leaving.

Reaching her, he came to a sudden stop, completely out of breath.

She looked up at him and gasped.

'Rosie, I…' He panted, trying to get his breath back. 'Rosie, I'm so sorry.'

He reached out his hand to her. She took a quick step back and clasped her hands tightly together, as if his touch was repugnant to her.

'Rosie, I'm sorry. Please let me explain.'

She shook her head and took another step backwards. 'There's nothing to explain. Nothing at all.'

She blinked several times and he could see tears in her eyes.

'Oh, and congratulations on your engagement.'

He stepped towards her. 'I'm not engaged, Rosie. That's what I want to tell you.'

She tilted her head. 'You're not… But I saw the engagement party invitation. It was sent to Arabella.'

He took in a few more breaths so he could speak more clearly. 'No. I am *not* engaged. My mother invented the whole thing. I don't think she expected me to find out, but she forgot that I do all the accounts, and the bill for one invitation was sent to me.'

'One invitation? But…' She shook her head in confusion.

'There was no engagement—no engagement party. Only one card was sent—to Arabella. She was obviously hoping that you'd return to America and we'd never see each other again. And it looks as if she almost succeeded.'

'So you're not engaged?' Rosie repeated, as if unable to comprehend this change of events.

'No, not yet.'

'Oh,' she said, lowering her head

'Not yet because you're going to have to marry me, Rosie. That's the only way I'm going to stop my mother from constantly interfering and matching me up with every passing heiress.'

Rosie's head shot up and her eyes grew wide. 'I'm going to have to *what*?' She gasped.

'Marry me, Rosie. I said you're going to have to marry me. That's the only thing that will let my mother know that her interfering won't work.'

'What?' she repeated, her face a vision of confusion, and he realised what he had just said.

'I'm so sorry, Rosie. I've been running like a madman since I arrived in London, and in my haste that came out all wrong. Let me start again.'

He took in a few deep breaths to try and slow his racing thoughts so he could explain himself better.

'What I mean to say is that if we have a long courtship then it will give my mother too much opportunity to put obstacles in our way. She will be constantly trying to thwart our plans. Even when she fails—which she will—it will be a constant irritation, so I think we should marry as soon as possible.'

She stared back at him, her dazed eyes even wider.

'I'm still doing this wrong…' He dropped down onto one knee and took hold of Rosie's hand. 'Rosie Smith— my darling Rosie. I adore you. I love you. I think I've loved you from the moment I saw you twirling down the entrance hall at Knightsbrook House. I've never seen anyone so free, so full of joy, and I've never experienced such happiness as I do when I'm with you. Without you it's as if there is no daylight—only a long, interminable night. I can't offer you immediate wealth, but I can offer you a title, and my undying love and devotion, and one day I hope to be able to lavish you with all the luxuries that you deserve. Will you do me the honour…the very great honour…of consenting to be my wife?'

'Of course I will,' she said, nodding her head vigorously. 'And I don't want luxuries. I don't even want a title. All I want is you. All I've ever wanted is you.' She looked around at the bustling crowd and laughed. 'Now, get up, will you? People are staring at us, and you know how much I hate making a scene.'

He looked around and saw that she was right. Even among this crowd that had seen virtually everything before, they had caused the bustle to come to a halt and people to stare in their direction.

'Oh, I have a confession to make,' she said as he rose to his feet. 'I'm not departing. We're meeting Mr van Haven. This is his luggage. He and Arabella have gone off to get a carriage. Your mother sent him a telegram, telling him what had happened, and he got the next steam ship over here. Poor Arabella's probably getting a severe telling-off at the moment, and when he comes back he'll probably try and offer you a deal you can't resist so you'll make his daughter a duchess.'

They looked towards where the carriages were waiting and saw Arabella and an older gentleman walking towards them.

'In that case we'll have to convince him that he's wasting his time,' said Alexander.

And with that he took his bride-to-be in his arms, lifted her off the ground and kissed her.

He knew that he had found his perfect duchess. A woman who would love him as deeply and passionately as he loved her, who would stand beside him and share his burdens the way he would stand beside her and share hers, and who would fill his days with love, laughter and happiness.

Epilogue

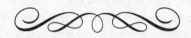

The wedding was to have been a simple affair: just family, a few friends and the tenants. But Mr van Haven had had other ideas. He was now connected to the aristocracy—albeit through a ward he had never really wanted, and to whom he had never paid more than the most minimal of attention—and he wanted to celebrate the fact. To that end he had arranged a lavish affair, no expense spared, and Rosie had conceded.

After being supported by Mr van Haven's reluctant charity for so many years, she had decided that letting him organise a large wedding at Knightsbrook and allowing him to invite almost every member of the British aristocracy was a small price to pay.

A lavish wedding would also go some way to appeasing the Dowager, who was still struggling to accept the fact that the next Duchess of Knightsbrook came with no dowry. But now that her attention had turned to finding a good match for Charlotte, she was at least leaving Rosie and Alexander alone.

And she wasn't the only one desperately matchmaking. With so many dukes, earls, barons and viscounts assembled in one spot, Mr van Haven was like a child in a candy shop. The wedding was providing him with the ideal opportunity to thrust Arabella in front of as many aristocrats as he could. He still most definitely had ambitions in that direction.

Well, Mr van Haven was in for a big surprise. Marriage did not figure in Arabella's future. She would soon be appearing on the London stage—albeit in a minor role, with a production company that was struggling financially to survive—but Rosie was sure it was the first step in what would be a brilliant career.

Rosie could only hope that Mr van Haven's business concerns would take him back to America before Arabella's opening night. A career on the stage was certainly *not* the future Mr van Haven had envisaged for his only child.

At least Rosie would now be able to act as Arabella's chaperon. After all, what was more respectable than being chaperoned by a member of the aristocracy—a duchess, no less? Aunt Prudence would be able to return to America with Mr van Haven, leaving the girls to enjoy themselves—and enjoy themselves is exactly what they were intending to do.

But they would think of that another day. Today they had a wedding to celebrate. *Her* wedding—something Rosie had never imagined would happen.

'Have I told you how radiant you look today, Rosie?' Arabella asked, joining her friend and linking arms.

'Only about a thousand times.'

'White lace definitely suits you. And it seems being a married woman also suits you. I've never seen you look happier or more beautiful.'

Smiling, Rosie hugged her best friend, who also looked radiant in a pale blue satin bridesmaid's gown.

It was hard to believe. She was now Rosie Ashton, the Duchess of Knightsbrook.

She looked over at her husband, who was in conversation with Annie, a delighted smile on his lovely lips. Alexander had insisted that all the tenants be invited to the wedding and the reception, much to his mother's and Mr van Haven's chagrin. But after much huffing and puffing they had been forced to accept his decision.

Alexander looked back at her. His smile grew larger and once again she was struck by how much he reminded her of a Greek statue—albeit one that now knew how to smile and laugh.

She smiled too, and a shiver of excited anticipation ran through her. Tonight she would finally discover whether he resembled a *naked* Greek athlete in all other respects.

He excused himself and walked towards her, causing her heart to beat faster. This handsome man, dressed in a dove-grey morning suit, his top hat long abandoned, was her husband. The man who had vowed to love and honour her until death did them part.

'I think I'll leave you two alone,' Arabella said with a light laugh. 'I'm sure my father has some man with a sizeable income and a country estate that he's dying to introduce me to.'

Alexander took Rosie's hands and lightly kissed her cheek. 'While the music, the dancing and the champagne are distracting everyone, there is something we really must do,' he whispered in her ear. 'Will you allow me to lure you away from our guests so I can satisfy a demanding urge that's starting to overwhelm me?'

Rosie nodded. Oh, yes, he could lure her away…and he could satisfy whatever urge he had.

He took her hand and led her across the grass, past the tables draped in white linen, laden with food and drink, and up the stone stairs leading to the entrance of Knightsbrook House—her new home. She looked back and saw that he was right. Everyone was distracted…talking, drinking and dancing. No one had noticed their departure. No one would know what they were up to.

He stopped when they entered the house, took both her hands and placed them around his neck, then encircled her waist with his arms.

Rosie's breath caught in her throat in anticipation. She tilted her head back, closed her eyes and parted her lips, waiting for a kiss.

'I know I should wait till our guests leave before doing this, but I've been waiting for so long I can't wait a minute longer.'

Rosie's hammering heart increased its tempo. 'Really? And what might "this" be?' she asked, her voice a breathy whisper.

'This…'

He began twirling, taking Rosie with him. They spun down the entrance hall, Rosie getting dizzier and dizzier. Her laughter joined his as the black and white floor tiles merged into one and the paintings, vases and statues that lined the walls whirled past.

When they reached the staircase they stopped suddenly, but the room continued to spin. He held her tightly, to stop himself from falling and to save her. But neither worked.

They collapsed in a tangled mass of arms and legs at the foot of the stairs.

Rosie continued to giggle—only to have her giggles stifled when his lips found hers. She kissed him back, her heart overflowing with love, passion and deep contentment.

* * * * *

AWAKENING
THE DUCHESS

To Jacqui, for starting me on this journey and for your continued support and encouragement.

And, of course, to Linda Fildew, Bryony Green and the talented editorial team at Mills & Boon.

Chapter One

London—1893

Oliver Huntsbury, the Fifth Duke of Somerfeld, was not usually a man to run from a fight.

But when faced with five armed assailants, all hell-bent on causing him as much harm as possible, and when one of those assailants was brandishing a knife and threatening to part him from his manhood, there was only one sensible course of action. Run.

So run he did down the backstage corridors of the Limelight Theatre.

He vaulted over props left carelessly lying in his path, dodged past stagehands moving scenery and flew past preening showgirls, their perfume wafting out like a floral cloud, masking the musky smell of the damp building. He ignored the temptation to stop and admire the scantily clad beauties. For once he had something more important on his mind: self-preservation.

'Come here, you guttersnipe, and take your punishment like a man,' Lord Bufford bellowed behind him. The irate peer of the realm raised his knife above his head, causing the corridor to clear immediately of showgirls and stagehands, as if a conjurer had waved his magic wand.

That left Lord Bufford, backed by his four burly henchmen, armed with an assortment of chains, knuckledusters and coshes, at one end of the corridor and Oliver at the other.

So once again he turned and ran. Somewhere in this labyrinth of corridors was Lucy's dressing room. He had to find it before the thugs caught him and stripped him of his most prized possession.

Oliver was loath to hide behind a woman's skirts, but Lucy would provide him with the necessary alibi to prove to these murderous marauders that he could not possibly be Lady Bufford's lover. Not when he had spent every night in the inviting arms of Lucy Baker. At least that's what he hoped the renowned actress would say. He had indeed spent many a night in her lovely arms, with her even lovelier legs wrapped around his waist, but he had also spent the occasional night sampling the abundant charms of Lady Bufford. And, yes, he had been known, on occasion, to have more than one woman at a time in his bed. But even he was not capable of servicing one woman in London while at the same time tupping another woman at her Essex estate.

As long as Lucy vouched for him and said he had spent every night with her, then his beloved body part would be safe. As would Lady Bufford's reputation. While the lady had never been reticent about taking a lover to her bed, she most definitely did not want that fact made public.

And having your lover dismembered by your irate husband would certainly get the tongues wagging. Not to mention putting a damper on your lover's ardour.

Lady Bufford had long ago lost interest in her boorish husband, but she had never lost interest in his money, or the comfortable life and position in society that their marriage provided. If Lord Bufford took the drastic action of petitioning for divorce on the grounds of adultery, it would be the ruin of her and such public shaming was not a fate Oliver wanted for any of his mistresses.

No, he had no choice but to keep running. He increased his speed as he rounded another corner. Where was Lucy's dressing room? He was sure he knew the way. Was he running down the same corridor he had just speeded down? Was he going in circles?

He overturned a rail of brightly coloured costumes, sending it crashing behind him. Hopefully that would slow down his assailants and give him time to think.

Hadn't Lucy mentioned something about taking up another position last time they had been together? He'd assumed she wanted him to get even more adventurous in their lovemaking, but perhaps he'd misunderstood and she'd secured another acting position in a different theatre. He really should pay more attention to what women were saying. He hadn't noticed her on stage during tonight's performance, but his attention had been taken by a new actress, one he hadn't seen before. She certainly had been a delight, with her midnight-black hair, ivory skin and that stunning body. But he should not be thinking of that now. He had to find Lucy. He had to keep running.

'It's blackmail, it's extortion, it's…it's…it's just plain wrong.' Arabella glared at her father, her hands placed firmly on her hips to emphasise her point.

'Call it what you will, my dear, but it's the best offer you're going to get.' Her father stared back at her, his stony face implacable. It was the look Arabella imagined he wore when he stared down any business rival foolish enough to try to get the better of Mr van Haven. Her father hadn't dragged himself up from poverty to become one of America's richest men by being faint-hearted. And now Arabella was on the receiving end of his merciless deal making.

But she shouldn't be so surprised. Hadn't she learnt from bitter experience that her father would do anything to get what he wanted, regardless of who got hurt and that included his only daughter?

'I'm being more than fair. Most men who discovered their daughter had defied them and become a professional actress would not be as forgiving as I'm being. All I'm saying is, you've had your fun and now you're going to have to do what I sent you to England to do: marry a man with a title. And to sweeten the deal, and to make sure you do nothing to undermine my plans, I'll save your precious theatre. It's as simple as that.'

Simple. There was nothing simple about this outlandish proposal. 'Basically, you're going to pay me to get married, or rather, you're going to pay the theatre if I marry.'

Arabella had hoped to shame him. Surely he could

see that blackmailing his daughter into marriage because he wanted the status that came with being related to a member of the British aristocracy was something any decent man would be thoroughly ashamed of.

But his expression showed no shame—instead he sent her a self-satisfied smile. 'Good. Finally you understand what's expected of you.'

Arabella shook her head rapidly, her bottom lip trembling. What was she thinking? Of course he would feel no shame. When it came to financial transactions nothing mattered to him except winning the deal. And in this instance, his daughter's marriage was nothing more than another financial deal to be won.

'I won't do it. I just won't.'

'Oh, yes, you will,' her father said, his voice a calm contrast. 'You can pout all you want. You can even throw a temper tantrum if you must, but you will marry into the aristocracy. And I won't be returning to America until you do. You've let me down once and it won't happen again.'

He drew in a deep breath and exhaled loudly. 'But I suppose I have only myself to blame. I should have known better than to let you come to England with my sister rather than accompanying you myself. All Prudence had to do was chaperon you when you met the man I had arranged for you to marry. But even that was beyond her.' He shook his head. 'And how the Duke of Knightsbrook ended up married to my ward instead of you I'll never know. But now I'm here, so there will be no more of your tricks. You *will* be getting married to a titled man.'

Arabella blinked away tears of anger and frustration. 'How can you possibly do this? It's…it's…'

'It's all for your own good. Left to your own devices you know you'll make the wrong choice—haven't you already proven that? So now you will do as you're told and I will generously inject the necessary money into this theatre. And if you're not convinced by that offer, I believe you should consider the alternative. You will have to come back to America with me on the next ship. You will never act again, even in amateur productions, and this theatre you inexplicably love so much might struggle on for a few weeks more at its present dismal level, before sinking without trace and all your new friends will be without a job. And unlike you, I doubt if any of them has a rich father to support them. Would you really see them thrown out on the streets, without money, without a job?'

'It's despicable, simply despicable,' Arabella muttered under her breath, sorrow clenching her heart. She could not stop acting, it was the one thing she lived for. Nor could she deny the theatre the chance of survival. It desperately needed more funds for advertising, for better props and scenery. Tonight's house had been less than half-full and, now that their leading lady, Lucy Baker, had left them for brighter prospects, they had also lost their main drawcard. The theatre desperately needed more money if it was to survive.

But this? Marriage? And to a man of her father's choosing. It was too much to ask.

'I can see you're upset, my dear, so I'll make you one concession.'

Arabella's tense shoulders eased slightly and she waited for him to throw her a lifeline.

'It can be any sort of title. I'm not that fussy. Duke, earl, viscount, even a baron will do, as long as you become Lady Something.'

Arabella's mouth almost dropped open and she stared at him in disbelief. It was hardly a concession. No matter how you looked at it, she was expected to sell herself in marriage to any man with a title to satisfy her father's need for self-aggrandisement. Being one of the richest men in America was not enough for him. Now he was going to use his daughter to get the social status that he'd always felt he lacked because he had been born poor. She was going to be sacrificed on the wedding altar just so that her father could feel superior in status as well as financially to those snobs back in New York. It was unconscionable.

'Oh, stop sulking, Arabella,' he barked at her. 'It's the first thing I've ever asked of you after a lifetime of indulging your every whim. Haven't I always given you everything you've ever wanted?'

Arabella continue to stare back at him, too shocked to answer. Yes, he had given her everything she could ever want in terms of material goods—fine clothes, expensive jewellery, music lessons, singing lessons and more—but as for affection, attention, they were areas which he'd severely neglected.

'I even forgave you when you acted in those little amateur shows back in New York, but I never thought you'd be so simpleminded as to do it professionally. Hopefully the substantial amount of money you'll bring to any marriage will counter the damage you've already done to your reputation. But now that I'm here in England we can put all this nonsense behind us. Once you're married you'll be a lady, living the life of luxury on your country estate, and all this acting nonsense will be forgotten.'

The ground wobbled under Arabella's feet. She wouldn't do it. She would not give up the life she loved and she'd find some other way to save the theatre that didn't involve her being sold off like a piece of chattel. She had worked so hard to get this acting job. It hadn't just taken skill as an actress, but had also involved scheming and planning so she could attend rehearsals without Aunt Prudence knowing. Her subterfuge had become more complicated when her father had arrived in England to attend his ward's wedding to the Duke of Knightsbrook. But she had succeeded. That is, until tonight.

'I mean you were born for better things than this,' he continued, looking around her tiny dressing room with distaste. He scraped a piece of flaking cream paint off the wall with his thumbnail, further exposing the rough grey plaster underneath, then glared at the dressing table with its split timber and tarnished mirror, and the racks of costumes and props cluttering up the corners.

It might be small and, yes, perhaps a little shabby, and it was unfortunate that it doubled as a storeroom, but Arabella was pleased to have a real dressing room in a professional theatre, to have her first part on the London stage, even if it was a minor role.

And she'd much rather be in this shabby dressing room than being bored to death at the tedious balls and social events that a woman of her class was expected to attend. Thanks to her father's constant absences she had been able to avoid most of the events hosted by New York society. And since her arrival in London, she had been given almost free rein. Her hypochondriac Aunt Prudence took to her bed most days with one imagined illness after another, and Nellie, her lady's maid, was more a friend than a servant and would do anything she could to help Arabella achieve her dream.

It had been her dream since she was a child to make her own way in the world as an actress. And now that she was on the cusp of achieving that dream, she would not have it snapped away from her by her father. She just had to find a way to do what countless businessmen and politicians had failed to do and get the better of her father, the notoriously ruthless New York banker, Mr van Haven.

The door flew open and Arabella's attention was drawn to a tall, blond-haired man barging into the room. Every inch the dashing leading man, he was staring straight at her with those deep brown eyes and heading in her direction, fast.

'There you are, my darling,' he said, sending her a roguish smile.

Before she could register who he was or what was happening he grabbed her firmly around the waist, tipped her backwards until one leg was off the ground and kissed her.

A gasp escaped Arabella's lips and she clung on to the stranger to stop herself from falling backwards. Although with him holding her so tightly falling was the least of her worries.

This was an outrage. She should stop this. Immediately.

So why didn't she? Was it because it felt strangely comforting to be held in his strong arms? Or was it because his fresh masculine scent, all musk and leather with the hint of a citrus shaving soap, was somewhat enticing?

She melted into his arms, her body moulding against his in a perfect fit. It was as if this was where she was meant to be.

No. That was ridiculous. This was not where she was meant to be. This had to stop. Right now. Especially as his tongue was running temptingly along her bottom lip, causing her to part her lips so she could fully appreciate the experience.

No. This was outrageous. She had to put a halt to this before he deepened the kiss. Stop it before she started kissing him back. She ran her hands through his tousled hair, telling herself it didn't matter how good his lips felt on hers. It didn't matter how nice it was to be held so closely. No, it didn't matter at all.

He pulled her in even closer, causing her to dissolve against his body. His strong body. How could she not fail to register the muscles of his chest? Hard, firm, powerful muscles.

Oh, yes, this was wrong. So wrong. But it felt so right to be kissed in such a manner. When that double-crossing Arnold Emerson had kissed her, it had been nothing like this. This time she was in the arms of an expert. Opening her mouth wider, she relished the masculine taste of him, loving the feel of his skin rasping against her cheek. She had no intention of stopping this pleasure. Not when she was enjoying herself so much.

But he had other ideas. He lifted her upright, back

on to two feet, and sent her a quick wink and the most devilish smile she had ever seen. She stared back at him as if in a daze. Blinked to clear the fog, then looked over at her father and waited for his outburst.

Her father would now do what she should have already done. He would reprimand this man in no uncertain terms for taking such a liberty with a woman's virtue.

But her father said nothing. Instead he took his time to scrutinise the stranger. Arabella watched expectantly as his gaze moved over the man's well-tailored three-piece black evening suit. He smiled as he looked at the solid gold chain of his fob watch suspended between his pockets, the mother-of-pearl cufflinks. His smile widened. Arabella could see he was staring at the large gold signet ring on the man's index finger, etched with a coat of arms. He then turned to the ruffians loitering at the door and his smile grew so wide he was baring his teeth, like a wolf who has spotted a tethered lamb.

'I'm Mr van Haven,' he said, extending his hand to the stranger. 'And after a kiss like that I can only assume that you are my daughter Arabella's fiancé.'

The stranger looked at her father, then over his shoulder at the ruffians, then back at the extended hand. 'Indeed, I am, sir. And I'm very pleased to finally make your acquaintance,' he said, giving her father's hand a brisk shake.

Chapter Two

The phrase out of the frying pan and into the fire seemed disastrously apt, as Oliver continued to shake the smiling American's hand while glancing back at the scowling Lord Bufford.

And it was a fire he was going to have to extinguish as quickly as possible. Being engaged was not for him and marriage was most definitely out of the question. Like his father before him, he was not a one-woman man. But unlike his father he would never subject any woman to the pain of being married to an unfaithful husband. He had vowed never to hurt a woman the way his father had hurt his mother and had sworn off marriage many years ago. That was why he only got involved with women like Lady Bufford and Lucy Baker, women who played by the same rules as him. Keep it fun, keep it casual and never expect commitment.

He looked over at the young woman he was now supposedly engaged to. She was certainly beautiful, the sort of woman many men would be happy to call their wife. But right now, his supposedly future wife was looking as disorientated as he felt.

Her long, slim fingers were gently touching her full red lips, her face was flushed a delightful shade of pink and those big blue eyes were quickly flicking from him to the older man and back again.

It was the same actress he had admired during this evening's performance. The one whose acquaintance he was hoping to eventually make, although most definitely not under these conditions.

It was obvious they were father and daughter. Both had jet-black hair, although the father was greying at the temples, and both had those blue eyes, although on the daughter they gave her a soft, gentle appearance, while on him the eyes were icy blue, accentuating his shrewd, calculating demeanour.

It was also obvious the father was up to something, but whatever it was, for now, it seemed, the plans of Mr van Haven would serve Oliver's needs as well.

He sent the young beauty a silent apology for what he was about to do and hoped that she would not just forgive him, but would also play along.

'Arabella has probably already told you all about me, but allow me to formally introduce myself,' he said, still clasping the American's hand. 'I'm Oliver Huntsbury, the Duke of Somerfeld.'

'A duke? Well, well, a duke,' Mr van Haven purred, his piercing eyes boring into Oliver's. 'My daughter really has made a good catch. We'd better be careful to make sure you don't get off the hook. So, are you going to introduce us to your friends?'

They both looked towards the menacing presence looming at the door.

Friends? That was an exaggeration if ever Oliver had heard one. 'Yes, of course. May I introduce Lord Bufford and his associates: Joe Butcher, Frank Thugger, Arthur Scarmaker, and Fred Killerman.'

Mr van Haven nodded a greeting, but got a line of scowling black looks in response. Perhaps Lord Bufford's associates didn't like the names he had assigned them, but at least they had the decency to hide their weapons behind their backs.

'Lord Bufford is Lady Bufford's husband,' Oliver continued, looking in Arabella's direction and giving her his most beseeching smile. She might not be Lucy Baker, but he could only hope she was as equally good an actress and would indulge in a bit of improvisation.

'Lady Bufford and Arabella are the best of friends,' he continued, turning to Lord Bufford. 'The two of them have spent many an evening together, gossiping the night away. I've felt quite neglected, I must say.'

'We have?' the American beauty asked. He sent her another pleading look and tilted his head in the direction of the door.

'Oh, yes, we have. Your wife is quite a delightful companion,' she added, giving Lord Bufford a tentative smile.

Oliver smiled with relief. He had his alibi. Hopefully now that would mean the departure of Lord Bufford and his murderous entourage. And his own departure. As much as he would like to get better acquainted with the young, black-haired actress, and as much as he'd like a repeat performance of that kiss, it was a pleasure he would have to forgo. This situation was complicated enough already. It was time to simplify things by exiting, stage right.

'As we're all such good friends I'm sure Lord Bufford and his associates would like to join us for a late supper so we can celebrate my daughter's engagement to the Duke of Somerfeld,' Mr van Haven said smoothly.

Oliver's smile faded. It seemed his departure was going to have to be delayed a while longer.

All three turned to look at Lord Bufford, whose lips curled back in a menacing sneer.

'We'd be delighted,' he growled, staring straight at Oliver.

Mr van Haven patted Oliver on the back. 'Right, Lord Bufford, you and I will go and find a couple of carriages to take us all to the Savoy, and while we're doing that you can tell me all about my future son-in-law.'

The four thugs turned to follow Lord Bufford and Oliver could see an opportunity to escape opening up. A quick apology and maybe a goodbye kiss to the young actress and he'd be off.

Mr van Haven held up his hand to halt the thugs' progress. 'Oh, no. You four can wait here. We won't be long.' He sent what could only be called a triumphant smirk in Oliver's direction. 'You can chaperon my daughter and the Duke while we're gone.'

Chaperons? More like prison wardens.

With a sinking heart Oliver saw his opportunity to escape close off. It seemed only an unwise man would underestimate Mr van Haven—the man was a veritable mind reader. And he had made sure that

Oliver would continue to be engaged to be married to his daughter, at least for a while longer.

Arabella stared at the stranger, this Duke of Somerfeld, her fiancé. He sent her an apologetic smile, a smile that was difficult not to warm to. It lit up his face and drew her eyes to his full, sculptured lips.

She was determined to be angry with him. This man who was obviously trouble with a capital T. But it was hard to maintain that anger while gazing into tawny-brown eyes that sparked with mischief, and a face so handsome that he should be on the stage. Arabella's appraising gaze took in the small crinkles round his eyes, lines that showed he laughed a lot. She moved to his strong jawline with the hint of stubble, then back up to his lips, those lips that had kissed her into a state of oblivion.

At the time, it had felt as though he was kissing her as if his life depended on it. Now it was apparent that was not far from the truth, if the murderous looks of the four burly brutes still looming at the door were anything to go by.

Arabella gave herself a small shake. There was no point thinking of that kiss now. This was an impossible situation and they had to find a way out of it.

She stepped towards him and his smile changed from apologetic to appreciative. Arabella ignored both that look and the way her heart was beating harder now that she was so close to him. So close she could feel the warmth of his body. So close that his masculine scent was once again filling her senses.

'So, who are you really and what are you doing in

my dressing room?' she whispered so the ruffians at the door wouldn't hear.

He raised an amused eyebrow. 'I really am Oliver Huntsbury, the Duke of Somerfeld, and I apologise for my somewhat unconventional entrance. I was looking for Lucy Baker.'

Arabella's spine straightened and she tilted up her chin. 'Oh, I'm sorry to disappoint you.' She heard the offended note in her voice and mentally kicked herself. Who cared if it was Lucy Baker he had meant to kiss? He just shouldn't have kissed her. He shouldn't be in her dressing room and he most certainly should not have agreed to be her fiancé.

'Believe me, I am not disappointed, anything but.' He smiled at her again, that heart-stopping, devilish smile that made his eyes dance with amusement. 'But you do deserve an explanation.' He nodded in the direction of the door. 'Lord Bufford and his associates have taken exception to my friendship with Lady Bufford. They were threatening to commit extreme acts of violence on my various body parts, so I was looking for Lucy, who is also a good friend, hoping she would provide me with an alibi to prove my innocence.'

Arabella's posture became more rigid, her lips more pinched. 'I take it Lady Bufford and Lucy Baker are actually more than just your *good friends*.' She hadn't meant to sound quite so judgemental. After all, this man meant nothing to her, so why should she care who he was or wasn't good friends with?

He ran his hand along the back of his neck. 'Well, yes, you could say that.'

Arabella huffed her disapproval. One of her questions had been answered. When he kissed her, she had suspected she was in the arms of an experienced man, a man who knew how to please a woman. And that was quite obviously the case. It explained why she had reacted to him the way she had. It was not her fault. It was simply his technique and experience that had caused her uncharacteristic response.

It also explained the high opinion he appeared to have of himself. His confident countenance was definitely that of a man who knew he could easily seduce any woman he chose. But she wasn't so easily impressed by a handsome face and a strong, masculine body. Nor would she swoon just because she had been kissed until she almost lost all ability to reason. No, none of those things would deter her from thinking he was just a rake, a man of no substance, to whom no sensible woman would give a second thought.

She placed her hands firmly on her hips and tilted her head to emphasise just how much he was not affecting her. 'Well, Lucy no longer performs at the Limelight Theatre. But that doesn't mean you can just burst into the dressing room of any woman you choose and…and…' She waved her hand in the direction of the place where he had taken her in his arms.

'And kiss her.' He sent her another devilish smile. 'You're right, that was a terrible affront to your virtue and I apologise if I upset you.'

Good, at least he had the decency to apologise, but that charming smile seemed to make a lie to any claim of regret.

'Just because I'm an actress doesn't mean you can treat me disrespectfully. People make all sorts of assumptions about actresses and they're just plain wrong. Most of us are respectable women who take our art form seriously.' It was an argument she had also had with her father, but it had fallen on deaf ears.

He nodded his agreement. 'Yes, I know, and I can see that you are a talented actress. I saw your performance tonight, very impressive.'

Arabella's hands left her hips. Her body relaxed and she couldn't help but beam with pleasure as warmth rushed through her. 'You saw my performance tonight? Really? And you enjoyed it? It's only a small part, but I do appear in every scene and have lines in most of them.' She was burbling, but couldn't stop herself, it was so delightful that he had noticed her on stage.

'You're a natural. And you certainly gave a stunning performance here in the dressing room, too. I've never been kissed with such conviction by a total stranger.'

The warmth engulfing her turned to a fiery blush, exploding on her cheeks. 'Well, you…you…caught me off guard. I was still in character. I was still acting. I was continuing to act as if I was still on stage. That was all.'

He gave a mock frown. 'Didn't you play a vestal virgin in tonight's play?'

Arabella shrugged, her cheeks still burning. 'Anyway, that doesn't explain why you pretended to be my fiancé,' she said sharply, hoping to move the conversation away from her overly enthusiastic response to his kiss.

He rubbed the back of his neck again. 'I'm sorry about that as well. At the time my choices were, become engaged or become the victim of a violent crime. And engagement seemed the less painful option.' He grimaced slightly. 'Forgive me, but I have no intention of marrying anyone.'

Arabella flicked her hand to dismiss his excuses. 'I'm not stupid. I realise that. And I have no interest in getting engaged either and even less interest in being married. It's all my father's idea. He wants me off the stage and married before he returns to America. It doesn't matter who my husband-to-be is, or what he's like, as long as he's got a title. It seems you fit the bill.'

He stared at her, his brow furrowed, concern in his eyes. 'And what of your mother? What does she have to say about this?'

Arabella gave a little shrug and ignored the hard lump that had formed in her chest. 'My mother is dead.'

'Oh, I'm so sorry.' He placed his hand lightly on her arm.

She shrugged again. 'It was a long time ago. Twenty-one years.'

He gave her an intense look and she could see him gauging her age and doing the calculations. Yes, she was twenty-one and, yes, her mother had died mere months after she was born, leaving her in the care of a man who had little interest in his daughter. And that lack of interest had continued throughout her life. It was only now that he could see how much use a daughter would be for advancing his position in both English and New York society that she had suddenly become something worth having.

'That must have been very hard for you,' he said.

Arabella shook her head. 'Well, I'm sure if she was

alive, she wouldn't want her daughter married off to just any man. But my father doesn't care who I marry and he's not going to relent until I've got a title. But that doesn't have to be your problem.'

He raised his eyebrows and looked towards the door, then back at Arabella and exhaled loudly. His look appeared to be saying that, for now, it was his problem as well.

'When does your father intend to return to America?'

'As soon as he gets me married off, which he's going to want to do as quickly as possible. He's already been away from his precious bank for over a month. I doubt if he'll be able to bear to stay away much longer. He's already starting to pine for the smell of freshly minted dollar bills.'

He tapped a thoughtful finger against his sensual lips. 'Then leave this to me. I think I can save both of us from an unwanted marriage, while getting your father off your back for the foreseeable future and saving my valuable body parts from dismemberment, all at the same time.'

Chapter Three

⧼⧽

The four thugs were starting to look bored. One thug was absentmindedly running his hand back and forth along his knuckleduster, another was tapping his cosh rhythmically against the door jamb. The third was repeatedly cracking the knuckles in his gnarled hands and, perhaps most surprisingly of all, the fourth one had wrapped a feather boa around his thick neck and was running his hands over the satin and silk fabric on the racks of brightly coloured costumes.

Oliver was unsure whether a bored thug was more dangerous than an angry one, but he didn't appreciate being in the company of either.

He knew that at some stage he could make an escape from Lord Bufford's henchmen, but that wouldn't solve the problem of the delightful Arabella van Haven. What her father was planning to do to this talented young actress was inexcusable. It was reprehensible to sell her off in marriage to any passing man, just because he had a title. And now it appeared he was in a position to save this rather enchanting damsel in distress, as well as saving his own skin and preserving Lady Bufford's reputation. In anyone's estimation that had to count as a good night's work.

As long as the thugs didn't get so bored that they needed a bit of entertainment, in the form of carrying out Lord Bufford's threat to his precious body part, he would be safe.

The four thugs all looked in his direction, as if reading his thoughts. The rhythm of the cosh thumping against the door jamb increased, accompanied by the sound of a knuckleduster being smacked into a fist and knuckles being cracked. This thumping beat of their weapons was not reassuring. When the fourth thug unwound the feather boa and tugged on it hard, as if testing its use as a garrotte, Oliver knew he was in trouble.

Mr van Haven and Lord Bufford entered the room and he released a surreptitious sigh of relief. He had never been happier to see the husband of one of his mistresses.

'All right,' the American said, rubbing his hands together. 'The cabs are ready and waiting so let's all depart for the Savoy and a spot of supper.'

Whatever Lord Bufford and Mr van Haven had been discussing during their absence it had obviously pleased the American banker. His wolfish smile had grown even more predatory. Presumably Mr van Haven was now even more certain he had Oliver right where he wanted him. That was heading up the aisle and tying the matrimonial knot with his daughter.

Marriage or a beating by four thugs and the loss of a vital body part—what a choice. Oliver suspected marriage would be the greater torture and both would be a threat to his manhood. But if his plan worked, he would have to suffer neither fate.

He looked around the room. Everyone was staring at him, waiting for his response, and none of the expressions was friendly. Five people wanted to tear him limb from limb and one wanted to use him for his own purposes. Only Arabella meant him no harm. She was the only completely innocent person in the room. He could not see her suffer. No matter what happened tonight, he would make sure he saved her from her father's outrageous plan of marrying her off to him.

'Excellent,' Oliver replied. 'Supper at the Savoy to celebrate our engagement sounds like a splendid idea. And I couldn't wish for better company.' He gave a small bow to the assembled party and received matching scowls of murderous intent from Lord Bufford and his henchmen, a resigned sigh from Arabella and a smug look of satisfaction from Mr van Haven.

He turned to Arabella. 'Let me help you into your coat, my dear.' Oliver lifted a jacket from the coat stand and held it open for her, but got a suspicious, narrow-eyed glare in return. 'Trust me,' he whispered in her ear. 'Before tonight I will have saved us both from the unwanted state of matrimony.'

She gave him another distrusting look, but turned her back to him and allowed him to slip the coat up her arms and over her slim shoulders.

He paused for a moment before he let her go so he could take a second to reacquaint himself with the scent of jasmine. It was the perfume he had inhaled when he had kissed her, fresh and youthful, just like the wearer.

Disappointment jolted through him as she broke away and picked up her reticule. After tonight he would not be holding her in his arms again, would not be kissing her, would not inhale her wonderful scent. But it had to be that way. It was the right thing to do.

He offered her his arm. 'Right, lead the way, Mr van Haven,' he said in his most cheerful voice as if he hadn't a care in the world.

The motley group left the dressing room and headed out the back door of the Limelight Theatre, where two carriages were waiting. Oliver helped Arabella into one and Lord Bufford and his angry mob entered the other.

Some jostling ensued between Mr van Haven and Oliver, until it became apparent to Oliver that he was expected to sit in the middle rather than Arabella, as manners would normally dictate. Presumably Mr van Haven was determined to stop Oliver from throwing himself out of the moving carriage and making his escape.

With a tap on the roof from Mr van Haven's silver-handled walking stick, they were off, winding their way through London's dark streets. The cab rattled over the broken cobbles, juddering the three occupants, something Oliver could hardly complain about as it caused Miss van Haven's legs to rub against his in a rather pleasant manner.

The ride became somewhat smoother as they approached the more affluent city centre. Under the modern electric street lights, fashionable men and women were climbing in and out of carriages and cabs, and some couples were walking along the West

End streets, taking advantage of the mild summer night-time air.

The Savoy appeared before them, the golden glow of its newly installed electric lighting illuminating the surrounding street, drawing them towards its promise of luxury.

The carriages stopped inside the courtyard and the ill-matched party disembarked and headed towards the doors of the hotel. The thugs for once were looking more ill at ease than Oliver as they adjusted their rough clothing with anxious fingers, straightened their spines and followed Mr van Haven and Lord Bufford inside the foyer.

The maître d' recognised Mr van Haven and immediately ushered them to an alcove, where they seated themselves on the plush sofas. 'Champagne all round and keep it flowing,' the American called, causing the maître d' to click his fingers at the nearest waiters.

As if by magic, silver champagne buckets arrived and with a flourish the maître d' poured the wine. When he departed, with much backward bowing, Mr van Haven raised his champagne flute and offered a victorious toast. 'To the Duke of Somerfeld and the future Duchess of Somerfeld.'

A quiet, unenthusiastic murmur went around the table. It seemed the assembled guests cared as little about the engagement as Oliver and Arabella did.

The four thugs quickly emptied their glasses. A waiter rushed forward and refilled them, which were downed in equal haste. The waiter lifted the bottle out of the ice bucket and almost dropped it when one thug growled for him to leave it.

At least the thugs were making the most of the occasion, Oliver smiled to himself as he sipped his drink.

'We should make the announcement as soon as possible and hold the engagement party next weekend,' Mr van Haven said, frowning slightly as the thugs continued to swill his expensive champagne as if it was cheap cider. 'I'm sure you will be available to host the engagement,' he added, turning his attention to Oliver. 'It will give me the opportunity to meet your family and to see your estate.'

His new fiancée rolled her eyes. 'That's a bit short notice, isn't it, Father? One week.'

'Nonsense. That's all right with you, isn't it, Son?'

Oliver smiled at the American's presumption. He presumably wanted it hosted at his estate so he could make sure that Oliver actually turned up for his own engagement party. 'Of course it's all right. Nothing would please me more.'

'And you are cordially invited, Lord Bufford,' the American added with a pointed look at Oliver.

Lord Bufford bared his teeth in what was presumably a smile. 'Nothing will stop me from attending Somerfeld's engagement party. And I will of course be bringing my wife. I can't wait to tell her that he's about to be married.'

He clicked his fingers at the now slightly tipsy thugs and they rose unsteadily to their feet. 'Thank you for your hospitality, Mr van Haven,' Lord Bufford growled. 'But if you'll excuse me I'm anxious to return to my wife and tell her the good news.' With that he bowed to Arabella, sent another angry glare in Oliver's direction and left the table. The four thugs staggered behind him, but not before one had grabbed a dripping bottle of champagne from the ice bucket.

'What charming fellows,' Oliver remarked. 'It's a shame they had to leave so early.'

'And I think we should start organising the wedding immediately, so it can be held as soon as possible,' Mr van Haven said, grabbing another wine bottle and refilling their glasses.

Oliver adopted his most concerned expression. 'Oh, no. I'm afraid that won't be possible. Won't be possible at all.'

The American paused, the bottle suspended in mid-air, Oliver's glass only half-full. 'And why not?' he barked and looked towards the door, as if intending to call back the tipsy thugs.

'There's the codicil on my title to consider.'

'The what?'

'Yes, the codicil,' Oliver said, taking the bottle from Mr van Haven's hand and filling up his glass. 'It's a clause in a will that…'

'I know what a codicil is, man,' he snapped. 'But why should it stop you from marrying my daughter?'

Oliver took a sip of his champagne while the older man's face turned a shade that could only be described as beetroot red. 'If I get married before I'm thirty-five, I lose my title, the estates, everything. That means, unfortunately, if your daughter is to become my Duchess, she will have to wait for seven years. But at that time I'd be honoured to make your beautiful daughter the Duchess of Somerfeld.' He raised his glass towards Arabella, smiled and drank it all.

She sent him a delightful, appreciative smile in return and turned to face her father.

Her father glared at her across the linen-covered table, his mouth twitching with anger, a dark flush moving up his face, from his neck to his hairline.

Arabella knew it would be wise to not react so obviously to this victory over her father, but she couldn't stop her smile from growing larger and larger.

Her so-called fiancé had done what business tycoons, bankers and politicians on both sides of the Atlantic had been unable to do. He had got the better of the ruthless Mr van Haven. And the pleasure of watching someone finally succeed where so many had failed was infinitely satisfying, especially after what had happened with Arnold Emerson back in New York.

In both cases the result had been Arabella not getting married. But this time it was her fiancé who had saved her rather than abandoned her. Oh, yes, this was a victory to celebrate and she raised her glass to Oliver and took a jubilant sip.

Her father continued to scowl. 'You can't marry before you're thirty-five?' His usual barking voice had taken on an uncharacteristically high pitch.

'Of course, I can marry at any time I want,' Oliver said, refilling everyone's champagne glasses. 'But if I marry before I'm thirty-five I lose my title, as will my wife, and of course we'll have no money. And, as I've never actually had to work for a living, I'm not sure how I'd make any more.' He looked over at Arabella and gave a mock frown. 'What do people actually do when they have to work for a living?'

She smiled as if he had asked a delightfully absurd question, raised her shoulders and shook her head. 'I'm sure it won't come to that,' she said, 'because my father can see now that there's no point us getting married after all. Can't you, Father?'

She glanced at her father, who was looking from one to the other, his brow deeply furrowed. He slowly flicked the side of his champagne glass as he silently contemplated this development for a moment. 'I suppose an engagement to a duke isn't to be sneered at,' he said quietly. 'It's still an engagement to a member of the aristocracy. Even if it does last seven years.'

He looked up at the pair of them. His wolf-like smile returned and Arabella's stomach fluttered with unease.

'Right, that's settled,' he announced decisively. 'We'll hold the engagement party next weekend. We'll announce your engagement in all the relevant newspapers, both here and in New York, and in seven years you'll be married, and my daughter will be the Duchess of Somerfeld.'

Arabella's smile died and her shoulders slumped. She wasn't going to get her victory after all. Her father still expected her to get married, eventually.

But what had she expected?

The last time she had fought her father about a man it had been over that treacherous Arnold Emerson. Her father had insisted that Arnold was just after her money, but Arabella was certain that the charming, handsome actor was in love with her, just as she was in love with him.

But she had been so wrong.

All it had taken for her father to prove his point

was for him to offer Arnold a substantial amount of money to take his amorous attentions elsewhere. He had immediately disappeared, out of Arabella's life, without even saying goodbye.

It had been devastating and humiliating and had shaken her faith in men and her own judgement.

But this time it was different.

She might know little about men, and she might have got it so wrong with Arnold Emerson, but even she could see that Oliver Huntsbury was not the man for her. Yes, he was stunningly good looking, with a devilish smile that could turn a woman to jelly, but he was an obvious womaniser. Not the sort of man any right-thinking woman would ever consider marrying.

But then he didn't want to marry her just as much as she didn't want to marry him. This time she had an ally in her fight against her father.

She looked down at her champagne glass and chewed the edge of her bottom lip. Perhaps this wasn't so bad. She was going to have to get engaged, yes. But a seven-year engagement was better than a marriage. And seven years was a long time. Her father would not want to stay in England that long. And with her father safely back in America and out of her life she would have seven years to dedicate to furthering her acting career. Seven years of glorious freedom, with only the easily duped Aunt Prudence as chaperon. And seven years for her and the Duke to think of a way out of this marriage.

No, it wasn't a complete victory, but they had won a decisive first battle.

Arabella raised her head, smiled and reached out her hand towards her father. 'All right, Father. The

Duke and I will become engaged, we'll marry in seven years, and in exchange you'll follow through on your promise and save the Limelight Theatre. And that is the best deal you're going to get.'

Her father eyed her for a second, then took her hand and gave it a firm shake. And with that handshake Arabella sealed her fate as a woman engaged to be married.

Chapter Four

His mission accomplished, Arabella's father spotted a business acquaintance across the room and departed, but not before reminding her new fiancé about the stiff penalties and the social disgrace imposed on men guilty of breach of promise. Her father was making sure the Duke knew that if he tried to get out of this engagement, he would suffer dire consequences.

But at least the theatre would be saved. When it came to business transactions, her father had a reputation for always keeping his word. And that was exactly what her marriage was, a business transaction.

She looked over at Oliver and sent him a doleful smile. Her new fiancé was as equally opposed to the sham engagement as she was. That had to be some consolation to being sold off by her father. Didn't it?

He refilled their champagne glasses just as the supper her father had ordered for eight people arrived. The waiters lay tray after tray on the table, until it was laden with silver trays overflowing with oysters, cheeses, thinly cut cold meats, truffles and *foie gras*.

Arabella looked at the feast and sighed. Her fellow

actors were staying in a boarding house close to the theatre and would be dining on thin soup and rough bread. Despite such humble fare and their dingy living quarters, she would much rather be with them, enjoying the camaraderie and excitement that always ensued after a night's performance, than sitting in this grand restaurant surrounded by London's most fashionable society.

'Don't worry, Arabella, it's an engagement in name only,' he said, misinterpreting her sigh.

She shook her head and sighed again. 'I know. I know. My father won't be able to stay away from his bank for much longer. He'll return to America and then you'll be free.'

He waved his hand in dismissal. 'It might not be ideal, but I think a long engagement of convenience is going to suit us both very well. So, drink up, eat up, we might as well celebrate. Even if all we're celebrating is freeing you from your father's matchmaking for the next seven years and saving me from being hanged, drawn and quartered by Lord Buffoon and his band of baboons.'

Arabella smiled at his deliberate mispronunciation. 'In that case, here's to long engagements.' They clinked glasses and she sipped her champagne, the bubbles tickling her nose.

Lowering her glass, she gave him a considered glance. 'I take it you don't really have to wait until you're thirty-five before you can marry?'

He gave her a conspiratorial wink, forcing Arabella to use all her acting skills to stop her heart from fluttering and cheeks from burning.

'I became the Duke of Somerfeld two years ago

on the death of my father and nothing can take that away from me. I'm the Duke until I die, but we don't need to tell your father that.'

'No, if he did find out your death would be the least of your problems. He can be somewhat ruthless when he's crossed.'

They both looked across the busy restaurant to where her father was sitting, now deeply engrossed in conversation, presumably making yet another deal. His daughter's future marriage settled, he had swiftly moved on to further business.

'Don't worry, Arabella, with both of us against him, your father doesn't stand a chance.'

His words held a note of reassurance. He might be going along with the engagement to save his own hide, but it was nice to have an ally, someone who also wanted to defeat her father.

Arabella raised her glass again in toast. 'To victory over my father.'

'To us.' He clinked his crystal champagne flute against hers.

'So, if we're going to be engaged for the next seven years, perhaps we need to know a bit more about each other,' Arabella said. 'All I know about you is your name and that Lord Bufford wants to tear you limb from limb.'

He rubbed his hand slowly around the back of his neck. 'You obviously haven't been in England very long if you haven't heard the scandals associated with the Huntsbury family and the Duke of Somerfeld. And I suspect if your father knew he wouldn't be quite so enthusiastic to be joined to our family.'

'Huntsbury? Yes, I have heard something about

them.' Arabella furrowed her brow and tried to recall where she had heard that name before. Hadn't the
other actresses been gossiping about someone called
Huntsbury? Their conversation suddenly jumped into
her mind and her hands shot to her mouth as she re-
called all the sordid details.

'I take it you know after all,' he said.

Arabella gulped and nodded. The actresses had described in explicit detail how Marcus Huntsbury, the
former Duke of Somerfeld, had died in the arms of
his mistress. And not just one mistress. The rumours
were that he'd had a heart attack while he was attempting a particularly strenuous sexual pose involv-
ing himself and four women, in a large four-poster
bed. A bed that had reportedly been designed spe-
cially so he could conduct his own personal orgies.

The actresses had found it particularly amusing as
both of them had taken part in the Duke's bedroom
athletics in the past. They were just surprised he'd
only had four women in his bed that night, as the bed
had been designed for eight.

Arabella took another sip of her champagne to try
to drive that image out of her mind.

'I don't think…' she coughed again '… I don't
think even that would deter my father. He doesn't care
who I marry, or what scandals surround the family,
as long as I get a title.'

'It seems we both have fathers who care only for
getting what they want and don't consider who suf-
fers as a result.'

Arabella nodded her agreement and they each sank
into their own thoughts.

The restaurant started to fill up with more diners,

many of whom were in high spirits, talking loudly and laughing boisterously. The Savoy was a popular venue for a late supper and many of the revellers would have come from the opera, the various playhouses and the array of illicit gambling houses in the neighbouring areas.

She spotted W.S. Gilbert and Arthur Sullivan enter, surrounded by a group of actors. The famous theatrical duo's comic operettas were performed in the adjoining theatre and they could often be seen in the restaurant. It was one of Arabella's most cherished dreams that she might one day appear in a Gilbert and Sullivan production. Certainly a more cherished dream than being married would ever be.

The group included numerous attractive young actresses and Arabella couldn't help but notice that several looked in Oliver's direction as they passed their table. Nor could she ignore the number of women throughout the restaurant who were smiling, nodding and even winking at her new fiancé.

Lady Bufford and Lucy Baker quite plainly weren't the only *very good friends* of the Duke of Somerfeld. But why should Arabella care? She had no illusions about the sort of man he was. He was most decidedly a lady's man, just like his father. But wasn't that all for the good? He would be less likely to interfere in Arabella's life if he was off chasing other women and she could get on with doing what she wanted to do, which was pursue her acting career.

Yes, it was definitely all for the best.

Another attractive woman passed the table and smiled suggestively at Oliver. Despite her resolve to not care, Arabella couldn't stop herself from frowning at the woman and she received a little, knowing laugh in return.

'Another one of your good friends, I take it,' she said, annoyed at the prissy sound of her own voice.

He shrugged apologetically. 'Yes, I suppose you could say that.'

'So how many of these good friends have you actually had and how many have you got at the moment?'

He turned in his seat to face her. 'Is that going to be a problem, Arabella?'

Heat shot to her cheeks. 'No, no, of course not,' she stammered. 'I'm merely making conversation. It's got nothing to do with me. You can have hundreds of good friends if you like. I don't care.'

He continued to stare at her, his brows drawn together, and despite her attempt to act nonchalantly her cheeks burned hotter under his questioning gaze. It shouldn't matter. It didn't matter. So why did a little stabbing pain strike her in the middle of her chest every time a woman smiled in Oliver's direction?

'You do realise this engagement is just one of convenience for both of us, don't you, Arabella?'

'Of course I do,' she shot back, her voice rising. 'I don't want to be engaged to anyone, least of all you, and I certainly don't want to be married. Yes, this suits us both. As you said, it saves you from a beating and it saves me from my father's incessant matchmaking.'

'And we'll both be free to pursue our interests, free from the other's interference?'

Arabella nodded and looked around the room at all the beautiful women. Her stomach clenched at the thought of Oliver pursuing his interests with his numerous *very good friends*. There would be other women in his life, women who he would take in his arms and kiss the way he had kissed her in the dressing room. Women with whom he presumably did more than just kiss, if the reaction of Lord Bufford was anything to go by.

She lightly touched her lips, remembering that kiss. After such a kiss she could see why so many women fell under his spell. It had been a kiss that had caused her to forget herself, to abandon all reserve, to want more, so much more.

She gazed back at him and he smiled. Even that wicked smile was enough to make her go all weak inside. When he smiled all she could see were those sparkling brown eyes, eyes that reminded her of rich brown chocolate, warm, inviting and satisfying, and those smiling lips, soft lips that had felt so good on hers, that had tasted so delicious.

A stray blond curl had fallen over his forehead and Arabella had to resist the temptation to sweep it back, and then, perhaps, to linger, her hands running through his thick hair, just the way they had when he had kissed her.

Yes, she could see why so many women fell for him.

She sat up straighter in her chair and looked back out at the crowded room. But she was not like most women. She had ambitions that did not include a man. And she had been badly burnt once. She wasn't about to be burnt again.

No, it did not matter to her, one jot, if other women were vying for his attention. They might be engaged, but she had only just met this man. He meant nothing to her. Nothing at all.

And she was determined to let him know that this was the case. 'So if I don't give a fig about you and all your *friends*, which I don't, can I also assume you won't do anything to interfere with my career on the stage?'

'That goes without saying,' he replied.

Arabella didn't know whether to be pleased or disappointed. Did that mean he didn't care one way or another what she did? That he didn't care about her at all? Again, that was a good thing, wasn't it? Of course it was. 'Right, that's settled.'

Another pretty woman passed the table and this one had the audacity to slip Oliver a note. It was outrageous. He was sitting at a table with another woman. Surely that should mean something. Surely other women should keep their distance, even if just for this one night.

But it was apparent that there were so many women in Oliver's life that none was accorded any special treatment. They presumably all knew very well what he was like and accepted him that way. It seemed a title was not the only thing he had inherited from the previous Duke of Somerfeld.

Oliver stared down at the note as if it were an unpleasant stain on the otherwise pristine white tablecloth. Normally a note from Lady Ambrose would be most welcome. It was presumably a reminder that he been invited to one of her notorious parties. Parties that never failed to provide him with an enjoyable diversion. Parties full of women who had no objection to the way he lived his life, who actively encouraged his more libertine ways.

But tonight, he was strangely embarrassed by its arrival.

He slipped the note into his pocket in what he hoped was a surreptitious manner. Out of sight, out of mind. But the disapproving look on Arabella's face showed clearly that it was not out of her mind.

For the first time in his life he almost felt the need to apologise for the way he lived. He was tempted to try to explain to Arabella that no one was ever hurt by his behaviour, at least no women. How their husbands felt was their own concern.

Most of those husbands had married women for their dowries, or for their social connections, and as long as they were discreet, they didn't care what their wives got up to and with whom. And, once freed of the constraints of society and marriage, his mistresses certainly liked to get up to a lot.

Even Lord Bufford was only annoyed because his wife's behaviour had been openly discussed at his club. He felt no jealousy about his wife having a lover, only rage that others had found out about it.

But why did Oliver feel the need to explain his lifestyle now? He had never felt the need to do that before.

Perhaps it was that kiss, which was still lingering on his lips, or the memory of the warmth of Arabella's body so close to his? Perhaps it was her enticing smile, or was it simply that she was not the sort of woman he usually associated with? Whatever it was, something was causing him a degree of discomfort.

It must be simply that she *was* so different from the women he usually associated with.

He fingered the note in his pocket, reminding himself of why he did not get involved with women like Arabella van Haven, no matter how enticing their kisses.

Oliver's father might not have cared about the damage he did in his headlong pursuit of hedonistic pleasure, but in one regard Oliver knew they were different. His father had seduced every pretty woman who came his way. He cared little if he broke hearts or ruined reputations, as long as he was getting what he wanted.

Oliver had definitely inherited his father's love of women, the more the merrier, but he ensured he only got involved with women who were as equally carefree as him. And that was obviously not Arabella.

She was sweet and innocent. She deserved to be with a decent man, not a man like him who shunned commitment with every fibre of his being. She might claim to not want to marry, and that was possibly true, but it was obvious from the way Arabella had scowled every time another woman tried to catch his eye, that she couldn't cope with a man she had to share. And he had never been a one-woman man. Never would be. That was why he only associated with women like Lady Bufford, Lucy Baker, Lady Ambrose, and all the other women who wanted to have fun with no strings attached.

But he would honour his promise to be engaged to her for the foreseeable future. While there were probably easier ways of getting out of a beating from Lord Bufford's baboons, and better ways of saving

Lady Bufford's reputation, what was done was done and he would stand by it.

If nothing else, it would save this lovely young woman from being pushed around by her odious father, a man who obviously saw her as nothing more than a pawn in his power game. It would free her up to be an actress, and a fine actress she was, indeed, if tonight's performance was anything to go by.

He smiled in memory of how she looked on stage. 'What is it you love so much about acting?' He wanted to know, but also wanted to move on to safer ground than his own reprobate behaviour.

Her pouting lips instantly turned into a smile and her blue eyes sparkled with enthusiasm. He gazed into those eyes, trying to determine what colour they really were. Blue didn't do them justice. Sapphire, perhaps, or aquamarine, or the blue of the sky on a warm summer's day. He wished he had the soul of a poet so he could describe them properly and not see them simply as beautiful blue eyes.

But whatever colour they were, they had him captivated.

'Oh, everything. I love absolutely everything about acting and the theatre. I love the smell of the grease-paint when we put on our make-up. I love the sound of the audience laughing or gasping at what they've seen on stage. I love the camaraderie of the cast. And most of all I love the applause at the end. There's nothing like it. It's like being wrapped in loving arms, being told how much all your hard work is appreciated. It's just wonderful.'

She continued to beam and he couldn't help but wonder if there wasn't sadness behind that smile. He looked over at her father, now writing out some plan on the linen tablecloth as the man next to him looked on with undivided interest. It was unlikely she had received much love from that mercenary man, a man who treated her like another commodity to be bought and sold. And she had said her mother had died when she was young. It was no wonder she craved the love and adoration that she would get from an audience.

He placed his hand over hers and lightly patted it as an unfamiliar emotion engulfed him. What was it? Was it the need to protect her from men like her father, to comfort her for the pain she had suffered, or even to provide her with the love she had missed out on?

He quickly withdrew his hand from hers as if it were on fire. Whatever strange emotion he was feeling, he should not be feeling it for a woman like Arabella. There was nothing he could offer her.

He poured himself another glass of champagne. Despite that kiss, she was an innocent and he needed to keep that foremost in his mind at all times. She did not need a man like him in her life.

He cursed himself for remembering their kiss. The scorching intensity of it had been so unexpected. She had been kissing a stranger, but had responded as if they were passionate lovers, desperate for each other. She might be an innocent, but it had definitely ignited a fire inside her, one that had almost engulfed both of them.

It was only the knowledge that they were in a room full of people that had stopped him from fanning the flame and seeing just how hot it would burn.

There could be no doubting that there was a passionate side to this young woman just waiting to be set loose, a passionate nature ripe for exploration.

He knocked back the glass of champagne in one quaff, horrified that he had allowed his mind to stray in that direction. Wasn't that just the sort of thing his father would think? Didn't his father look at every woman and see her as yet more prey waiting to be seduced? But he was not like that. He would never be like that. And he would not be like that with Arabella.

The sooner their engagement was signed, sealed and delivered and they could go their separate ways, the better. Only then would he be safe from these inappropriate desires and only then would Arabella be safe from him.

Chapter Five

Arabella was under no illusions. It was only because of her father's manoeuvring that Oliver was still sitting at this table with her and not off pursuing one of the other women in the restaurant. He had not chosen to be with her, he had been forced to be with her against his will.

And he had made it clear to her that he expected to be free to pursue any woman he wanted, even though they were to be engaged to be married.

She shrugged and took another sip of her cold champagne. He had every right to chase any woman he wanted to and she had no right to try to stop him. And she would *not* try to stop him. She would abide by their agreement. It was the very least she could do. After all, she should be grateful to him. He did not have to agree to become engaged to her. He could have made his escape and left her to her fate. She knew her father well. Her fate was sealed. He would move heaven and earth to ensure she married a man with a title. She had much to thank Oliver for. It was also down to his quick thinking that she would not have to face the prospect of a forced marriage for seven more years.

Thanks to him, she now had a long-term engagement of convenience. It was more than she could have hoped for when her father gave her the ultimatum of getting married or returning to America with him. And if it meant she was engaged to a man who had countless other women in his life, well, so be it. It was not as if they meant anything to each other. They had only just met. And surely, if she really was grateful to him, she would put no obstacle in his way when it came to pursuing other women.

Yes, she owed him his freedom. And that was exactly what she would give him. There would be no more pouting when a woman gave him *that* look. No more snide comments about his *good friends*. No, he could behave in any way he wanted, with whomever he wanted, and he would get no objections from her.

She smiled at him as if to underline this firm resolve. 'I hope you've got some enjoyable entertainment arranged for the rest of the evening. I'd hate to think my father interrupted your plans.'

Despite her determination to feign nonchalance, she couldn't stop her eyes from straying to his pocket, where he had stored the note from that particularly attractive brunette.

He smiled back at her; a smile that was this time more sheepish than devilish. 'It was a particularly pleasant interruption and I have no regrets about how I'm spending this evening.'

He found her company pleasant. He had no regrets about spending his evening with her instead of all those other women vying for his attention.

She returned his smile and his became wickedly tempting, drawing her gaze to his sensual lips. Arabella imagined touching her finger to those enticingly smiling lips, gently stroking the line where they met his olive skin, before she kissed him again. Running her tongue along…

Where on earth had that image come from?

Shocked at where her thoughts had led her, she closed her eyes and shook her head to drive it out.

Yes, he had kissed her once, but it had been for one reason, and one reason only: because he was being pursued by the husband of one of his mistresses and he'd needed an alibi. And it wasn't her he'd intended to kiss, but Lucy Baker. And even if he ever did want to kiss her again, which she was sure he didn't, she could not let it happen. She had made a fool of herself over one man before and she was not about to let history repeat itself. No, if Arnold Emerson had taught her anything, it was to not trust herself when it came to men. And if she couldn't trust herself with Arnold Emerson, then she most certainly could not trust herself with this seductive, charming rake. Their kiss was proof of that.

Opening her eyes, she saw he was still staring at her, his eyebrows drawn together, questioning her unusual behaviour. How long had her eyes been closed while she tried to drive out that image of him kissing her?

Heat tinging her cheeks, she picked up her napkin and dabbed the edge of her eye. 'I think I might have something in my eye,' she said, her embarrassment rising with every word as she tried to explain her discomposure and odd reaction to his attention.

'Here, allow me.' He took the napkin from her hand and began dabbing at the edge of her eye himself. This was worse than Arabella could have imagined. He was now so close she could feel the warmth radiating from his body, smell his intoxicating masculine scent, picture the hard muscles under his crisp white shirt. She tried not to breathe, not to feel, not to think.

'Open your eyes wider so I can see what the obstruction is.'

She did as he commanded, but stared up towards the ceiling so she would not have to look at his handsome face. This situation was uncomfortable enough. She did not need the extra discomfort of looking at that strong, chiselled jawline, or those full, inviting lips.

'I can't see anything. Perhaps when you closed your eyes you dislodged it.'

He lowered the napkin and Arabella lowered her gaze. That was a mistake. Now she was staring straight into his velvet-brown eyes and a delicious sensation of rich chocolate slowly melting on her tongue engulfed her.

She swallowed the sigh of pleasure that was threatening to escape and quickly looked down at her lap in a desperate attempt to still her fevered imaginings.

Why did he have to be so handsome? This whole encounter would be so much easier if he didn't make her turn to jelly every time she looked at him.

There was absolutely no denying he was charming, but he wouldn't have much success as a womaniser if he wasn't charming, would he? And the one thing she did not want was to be charmed by a man who was well experienced in the art of seduction.

She drew in a deep breath. No, it did not matter how charming he was, or how handsome, or how captivating that mischievous smile, she would not succumb. She would keep firmly in her mind at all times the type of man he was. He was a rake, a reprobate, a debaucher. Not the sort of man she wanted in her life.

He handed her the napkin, which she tentatively took from his outstretched hand, taking every precaution to avoid contact with his skin.

If she couldn't trust her body to act as sensibly as her mind, it was time to put some distance between herself and the Duke of Somerfeld. 'Well, I think I'll call it a night and let you get on with enjoying the rest of your evening.'

'I'm in no hurry and you've eaten nothing of the supper.'

She looked at the array of dishes. The last thing she felt like was eating. 'I'm not hungry, but please, don't let me stop you.'

He waved his hand in dismissal, so she signalled to the waiter. 'Would you please parcel up all this food and have it delivered to this address.'

She took a blank white card out of her beaded purse, wrote the address of the boarding house where her fellow cast members were staying and handed it to the waiter. They would appreciate the feast that would otherwise go to waste.

'But as I said, I'm tired and I think it is time I went to bed.' Heat exploded on her cheeks at the mere mention of beds and she was reminded of how his father had died. Had Oliver inherited that bed, the one made to take eight women? Was that where he would be spending this evening? And which of the women in this room would be joining him?

She threw the napkin on the table and stood quickly, anxious to get away from him and away from such disturbing images. 'Yes, I really must be going,' she said and looked around the room as if suddenly unsure of where she was.

'Then allow me to escort you home,' he said, rising, a teasing quirk to his lips.

He knew what she was thinking. That was why he was smiling at her like that.

Arabella's embarrassment intensified. How could she be so transparent? She was an actress, for goodness sake. Surely she should be able to keep her feelings hidden from view. And surely she shouldn't start blushing just because the word bed had been mentioned.

'There's no need to accompany me home. I'm staying here at the Savoy. I'd much rather be staying with the other actors, but Father would be horrified if I did. He sent me over to England a few months ago to marry an aristocrat, not to become an actress. He had one duke lined up for me, but my father's ward, Rosie, married him instead. That's why he is so determined to not let another aristocrat get away.' Her words had tumbled out in a rush, but she seemed incapable of stopping herself from talking.

He smiled at her. 'So you eluded one duke and got a job as an actress, now you're trying to escape from another one. I can see you're an enterprising young lady if you're able to keep your plans secret from your father.'

'Fortunately Father has spent so much time making deals and looking for good financial investments while he's been here he's hardly noticed what I've been doing, so it hasn't taken too much enterprise on my part to creep out.'

The fire on her cheeks moved to her neck and the room suddenly seemed unbearably hot. 'Not that I ever do creep out, except to go to the theatre. And afterwards I come straight home, where Aunt Prudence is always waiting for me. And if I don't go to the theatre I always take a chaperon, either Aunt Prudence or my lady's maid. So I never really creep out.' Arabella knew she was still burbling, but it was essential that he knew she was not the sort of woman who flirted with men in public, or passed them secret notes, and she certainly had no intention of creeping out with him, tonight or any other night.

'Well, at least let me walk you to your room,' he offered.

'No, there's no need.' The last thing she wanted was Oliver anywhere near her hotel suite. It wasn't that she didn't trust him. It was that she wasn't entirely sure she could trust herself. Her own behaviour tonight had been so uncharacteristic and unpredictable, she was in danger of doing something reckless. She might even be tempted to encourage just one more kiss from him. She bit her bottom lip lightly to try to stop it from tingling at the memory of it.

She held out an unsteady hand to shake goodbye. 'That won't be necessary, I can find my own way to my room,' she said more emphatically than she intended.

Oliver took her hand in his, but instead of shaking it, he leant over and gave her a light kiss on the cheek.

Arabella froze.

His lips lingered.

Would he kiss her on the lips, too? Would he take her in his arms? Would he hold her body close to his? She knew she shouldn't want that. But she did. Like so many other women in the room, Arabella was falling for the charms of Oliver Huntsbury.

But she was not like every other woman in the room. She *refused* to be like every other woman in the room.

She took a step backwards, almost colliding with the wall. 'Well, goodnight,' she stammered. 'I suppose the next time we see each other will be at our engagement party.' She gave a fake laugh.

He released her hand and Arabella released her held breath.

'Until our engagement party.' His eyes once again sparked with wicked amusement.

Arabella turned and all but ran out of the restaurant, not bothering to say goodbye to her father who was still engrossed in his latest deal.

She hurried away, sure her almost-fiancé's eyes were still on her. Next weekend she would be engaged to him. Engaged to a man she didn't want to be engaged to. A man she didn't want to marry and, worst of all, a man who made her feel things she knew she shouldn't be feeling.

Oliver watched his fiancée leave, her silk dress rustling as she departed rapidly without a backwards glance, then slumped back down on to his chair.

On most nights the evening's entertainment would just be getting started at this late hour, but tonight he had no interest in visiting any of his usual haunts, no desire to see Lucy Baker or any of the other women who were currently providing him with delightful diversions.

Is this what happened when you became engaged? Oliver shuddered. Perish the thought. That was not him.

He pulled Lady Ambrose's note out of his pocket and read the contents. As expected, it was a reminder that she was hosting yet another party. A particularly salacious party, if the wording on the note was any indication, and it was being held at her town house later this evening. Normally Oliver would be pleased by such an invitation. Lady Ambrose's parties could even top his father's when it came to inventiveness. But tonight, it seemed he wasn't in the mood.

He looked towards the door through which Arabella had departed.

Nor, for some reason, did he feel compelled to follow up on any of the unspoken invitations he had received throughout the evening.

Instead he would return to his estate and tell his mother the news, that he was now engaged to be married.

At least his betrothal would bring pleasure to his dear mother. She, too, was an innocent and, despite being married to one of England's most notorious rakes, she refused to think anything bad about her husband and still saw marriage as a wonderful thing.

To maintain his mother's innocence, he had been forced to deceive her for many years. Oliver knew it would have destroyed her to know the man she loved and revered had been repeatedly unfaithful to her, with countless women throughout their marriage. So far his mother had continued to live in blissful ignorance, rarely coming to London and preferring to socialise with the genteel ladies in the Surrey countryside.

And now he was about to lie to his mother about himself. But it would only upset her if she knew the truth. That his engagement was not a love match, but merely a way to save one woman's reputation and allow another woman to defy her father and to continue to perform on the stage.

But even if he was forced to lie to his mother, he would not lie to Arabella. While his mother was never aware of what her husband was really like, at least Arabella knew exactly what sort of man she was now engaged to. She was entering this arrangement with her eyes wide open and had accepted him for who he was.

He had vowed he would not be like his father in the way he treated women as mere playthings, with no feelings of their own. He would do everything he could to avoid causing Arabella emotional pain and the best way to do that was for him to never see her again once the engagement party was over.

He looked again at the door through which she had departed. Keeping that vow would be so much easier if he was engaged to a woman who wasn't so damned attractive, a woman whose kiss did not hold so much promise of a passionate nature. But he had kissed her once, he would not do so again. He would not take her in his arms again. He would not feel that beautiful body pressed up against his, or taste those tempting lips again, not run his hands over her wonderful curvaceous figure.

He might not be able to forget their kiss, that would be asking too much, but it must never happen again. If it did, he was unsure whether he'd be able to stop at just a kiss and that would be a disaster. Arabella must retain her innocence until she met a man who was worthy of her, a man who could love her in the way she deserved to be loved.

He continued to stare in the direction she had departed and drained his champagne flute for the last time. No, a woman like Arabella was most definitely not for him.

He summoned the waiter and asked him to hail a hansom cab. Oliver would return to his town house, then catch the first train back to his Surrey estate and break the supposedly happy news to his mother. Then, next weekend, Arabella and he would go through the motions of an engagement party. After that, they would never have to see each other again.

Chapter Six

An engagement party should be a joyous time of celebration. Family and friends gathering together to mark the happy occasion. And the happy couple should be just that—happy.

But Arabella could see nothing to be happy about. As Nellie, her lady's maid, curled her hair, then lifted it into a bun high on her head and added the hair pieces that would give her already abundant hair an even more voluminous look, Arabella stared at the face reflected in the mirror. It was a face of a woman about to start a long prison sentence, not the look of a woman about to celebrate her engagement.

She just had to keep reminding herself it was not a real engagement. She was not going to be married. She had seven years in which to come up with a way to get out of this unwanted predicament. And it could be much worse, she could be tied to a man who repulsed her, instead of a handsome duke who made her heart beat faster every time he looked at her, whose kisses had caused her to forget who she was and what she was doing.

Arabella sighed. Was that better or was that worse?

Perhaps it would be better if he was some horrid old duke with bad breath and rotting teeth. Then there would be no problem, no confusion, she would know exactly how she felt and what she wanted.

Nellie teased out a few curls and allowed them to deliberately fall loose, so they had a carefree look about them, then stood back to admire her work. 'Perfect, if I do say so myself. It's just a shame that my perfect hair style is being worn by someone who looks as though she's about to have her head cut off.'

Arabella sent Nellie a sad smile. Originally from Ireland, Nellie had joined the van Haven household when she first arrived in America at the age of thirteen. Arabella was only fourteen herself at the time. They had grown up together and were more friends than servant and mistress.

'Sorry, Nellie. Yes, it looks lovely, as always.'

Nellie placed her hand gently on Arabella's arm. 'No, it's me that's sorry. I'm sorry you have to go through this, Arabella. Sorry your father is selling you off like this. Sorry that you can't just be left alone to live the life you want to live.'

Arabella patted Nellie's hand. 'I could say the same for you, Nellie. You could be so much more than just a lady's maid, if the world treated women better than it does.'

Nellie raised her eyebrows and sent her a mysterious smile. 'Oh, I have my plans and I'm not going to let the world tell me what I can and can't do.'

Before Arabella could question Nellie over what she meant, there was a knock on the door, and Nellie opened it to admit Rosie, Arabella's best friend. Recently married to the Duke of Knightsbrook, Rosie was glowing with health and happiness.

She hugged Nellie and gave Arabella a kiss on the cheek. 'Oh, Arabella, I was so sorry to hear about your engagement. I wish I'd been here to stop it.'

Arabella shrugged. 'Never mind, Rosie. It's only an engagement of convenience. Oliver is just as set against marriage as I am. He's like you, a great one for coming up with clever plans, so I'm sure we will never actually have to get married.'

Rosie screwed up her face. 'I hope he thinks things through a bit better than I did.'

Arabella smiled at her friend. She was referring to Rosie's plan to save Arabella from her father's last attempt to marry her off. Rosie had come up with what she thought was the perfect plan to put the duke off Arabella. While Arabella was pursuing work on the London stage, Rosie would meet him and pretend to be Arabella, then behave so badly that the Duke of Knightsbrook would have no interest in marrying her. Instead it had all gone terribly wrong, or gloriously right, depending on how you looked at it, and they had fallen in love.

'I'm sure Oliver knows what he's doing. And he has even more reasons for not wanting to get married than I do. So, no matter what, I'm sure he'll make sure this marriage never happens. In the meantime, while I'm engaged to be married, it stops Father from throwing me in front of every passing duke, earl or viscount.'

'Yes, I've heard the Duke of Somerfeld has quite a lot of reasons for not wanting to get married,' Nellie said and exchanged a knowing look with Rosie.

It seemed Oliver's reputation as a womaniser was known far and wide.

Nellie helped Arabella into a peach-coloured silk skirt and a matching embroidered jacket with a lacy neckline. Arabella had been tempted to wear black for mourning, but in the end had decided that might be taking things a bit too far.

While Nellie used a buttonhook to do up the buttons on Arabella's white boots, Rosie told them of all the plans she and her new husband had for modernising the Knightsbrook estate. She was so full of enthusiasm and Arabella had to admit that marriage suited her friend. She had never looked more lovely. But she had married the man she had fallen in love with. She hadn't been forced to become engaged to a man who was a notorious rake, whose sexual conquests were legendary.

Getting caught up in Rosie's excitement, Arabella found herself actually smiling and laughing. It might not be a day of celebration for her, but it was good to be with her two friends and with Rosie by her side she knew she'd get through this horrid engagement party.

Once Arabella was dressed, Nellie gave her a critical once over, then departed.

'Well, I suppose I had better get this over and done with,' Arabella said. The best friends left the room arm in arm, walked down the grand staircase, through the expansive hallway of Somerfeld Manor, and out through the heavy oak doors at the entranceway.

When Arabella and her father had first arrived at Oliver's estate, her father had wandered around, inspecting the house and the surrounding grounds with a satisfied smile. He had admired every piece of antique furniture and every ancestral portrait, and each time he saw the family crest, bearing two rampant stags and a shield, his smile had grown so wide he looked fit to burst. Arabella had quickly lost count of the number of times he had mentioned that the Huntsburys could trace their family back to the fifteenth century.

It was exactly what her father wanted. He could now boast that he was about to become related to a family with a country estate that had been in their family since before the time America was first settled.

Joining 'old money' was something he had desired for a long time. Despite being born in poverty, he now had more than enough money to gain entry to New York's highest social echelons. But Arabella was aware that, despite his money and his power, he was still looked down upon by those members of society who had been born to wealth and privilege. Now, through his daughter's marriage, he finally expected to gain the status that being part of such a long-established family would bring him.

And he didn't care that his daughter had to be sacrificed to achieve his dream.

While her father had walked round the estate with a self-satisfied air, Arabella had found herself somewhat overawed by the grandeur of the enormous four-storey house, with its maze of expansive rooms.

She had been raised in a luxurious mansion on Washington Square, which her father had spared no expense when it came to decorating, but Oliver's estate almost made their home seem humble. With its thousands of acres of land and countless rooms decorated with priceless objects and paintings acquired over many generations, it was impossible to ignore the fact that the Huntsbury family had been fabulously wealthy going back hundreds of years.

Under normal circumstances spending the weekend at such a grand stately home would have been a delight, particularly as the view from her room was so picturesque, with its outlook on to formal gardens, green rolling parklands, and woodland areas. But as the weekend had progressed her anxiety had only grown. Particularly as, despite the size of the house, it had been virtually impossible to avoid Oliver.

Every time she had been in his company, her nerves had taken another shredding, until she was now exhausted and just counting off the hours until the engagement party was over and she could put this all behind her.

She would have much preferred to have spent the weekend in London, doing what she loved. But instead she had been forced to get the understudy to take her part so she could take on a different acting role, that of a woman who was happy to be engaged to a man she knew little about, except that he was not the sort of man any woman in her right mind would want to be married to.

Standing at the top of the tiled steps that led down to the garden, she paused and looked out over the sweeping lawns in front of the house.

It was a pleasant summer's day, so the engagement party was being held outside. Linen-covered tables, laden with food and drink, had been set up on the grassed area beside the lake. An army of liveried servants were lined up, ready to serve the guests with as much food and drink as they required, and maids were at the waiting, to clean away dishes as soon as they emptied and keep the sumptuous banquet replenished.

It was a perfect day for an engagement party. The sun was shining brightly in a blue sky, dotted with fluffy white clouds. There was even a gentle breeze, so the guests would not get too hot. But this day was far from perfect.

Arabella's gaze moved to her fiancé, who was talking to his auburn-haired mother. Arabella had been introduced to Oliver's mother when she first arrived and had been surprised that the woman was so happy and carefree. Arabella had expected the wife of a man who had died in the arms of four women to be bitter and cynical. Instead his mother gave every appearance of being someone who had never been exposed to any of life's harsher lessons. And she was still an attractive woman, even though she was now in her early fifties. She must have been quite stunning as a young woman, but even that had not been enough to keep her husband from straying.

Oliver's affection for his mother was obvious. He treated her as if he was the parent and she the child, a delicate young child who needed to be protected and cherished.

Oliver turned and looked at Arabella and her breath caught in her throat. She wished that wouldn't happen every time they made eye contact. It was so hard to pretend she wasn't affected by how handsome he was when it was difficult to breathe and when her cheeks were glowing as if she'd caught too much sun.

Rosie gave her arm a small squeeze of reassurance as Oliver excused himself from his mother and walked towards them. Arabella tried to get her breathing under control and still her racing heartbeat, but she was fighting a losing battle. Every time she saw him, her heart responded in this inappropriate manner. And today was no exception. But then, he was looking particularly handsome, dressed in a cream three-piece suit with a waistcoat embroidered with silver thread. His perfectly cut jacket showed off the breadth of his shoulders, the tailored trousers draped around his lean hips, and she could see the faint outline of firm muscles under the fabric as he walked towards her.

Why did he always have to look so damn handsome?

As he crossed the lawn, those laughing brown eyes were fixed on her. Arabella couldn't ignore how mischievous he always looked, like a young boy who had just committed a prank that he knew his elders would thoroughly disapprove of.

When he reached the bottom of the steps those full, highly kissable lips smiled in welcome.

'Darling,' he said, amusement sparking in his eyes. 'You look beautiful.'

The term of endearment might be a joke, but the way his gaze swept up and down her body was nothing to laugh at. Nor was Arabella's reaction. Her body came alive under his gaze as if every inch of her skin was being caressed.

She coughed to clear her throat and to give herself time to get her traitorous reactions under control. 'May I present my friend, Rosie, the Duchess of Knightsbrook. Rosie, this is Oliver, the Duke of

Somerfeld. Rosie is my closest friend and she knows all about this sham.' She waved her hand in a circle to encompass the entire engagement party.

Oliver was standing two steps below Arabella and Rosie, but his six-foot-something height meant he was at eye level with the two women. He took Rosie's hand and bowed formally.

'It's a pleasure to meet you, Duchess.' Releasing her hand, he turned to Arabella. 'And I believe if we're to maintain our charade it might be more appropriate if you called me Oliver, or darling, sweetheart, my love, my cherished one, the love of my life, the light of my dreams, or some such,' he said with a laugh.

Arabella pulled a slight frown of disapproval. 'All right, Oliver it is, then.' A statement that caused Oliver to send her another of those heart-stopping mischievous smiles.

The Duke of Knightsbrook joined them, shook hands with Oliver and led his new wife away. Rosie was smiling at him coquettishly, her happiness making her glow.

Oliver's smile turned from mischievous to warm and tender. 'You *do* look beautiful today, Arabella. Only a fool would not want to marry a woman as beautiful as you.'

She gave a false laugh. 'Then I take it you consider yourself a fool.'

His responding laugh was genuine. 'I've never thought otherwise.' He held out his arm for her and Arabella fought the temptation to flee back inside the house. It was so hard to maintain a composed demeanour when she was being told she was beautiful by a man who made her pulses race, causing her to gasp for breath as if her corset was laced too tightly.

'Shall we greet our guests?'

She nodded and joined the receiving line with her father and Oliver's mother. The guests filed past and had already divided themselves into two groups, Oliver's friends in one and Arabella's friends from the theatre in the other. It appeared the two worlds were reluctant to merge, just like the engaged couple themselves.

She exchanged pleasantries with the elegantly dressed men and women, and tried to remember their names, but each one slipped immediately from her mind. All she could focus on was the way the women looked at Oliver. Some sent him looks that suggested they wanted to devour him, others gave him shy but equally inviting smiles, and many looked at Arabella in much the same way that Lord Bufford's thugs had looked at Oliver.

While these women were sending silent signals of invitation, the men on their arms seemed oblivious to what was happening. Oliver was seducing their wives right under their noses and the husbands were either completely unaware of it or didn't care.

Only Lord Bufford showed evidence that he did not trust Oliver with his wife, gripping Lady Bufford's arm tightly in a proprietary manner and smiling humourlessly, as if he had achieved a great victory over Oliver.

The introductions were no less irritating when they greeted the cast from the Limelight Theatre. Arabella had been pleased when her father had relented and agreed to hold the party on a Sunday which meant the cast were able to attend. But now she was having a small regret about making such a demand. It was obvious that some of the actresses had met Oliver before, but they were respectful enough to not make obvious overtures towards him. Well, not in front of Arabella, anyway.

But why should she be surprised? After all, weren't the women's reactions what she had already come to expect? Hadn't their first encounter been one where he was being pursued by the angry husband of one of his mistresses? And hadn't a woman blatantly slipped him a note while they were dining together at the Savoy? An invitation which she very much doubted had been one to take tea with a group of maiden aunts.

No, nothing about the women's reactions should come as a surprise to her. But that didn't mean it wasn't annoying.

But there was one person who was thoroughly enjoying the party. Throughout the introductions Oliver's mother had smiled with unabashed joy. She was obviously pleased that her son was to marry. With a stab of guilt Arabella was shamed that she, too, was now deceiving this kind, trusting woman.

Once the introductions were over Oliver took two glasses of champagne off the tray of a passing footman, handed one to Arabella and they walked slowly around the party.

'Your mother is lovely, Oliver. Not at all what I expected,' Arabella said.

'You probably expected someone who was worn down from years of misery living with my father, did you not?'

'Mmm.' That was the politest response Arabella

could give. That was exactly what she had expected. Exactly the effect being married to a rake would have on his wife. Exactly the reason why she would never consider a marriage to such a man.

'My mother managed to stay sweet, despite being married to my father. I believe it's because on their honeymoon she caught him in a compromising position with a young maid who worked in the Italian hotel in which they were staying. My mother was naturally distraught and my father managed to appease her by vowing she would never catch him with another woman again. And he stayed true to his vow.'

Arabella stopped walking and stared up at him. 'But I thought…'

'He stayed true to his vow that she would never catch him doing it again. And she didn't. He never vowed that he would remain faithful to her. And the trusting woman that my mother is, she thought her husband remained faithful to her from that day onwards.'

Arabella shook her head. 'But didn't she hear any of the rumours?'

'It helps that she rarely leaves the county, can't abide London and prefers the company of local people rather than society. My father was also a master at keeping rumours from her. Then as I grew into adulthood, I also did everything I could to protect her. Between us, we managed to stop any rumours from reaching her and to save my mother from a great deal of heartache.'

They resumed their slow stroll. Arabella was unsure whether that was a good or a bad thing. It meant he was kind to his mother, a good thing. But it also meant he was well experienced in keeping women in the dark. He was a master of deception. A very bad thing.

A friend of Oliver's joined them, and Arabella made her excuses so she could join Rosie and her new husband.

She walked across the lawn, wishing this party would finish so she could return to London, back to her life, away from all this emotional confusion. Her progress was halted when Lady Bufford suddenly accosted her. Arabella looked down at the fingers tightly clasping her upper arm, then back up at the woman, waiting for an explanation.

Lady Bufford sent her a false smile that was close to a sneer. 'So, you're the actress who managed to capture the Duke of Somerfeld.' The grip on Arabella's arm tightened. 'I wonder what you were able to do for him that no other woman before you has? It must have been quite something, but do you think it will be enough to keep him satisfied?'

The venom in her words sent a cold shudder running up Arabella's spine and she dragged in a deep, steadying breath. 'I don't know what you're talking about, Lady Bufford, but I insist you release my arm. Now.'

Lady Bufford shrugged and released her grip. 'You may think you've caught him, but you certainly won't be able to keep him.' She looked Arabella up and down. 'It won't be long before he tires of the novelty of being with an actress and wants a woman from his own class. Your father might have money, but I hear his father was some sort of miner. I mean, really?

A miner? What was Oliver thinking?' With a harsh laugh the loathsome woman walked away.

Shaken, Arabella took a moment to compose herself, then put on her sunniest fake smile and continued walking towards her friend.

Lady Bufford was wrong and she had wasted her anger on Arabella. She hadn't captured him. The only reason she was engaged to Oliver was because of her father's skulduggery.

No, she meant nothing to Oliver. She might not be like Oliver's mother, who was completely unaware that her husband was repeatedly cheating on her. Arabella knew that the man she was now engaged to was a complete philanderer, a fact he hadn't even tried to hide from her. But it was still humiliating to be engaged to a man who wanted just about every woman who came within range of his charming smile.

Her false smile faltered. And hadn't she been humiliated enough by men in the past?

Arnold Emerson's rejection had left her shaken and shamed. And now it seemed she was once again being humiliated in public.

She increased her pace. But it was almost over now. Her father had his engagement. Soon she would be able to leave Oliver to women like the poisonous, arm-grabbing Lady Bufford. A woman, who, unlike Arabella, was happy to share him with his multitude of mistresses.

Chapter Seven

It was wrong. So wrong. If Oliver needed further proof that Arabella van Haven was a woman he should not be involved with, the expression on her face during her encounter with Violet Bufford would provide it. Her lovely face had been contorted with an array of emotions, including shock, disdain and contempt.

Oliver had tried to intervene, but the encounter had happened so quickly he had been unable to cross the lawn in time. Now Arabella was in the company of her friends, where she was safe. Safe from him and safe from the likes of Violet Bufford.

Whatever the other woman had said had shaken Arabella. Violet had presumably taken delight in telling Arabella about their relationship and the details of their sexual activities.

But all it had ever been for either of them was a fun diversion. If it was jealousy Violet had been expressing, she had no more right to be jealous of him than he did of Lord Bufford or any of Violet's other lovers. And he doubted it would be genuine jealousy, but whatever it was, it was completely unacceptable. It was apparent he was going to have to have a discreet word with Violet so Arabella did not have to suffer such an indignity again.

But one thing the encounter had absolutely confirmed to him was that Arabella was unlike any other woman he knew. If Violet Bufford had confronted anyone else he was involved with, she would have merely ignored it, or laughed it off.

But Arabella had been visibly upset. Despite being an actress, which usually equated with a certain degree of worldliness, she had an air of innocence about her. And a man like he most definitely did not deserve the love of a woman who was so uncorrupted.

Not that Arabella would ever be silly enough to fall in love with him. She was far too sensible and intelligent for that.

But she did deserve to love and to be loved. She deserved a man who appreciated her, who would adore her, who could commit to her and her alone. And it simply was not in him to provide her with those things. She needed to be protected from him, just as his mother had needed to be protected from the knowledge that she was married to a serial adulterer.

He looked over at his mother, deep in conversation with Mr van Haven. To his horror he watched as his mother sent the wealthy American a shy smile and coquettishly rose one shoulder. Was his mother flirting with him? He prayed not. His mother could not fall for that odious man, a man who was using his daughter to further his own ambitions.

It wasn't inconceivable that his mother would marry again. But to a man like Mr van Haven? After marriage to an inveterate philanderer, surely she wouldn't now set her sights on a man who put money above people? It was an unfortunate side to his mother's innocence; she could not see the bad in anyone.

He strode across the lawn, determined to save her from the rapacious Mr van Haven.

'Mother, I think you're monopolising Mr van Haven. Perhaps you'd like to circulate,' he said, ruthlessly interrupting their conversation and taking his mother by the arm. He nodded to the older man as he led his mother away and received a glacial glare back from those cold blue eyes.

'You seem to be enjoying yourself, Mother. What were you discussing with Mr van Haven?' Not anything romantic, he hoped. Not marriage. Please, not marriage.

'Oh, he was very interested in the family's history. He's so happy that his daughter is marrying into a family with such a long and distinguished lineage. And so am I, Oliver,' she smiled at him, her eyes shining with tears of joy. 'You couldn't be marrying a more delightful girl. And fancy her being an actress.' His mother smiled playfully. 'I always knew you'd marry someone unconventional. You've always been such a rascal.' She looked around at the assembled guests, still smiling. 'Having these acting people here is causing such a stir.' She giggled quietly. 'We're becoming quite the bohemians, aren't we?' She turned back to Oliver. 'But she really is a beauty and I'm so pleased that you're marrying her. Your dear father would have been delighted by your choice, I'm sure. He was never a snob and he did admire actresses so much.'

Oliver cringed inside. There was no denying how much his father had admired actresses.

'You're right, Mother, she is a beauty,' he said, looking over at Arabella, still talking to her friends the Duke and Duchess of Knightsbrook. She turned and looked at him. When their eyes met, she blushed slightly and quickly turned back to her conversation.

Oliver exhaled loudly. Even this engagement party was more than Arabella should be subjected to. She should not have had to meet Violet Bufford, but her father had invited Lord Bufford so there was not much he could do.

A gong boomed out loudly above the sound of the chattering guests, causing every head to turn in the direction of Somerfeld Manor's entrance steps, where Mr van Haven was standing, his glass raised.

'Ladies and gentlemen, I'd like to propose a toast,' he shouted out. 'Arabella, Oliver, if you would please join me.'

Oliver looked over at Arabella and saw her take a deep breath, as if to brace herself for the ordeal ahead. Excusing himself from his mother, he walked across the lawn and offered his arm to Arabella. 'Don't worry. This will soon be over,' he whispered in her ear.

Like a couple heading up the steps to the gallows, they climbed the stairs and took their place beside Mr van Haven. Oliver sent Arabella a reassuring smile and took her trembling hand in his, trying to still her obvious nerves. She smiled back at him, but even her acting abilities couldn't stop the smile from quivering.

Her beaming father raised his glass higher. 'I'm pleased you have all been able to join us today here at Somerfeld Manor to celebrate the engagement of my daughter, Arabella, to Oliver Huntsbury, the Fifth Duke of Somerfeld. So please, raise your glasses to Arabella and Oliver, the Duke and future Duchess of Somerfeld.'

A sea of glasses raised in front of them. 'Arabella and Oliver,' the guests cried out joyously.

'But I'd also like to make an announcement to the cast and crew of the Limelight Theatre.'

Oliver felt Arabella tense beside him. He rubbed his thumb across the back of her hand to offer reassurance, but he could see the growing strain on her face from maintaining that false smile.

'I intend to make a sizeable contribution to the theatre.'

A murmur of surprise and excitement rippled through the guests.

'It can go to modernising your facilities, renovating the building, buying props, increasing the wages of all the cast and crew and it can provide all the necessary advertising to make your next production a success. Such improvements will increase patronage and make the theatre much more profitable. This is all part of my engagement present to my daughter.'

'Engagement present? Engagement ransom would be more accurate,' Arabella murmured so only Oliver would hear.

Enthusiastic clapping erupted from the cast and crew. They had no idea what a sacrifice Arabella was making so the theatre could survive. But Oliver did and it only increased his admiration for the young woman standing beside him.

'Three cheers for Mr van Haven,' one shouted,

followed by a resounding chorus of hip-hip-hurrahs, and the waving in the air of many hats.

Even Oliver's friends were getting caught up in the excitement, smiling and clapping approvingly.

Eventually Mr van Haven waved his hands, palms downwards, to bring an end to the rapturous applause. 'And after discussions with Oliver's mother, the Dowager Duchess, I have one more piece of good news to share with you.'

It was now Oliver's turn to become tense, for his false smile to become strained. He wasn't going to announce his engagement to Oliver's mother. Was he? Such a thing could not happen so quickly. Could it?

'The Dowager Duchess has recently shared some delightful information with me.' Mr van Haven turned to Oliver and smiled victoriously. Oliver narrowed his eyes and glared back at Mr van Haven, letting him know that an engagement to his mother would be a step too far. It was something he would never countenance. He would do everything in his power to protect his mother from that grasping, despicable social climber.

'I had been under the impression that the Duke would lose his title if he married before the age of thirty-five. It seems that my future son-in-law was mistaken.' Mr van Haven's victorious smile became a satisfied smirk. 'Personally, I would like to see the happy couple married off right here and now, but it seems I must abide by tradition. The banns will be read in the local church, and in four weeks' time my daughter and the Duke will be married. The Dowager Duchess has kindly consented to hosting the wedding at this magnificent estate, so I'd like to invite you all to return four Sundays from today to join the celebrations.'

The already excited crowd erupted into even louder cheers of enthusiasm. More hats were thrown in the air and a few couples were even dancing a jig. Everyone was excited by this wonderful announcement. Everyone, that is, except the future bride and groom.

Her father had won after all. How could Arabella have ever thought that he wouldn't? She should have known he'd have an ace up his sleeve. Didn't he always?

And now she was to be married. Married to a man who didn't want her. A man who no woman in her right mind would want to be married to.

But what choice did she have? Looking out at the jubilant crowd, she knew she could never disappoint her colleagues and tell them that there would be no wedding, that there would be no money for the theatre, that their jobs and their futures were not secure. She could not be so cruel as to take away from them something that had secured their futures, even if it meant destroying her own.

She looked at Oliver, his face as crestfallen as her own. Obviously, the thought of marriage to her was filling him with the same sense of foreboding.

But he was not trapped the way she was. He had choices. There was nothing to stop him from calling off this engagement, from refusing to get married. The cast and crew of the Limelight Theatre meant nothing to him. He was safe now from Lord Buford's ruffians. He could walk away from this ridiculous proposal.

He smiled down at her and gave her hand a gentle squeeze. 'Don't worry, Arabella. Even if we do have to tie the knot, our marriage will be as false as our engagement. You have nothing to fear.'

She could not return his smile. It was easy for him to say there was nothing to fear. He was a man. He wouldn't be bound by the laws of the land that gave few rights to a married woman. When a woman married, she became essentially a man's property. While he had said he cared not a bit if she appeared on the stage, once they were married there would be nothing to stop him from changing his mind and insist she give up the life she loved. She did not want to give that power to any man and certainly not to this man she had only just met. No, there were many reasons for her to fear being married to Oliver Huntsbury.

The greatest fear being that, for her, she would actually want more from Oliver than he was prepared to give. She pulled her hand from his grasp. Having his hand touching hers was doing nothing to calm her agitation. No, she needed a clear head, so she could think about how she was going to cope with this intolerable situation.

Because it *was* intolerable, intolerable to be forced into a marriage with a man who didn't want her, intolerable to be engaged to a man who gave every appearance of wanting to bed just about every other woman in England.

'We're still not defeated, Arabella,' he whispered in her ear. 'Let's leave the guests to their celebrations and slip away so we can formulate a plan of action to get us out of this situation.'

Slipping away together was not a wise idea. Being

alone with him was never a good idea. But they did need to formulate a plan. She had no idea how they were going to stop this marriage, but perhaps Oliver did. After all, he had come up with the seven-year engagement idea. Perhaps he was capable of doing the impossible and thwarting her father's plans while still saving herself and the theatre. Arabella knew she was grasping at straws, but she nodded and followed him down the steps around to the side of the house, away from the sound of the celebrating crowd.

He took her to a small, white-painted pergola and once again he took her hands gently in his. And once again Arabella fought against her unwanted reactions. Her hands should not be burning. Her heart should not be racing at such a furious pace because he was touching her. And she most definitely should not be wishing he'd do more than just hold her hands.

'I am so sorry, Arabella. I should have told my mother not to say anything. Although, unlike my father, she is a terrible liar, so even if I had informed her of our plans she probably would have told the truth anyway.'

'You have nothing to apologise for.' She looked up into his brown eyes, eyes that were no longer sparkling with mischief, but were gazing down at her apologetically. Arabella was unsure which was harder to bear, that wicked glint in his eye, or this look of concern. Both ignited a strange response deep within her core, causing her to lean towards him as if drawn by an invisible but powerful force.

She told herself to stand up straight. 'None of this is your fault. It's all my father's fault. He has made it impossible for me to get out of this marriage without threatening the jobs of people I care about, but that shouldn't affect you. You don't have to go through with this.'

He stared at her for a moment, then slowly shook his head. 'I don't want to be the cause of your friends losing their livelihoods. They've done nothing wrong, so why should they suffer?'

She smiled at him. He cared about people he didn't know. He cared about his mother and had protected her from the pain of being married to a reprobate. Despite the way he lived his life, there was definitely a lot of good in Oliver Huntsbury.

He smiled back and she wished he hadn't. Not when it drew her gaze to his soft, sensual lips. Lips that had once kissed her. She bit the edge of her bottom lip and, with as much nonchalance as she could muster, she forced her eyes to move from his lips to his eyes. But that was no better. His warm dark eyes glittered, like sparkling black onyx, accentuating their devilish quality, causing her cheeks to erupt with heat and a tingling sensation to radiate out from her lips and race around her body.

She looked down at the ground. 'That's very thoughtful of you,' she said, her voice barely a whisper. She swallowed and slowly raised her gaze. 'It's very good of you to care about my colleagues,' she repeated in a more assertive voice. 'But it doesn't solve our problem. If we don't get married, my father will withdraw his money and the theatre and all the cast and crew will soon be ruined. But we don't want to get married, do we?'

He shook his head. Then that delicious smile grew wider. 'So, I'll make them a better offer.'

'You'll what?' she asked as he continued to smile that glorious smile.

'My money is just as good as your father's. There's nothing to stop me from offering the theatre whatever your father has offered them and more. Then your friends will be safe. You won't have to get married. We can tell your father we still plan to wed, but that we want a long, long engagement for propriety's sake. You'll be safe for a while yet from his matchmaking.'

Arabella's heart leapt. He had done it. He had done the impossible. He had found a way out of their dilemma. 'Oh, Oliver, that's a wonderful idea. You're so clever.' In her excitement she threw her arms round his neck.

His hands slid to her waist and he laughed. 'I never realised that one day a woman would become ecstatic because I promised I wouldn't marry her.'

'Oh, but that is the kindest thing you could do.'

He looked down at her, his laughter dying away. His dark brown eyes grew intense, staring into hers. As if mesmerised, she felt incapable of looking away. As she continued to gaze into the deep, fathomless depths a shiver rippled through her body. His hands were still on her waist, holding her firmly. His touch burned into her, through the fabric of her gown, into her skin, making it tingle with awareness. Her heart beating so hard she could feel it hammering against her chest, she knew she was incapable of breaking from him, did not want to break from his touch. Slowly, she moved her hands up his neck, her fingers curling through his thick blond hair. Parting her lips, she rose on her toes, moved her body closer to his, needing to feel the touch of his chest against hers, desperate to feel his arms close tightly around her. As if under the command of a puppet master, she pressed herself against him, rose even higher on her toes and tilted her head until her lips gently touched his.

And then he was kissing her.

Oh, this man definitely knew how to kiss! She had repeatedly dreamt of him kissing her again since the first night they'd met and now her dream was coming true. She parted her lips wider, her tongue lightly stroking his bottom lip, loving the masculine taste of him, the feel of his skilled mouth on hers.

He groaned slightly and pulled her in closer, his arms encasing her, holding her firmly. As if she was in one of her fervid dreams, she felt his tongue entering her mouth, tasting, probing, possessing her. She was hardly aware of what she was doing. All she knew was that she wanted this, wanted it with every inch of her aching body.

Like a starving man who had been invited to a feast, he deepened the kiss, pulling her in even closer. His powerful chest was now hard up against her breasts, breasts that were swollen with desire. Without thought she rubbed herself against him, desperately needing to be touched by him, to be desired by him, to be caressed by him.

As if following her unspoken command, he ran his hands down the back of her body, cupping her buttocks. His touch on so intimate a place released a tempest of need within her that was both exciting and frightening. Oh, yes, she wanted this man, wanted to experience every sensual pleasure he could give her. She arched her back, her buttocks moving sensually under his hands, letting him know how much she needed him, how much she had to have him, how desperate she was for him to relieve the fiery need burning within her.

'Marking the happy occasion, are we?' She heard a voice behind her, as if coming from a distant place.

He broke from her and she fell forward against him, her head tilted, her throbbing lips still desperate for his kisses.

'I'm pleased to see you two getting on so well. But you should leave all this until the wedding night, you know.'

Her father's voice invaded her foggy consciousness and she jumped back from Oliver as if from a raging inferno that was threatening to engulf her.

'Father? What are you...why are you...?'

'It looks like I'm saving you from giving yourself to this man before he's even sealed the deal and put a ring on your finger.'

He took hold of Arabella's arm and forcefully pulled her away. Oliver stepped towards her father, his eyes blazing with fury. But a fight between Oliver and her father would serve no purpose. Arabella had acted like a fool. Her kiss had revealed to Oliver exactly how much she desired his touch, something she had fought so hard to conceal. This whole incident had been embarrassing enough, without them fighting over her honour. An honour she had been more than happy to surrender to a man who was a master at the art of seduction.

She shook her head and placed her hand in the middle of Oliver's chest to halt his progress. 'It's all right,' she murmured, her voice cracking.

He continued to glare at her father but halted his progress and unclasped his clenched fists.

What had come over her? She was not going to marry Oliver Huntsbury. And she most definitely did not want to become one of his many mistresses, even if he *was* capable of kissing her into oblivion. This was all her fault. She should never have let her guard down and kissed him in the first place.

For once she had to admit her father's interference was all for the best. If he hadn't come along, who knew what might have happened. She might have given herself to him, just as countless other women had done before her and no doubt countless other women would do in the future.

Without another word to Oliver she turned her back on him and allowed her father to escort her back to the party, for once pretending to be the dutiful daughter she most certainly was not.

Oliver watched Arabella and her father walk away through narrowed eyes. 'Leave it for the wedding night,' her father had said. But there would be no wedding night. That meant he would never get to explore her tempting body, never get to fully taste what she had to offer. And if that kiss was anything to judge by it would be spectacular. She had kissed him with such passion, such urgency, such need. And the effect it had on him was devastating.

He had long ago lost count of the number of women he had kissed, the number of women he had bedded. He was all but blasé about kissing yet another woman. But Arabella, she was different. He didn't know what it was, but there was something special about her. It wasn't just her pretty face—he had kissed plenty of pretty women before—nor was it her gorgeous body, as tempting as it was. It couldn't be her innocence. He had always shied away from virtuous virgins, seeing them as nothing but trouble. And *he* most definitely would be trouble for *them*. While the idea of deflowering a virgin appealed to some men, it most definitely did not appeal to him.

Perhaps it was her passion. A passion that was also evident in her determination to succeed as an actress, to succeed against her father's wishes, despite the odds that were stacked against her. Perhaps it was that which made her so appealing to him. Or was it that she was utterly unimpressed by his title? For so many women his title was like a red rag to a bull. The thought of being the next Duchess of Somerfeld had seen many a young debutante throw herself in his path. But Arabella would rather have a minor acting role in a play at a rundown theatre than all the social prestige that came with being a duchess. Perhaps that's what he found so attractive. That and her pretty face, gorgeous body and very kissable lips, of course.

With that riddle still unsolved he headed back to the party. As the joyous crowd surrounded him, he could not get the conundrum of Arabella van Haven out of his mind. But the mystery would have to remain unsolved. They would not be marrying. He would make sure of that. He most certainly had no interest in marriage to anyone. She had no interest in marriage to him. So, he would make sure he found a way to halt this wedding.

Her father had said leave it till the wedding night and it was most definitely a shame that there would be no wedding night. But it could not be. He was not so much of a cad that he would subject such a lovely woman to the horror of being married to him just because he wanted to fully sample all that her passionate nature and beautiful body had to offer.

He looked over to where Arabella was talking to a group of excited actors, a fake smile once again on her lips, those plump red lips that had just moments ago been pressed up hard against his.

He sighed deeply. It was most certainly a shame that he would not get to experience the pleasure of their wedding night. And, of course, he would never take a woman like Arabella as his mistress. It was extremely tempting, but it was out of the question. He might not have much of a code when it came to women, but one rule he did abide by was that no one got hurt. And Arabella was a woman who could so easily get hurt.

He took a glass of champagne offered to him by a footman. As there would be no wedding, and hence no wedding night, the only thing left for him to do was to try to enjoy his own engagement party.

Chapter Eight

'What do you mean, you sold the business?'

'Exactly that. I've sold the lot. The entire building, which includes the theatre, the props and costumes, along with rights to the plays. Everything. I was made an offer I couldn't possibly refuse.'

Oliver glared down at the theatre owner seated behind his messy desk. The *former* owner of the Limelight Theatre. 'And dare I ask who bought it?' It was a question to which Oliver already knew the answer.

'Mr van Haven bought it.' The owner leaned back in his squeaking chair, put his hands behind his head and smiled. 'He offered me a ridiculous amount of money. He's closed the theatre for renovations, laid off the staff on full pay and pouring money into the place as if it's a bottomless pit. I must say I was a bit taken aback. I would have thought a man like Mr van Haven would have more financial sense than to spend such money on a third-rate theatre like this.' He waved his arms in the air as if to encompass the entire Limelight Theatre, the shabby office, the run-down auditorium and the severely neglected backstage area. 'But there you go. He can't be as clever or as good a businessman as people say he is. It looks as though when it comes to the theatre, he doesn't know what he's doing, but I made a tidy profit, which is all that really matters.'

Oliver shook his head in dismay. The theatre owner was wrong. Mr van Haven knew exactly what he was doing. He had spent that money to make sure his daughter was compliant with his plans to marry her off to a man with a title. To Mr van Haven it would be money well spent. Once again, the older man had outsmarted them and thwarted Oliver's plan.

'Well, at least his daughter will be happy that the theatre is doing well out of her father's money.' Oliver was desperate to see the bright side of this dismal situation. It had to be some consolation that the theatre would now be a success. He had to have some good news to take back to Arabella. Perhaps telling her that the theatre was to be greatly improved by her father might be the small silver lining to an otherwise very black cloud.

'His daughter? Why?' the former owner said, standing up and placing a wooden crate on his desk so he could pack up his belongings.

'Arabella van Haven. She's an actress here at the theatre.'

'She used to be.'

Oliver grabbed the man's arms and pulled him across the desk, halting his packing. 'What are you saying? What do you mean, used to be?'

The former owner stared back at him with wide eyes, a pile of old theatre programmes dropping from his hands. 'Just that—she used to be an actress here.

Apparently, her father told the director to find someone to replace her. He said he didn't want to see Arabella van Haven's name on the bill ever again.'

Oliver froze, his face still inches from the other man's, then sunk down into a chair. With his head in his hands he released a growl of frustration. This was getting worse and worse. Not only would he have to tell Arabella that his plan to pay the theatre so he could stop their marriage had failed, but she was now also out of a job. She would be crushed. All her dreams would be shattered. This could not happen. He had to think of something to stop this ridiculous marriage and save Arabella's job. But what? That was a question to which Oliver had no answer.

He had agreed to meet Arabella at Hyde Park to tell her the good news. When he had set off to the theatre this morning, he had been full of confidence, certain that he would make everything right. All he had to do was offer the owner a better deal, give him more money than Mr van Haven. He had even considered buying the theatre himself. Then it would be safe. All Arabella's colleagues would keep their jobs and Arabella would be saved from the terrible fate of having to marry him.

Instead, the only bit of good news he could give her was the theatre was indeed saved and everyone's job was safe. Everyone's, that is, except hers.

As he walked towards their agreed meeting place by the Serpentine, he felt like a man going to his execution. And not just because he was now committed to marrying in less than a month's time, but because he was going to have to disappoint Arabella on two counts. Her father could still hold the threat of destroying the theatre over her head and her dream of becoming an actress was now in tatters.

She was sitting on a bench staring out over the lake, looking as enchanting as she did on that first night when they met. Dressed in a blue-striped dress, with a jaunty straw hat sporting a blue ribbon on her ornately styled black hair and protecting herself from the warm sunshine with a cream-coloured lacy parasol, she was as pretty as a picture.

He paused to watch her and enjoy the sight before he had to destroy any sense of hope she might be feeling. She was staring straight ahead with unseeing eyes, not taking in the small boy in front of her, floating his ornate toy sailing ship on the placid water, or the little girl jumping around with an excited pug dog.

Oliver inhaled deeply to give himself courage and strode towards her in a manner more confident than he felt. The young lady's maid chaperoning her stood up as he approached and, as if by arrangement, she wandered off to give them some privacy.

Arabella looked up and sent him an expectant smile, then registered his stern look and her smile faded. 'It's bad news, isn't it? What has he done now?' Her shaking hands folded up the parasol and she gripped the wooden handle tightly.

He sat down beside her, his heart in his mouth. 'Your father has bought the theatre,' he stated bluntly, not knowing any way to soften the blow.

She released an annoyed sigh. 'I should have known he'd do something like that. He's got a reputation for anticipating what his business rivals will do and I guess that's what we are now, his business rivals.'

They both looked out at the lake and Oliver steeled himself to impart the next bit of bad news. 'I'm afraid that's not all he's done.'

Her body tensed beside him and he heard a sharp intake of breath. 'What else could he do? He's got everything he wants now.'

'I'm afraid he's told the director that you can't work at the theatre any more.'

He had expected an immediate response: tears, foot stamping, angry words. But she continued to stare out at the lake, her body rigid as she silently seethed. 'Now he has gone too far,' she eventually said, through clenched teeth. 'He's already won, so why does he have to punish me even further?'

Pain gripped Oliver in the middle of his chest. Somehow, this all felt like his fault. Perhaps if he hadn't crashed into her room that night, if he hadn't taken her in his arms and kissed her, none of this might have happened. In some ways it was indeed his fault. And it was up to him to make it right. 'Please, Arabella, don't upset yourself. He might have stopped you acting at the Limelight, but he can't stop you acting altogether. You got the job there without him knowing, you can use your wits to find another job somewhere else. There are other theatres in London. He can't buy them all. It will be all right. I'll make sure it is.'

He didn't know how he would do that, but he would try. He couldn't bear to see her so unhappy, couldn't bear to see her dreams shattered.

'You're very kind, but this is not your problem.'

She turned to face him and he could see unshed tears in her eyes. 'I've said it before and I still mean it. You don't have to marry me. You don't have to get caught up in my father's scheming. He said he'd sue you for breach of promise, but he'd never do that, because the scandal might ruin his chances of marrying me off to someone else.'

Oliver shrugged. She was wrong. He didn't have a choice. If he didn't go through with this marriage, he would leave Arabella in a worse position than she already was. If they didn't marry, her father would withdraw all his funds from the theatre and it would be forced to close. And it was obvious that would not stop her father. He would eventually find some other titled man for her to marry and it might be one who did not respect and admire her the way Oliver was coming to, more and more.

'I've said I'd go through with it and, even though I've got too many faults to list, I'm always true to my word. Unless we can think of something your father hasn't already anticipated within the next four weeks, it looks as though we're about to become newlyweds.'

She gave a resigned shrug of her slim shoulders and sighed loudly. 'Thank you. It's very kind of you to go to all this trouble.'

Oliver swallowed a sudden ironic laugh. Many women had pursued him over the years, desperate to become the next Duchess of Somerfeld. They had all chosen to ignore the fact that they would be marrying a man incapable of committing to one woman. All they could see was a title, nothing else. He had dodged a bullet many times, saving himself and many a young woman from that terrible fate. Now he was to marry someone who mistakenly thought he was a kind man, that he was kind because he was trying his best to save her from such a marriage. He could almost see the funny side of the situation. Almost.

'Hopefully it won't come to that,' he said. 'We've still got a month to think of a way out of this situation.'

She shrugged again and slowly shook her head. 'I've never known anyone to get the better of my father and he's been up against equally ruthless businessmen, ambitious politicians and bankers who are just as much in love with money as him, and he's thwarted them all. I don't think we stand much of a chance.'

They sighed simultaneously and looked out at the lake.

'I suppose being married to one another won't be that bad.' Oliver gave her an apologetic smile.

'No, I suppose there are worse things that happen to people. And I guess it could be much worse. He could be marrying me off to someone like Lord Bufford.'

He shuddered at the thought of Arabella married to a man like that and took heart from the fact that she considered him a better catch than a sixty-year-old man with a deeply florid complexion, bushy grey eyebrows, an overly waxed walrus moustache, a bulbous nose and a decidedly aggressive and irritating disposition.

Yet Violet Bufford had been more than happy to marry him. She, and her family had ignored Lord Bufford's flaws because it meant moving up the social hierarchy. But Arabella was not like that. She did not want to marry a title. Instead one was being thrust upon her.

'But I promise you, once we're married, we can part company,' he said, in his most reassuring voice. 'I'll make no further demands on you.'

Her smile was sad and suggested she didn't believe him. And why *should* she believe him? After all, all she really knew of him was that he was the sort of man who crashed into strange women's dressing rooms, grabbed them and kissed them. A man who had to run from irate husbands. A man with a scandalous reputation.

'And if nothing else, you will at least be safe from your father, Arabella.' He couldn't offer her much, but at least he could offer her that. 'After all, you'll be my wife. You'll be under my care, not your father's. He won't be able to stop you from doing anything, ever again. And I promise you your freedom.'

Arabella breathed in deeply, then exhaled slowly. 'It is so unfair,' she said, emphasising every word. 'I always have to be under someone's care, my father, my husband and, under normal circumstances, it would eventually be my son, just the way your mother is under your authority. It's simply not fair.'

Oliver shrugged. 'I can't agree more. And often women are under the authority of men less competent than themselves, but that, unfortunately, is the way of the world.'

'But it shouldn't be.'

'No, it shouldn't be.'

Once again Oliver felt as if that, too, was his fault. But he hadn't made the world the way it was. All he could do was ensure that one woman, Arabella, his future wife, was free to live her life the way she wanted to, without the interference of any man, including her husband.

'And it's not fair to you either. You should be allowed to marry whomever you want, not be manipulated into marriage by my father.' She bit the edge of her lip. 'Is there anyone you really do want to marry?'

Oliver shook his head and smiled. 'No, there never has been and there never will be.'

She turned slightly on the bench and looked at him, her head tilted in question. 'But you're a duke. Don't all dukes have to marry, whether they want to or not, so they can produce the heir and the spare and keep the line going?'

Oliver laughed at her misplaced concern. 'I suppose the ones who care about such things do, but there's other members of my family who'll more than happily take up the title of Duke when I kick the bucket. And I think the world would be a better place if I didn't procreate.'

His smile died and he turned to face her. 'But what about you, Arabella? Don't you want children?' He held his breath while he waited for her answer. No matter what her response was, it was an added complication and one he hadn't considered.

Her gaze dropped and she stared at her hands, clenched tightly on her lap. 'I don't want to think about that now,' she said, her voice barely a whisper. 'We've only four weeks to think of a way out of this, that's what we should be concentrating on.'

Four weeks. That's all they had to think their way out of this impossible situation. Arabella looked back out over the calm water of the Serpentine and contemplated how they were going to achieve the impossible.

'So, do you have any more thoughts on what we can do to stop this marriage?'

He shook his head. 'I'm sorry, Arabella, I'm out of ideas at the present.'

Then it truly looked as though her father was going to win. Didn't he always?

The one time she had thought she had won a victory over her father was when she had insisted that he allow Rosie to live with them after Rosie's mother died. At the time Arabella had thrown a temper tantrum, had threatened to run away, until her father relented. She had thought she had won a victory. Now she suspected her father had merely decided that it would be to his advantage to make Rosie his ward. It gave Arabella a friend, someone to play with and entertain her when he was away from home pursuing his latest business venture. So, to some extent Rosie had become just another possession that he had given to his daughter. It had not been her victory. If her father hadn't seen all the advantages of having a ward, he would have made Rosie leave, despite the devastation it would have caused to an innocent young girl.

And Arabella was no different. She, too, was just a possession.

It was a terrible thing to think, but that was all she had ever been to her father. And now she was going to have to repay him for all the money he had spent on her over the years by giving him what he wanted, an entry to the British aristocracy. He didn't care who she married, whether the man loved her or not was of no concern, whether he was a scoundrel or a good man did not matter, as long as he had a title.

Was it even worth fighting a man who always won? 'Perhaps we should just go through with it,' she said, her voice resigned. 'After all, it won't be a real marriage. I wouldn't interfere with the way you live your life. My father will get his victory and we'll both be free to do as we please.'

It was most definitely not what Arabella wanted. She had no immediate plans for marriage, but when it happened, she had expected to be married to a man she loved, a kindred spirit who wanted to pursue the same dreams as herself. But then, wasn't that what she thought Arnold Emerson was? And hadn't she been wrong about him? Hadn't she completely misjudged the man she'd once thought she loved?

His love had been as phoney as her marriage would be. But with Oliver at least there would be no pretence. He didn't love her and he had no intention of pretending he did. And it could be much worse. She could be marrying someone who did not respect her work as an actress and would forbid her from continuing her life on the stage.

She would just have to resign herself to being married to a man who had countless lovers.

And she would just have to keep that thought foremost in her mind at all times if she was to avoid humiliating herself.

She had forgotten it when she had shamelessly thrown her arms around his neck at the engagement party and kissed him with an intensity that had surprised and shocked her.

And even this morning she had almost forgotten

who he was and what he was like. She had chosen her gown with such care and had even been tempted to apply a touch of rouge and lipstick, just to enhance her appearance. She applied make-up every time she appeared on stage, but never before today had she even considered doing something as risqué as wearing it in public.

It had all been so ridiculous. She should not be trying to make herself appear attractive to him. After all, she did not want to attract him. Did she?

No, of course she didn't. These affectations were going to have to be kept well under control if this marriage of convenience was to work. If her marriage was to be a success, she would need to ensure she had no feelings for her husband and that any physical attraction she felt towards him was squashed down so small that she was able to ignore it.

She glanced over at her husband-to-be. Except, squashing her feelings of attraction for him was going to be no small task. While she was pleased he wasn't an old duffer like Lord Bufford, being married to a man as handsome as Oliver Huntsbury was going to have its own complications. He was undeniably the most attractive man she had ever met and she had met some handsome men working in the theatre. But it wasn't just his stunning good looks that caused her to so easily forget her resolve. Nor was it just his easy, confident manner. There was something special about him. It was a quality that leading men strove hard to capture. It was a magnetism that caused every eye to turn in his direction and for women, even sensible ones like herself, to suddenly start preening themselves and acting in a ridiculously coquettish manner.

Yes, his masculine appeal was undeniable. But she was most certainly not the first woman to feel its attraction and she would not be the last. If she was to deny its pull, she had to keep reminding herself of Lady Bufford, Lucy Baker and all his other *very good friends*. She could not allow herself to be lured in, just because he was handsome. It did not matter what effect his kisses had on her. It did not matter that she could hardly remember who she was, where she was and why she was doing what she knew she shouldn't.

It was not going to be easy, but this unwanted marriage would only work if she kept her distance from Oliver, the reprobate Duke of Somerfeld.

Chapter Nine

A wedding day should be the happiest day of a woman's life. Isn't that what everybody said? But when you're being married against your will to a man who has been tricked into becoming your husband, happiness doesn't tend to be an emotion in great abundance.

A solemn Arabella stared at her reflection in the ornate mirror. It was like déjà vu. Just four weeks ago she was sitting in exactly the same place, staring at an equally sad reflection. The only difference was that time she was facing an engagement party. Today it was a wedding. And after today she would be a married woman.

'Cheer up, girls,' Arabella said with false enthusiasm, as an unusually gloomy Nellie dressed her hair, watched on by an equally despondent Rosie. 'It could be worse. I really could be going to my execution, instead of just becoming a bride.'

Her two friends sent her reassuring smiles.

'You're right,' Rosie agreed. 'It could be much worse. You could be marrying a man who wouldn't let you act on the stage.'

'And he could have bad breath and be desperate for an heir,' Nellie added. 'One thing about the Duke, he's definitely easy on the eye.'

Arabella smiled. There were some consolations, she supposed.

Her hair completed, Nellie tightened the laces of her corset, helped her into her silk petticoat and removed the wedding gown from the wardrobe. Using a pattern from a French fashion house and hand-embroidered ivory material, the London dressmaker had created an exquisite bridal gown. Despite her reluctance to marry, she experienced a slight thrill of excitement as Nellie helped her into the flowing folds of white satin. She did a small twirl in front of the mirror and watched the soft fabric of the long train swirl gently around her ankles. The gown was the epitome of elegance and romance even if today's wedding was nothing more than a business transaction.

Nellie fastened the line of small pearl-coloured buttons at the back of Arabella's gown, placed the gossamer-fine veil carefully on her head and secured it in place with a simple garland of orange blossoms. She removed a silver and diamond necklace from the jewellery box and placed it around Arabella's neck.

At the sight of the necklace Arabella bit her trembling lip. It had belonged to her mother, a gift from her father when they got married. Arabella couldn't help but wonder what her mother would have thought of this hastily arranged marriage. Would she have approved? Or would she have forbidden it and insisted that her daughter marry for love, not for social advancement?

Arabella would never know, but she could only

hope that her mother would have been a loving parent who wanted the best for her daughter.

As she buttoned up her lacy white gloves she looked at her sad reflection and sighed. The happiest day of her life? Not in the slightest.

'Well, I suppose we should get this over and done with,' she said to her friends. Rosie was dressed as her maid of honour and was wearing a flattering cream gown with a blue waistband. Unlike Arabella, marriage suited Rosie and every time she mentioned her husband her voice softened and her face lit up with pleasure. That's what a marriage should be like. It should be a love match. It shouldn't be about titles and improving one's social status.

The two girls made their way down the grand staircase of Somerfeld Manor, followed by Nellie, who was still fussing about the gown and straightening out the train.

Arabella took a few minutes to compose herself before walking out of the front entrance.

Her father was waiting for her, standing beside an open carriage decorated with garlands of flowers. The liveried footman moved forward. He offered his hand to help Arabella and Rosie into the carriage that would take them to the local church where the supposedly happy event would take place.

Her smiling father climbed in beside them. Dressed in a formal grey morning suit, a white orchid in his buttonhole, she had never seen him look more pleased with himself. This wedding might not be the happiest day of Arabella's life, but it was evidently the happiest day of her father's.

He had stopped her from marrying Arnold Emerson, the man she'd thought she loved, because he wasn't going to waste a potential asset on a man who would bring neither money nor prestige into the family.

Arnold had not loved her and had been easily bought off. Her father had inadvertently saved her from making a match that would have been a disaster. But that had not been his reason for offering Arnold money so he would withdraw his affections. If Arnold had possessed a fortune, or better still a title, they would now be wed.

And now her father had found someone with both money and a title. So, whether they were in love or not was of no matter to him, her father had what he wanted.

As they rode down the long, oak-lined driveway, the leaves rustled in a slight breeze and the carriage wheels crunched over the gravel. It was another perfectly sunny day. But that was the only thing perfect about this day, the weather.

The closer they got to the church the more Arabella's nerves jangled. She was about to be married. Her life was about to change for ever. She had no idea what it was going to be like to be married to the Duke of Somerfeld. He had promised her freedom, had said that nothing would change for her, but she had known him for such a short time. She knew virtually nothing about him. Nothing, that was, except the rumours she had heard and that did little to still her rampaging nerves.

The temptation to throw herself out of the carriage and make a run for it was becoming all but overwhelming. But where could she run to? Nowhere.

She was in the middle of the Surrey countryside and dressed in clothing that was hardly suitable for fast escapes. And if she knew her father well, and she did, he probably had burly men stationed along the path to drag her kicking and screaming back to the altar.

There was just one possibility left, that Oliver might have even colder feet than she did. Perhaps he had already decided to flee, back to the arms of one of his many mistresses. After all, there was nothing in this marriage for him. He said he didn't break his word, but how was she to know if that was true? He might have kept his word in the past, but he had presumably never been faced with the prospect of marriage before.

She shivered, as if the weather had suddenly turned cold, even though the sun remained shining in the cloudless blue sky.

Would it really be a good or a bad thing if Oliver didn't turn up? It would be good that she wouldn't have to get married, but bad as her father might withdraw his funding for the theatre. It would also be bad to once again endure the humiliation of being jilted, albeit this time by a man she didn't want to marry in the first place.

And all it would do was postpone the inevitable. Her father would find some other hapless member of the aristocracy to marry her off to and he would find some other method of tricking her into walking up the aisle. With a small dejected sigh Arabella knew she just had to accept the inevitable.

No matter how she looked at it, she was doomed. Doomed to become a wife.

The carriage pulled up outside a quaint stone

church, surrounded by happy villagers, all eager to get a view of the bride. No doubt many were wondering what sort of woman had actually captured the notorious rake, Oliver Huntsbury.

Arabella tried, with all her might, to look happy for their sake.

To the sound of an organ playing the wedding march, she entered the church on her father's arm, with Rosie walking behind. The sweet scent of roses from the flowers bedecking the church filled the air as they made their slow funereal walk up the aisle.

The congregation stood in the wooden pews and every head turned in her direction. Some were smiling, some were scowling and many had bemused expressions on their faces, as if they, too, could not believe this was actually happening.

Oliver turned to look at her and Arabella's slow progress momentarily faltered. Her husband-to-be looked magnificent. Dressed in a dove-grey morning suit, with a cream waistcoat and white cravat, he was more sublimely handsome than she remembered. Even from this distance she could see that seductive spark in his eyes. He was smiling with reassurance and Arabella tried to feel reassured. But how could she possibly feel calm when she could feel the blood pumping through her body and the hammering rhythm of her heart was so loud it was almost drowning out the sound of the wedding march?

And tonight would be their wedding night, their first together as man and wife. If Arabella's nerves weren't jittery enough already, reminding herself of that fact was enough to send them into agitated spasms.

She reached the altar and, like the possession she was, her father handed her over to Oliver. He smiled down at her and a frisson of awareness rippled through her. This man was to be her husband. This man with his laughing eyes and his devilish smile was to be her husband. This man, with a seductive charm that made him notorious among actresses and aristocrats alike, was to be her husband. Once again, she wondered whether it wouldn't be better to be forced into a marriage with a man who wasn't so attractive. Then she'd know exactly how to feel about this situation. She wouldn't be standing beside a man who caused her to feel disorientated every time he looked at her. A man whose kisses caused her to respond with a passion she had not thought she was capable of. A man who she knew she should never, ever fall for.

Arabella closed her eyes. She had to keep reminding herself of that fact if she was not to lose all sense of reason. No matter how much Oliver's charm and seductive manners disorientated her, she had to remember her resolve to keep her distance from him. She was not a real wife and she did not want to be one of the many women in his life. She did not want to be like his mother, in love with a man who was incapable of fidelity.

No matter what happened on their wedding night, and every other day and night that followed in their marriage, she would not let herself fall under his spell.

She opened her eyes and looked up at the vicar, dressed in his ornate vestments. Despite her determination to focus and not be distracted by the man standing beside her, she hardly heard a word the vicar said, apart from when he asked if anyone had just cause why this man and this woman could not be joined together in holy matrimony.

Arabella waited for someone, anyone, to say yes, because it was a joke, a farce, that it wasn't holy matrimony, it was a holy mess.

But the congregation remained silent.

She also heard Oliver promising to love and honour her, two things she doubted he would do. And as for *forsaking all others*—well, they had already agreed that would not be happening. But then again, she also promised to obey him in her own wedding vows. Something she had no intention of doing.

The vows completed, the best man held out the wedding ring for Oliver to place on Arabella's finger. Arabella removed her gloves, lifted her left hand and was horrified to see that it was shaking. Oliver gently took hold of it and covered it with both his hands, as if trying to calm her down and allow his strength to flow into her. But the touch of his skin on hers had the opposite effect. A rippling sensation rushed up her arm, causing her heartbeat to increase its furious tempo and her already agitated nerves to strain further until she was close to fainting.

She closed her eyes, took in a series of steadying breaths, then looked up at him and sent him what she hoped was a composed smile. But the tremor at the edges of her lips made a lie of any such pretence to composure.

'It's all right, Arabella,' he murmured quietly. 'Try to see this as a victory over your father. Once you're married you will be a free woman.'

Arabella nodded slightly and tried to smile with stiff lips.

The vicar coughed and sent Oliver a pointed look, reminding him to continue with the service.

Oliver picked up the ring, gazed down at Arabella and smiled. 'With this ring I thee wed, with my body I thee worship and with all my worldly goods I thee endow,' he said as he gently slid the ring up Arabella's finger.

With my body I thee worship.

A blush rushed to Arabella's cheeks. The last thing she wanted to think about right now was Oliver's body and she certainly didn't want to visualise him worshipping her. An image of being held by him, kissed by him, invaded her thoughts. Her cheeks grew hotter. Her heart pounded harder. She had to get her reactions under control. She just had to. She turned to face the vicar, who smiled at her benevolently and proclaimed them man and wife.

It was over. They were now married. Her fate was sealed.

'You may now kiss the bride,' the vicar said. No, it wasn't over. She had one more ordeal to endure.

She looked up at him and could feel her lips trembling. In fear? In anticipation? Arabella was unsure.

Oliver sent her one of those devilish smiles that always seemed to make her body react in the most inappropriate of manners. Although perhaps it was no longer inappropriate to react in such a way, now that he was her husband. Arabella pushed that thought away. He was her husband in name only, so, yes, it was still inappropriate.

He leant down and lightly kissed her on the lips. She closed her eyes. Despite herself she loved the touch of his lips on hers, even if it was just a formality.

She parted her lips slightly, willing him to kiss her more deeply. But unlike herself, he had the sense to remember they were in a public place and his kiss remained light. Or was it because he was being watched by a congregation that included at least one of his mistresses and possibly several more?

The church bells rang out joyously and, as if in a trance, Arabella was led back down the aisle on the arm of her new husband.

A cascade of red rose petals descended on them as they stood in the entrance of the church and the full reality of the situation hit Arabella. She was now married to Oliver Huntsbury. Married until death parted them. No matter what he said about nothing changing, her life had just changed for ever in a fundamental way. She was now a married woman. Nothing would ever be the same again.

Oliver tried to smile as the rose petals danced around them, caught in the light breeze. He was now married, married to Arabella van Haven. A woman he hardly knew. Just one short month ago, he had no intention of marrying anyone, ever. And now he was a married man. He had promised to honour this woman in sickness and in health, for richer and for poorer, and that, at least, he would do. But it was all so much to take in. What sort of marriage would they have? Would they really be able to work out an arrangement that suited them both?

Oliver hardly noticed the many people who shook his hands, slapped him on the back and congratulated him. All he could think was, *I'm now a married man. I've done what I vowed I would never do.*

And he had good reason for making that vow. He knew he was incapable of committing to one woman. He had discovered as a young man that he was exactly like his father. He loved women, but it was all women he loved—it would never be just one woman. And if he couldn't commit to one woman, then he wouldn't ever get married. It was a simple solution that had worked well for him in the past. But now he was married and to the type of woman he never, ever got involved with.

His gaze moved from his young bride to his smiling, happy mother.

He was not letting history completely repeat itself. Unlike his father's marriage to his mother, his bride was under no illusions about the sort of man she had married. He had not deceived his new bride, had never pretended to be someone he wasn't.

He looked back at Arabella, who was being hugged by her best friend. Remembering that she was not his would be so much easier if she didn't look so damn attractive. From the moment he saw her on the stage at the Limelight Theatre he had been entranced by her gentle beauty. Those crystal-blue eyes that sparked with intelligence, that heart-shaped face was undeniably attractive and she had immediately caught his eye. And how could he not be attracted to a woman who was so fiercely independent? She was determined to become a successful actress, to make her own way in the world. She had a father who was fabulously wealthy, who could buy and sell many members of the aristocracy. Yet she wanted nothing from him. She preferred to work in a shabby theatre in a rundown part of London rather than live a life of privilege and idleness. Her single-minded determination was something for which he had immense admiration.

His mother approached him, beaming with happiness. 'Oh, darling, that service was so touching.' She dabbed at her eyes. 'And Arabella makes such a beautiful bride.'

He kissed his mother's cheek and looked over at his bride. She did indeed look beautiful. The white gown suited her so much. It was a shame she was not a real bride, getting married to the man she loved. It was something she would never now experience and for that Oliver felt a deep sense of guilt. She should be marrying for love, to a man who loved her. She deserved that. She did not deserve this forced marriage. She did not deserve to have him in her life. If he hadn't burst into her dressing room chased by a group of thugs, her father might not have felt he could blackmail him into marriage. There was no doubt that her father would not have given up until his daughter was married to a titled man, but if she hadn't been forced to marry him, she might have met a titled man she could love, who could love her. He did indeed have a lot to feel guilty for, a lot to make up to Arabella. And the best way he could do that was to leave her alone, to let her live her life the way she wanted, without his interference.

Chapter Ten

Somerfeld Manor had been transformed for the wedding. Even to Oliver's undiscerning eye he could see that a great deal of effort had gone into making the house festive and inviting. Large bouquets of fragrant flowers decorated the great hall where the wedding breakfast was to be held. And musicians were tuning up in the adjoining ballroom in preparation for the dance that was to take place later that evening.

Tables had been set out for the large party of guests. Crystal sparkled, silver glistened and the tables were strewn with ivy leaves and scented lilac flowers. The house servants, along with an army of extras recruited for the day, were rushing about, attending to every need of the guests.

Oliver escorted Arabella to the head of the table, and, when she had seated herself, the wedding party sat down to the accompaniment of shuffling chairs and the sudden eruption of chatter.

Champagne began to flow immediately and the footmen made sure that glasses were topped up before they had a chance to be emptied. But Oliver took pains to ensure he moderated his drinking. It was essential that he keep himself under complete control. Something which he could tell was not going to be easy to achieve. Not when his new bride was sitting so close to him that he could smell her delightful jasmine perfume. But he knew from past experience that if he wanted to keep his amorous inclinations in check, then imbibing champagne would not help.

While the rest of the wedding party chatted, laughed, drank and ate, the couple at the head of the table exchanged only a few words as they picked at each successive course. Speeches were made, but Oliver hardly heard a word of what was said. He laughed when others laughed, looked solemn when others talked of the sacred importance of the institute of marriage. He even made a speech of his own, saying all the appropriate things about how beautiful his new bride was and how he would do everything he could to make her happy, all of which was true.

But it all happened as if he was watching someone else going through the motions of a wedding. One that had little or nothing to do with him. But then, that was exactly what he and his wife were doing, wasn't it? Going through the motions.

The wedding breakfast finished; he escorted his new wife through to the ballroom.

'It's almost over, Arabella,' he whispered in her ear as the band played and he led her out on to the dance floor for their first waltz together as man and wife.

As he slid his arm round her slim waist she gasped slightly and blushed, as if caught doing something that was forbidden. She placed her hand tentatively on his shoulder, standing well back from him as if she would get burnt if she came too close.

Oliver smiled. They must look a peculiar pair, a couple just married who were reluctant to even touch each other. He pulled her in closer. *Just for appearances' sake.*

They glided round the dance floor and her rigid posture relaxed as her soft curves moulded into his body. Unable to resist, his arm moved further round her small waist, pulling her still closer, until her soft breasts were touching his chest.

He registered the touch of her tight nipples against his chest and forced himself to suppress a growl of pleasure. Oh, what he wouldn't give to feel those lush breasts without that barrier of her clothing. To caress them, to rub his fingers along those hard nipples, to take them in his mouth and nuzzle them until she was screaming out for him.

It seemed his abstinence from champagne was not working and his amorous intentions were becoming painfully clear to him. He could only hope his new wife did not notice.

He loosened his grip on her waist and moved back, to minimise the contact he was having with her, so she would not be able to feel the effect she was having on him. He continued to lead her round the floor. How quickly he could forget his vow to himself when he had her in his arms. But it was a vow he had to abide by. He just had to remember she did not want to be in his arms. She had been caught up in things beyond her control. Under normal circumstances she would not even be dancing with a man like him and certainly not married to him.

She was in an intolerable situation and she needed his reassurance, not his lust.

Only a complete cad would allow himself to forget that. And he hoped he wasn't a *complete* cad.

He coughed lightly to drive out any lingering inappropriate thoughts, looked down into those soft blue eyes and sent her what he hoped was a comforting smile that was completely free of desire.

'Just remember, Arabella, that tomorrow everything will go back to how it was and we can try to pretend this wedding never happened.'

She sighed and tried to smile back. 'Except I'm no longer an actress. I'm just another young society wife. And I'm not even that, not really.'

He shook his head. 'You *are* an actress. And one day you'll be a great actress. You're just between jobs. Resting, isn't that what actors say when they're not working?'

She gave a small, resigned smile as he twirled them around one more time.

'And if it's any consolation, you're now completely free of your father's interference. You can do anything you want. As a married woman you won't need to be chaperoned. You can go anywhere, do anything, see anyone you want.'

A sudden thought hit him like a thunderbolt and he almost halted on the dance floor. What he had said was true. She would be just like all those married women he had taken as his mistresses. They, too, were women who could do anything, go anywhere and see anyone they wanted.

Arabella would indeed be free. Free of her father and also free of him. Just like him she could take a lover if she chose. Bile burned up his throat and his muscles suddenly clenched into tight knots at the thought of Arabella with another man.

Some other man would experience what it was like to make love to her. She would give herself to some other man, a man she actually loved.

But what right had he to object to such an arrangement? If she wanted to take a lover, who was he to stop her? Well, he was her husband, but he had said he wouldn't stop her from doing what she wanted and surely that had to extend to her taking a lover.

It seemed he was a complete cad after all. He could hardly bear the thought of his lovely wife having that amount of freedom. But bear it was exactly what he was going to have to do. He gritted his teeth more tightly. He had promised her freedom, even if that freedom meant she took another man to her bed.

Free. Is that what she was? All Arabella was feeling was confused. But it was good to be in Oliver's arms again, to have him hold her as he glided her gracefully round the ballroom. She could almost imagine that she really was his bride, that he loved her, wanted her. And her traitorous body was reacting as if that was true. It was as if this was where she belonged and it hadn't taken long for her to sink back into his arms, to surrender herself to him as he took the lead for their first dance as man and wife.

But even if her body was being deceived, her mind knew differently.

He didn't want her. He didn't want any woman. Or, rather, he wanted virtually every woman he met, but no woman in particular.

And he was free as well. Free to pursue any woman he wanted. And from what she had heard from the other actresses at the Limelight, his reputation for pursuing, and catching women was even more notorious than his father's.

She had let it slip that this was a marriage of convenience, that Oliver would be her husband in name only. Once the other actresses had heard that, then all attempts to keep the truth from her were extinguished. She had then been regaled with gleeful tales of Oliver's conquests and his athleticism in bed until her head had reeled with images that should not invade a young woman's mind. Images that were equally exciting and upsetting.

Several of the actresses had experienced that athleticism first-hand and Arabella had no doubts that Lady Bufford wasn't the only woman present at this wedding who had been his lover.

Yet tonight, would be her wedding night. He had kissed her twice before and she wondered if he would try to kiss her again tonight. Perhaps he would do more than just kiss her. He was her husband now, after all. In law that gave him certain rights. Would he try to exercise those rights tonight?

Would she finally discover what so many other women had done before her, what it was like to be seduced by Oliver Huntsbury?

She had little experience of men. Arnold Emerson had been as inexperienced as herself and had never done anything more than kiss her. And those kisses had been somewhat chaste affairs compared to what it had been like to be kissed by Oliver.

When Oliver had kissed her, it had been as if he

wanted to possess her. His fervour had been almost overwhelming, but it had also been exciting and had elicited feelings deep within her that she did not know existed.

Even now, in this crowded ballroom, she was feeling things she knew she shouldn't. She had loved the feeling of his body up against hers. Would she feel the touch of his body again tonight? Would he hold her again? Would he try to seduce her by kissing her, caressing her, relieving that demanding need for him that was almost painful.

She released a soft sigh, moved closer to him and looked up into his eyes. Eyes that weren't smiling. Eyes that were sparking with fire, burning into her with an intensity that was all consuming. And she wanted to be consumed, to be taken by him, to feel the heat of his passion.

Her breath coming in quick gasps, she was incapable of breaking free from his gaze. A small, sane part of her mind was telling her she should be wary. But she would not listen to her cautious brain. She loved having him look at her like that. Yes, perhaps he had looked at many other women like that, but tonight he was looking at her. And it felt wonderful.

Many other women.

Those three words that said it all hit Arabella like a lightning bolt coming out of a clear blue sky. Many other women.

Of course he knew how to make a woman feel special, to feel desired, as if she was the only woman in the room. He was an experienced seducer. That would be part of his usual technique.

And she had naively fallen for it.

Well, if he thought she would succumb to his charm he was going to be sadly disappointed. Tonight might be their wedding night, but this was a wedding in name only and he was going to find that out loud and clear. She would not be seduced by Oliver Huntsbury.

The music ended and the band struck up another piece. Arabella quickly released her hold on his shoulder and hand as if she were being scorched by his touch. She needed to get away from this man who made her forget herself so easily.

'Please excuse me, I think I should circulate with our guests.' Arabella all but ran off the dance floor. She wanted to talk to her friend Rosie. Rosie would be able to guide her out of this fog of confusion that Oliver seemed to wrap around her. But Rosie and her new husband were dancing, holding each other close and looking adoringly into each other's eyes. She didn't have the heart to break them up.

Instead she turned to the nearest person standing on the edge of the dance floor and used all her acting skills to force her lips into a welcoming smile. She had to talk to someone, to distract her mind and body away from treasonous thoughts of Oliver.

'How do you do? I don't believe we've been introduced.'

'I'm pleased to make your acquaintance, Your Grace. I'm Greta Jones,' the woman said, to Arabella's surprise. She had called her *Your Grace*. Then, to her even greater surprise, the woman bobbed a curtsy.

That's right, she was now a duchess, of all things, and people would start deferring to her in that manner.

'Please, there's no need to address me as Your

Grace. My name is Arabella van… Oh, no, it's not—
it's Arabella, Duchess of Somerfeld now. Anyway,
I'm still just Arabella.'

The woman smiled at her. 'Yes, Your Grace.'

Arabella smiled and ignored the woman's refusal
to drop the formality. 'And how do you know the
Huntsbury family?'

'Has the Duke not told you about me?' she said, her
voice hushed as she gazed sideways at Oliver across
the room talking to his mother. Arabella braced herself for yet another shock about her new husband. The
woman looked too old to be his mistress. She was not
much younger than his mother, but with a man like
Oliver you never knew.

'Oh, you're Greta Jones. Yes, of course Oliver has
told me all about you. I'm pleased you could make it
to the wedding.'

She did not want the rest of the world thinking
that Oliver kept her in the same state of ignorance
as his father had kept his mother. This marriage was
humiliating enough without having the world laughing at her for being Oliver's ignorant, gullible wife.

The woman beamed a delighted smile. 'I'm so
pleased everything is so open between you and Oliver. That man really is a saint.'

A saint? Was this woman actually talking about
her husband? She looked over at him. He had moved
on from talking to his mother and was now chatting
to a young woman, who was gazing at him wistfully.
Arabella was sure it wasn't his saintliness that was
causing her to give him coy, flirtatious looks.

'You're talking about Oliver, the Duke of Somerfeld?' Perhaps the woman was mistaken, perhaps

there was some other man in the room who could more easily wear the title of saint.

'Oh, yes, such a wonderful man. When he found out that I'd had a child out of wedlock he did everything he could to help us. He bought me a really nice house. He provided me with a regular income and he's even paying for my Jenny's education. Oh, yes, the man's a saint.'

It wasn't her definition of a saint. Saints did not usually go around impregnating women. But instead of saying that, Arabella merely kept on smiling and nodding. 'So, does he see much of you and Jenny?'

'Oh, yes, he sees her all the time. After all, she is his half-sister.'

Half-sister?

Arabella tilted her head, unsure that she had heard correctly. 'She's what?'

'Half-sister. Didn't he tell you about Jenny? Oliver's father is also Jenny's father. They're half-siblings.' She gave Arabella a sideways glance, her brow furrowed.

'Oh, yes. That Jenny. Of course he did. I was forgetting.'

The woman gave a little laugh. 'Well, I suppose it is easy to forget. After all, his father did have a lot of children, so Oliver does have a lot of half-brothers and half-sisters. That's my Jenny over there, talking to the Duke.'

Arabella looked back at Oliver. She could now see that the young woman wasn't so much flirting with her husband as looking at him with affection and admiration. Perhaps she had merely seen what she had expected to see. Perhaps she *had* judged her husband a bit too harshly.

She looked back at Greta Jones, who was looking over at Oliver with the same smile of affection. 'And the Duke has made arrangements for all his father's children,' Greta said. 'The only condition he puts on his money is that we keep it secret from his mother. Oh, yes, he really is a saint. To us and to her.'

Arabella looked back at Oliver. Perhaps there was a small bit of saintliness hidden inside that sinner after all.

'And you've all managed to keep this a secret from Oliver's mother?' It was hard to believe when there were so many ex-mistresses, so many children.

Greta laughed lightly. 'Oh, yes, we're all so grateful that we're happy to abide by that one condition and an ability to keep secrets from women is something else Oliver inherited from his father.'

All Arabella's warm feelings towards Oliver instantly evaporated. Greta looked up at her and registered Arabella's expression and her smile faded. 'Oh, but now that he's married that will change, I'm sure he tells you the truth about everything. Now, if you'll excuse me.' Greta Jones quickly walked away, her face burning with embarrassment.

No, Arabella's initial assessment was right. There might be a saintly side to Oliver, but he was still more sinner than saint and that was something she would be wise to remember.

Chapter Eleven

The saint—or was it the sinner?—excused himself and walked across the room to join Arabella. She watched him stride towards her, unable to look away. There was no denying he was the most attractive man in the room. And Arabella's eyes weren't the only ones fixed on him as he cut a swathe through the crowded ballroom.

Yet, despite the numerous admiring gazes he was getting, his eyes never left hers and the effect on her nervous system was decidedly unsettling.

'Arabella, I'm sorry I've been neglecting you. But I see you've started talking to the guests.' He looked in Greta Jones's direction. 'What were you talking about?'

It was a casual question, but there was an underlying apprehension in his voice. Why he should be concerned that she was talking to her father's ex-mistress she didn't know? Was he worried that she had found out that he was financially supporting Greta and many more of his father's ex-mistresses and children? Surely what he was doing was a good thing. Or was he worried that she might start to see a side to him that didn't fit in with the way the rest of the world saw him, as an unmitigated rake? There was only one way to find out.

'She was telling me about the house you bought for her and how grateful she is that you're paying for Jenny's education.'

'Oh, that.' He rubbed his hand along the back of his neck and gave a strained smile.

Was the sinner embarrassed that his saintliness had been exposed?

'She also mentioned that you are supporting all of your father's ex-mistresses and children, and there's rather a lot of them.'

He gave a snort of derision. 'Well, someone has to. These women would be left on their own otherwise, struggling to survive in a world that is not easy for any woman and especially not a woman who has a child out of wedlock.'

'And did your father not make provisions for them?'

His jaw tightened. 'My father had no objection to me organising the allowances for them, but I'm afraid once he lost interest in a woman that was it. It didn't matter how much harm he had caused, it simply never occurred to him to even try to undo some of the damage. He would be too interested in moving on to his next conquest.'

There was anger in his voice. Like her, he'd had a father who pursued his own goals without caring about how much harm it might cause others.

'And you invited them all to the wedding?'

He looked down at her, his face serious. 'Only

Greta and her daughter. I've become quite close to them over the years and I didn't want them to feel excluded. I hope you don't mind.'

'Of course I don't mind. I think it's an admirable thing to do. I'm just surprised you've managed to keep all these secrets from your mother.'

Once again, he rubbed his hand slowly across the back of his neck. 'Well, unfortunately, thanks to my father, I've had a lot of experience in keeping things from my mother.'

Arabella couldn't stop a disapproving sigh from escaping. There might be a saintly side to this sinner, but he certainly had a lot of experience in keeping women in the dark. He was obviously a master at it.

She looked across the room at his mother. Was that to be her own fate, as well—to be kept in the dark and to have no idea what her husband was up to?

The Dowager Duchess looked in their direction, beamed a happy smile and walked over to join them.

'Oh, Oliver, Arabella,' she said. 'I don't think I've ever been happier, not since my own wedding day.'

'And you look beautiful, Mother,' Oliver said, leaning down and kissing his mother on the cheek.

His mother smiled coyly. 'But not as beautiful as this young lady. Arabella, you make a lovely bride. I'm sure you're going to be a wonderful Duchess of Somerfeld and wife for Oliver.'

Arabella forced herself to smile and hoped it looked genuine.

'And I truly hope the two of you are as happy as Oliver's late father and I were.'

Arabella looked sideways at Oliver, who looked somewhat uncomfortable.

'Mr van Haven was so excited that you and Oliver had married,' she continued. 'It was just a shame he had to leave so early. He said he had some urgent business to attend to.'

An exasperated sigh escaped Arabella's lips. Her father had been the first guest to leave. As soon as the wedding breakfast had finished, he had departed, not even staying for the ball. Now that he had achieved his goal, he obviously saw nothing to detain him. She had little doubt that he would now be taking the first steamer back to America, to his beloved bank.

'Yes, that was a shame,' Arabella replied truthfully. Everything about her father forcing this marriage upon her had been shameful.

'Well, I must circulate. There are so many lovely people here tonight.'

With that she departed and joined another group of women and Arabella wondered if they were yet more of her husband's ex-mistresses, causing Arabella to wince in sympathy for Oliver's poor, deluded mother.

'My mother is talking to her cousins,' Oliver said, seemingly reading her mind. 'And, as surprising as it is, even my father wouldn't try to seduce his wife's relatives.'

'No, he might have broken his vow and been found out.'

Oliver raised his eyebrows and gave a slight nod. 'Yes, unfortunately you're probably right. That most likely was his reasoning.'

The band leader announced the quadrille and couples took to the floor. Oliver sent her another of those mischievous smiles. 'So, Your Grace,' he said, performing a low bow. 'Would you do me the honour of this dance?'

Despite herself Arabella smiled back at him. Why did his smile always cause her to feel warm inside, even when she told herself not to succumb to his charms?

He held out his hand and she lightly placed her gloved hand on his. As he led her on to the dance floor, she caught sight of Lady Bufford, grabbing her husband and dragging the reluctant man in their direction. The assembled guests formed themselves into groups of four couples and it became apparent what Lady Bufford was up to. She bustled herself and her now red-faced husband into their set. She was obviously determined to get an opportunity to dance with Oliver.

Arabella forced her jaw to unclench and her body to relax. What did it matter if Lady Bufford wanted to dance with her husband? She had no right to be jealous. But still, this was her wedding night after all and she didn't want to share it with one of Oliver's mistresses.

The band struck up. Oliver took her hand and they danced the first set of steps. They parted and he joined Lady Bufford for the second set.

Arabella fought hard to keep that little green monster under control as she watched Lady Bufford simper and smile, and whisper something in Oliver's ear. Lord Bufford also appeared to be battling with his own demons and gave every appearance of a man fighting to restrain himself from leaping forward to pull his wife away from her lover.

Lord Bufford might be entitled to feel jealous at

this blatant display, but Arabella did not. Hadn't she promised Oliver freedom? Hadn't she said that she didn't care how many *good friends* he had? No, this was something she was going to have to learn to cope with. She was going to have to control her impulses to stamp her feet in rage, to pout, and to send her rivals looks that were designed to cut them to the quick.

But at the very least, she just wished Lady Bufford had the good manners to not be quite so obvious. Each time she danced with Oliver her face lit up like a modern electric lightbulb. She smiled up at him, giggled girlishly and continued to whisper in her ear. Surely she should have enough decency in her to restrain herself and keep her hands off the groom, even if it was just for this one night.

When the dance finally came to an end Arabella released her tightly held breath, pleased to be led off the dance floor, away from that despicable woman.

The temptation to ask Oliver what Lady Bufford had been whispering to him was almost overwhelming, but she would not do it. She clamped her teeth tightly together to stop the words from escaping.

They were joined by Greta Jones, who was all smiles. 'You two look perfect together,' she said, taking Oliver's hands.

Oliver bent down and kissed her cheek. 'I hope you're enjoying yourself, Greta.'

'Oh, I am, I am, Your Grace. I'm so happy to see you married. But it's time I went home. I just wanted to say goodbye to you and your bride. She really is delightful, Oliver. Just the sort of woman a good man like you deserves.'

Oliver and Arabella exchanged disbelieving looks.

Arabella knew she was neither the woman Oliver deserved nor wanted for his wife, but wondered what sort of woman he actually *did* deserve. Greta had called him a saint. Did he deserve a saintly woman? That most certainly was not Arabella. Surviving a marriage to a man like Oliver was going to demand the patience and forbearance of a saint, but her reaction to Lady Bufford's performance on the dance floor had shown her she definitely did not possess those qualities.

And as for the sinner, well, that man was obviously more than capable of getting as many women as he wanted, but whether he deserved them all was another question entirely.

They said their goodbyes to Greta and several other guests approached them to say farewell. The ball was starting to wind up and she would soon be alone with Oliver. Alone with her new husband.

While some guests would be staying overnight, they would be in a separate wing, far away from the rooms occupied by her and Oliver. Even his mother had announced that from the date of the wedding she would be moving into her own home on the estate and leaving Somerfeld Manor to the new Duchess.

So she would be alone with Oliver. What would happen then?

Several other guests approached them to say their goodbyes. Arabella made polite conversation, hardly aware of what she was saying. All she could think was that, with each departing guest, she was coming closer and closer to being alone with Oliver. Alone with a handsome rake with a notorious reputation. And she was his wife. Would it now be her turn to be the sole focus of his seductive charms? And how was she going to react if it was?

A tingling awareness raced round her body as heat erupted deep within her core. *She would be alone with him.*

As if sensing her body's reaction, he looked up from a departing couple and stared intently at her. Her nerves jumped in response and she stared back, transfixed. Fire flickered in those dark brown eyes as his gaze scanned slowly from her face down her body, then back up again. Every inch of her body burned under his gaze, as if his eyes had softly caressed her sensitive skin. He was looking at her as if she really was his. It was a look of possession, of desire, of passion. It was how he looked at her when he kissed her. Was it how he would look when he took her in his arms, when he laid her down on his bed? Was that how he would look at her when he made love to her?

A mixture of panic and excited awareness raged a war within her. She would soon be alone with this man. A man who could bring her body alive with just one look. A man who made her feel things she had never felt before, who made her body ache with need. A man she knew she had to resist.

A woman pulled at his sleeve and dragged his attention away, breaking the spell between them. Arabella blinked several times to bring herself back to reality.

What had just happened?

Had she just experienced a taste of his seduction routine? Was that how he looked at women when he was planning to bed them? She could see why he was so successful with women. It had certainly worked on her. One intense look from those dark brown eyes and she had lost all ability to reason. That one look had driven her imagination wild, sent thoughts of giving herself to him running through her mind, of letting him do anything he wanted with her, of *wanting* him to do anything he wanted with her.

She closed her eyes and took a series of deep breaths to force some control over her riotous nerves.

Well, if Oliver was planning on using his tried-and-true seduction techniques on her he would be wasting his time. He would not be seducing her, tonight or any other night. He was about to learn a valuable lesson: that not all women were his for the taking.

With each departing guest Arabella could feel that firm resolve fray more and more at the edges. She knew she was going to have to be strong. She just had to remember who he was, to keep in mind all those other women in his life. She might be his wife, but she did not want to be yet another one of his women, yet another *good friend* to add to the long list.

Finally, the last guests headed out of the room and departed in their carriages, leaving the couple alone in the suddenly quiet grand ballroom, with only a few servants remaining, who discreetly ignored the couple as they continued to clear the tables.

Now Oliver was about to learn his lesson. He was about to find out that she was not like other women. She would not be his latest conquest.

He turned towards her and Arabella's heart seemed to jump into her throat, her cheeks grew hot and her skin burned under his gaze. A reaction she knew she should not be having if she was to remain strong. She closed her eyes briefly and forced herself to take in a few calming breaths.

'It's been a long day, Arabella. Now we can finally retire,' he murmured. 'Shall we?' He held out his arm for her. Arabella nodded, unable to speak, and with trepidation she placed her arm through his.

This was it. They walked towards the stairs that led them up to their bedroom suite.

Arabella's mind blurred with confusion. All she was conscious of was his strong body close to hers as they ascended the staircase, so close she could feel his warmth, imagine the strong muscles under his shirt and jacket. Unable to stop herself she drew even nearer to him, their bodies almost touching, sending a thrilling ripple coursing through her body.

In silence they walked down the long corridor. Arabella could not imagine what was going through Oliver's mind as he led her towards their bedroom, but her own mind was a swirl of chaotic thoughts. Her body was even more confused and Arabella fought to slow the rapid drumbeat of her heart and get her breathing under control.

They reached the bedroom door and he stopped. Her breath caught in her suddenly dry throat as she looked up at him. He gazed down at her, those rich brown eyes staring deep into hers, as if penetrating through to her very soul. She waited, her treacherous body aching to feel his touch, a touch she knew she should not be wanting, but one her body desired with an insatiable need that could not be ignored.

He leant down towards her. Her lips parted in anticipation. She closed her eyes and moved towards him, her heart racing, her body throbbing. His lips caressed her warm cheek and she sighed. 'Goodnight, Arabella. I hope you sleep well.'

Her eyes flew open and she watched in disbelief as he turned and walked off down the corridor. Without a backward glance he opened the door to the adjoining room and entered.

As if frozen to the spot, Arabella continued to stare down the now empty hallway.

Was that it? Was that to be her wedding night? She'd had every intention of rejecting his advances, but he hadn't even tried to seduce her. The notorious rake, who desired almost every woman he met, did not desire one woman. His wife.

Well, so be it.

Abruptly Arabella turned and pulled open the door to her bedroom, slamming it shut behind her. Her hand flew to her mouth and she looked in the direction of Oliver's bedroom. She hoped he hadn't heard the bang of her door closing. It would be too humiliating if he thought she was in any way concerned that he had just rejected her.

She tiptoed across the room and reached for the bell pull to summon Nellie. Her hand paused in midair. If she called Nellie to help her undress, then her lady's maid would know that she was spending her wedding night alone. Nellie was her friend and she would not judge, but still Arabella felt ashamed that it would not be her husband who removed her wedding gown, her stockings, her undergarments.

Instead she would do it herself. With much wriggling and contortions, she managed to undo the small pearl buttons up the back of her gown and release herself from the tight corset. When she was finally free, she threw the dress across the room. It landed on a chair in an abandoned pile of white embroidered satin and lace.

She released her hair and tossed the clips on to the dressing table.

Dressed in her virginal white linen nightdress, she climbed into the four-poster bed and scowled at the closed adjoining door that separated her room from Oliver's.

The door was only made of oak, but it might as well be made of iron and be shut with a lock and chain, it presented such a barrier between them.

Leaning over, Arabella blew out her lamp with a decisive puff of air. The best thing she could do now was to sleep and forget all about the man in the next room. After all, it had been a long, tiring day. Instead she lay on her side, staring at the carved wooden door that connected their rooms.

Candlelight flickered along the gap under the door and she could see a shadow moving around. He was still up. Not yet in bed. Was he thinking of her? Was he going to change his mind? Would the door open and he would join her after all?

The shadow approached the door. It stopped moving. She sat up, pulled up the sheet to her chest and gasped in a breath. The doorknob appeared to move slightly. Or was that just a trick being played on her eyes in the darkened room?

The shadow moved away. The light under the door went out. He had retired for the evening. Arabella released her held breath. She lay back down. If he could go to sleep as if today had been just another normal day, then so could she.

But instead she stared up at the ceiling for hour after hour, willing sleep to come.

Chapter Twelve

Oliver remained in bed until late in the morning, listening to the sound of carriage wheels crunching on the gravel driveway as the last of the wedding guests left the estate.

Perhaps he should have risen early to say goodbye. Although his absence would be excused—they would assume he was still in bed with his new bride.

But they would be so wrong. The first day of his life as a married man would not be spent in the arms of his wife. Nor would any other day or night during this arranged marriage.

Last night he had proven to himself that he *was* capable of achieving the seemingly impossible, he could walk away from his enchanting wife.

But it had taken every ounce of self-control he possessed to do so. When he'd looked down into her face, at her inviting lips, her blushing cream cheeks, her softly closed eyes, the temptation to kiss her had been so strong. As had the temptation to rip off that restricting wedding gown, to see her naked, to take her into his room and make her his own.

But he had done the unimaginable. He had resisted temptation.

Even though his mind had been clouded by desire, one rule had been able to cut through the obscuring clouds, a rule by which he had always lived.

He did not seduce virgins.

He had never done it before and he wasn't about to start now. Even if that virgin was his wife.

When it came to women, he might not have many restrictions, but even a man like him had to have some sort of code of conduct.

Arabella needed his protection, not his lustfulness.

But despite that rule nagging in his head, he had almost succumbed.

When she had tilted back her head, her pink lips parted, her blue eyes closed, the memory of kissing her had almost undermined his resolve. Virgin or not, there was no denying that when he had kissed her, he had felt a fire burning inside her. There was definitely untapped passion in his new wife and the pull to be the one to fan those flames until she burned up had been hellishly strong.

Yet he had resisted. He had walked away. Amazing.

Now he just had to ensure he continued to walk away from temptation.

He threw back the bedcovers. It was time to start his day. And this was to be a day like no other. After all, he was a married man now. That was going to take some adjustment.

He walked through to his dressing room, where his valet had discreetly laid out his clothes and shaving gear, presumably to avoid disturbing the newly married couple.

He washed and shaved, then pulled on his trousers, shirt and waistcoat, and stared at his reflection in the full-length mirror as he adjusted his cravat. Just how was he supposed to behave now he was a married man? he asked his reflection. They had promised each other complete freedom as if they were not married to each other, but she was still his wife. She was living in his house. She had taken his name. The world thought of them as a couple.

So how *were* they supposed to behave towards each other? As if they were friends? Acquaintances? Business partners?

He buttoned up his jacket. And if this was confusing for him, it must be even more so for her. In just a few short weeks her life had been turned upside down. She had gone from being a single woman pursuing a career on the stage to a married woman whose career had been destroyed.

While little had really changed for him, she must be devastated.

He must remember that at all times. He nodded to his reflection.

She wanted this marriage even less than he did, if that was possible.

He headed out the door and down the corridor to the breakfast room. As he walked through the house, he could see the servants had returned everything to how it had been. It was as if a wedding had not taken place the night before. And his new bride was nowhere in sight.

Perhaps she had already left and returned to London, or ridden off with her friends, the Duke and Duchess of Knightsbrook, to stay at their estate in Devon.

If that was what she had chosen to do, she had every right to do so. She did not have to explain herself to him, or even tell him of her intentions.

He served himself a generous breakfast and shook open the newspaper. No, the new Duchess of Somerfeld did not need to keep him informed of her plans. She was a free woman. She could go anywhere, do anything, see anyone she wanted. That was their agreement.

But she could have said goodbye to him, couldn't she?

He folded up the paper and pushed aside his plate, no longer feeling hungry as these questions continued to whirl through his mind.

Perhaps he could divert himself with a vigorous ride round the estate. Strenuous exercise would put an end to this unsettled state. It would drive out these constant thoughts of his marriage.

As he headed for the stables, he saw his bride, walking slowly in from the rose gardens, a posy of flowers in her hand. He stopped on the top of the steps and looked down at her, taking the opportunity to observe her before she was able to see him watching. Her black hair was tied back in a simple plait, making her appear even more innocent, and she looked so sad and wistful. The enormity of the grounds of the Somerfeld estate seemed to make her appear small and alone, and the expression on her face was so forlorn it broke his heart.

He rushed down the steps and crossed the formal garden.

'Arabella.' He hesitated, suddenly unsure what to say, uncharacteristically uncertain of himself.

She looked up at him and sent him a tentative smile. It seemed she, too, was unsure of how they were supposed to act with each other now that they were husband and wife.

With dark shadows under her big blue eyes, she looked tired. Had she spent the night worrying about what marriage would bring, what her duties would be? Well, she should have no worry on that account. He would expect nothing of her.

'Good morning, Oliver, I was just taking a walk round the gardens. They really are stunning.'

He nodded. 'Do you mind if I accompany you?'

She shrugged slightly. 'I can hardly stop you. After all it's your garden and I'm your wife, just another of your possessions.'

He dragged in a breath and winced. 'Please, Arabella. You know I don't think like that. You are not my possession. You are your own person. You are free to do as you want, to go where you want.'

She shrugged again and clasped her posy of flowers more tightly. 'I'm sorry, you're right. I should not have said that.'

They walked through the sculptured formal garden. Oliver was tempted to take her arm. Would that not be the polite thing to do? But his new wife appeared so tense, her body so rigid, he suspected she would be affronted by such a gesture.

He had to let her know that he meant what he said. 'Arabella, you have nothing to worry about. I will arrange with my man of business for you to have a regular allowance that is generous enough that you never have to worry about money,' he announced. 'That money will give you complete independence to live your life however you choose.'

She stopped walking and looked up at him. 'So, I'm to have an allowance, just like your father's ex-mistresses.'

There was bitterness in her voice. Why was she so annoyed with him? What had he done wrong? Couldn't she see that he would do everything in his power to ensure that marriage to him changed nothing for her, that it did not impede how she lived her life?

'An allowance will give you freedom,' he said softly, as if trying to calm a skittish colt.

'Freedom to do what? My father has destroyed my career and forced me into a marriage I didn't want. You say I have freedom, but what am I supposed to do with it now that I have it? I'm nothing if I'm not acting on the stage and that is all over now. All I am is a wife and I'm not even that.'

Oliver shook his head, unsure of what he could say or do to make things better. 'Well, my town house will be at your disposal any time you want. You can use that as a base to contact as many theatres as you like so you can secure another part.'

She exhaled a deep breath, shook her head and resumed walking. 'I'm so sorry, Oliver. None of this is your fault and I should not be getting angry with you. I'm feeling so confused by everything that has happened and I didn't sleep very well last night.' She blushed slightly and looked down at her posy of flowers. 'I just don't know what my role is now.'

He took her arm, determined to offer her reassurance. 'Nothing's changed for you. You can still act.'

She looked uncertain.

'You could even contact the Limelight Theatre again if you choose.' Oliver smiled as a thought occurred to him. 'After all, the manager was told he could not employ Arabella van Haven. He was not told he couldn't hire Arabella, the Duchess of Somerfeld.'

She paused, turned and looked up at him, her frown turning into a smile. A bright, delightful smile, as if the warm sun had just emerged from behind a grey cloud. 'You're right. My father *did* tell them they couldn't hire Arabella *van Haven* and she doesn't exist any more.'

The sadness had disappeared from her face and Oliver smiled back, pleased that something he had said had actually made her happy.

'That's exactly what I'm going to do.' Her walking pace increased; her body no longer rigid. 'I'm going to ask for my part back at the Limelight. It will be so good to pull the wool over my father's eyes after what he's done. He's such a stickler for contractual agreements. He's managed to fool many an opponent who didn't take the time to read the fine print. And now we'll return the favour. Oh, you're so clever, Oliver.'

Clever? That was not a trait usually attributed to him, but he rather liked the sound of it. Especially when being clever made her so happy.

'Right. Let's do that immediately,' he said. They turned around and walked briskly back to the house. 'And I'll send a telegram to the manager, so he knows that I, too, approve of you returning to the stage.'

Her smile faded, and she sighed audibly. 'Yes, I suppose now that you're my husband you do have to approve my actions, don't you? And I suppose that as a duchess the manager at the Limelight will feel obliged to hire me, whether they think I'm talented or not. It will be such a drawcard to have a member of the aristocracy on the bill. I'll be the freak that everyone wants to see.'

Her sadness had returned and Oliver knew he had to make things right for her. 'Then act under another name. Yes, some people will still know who you are, but the majority of people who go to the Limelight Theatre won't. You don't have to call yourself a duchess if you don't want to. You can be just plain old Arabella Huntsbury.' Although there could never be anything plain about the young woman standing beside him.

She stared up at him, her brow furrowed. 'Yes, that might work, I suppose.'

'Of course it will. And I assure you, I will never interfere in your life. You have my word. I can even draw up legal documents to ensure it, if you would like. With a substantial allowance and such legal agreements, you'll be more independent than you ever have been before. Marriage will not hold you back. I guarantee it.'

Her furrowed brow smoothed over and she sent him another of those heart-warming smiles. 'That's very kind of you.'

Clever and now kind—two descriptions largely unfamiliar to him. He was fearing she was starting to get the wrong idea about the sort of man he was.

They reached the foot of the steps and she paused.

'So, what about you? Will this marriage hold you back?'

It was his turn to furrow his brow. He was unsure how to answer that question.

'Don't worry,' she said before he could formulate an answer. 'I promise I won't restrict your freedom either. Like your father, your wife will never get in your way.'

At the mention of his father a pang of pain pierced Oliver's chest. He might be like his father in many respects, but he hoped he would never treat a woman the way his father had treated his mother.

'Arabella, I…' He was unsure how to continue. What could he say? *I won't be like my father?* He knew that would not be completely true.

'You don't have to say anything. I know the man I married.'

He cringed as they walked up the steps in silence. *She knew what sort of man he was.* Oliver also knew what sort of man he was and it had never bothered him before. So why was it bothering him now? That was a question he did not want to even try to answer. Instead he would focus on helping Arabella resume her career.

They walked into the drawing room. Oliver headed for the rolltop desk, sat down, removed a piece of paper and smiled up at her. 'Right, let's get your life back. You can tell me what to write. That way the letter to the manager will be from me, but you'll be completely in control.'

Arabella smiled back, regretting her earlier petulance. He was doing everything he could to make this easy for her and she was acting like a spoilt child, just because she was confused by her conflicting emotions. So what if she was the only woman in England this notorious rake had no interest in? That was what she wanted. She should be grateful that he did not try to seduce her last night. And she *was* grateful. So, it was time she acted that way instead of pouting and snapping at him.

She looked over his shoulder and laughed. 'If I'm to downplay the fact that I'm now a duchess, I don't think that stationery will be entirely appropriate.' She removed the piece of paper in his hand bearing the Somerfeld crest, returned it to the small shelf, took a plain piece of paper and placed it in front of him. All the while she tried to ignore the scent of him, all musk and masculinity, and the warmth of his body. She would not think of that now. She would focus on the task at hand, returning to the life she had before she met Oliver.

He dipped his pen in the ink pot and looked up at her expectantly. 'Right, what shall I write?'

She paced the room, thinking about the best way to convince the manager of the Limelight that they should rehire her. 'Well, I guess you can put the address of Somerfeld Manor at the top of the page. After all, they already know that I've married a duke so there's no point trying to hide that. I just don't think I should emphasise it by using stationery bearing your crest.'

Oliver nodded, and his pen scratched across the paper as he wrote out his address. 'Right, what next?'

'Well, *Dear Mr Hackett* might be a good start.'

Oliver dutifully wrote that down.

'*I would like to announce that Arabella Huntsbury is now available for consideration in the part previously played by Arabella van Haven.*'

She paused and looked over Oliver's shoulder as he took down her dictation. 'That way we're letting him know I go under another name without actually saying so.'

'Good idea.' Oliver finished writing and looked up at her, his pen poised above the paper.

'*I am aware that my wife...*' Arabella paused, finding it difficult to take in that she was referring to herself as Oliver's wife. '*My wife has been denied a part in your present production under orders from the new owner, Mr van Haven. Please be informed that Mr van Haven has since returned to America.*'

Arabella hoped the manager could understand that that meant her father was far away and would have no direct influence on the Limelight, so they were free to hire whoever they chose.

'*While he has forbidden Miss van Haven from appearing at the Limelight, he did not forbid my wife from appearing, so I urge you to consider hiring her.*'

Oliver wrote that down, but then his pen continued to scratch along the page. '*In doing so, you will be hiring a talented actress who I am sure you appreciate is destined for greatness.*'

'I didn't say that,' she pointed out.

'No, but it's what the writer thinks.'

Warmth flooded through her. He might just be saying that to encourage the manager to rehire her, but she loved hearing him say he thought her talented.

She resumed her pacing. 'Well, I suppose you'll also have to add that you give your permission.'

Oliver nodded, and continued writing. *'I have no objection to my wife, Arabella Huntsbury, appearing on the stage...'*

Arabella fought not to be annoyed. She should not have to get Oliver's permission. A woman should be free to choose her own path in life, whether she was married or not, but that was the way of the world. However, unlike many other women, she had a husband who would put no obstacles in her path.

'...and I feel I would be doing the world a disservice if I kept this superb actress from her public.'

He sent her a devilish smile that washed away her annoyance and she smiled back at him.

With a flourish, he signed his name at the bottom, blotted the ink, folded up the letter, addressed an envelope and rang the bell for a servant.

'Hopefully that will do the trick. And it seems I've acquired a new skill, being your secretary. How did I do?'

His teasing made her laugh. 'You were perfect.' And perfect he was, in so many ways.

'And as your new secretary, I will point out that we shouldn't put all our eggs in one basket. There are lots of theatres other than the Limelight. Why don't we contact a few more and see what response we get?'

When the footman arrived, Oliver handed him the letter and asked him to send it immediately so it would catch the next mail train to London. He also requested copies of the day's newspapers and for Cook to prepare some sandwiches for their lunch so they could eat while they worked.

'We'll scour the papers and get a list of the main

theatres and write to them all. I'm sure lots of them will have a part for a promising young actress.'

This was more than Arabella could have hoped for. Not only was he keeping his promise to not interfere in her career, but he was also helping her find work. Then a small voice inside her head questioned his motives. Was he trying to get rid of her? Was a wife going to be an encumbrance to his lifestyle? Would it suit him to have her busy on the stage so he could pursue his own interests? She forced that little voice to stay silent. It didn't matter what his reasons were, he was helping her and that was all that mattered.

When the newspapers arrived, they spread them out on the table and leant over next to each other so they could peruse the entertainment sections together. Arabella forced herself to focus and ignore the fact that she was now standing close to Oliver, so close that their arms resting on the table were nearly touching, as they scanned the list of theatrical establishments.

She moved her arm slightly away from his in an attempt to stop the tingling that being this near to him always elicited. 'The best ones to look for will be ones where the play is coming to an end.' Her voice came out unnaturally high. 'That means they'll be casting for the next play and starting rehearsals soon.'

Oliver picked up another piece of paper and dipped his pen in the ink pot. 'Right, I'll compose a list of likely candidates.'

He pointed to the advertisement for the Lumière Theatre. 'We should add that one as well. I know that their lead actress has recently left because she ran off with a viscount. I heard they're living together in Italy, so they'll be needing a replacement.'

He wrote that on the list and leaned back over again to survey the ads.

He showed her another advertisement. 'And the Neptune Theatre is probably a good bet, but they prefer actresses who can also sing and dance.' He leant on one arm and looked at her. 'Can you sing and dance?'

She quickly stood up. He was now far too close for comfort. 'You seem to know more about this business than I do,' she said more curtly than she'd intended.

He smiled up at her. 'Well, I have known a few actresses over the years and my father knew even more. I almost grew up in the theatre, you could say.'

Arabella's body tensed and she fought hard to stop her lips from compressing in a disapproving scowl. Of course he knew a lot of actresses. She already knew that. And it was not something she should care about. It *was* something she *didn't* care about.

'Yes, I can dance and sing,' she said as evenly as she could.

'Right. Well, let's put the Neptune Theatre on the list as well.'

He turned back to the newspaper and added a few more to the list. Arabella told herself to stop being so sharp. She knew that she was married to a rake. If she reacted like that every time she was reminded that he'd had countless lovers she was going to drive herself mad. So she breathed slowly and steadily, forced herself to smile and pointed to another advertisement. 'Add the Savoy Theatre to the list, it's worth a try, and I'd love to perform in a Gilbert and Sullivan production.'

When they reached the end of the advertisements, she realised Oliver had been right. There really were a lot of options available if the Limelight turned her down. And they'd only covered the theatres in London. If they got no response from them, then they could branch out and try the other cities, even the smaller towns. Her father might have forced her to marry, but in one respect he couldn't have chosen a better husband for her. Oliver really was determined to help her in her career.

He stood up, held up the list and smiled at her.

'Right, now we need to compile a list of your previous performances, so they know how versatile you are. Do you have any clippings of your reviews? We can include a few good quotes from them. And I'll arrange with a photographer to take your portrait and we can send copies to the theatres.'

Arabella laughed. He looked so serious and committed to what he was doing. 'You really do know the industry, don't you? Perhaps you should manage my career.'

He smiled back at her. 'That's not a bad idea. I'd prefer that to being your secretary.'

'I'm not joking, Oliver. Sarah Bernhardt and Lillie Langtry and all the other successful actors and actresses have theatrical agents. They deal with theatre managers, publicity and so on. It would put my career on a much more professional basis. What do you think?'

He tapped the end of the pen against his teeth as he considered her proposal.

Arabella instantly regretted her suggestion. If he was her agent, he would be in the company of a lot of actresses. Would she be able to bear it if he took one of her colleagues as a lover? She doubted she had such strength that she could bear such humiliation.

'On second thoughts. I don't think that would be a good idea. After all, we did agree to live separate lives.'

He lowered his pen and frowned. 'Yes, you're right. We did agree on that. But I do know a lot of people in the industry, so I'm sure I can be a help to you.'

It seemed he was disappointed that he wouldn't be spending his days in the company of young and available actresses. But he was right. He could help her career and she would be unwise to let her ridiculous jealousy get in the way.

'All right, you can be my agent,' she said tentatively.

'Excellent.' He smiled and held out his hand for them to shake on their new arrangement. As if putting her hand into a fire Arabella forced herself to extend her hand. At the touch of his skin a burning sensation ripped up her arm, causing heat to explode throughout her body. Her heart was beating so loudly he must be able to hear it, as Arabella could hear nothing else.

Why did his touch always do that to her?

She drew in a strained breath and looked up at him, fighting to keep her face impassive so she would not expose to him to her reaction.

But looking into those deep brown eyes was the worst thing she could do. Her heart thudding fast, she knew she should look away, but she couldn't. They imprisoned her. She held her breath as his gaze moved from her eyes to her lips, then back again. When his gaze returned to her eyes, she could see a change had come over him. He was no longer looking at her like a helpful friend, but like a hungry man staring at a feast. Her frantically beating heart increased its fierce tempo. She was the feast. He wanted her. He desired her.

She dragged in a slow breath and held it, waiting. Wanting him to do more than just look, to act on what he was feeling, to satisfy his hunger.

He inhaled long and deep, then looked away, released her hand and took a step backwards. Her burning hand now free from his grasp, she wanted to sink to the ground, her legs too weak to hold her. She had expected him to kiss her again. Had wanted him to kiss her again. To do more than kiss her. But he hadn't.

Humiliation and disappointment engulfed her. Why did she have to expose her need to him? He quite obviously did not want her. Hadn't he proven that last night? Hadn't he just shown her yet again?

Yes, he had fleetingly been interested in her, but just as quickly that interest had disappeared. And if he had satisfied his hunger, wouldn't he have then moved on to his next conquest?

Why did she keep forgetting that? Yes, his kisses had been earth-shattering. But they would be, wouldn't they? Of course he was a good kisser, a man who'd had an endless stream of lovers would be.

Arabella smoothed down her skirt and coughed delicately. 'As my theatrical agent you'll probably need to know all about my career to date.' Her voice was a little breathless, but there was nothing she could do about that.

He nodded his head rapidly, sat down and picked up his pen again. It was all business now. 'Yes, the first thing we need to do is make a list of all the plays you've appeared in and all the theatres you've performed at. You've worked in America so we'll also be able to say you've got international experience.'

She sat across the table from him. With a table between them she would hopefully not reveal to him just how much his touch, his look, affected her. 'Well, there was the Atrium Theatre in New York. It's just a small amateur theatre, but no one in England will know that. I played Lady Macbeth.'

He raised his eyebrows. 'I can't imagine you as someone capable of plotting murder, you seem too sweet for that.'

'I'm an actress, remember? I can be lots of different women,' she retorted.

'And do you have any reviews from that?'

'Yes. They were very good reviews. And not one of the reviewers said I was sweet.'

He sent her a long, appraising look, causing heat to rush to her face. Why was it so important to her to convince him that she wasn't a sweet little girl, but was as much a woman as every other he had known?

She looked away and in a garbled rush listed all her other performances until he had to ask her to slow down so his writing could keep up with her torrent of words.

At a slower pace she repeated the list of productions she had appeared in, and the parts she had played, while he wrote it all down.

When she had finished, he held up the page and smiled at her in satisfaction. 'That's quite a list. We should get it printed so it looks professional. We can send it out, along with your picture, then sit back and wait for the offers to come flooding in.'

Arabella smiled back at him. He really was being helpful and he would be a great asset as a theatrical agent. It was just a shame that she couldn't trust herself to keep her traitorous reactions to him under control.

A footman knocked on the door and entered. 'Your Grace,' he said with a bow, 'Cook would like to know when you would like dinner served.'

Oliver looked over at the engraved brass clock ticking on the oak mantelpiece and Arabella followed his gaze. To her surprise she realised they had spent the entire afternoon together and it was now late in the day.

'Tell Cook we'll be ready in an hour.' He looked in Arabella's direction and she nodded her agreement. 'And we'll dine on the terrace tonight. There's only the two of us and I believe it's warm enough.'

'Very good, sir.' The footman bowed and withdrew.

Oliver put his pen and ink away and picked up the lists they had compiled. 'I believe that is what you'd call a productive day. We'll have you back on the stage before you know it.'

He smiled at her. She smiled back. It was what she wanted with all her heart, to return to the stage. So why was that anticipation tinged with an edge of regret?

Chapter Thirteen

Oliver never felt nervous and certainly not because of a woman. Never. And yet, as he sat on the terrace and waited for Arabella, nerves were indeed getting the better of him. Ridiculous. Perhaps it was simply the unfamiliar situation of having dinner with a woman with the simple intention of eating, of making polite conversation and nothing more. Usually when he dined with a woman, both of them knew it was just a precursor to their time in bed together. And their conversation would be far from polite. It tended to consist of sexual innuendo, flirting and teasing.

But tonight, there would be no flirting, no teasing and definitely no sexual innuendos. And this dinner was most certainly not a precursor to bedding Arabella. It was to be food, drink and polite conversation, only. Nothing to be nervous about at all.

The footman opened the doors to the terrace and Arabella emerged. He rose slowly from his seat as if transfixed and took in the vision that had appeared before him. She looked stunning, wearing a light yellow, low-cut gown. There was more of her enticing soft flesh on display than he had seen before. He fought and lost the battle to stop his eyes from straying to that delightful décolletage, to those enticing cream-coloured mounds, rising and falling with each breath. How could he not look? After all he was just a man, a weak man, powerless in the face of such tempting beauty.

Exercising supreme willpower, he forced his gaze to move up to her face, her beautiful face. She had made quite the effort for tonight's meal. Not just with that wonderful gown, which exposed the tops of her breasts and the soft skin of her shoulders to his appreciative gaze, but also her midnight-black hair, which had been intricately styled. Although he had to admit, he preferred to see her with her hair in a long plait flowing down her back, as it had been today. Or, better still, he would like to see it loose, free from all restraint, so he could run his fingers through it, before…

He coughed to drive out that thought before it led him to places he knew he should not go. He pulled out her seat. As she sat down he inhaled her delightful scent—jasmine. He remembered it well from when he had taken her in his arms before. He paused, his hands still on the back of her chair, his body close to hers.

He felt her grow tense, reminding him that this was just a convivial meal between two people who had been forced together against their wills and his behaviour was becoming inappropriate.

He returned to his own chair and rang the small brass bell on the table. Two footmen immediately emerged from behind the doors, one to serve the soup, the other to fill their wine glasses.

Oliver raised his glass in a toast. 'To your brilliant acting career.' He smiled inwardly. That was the right approach. Keep it light. Keep it friendly.

She clinked her crystal glass against his. 'And to your new career as a secretary and theatrical agent.'

'Well, I don't know if it's going to be much of a career. There's only one actress I want to look after.'

He took a sip of the white burgundy, savoured the distinctive nutty taste, and tried to laugh off what he had just said. Yes, he was looking after one actress. But it was only Arabella's *career* he was going to look after. *Nothing more.*

He picked up his spoon and tasted the clear vegetable soup. 'I'm afraid there will only be three courses this evening. I hope you don't mind, but as there is only the two of us, I didn't want to put Cook to too much trouble.'

She smiled at him, that enchanting smile. 'Of course I don't mind. Compared to what actresses usually eat I'm sure it will be a feast.'

He took another sip of his wine and watched her as she ate her soup. She really was quite different from any woman he had known. 'The life of an actress is not one I'd have expected the daughter of a wealthy man to choose. After all, it's often long hours for low pay.'

She lowered her spoon and tilted her head in thought. 'I don't think I actually did *choose* to become an actress. I think the life chose me. The first time I appeared on stage I felt as though I had come home. It was like the other actors were the family I never had. And the audience—when they applauded it was like nothing else on earth. I felt so happy and being on stage continues to make me happy.'

They exchanged smiles. She lit up when she spoke of the stage, her blue eyes shone and her smile was nothing less than radiant. 'But what about your father? I suspect you being on the stage doesn't make *him* happy.'

She nodded and her forehead furrowed as her eyebrows drew together. 'Fortunately, for a long time my father took very little interest in what I did. I'd appeared in numerous performances before he even realised what I was doing. If it hadn't been for...'

She looked down and picked up her spoon again.

'If it hadn't been for what?'

She placed her spoon back in the soup bowl with a decisive clink and pushed the bowl away. 'I suppose you might as well know. After all, you are my husband, even if, you know, you aren't really.'

He waited. She had him intrigued. What on earth could she tell him that she thought he should know? He doubted there would be a scandal. And if there was, it was unlikely to be anything worse than many of the scandalous things he had done. Whatever it was, he would forgive her.

'My father found out about my acting because I wanted to become engaged to be married to an actor.'

Oliver sat up straighter in his chair. That was not what he'd expected. She now had his undivided attention. 'You were previously engaged? You wanted to get married? Who to? What happened?'

She inhaled deeply and exhaled slowly through pursed lips. 'It was an unofficial engagement. His name was Arnold Emerson and we appeared together in that amateur production of *Macbeth* in New York. I thought he was in love with me. He said he was in love with me and I believed him. When he approached my father to ask for my hand my father was horrified. He said he was a charlatan and was only after my money. I was sure my father was wrong and was only saying that because Arnold had no money and no status. Not exactly the sort of man my father wanted me to marry.' She picked up her spoon and clenched it tightly. 'But it turned out that my father was right. To prove his point, he offered Arnold a large amount of money to leave New York and never see me again. And that's exactly what he did.'

'That's appalling. The man's a complete bast— dastard.'

She looked up at him. 'Who, my father?'

'Well, yes, him, too, but, no, this Emerson fellow. He's a dastard and a fool, and you're better off without him.'

'Yes, that's what my father said.'

'For once I'm in agreement with him.' Oliver steeled himself to ask the question to which he both wanted and did not want to hear the answer. 'Did you love him very much?'

She shrugged. 'I thought I did. But I didn't really know him, did I?' She gazed at him, those big blue eyes staring into his. 'I was angry at the time, but I think I was more angry that Father had been proven correct than because I wouldn't be getting married to Arnold. So I suppose that means I wasn't really in love with him after all.'

Relief flooded through him and his tense shoulders relaxed. 'I'm so sorry, Arabella.'

She shrugged again. 'Well, it's all in the past now.' She bit lightly on her lip and looked over at him. 'So what about you? Have you ever been in love?'

Oliver couldn't help but laugh at the absurdity of the question. Him? In love? Never. 'No, most certainly not. In fact, I doubt if such a thing actually exists. Countless women thought they were in love with my father, including my mother, but like you with Arnold Emerson, they never really knew him. If they did, I doubt that there would be much love in their hearts for that scoundrel.'

'So your father taught you that love doesn't exist and my father taught me that when it comes to love and to men, I can't trust my own judgement. What a great married couple we make.'

Oliver lifted his wine glass. 'In that case, shall we toast our fathers, the old scoundrels.'

'Our fathers.' She laughed and clinked her glass against his.

The footman arrived, removed their soup bowls, replaced them with the fish course and began serving out the vegetables.

'Just leave them, thank you,' Oliver said. 'We can serve ourselves.'

With a bow the footman departed.

'But your mother loved your father?' Arabella asked as she served vegetables on to their plates.

'Yes, she did. And in her case love was very, very blind.'

She looked up at him, a spoonful of carrots suspended in mid-air. 'So how many mistresses do you think your father had?'

Oliver frowned. That was a question he couldn't possibly answer. 'I don't know. I doubt if I could even take a tally of how many he had each year.'

She nodded; her face thoughtful. 'So, they were all short-lived affairs?'

'I suppose some lasted longer than others, but none for very long. They only lasted until the next pretty face caught his attention.'

She bit the edge of her lip. 'And how many children did he have, apart from you? How many half-siblings do you have?'

'At the last count there were eighteen.'

'Eighteen.' The serving spoon clattered back into the silver terrine and she stared at him with wide eyes.

'Yes, but I suspect there are more. I have people investigating to see whether there are any that I have missed, so that I can make sure they are supported by the estate and not left to try to cope in poverty.'

'And what about you, Oliver? Do you have any children?' she asked quietly, picking up the serving spoon and clenching it tightly.

'No,' he stated emphatically.

She tilted her head, as if waiting for him to prove why he was so certain. Oliver coughed, unsure how he should explain, without going into details that might embarrass her, the precautions he and his mistresses took to avoid pregnancy. 'I know I have no children because there are things a man can do to prevent such things happening. And the women I am involved with have their own methods of...' He waved his hand in the air. Was it her embarrassment that he was trying to prevent or his own?

'I see,' she said, colour tingeing her cheeks. 'So why did such techniques never work for your father?'

Oliver laughed, a humourless laugh. 'Because he didn't use them. He didn't care. It was as simple as that.'

'Oh, I see.'

Oliver hoped that was the end of her questioning. With most of the women he associated with the conversation could quickly get downright bawdy and he would be far from embarrassed, but discussing how to prevent pregnancy with Arabella was a decidedly disconcerting experience.

They ate their meal, with only the sound of silver cutlery on porcelain breaking the silence. Once the fish course was over the footmen served the dessert. Oliver waved it away, but Arabella's face lit up at the sight of the strawberry tart and cream. She ate the sweet treat with obvious enjoyment, occasionally closing her eyes and licking her lips, causing Oliver to smile.

When she had finished, she looked at him and winked. 'Delicious.'

As if by sixth sense the footman reappeared and removed her plate. Oliver refilled both their glasses and sat back to look out over the estate. He took in the long shadows cast by the plants and topiary in the formal garden and watched as a group of swallows dived and swooped in the soft early evening light, as if putting on a show for their benefit.

He smiled again at Arabella and she smiled back.

He couldn't remember the last time he had done this, just sat outside and watched the last of the sunlight disappear. It was such a pleasant evening he was pleased he could enjoy it with Arabella. But such pleasure was just an interlude before their real lives recommenced.

'Hopefully you will hear from the Limelight Theatre soon,' he said. 'Then you can get back to doing what makes you happy.'

'Hmm, and what about you, Oliver, what makes you truly happy?'

She waited for his answer, then colour exploded on her cheeks and she looked away. She had obviously answered the question herself.

Oliver smiled. 'I take it from your blushes you think you know exactly what makes me happy.'

She picked up her glass and took a nervous sip. 'Well, I wouldn't know about that.'

He stifled a laugh. 'But there are *other* things that make me happy, too.'

'Really? I wouldn't have thought you'd have the time or energy for anything else.'

He laughed lightly. 'I suspect my reputation far exceeds reality.'

'Well, I should hope so.' She placed her glass firmly on the table, the wine nearly spilling over the rim. 'Just so I don't experience any surprises, how many *good friends* do you actually have at the moment?'

'At this precise moment?'

She nodded.

'None. I know you have a poor opinion of me, but I'm not quite the rascal you think I am. And I do have some rules that I live by, you know. I'm not a complete cad.'

She shook her head, her lips pursed. 'Rules? What sort of rules?'

He took another drink, not sure if he liked the direction the conversation was going, but she deserved to know about the man she was now tied to. 'I've already told you I only get involved with women who want to have fun with no commitment and that is almost invariably married women who are unhappy with their husbands for various reasons. But I also have a rule that I never seduce anyone, ever.'

'You *never* seduce anyone?' She gave a small, fake laugh and a deeper blush tinged her cheeks. Her discomfort at this conversation was obvious, but despite that she continued. 'You can't be much of a rake if you don't seduce women—isn't that the very definition of a rake?'

'I never said I *was* a rake. And, no, I don't seduce women. I would never take a woman to my bed unless she was more than willing.'

Her lips pinched into a narrower, more disapproving line. 'So, is that your only rule? You never seduce anyone?'

He shrugged. 'No. I have another rule, I never bed virgins.'

The colour on her cheeks burned a deep crimson red. She picked up her wine glass, put it back down on the table, then picked it up again, her hand clenching the stem. 'That rules me out then, doesn't it?'

she said with another false laugh. 'I might be a married woman, but I'm a virgin and I guess I'm going to stay that way.'

It was Oliver's turn to feel embarrassed. He looked over at her, both shocked and surprised by her frank statement. 'I'm sorry, Arabella. This situation should not have been forced on you. You should have been allowed to marry whomever you wanted. To marry a man who loved you.'

'I thought you didn't believe in love, said it didn't exist.' She looked up at him, a challenge in her eyes.

Oliver squirmed in his seat. 'I don't, but I suspect you do. All I'm saying is, don't give your virginity to just any man. Wait until you think you are in love.'

'Well, that's hardly your business, is it?' She stared at him defiantly. 'If I don't object to whom you take as a lover, you can hardly object to any man who becomes mine.'

Acid burned up his throat at the thought of Arabella with another man. His hands clenched into tight fists, as if he wanted to commit an act of violence on this unknown lover. 'You're right, I'm hardly in a position to object,' he said through gritted teeth.

'Well, I'm pleased you have accepted that,' she said, her voice sounding anything but pleased. 'So, perhaps you can find a suitable lover for me, one who doesn't live by your rules.' Her false laugh now had a jeering quality. 'A man who doesn't mind seducing married virgins.'

Her words were like bullets fired straight at his heart. Rage boiled within him and blood pulsated in his ears. He stared at her in shocked disbelief, hardly able to believe what she had just said. He knew she had a low opinion of him, but this…? This was sinking to lower depths than even he was capable of plummeting.

He glared at her; his jaw so tense it ached. 'I…will…do…no…such…thing.'

Chapter Fourteen

Arabella stared out at the garden, seeing nothing. She had gone too far. But his so-called rules had made her angry. How could he have rules when it came to women? This one he could take to his bed, but not that one. It was outrageous. And it didn't help that all this talk of bedding and seduction had caused a decidedly unsettling reaction deep within her. All those women he had bedded, they knew what it was like to be held by him, to be caressed by him, to be desired by him. Something she would never experience.

There was no denying she *did* desire this man, her husband. The way her heart beat faster every time he looked at her told her that, loud and clear. But it was a desire she should not be feeling. And it was a desire he did not feel for her in return. She was a virgin. She might be his wife, but she was against the rules.

But her anger at his ridiculous rules did not excuse what she had just said. She had wanted to shock him, and the anger flashing in his eyes showed that she had succeeded.

Perhaps she was acting so out of character because last night she had hardly slept a wink. Instead, she had tossed and turned in her bed all night, unable to get comfortable, unable to stop her mind from going over and over everything that had happened during their time together. When she wasn't tossing and turning, she was lying on her side, staring at the closed door that separated them, thinking about the man behind it.

No wonder she was tired. No wonder her nerves were strung as tight as a long bow. No wonder she was so quick to become offended. But still, that didn't excuse what she had said.

She took a tentative sideways glance in his direction. His strong jaw was clenched so tightly she could see the bulge of muscles at the side of his face. He, too, was staring out at the garden, but she doubted he was taking in the scenery and his hand was gripping the wine glass so tightly he was in danger of breaking the stem.

Only the sound of the birds tweeting in the trees interrupted the uncomfortable silence stretching out between them.

She had to put this right. She had to apologise for saying something so offensive to him.

'I'm sorry, Arabella,' he said, still staring straight ahead. 'I should not have reacted so strongly to what you asked.'

He was sorry? *He* had nothing to be sorry about.

'No, Oliver. I'm the one who should apologise. What I said about…' She waved her hand in the air, not wanting to repeat the words. 'I didn't mean it. And I should not have said it.'

He turned slowly to face her. Despite his apology,

rage still burned in those dark brown eyes. 'So, I take it you don't want me to find you a lover?'

She swallowed and shook her head.

He held her gaze and heat burned brighter on her already flaming cheeks. She swallowed again, aware that there was only one man she wanted as her lover and he was staring at her right now.

The realisation hit her, hard. She struggled to breathe, her eyes grew wider and her heart thumped so wildly she could feel its pulsating rhythm throughout her body.

It shouldn't be true, but it was. She wanted Oliver, not just to be her husband, but to be her lover. How had she let this happen? She hadn't wanted it to happen, had been determined that it wouldn't happen, but it had and she couldn't deceive herself any longer.

She lowered her eyes and dragged in a breath to try to slow the turbulent beating of her heart.

This was an impossible situation. He was a rake, for goodness sake, a man who moved from one woman to another without a backward glance. And she wanted him. Desired him. Had her experience with Arnold Emerson taught her nothing? It would seem not. She was once again falling for the wrong man.

'No, I don't want you to find me a lover,' she stated with all honesty. The only one she wanted was sitting beside her, glaring at her with his hard, brown eyes.

He looked back out at the garden and took a sip of his wine. 'Good.'

'Obviously that would be an inappropriate role for a husband.'

He laughed without humour. 'Obviously.'

'When I take a lover, it will be a man of my own choosing.' But how was any other man going to match the man she was married to? Arabella shook her head and looked up at Oliver.

His grip on the wine glass intensified and those clenched muscles at the side of his jaw reappeared. He breathed out slowly and deeply, then drained his glass in one long draught.

He was still angry. But why should he care who she took as a lover? Was it simply because she was his wife, his possession and, even if he didn't want her himself, he didn't want any other man to have her? Would he be so petty? Nothing about him had suggested he was a petty man.

But there was no denying that he was enraged. Was there a possibility that the thought of her with another man was making him jealous? His reaction to her taunt that she wanted him to find her a lover could have been due to his pride, but his obvious anger at her statement that she could find her own lover, that was different.

Or was it merely wishful thinking on her part? If he was jealous, did that mean he desired her, wanted her?

A footman appeared with a lamp and placed it on the table. Arabella had hardly noticed that the last of the twilight had faded and they were now surrounded by darkness. The lamp cast an arc of yellow light around the table, enclosing them in an intimate circle.

Slowly Oliver turned towards her. 'Arabella, you are a free woman,' he stated in a clipped monotone. 'I have said it before, but it is worth restating. I will do nothing to interfere in the way you live your life. But I know men. You should be careful whom you get involved with.'

She stared him straight in the eye, determined not to be cowered by the turbulent emotions that were waging a war within her.

'So, do you think I should also compile a list of rules for choosing a lover the way you have?'

She watched his reaction carefully. His jaw clenched tighter as he gripped the now empty wine glass. 'Perhaps,' he said in that same monotone.

'Well, obviously they will have to be different from your rules,' she said ruefully.

'And whatever those rules are, Arabella, they are ones you are going to have to compile yourself. I have no interest in helping you.'

He stared down at her, his unflinching eyes making it clear that this conversation was over. Arabella was now seeing a completely different man from the brazen one who had rushed into her dressing room and taken her in his arms, or the man with the mischievous smile and devilish sense of fun.

This man was serious. He saw nothing funny in her taunting.

And nor did Arabella. She did not want any rules. She did not want a lover. She only wanted him.

'I shall leave you to think about your list. Now, if you'll excuse me, it is getting late. It is time to retire for the night.' He stood up and bowed formally. 'I believe you can find your own way to your room.' With that he departed, leaving Arabella sitting alone, staring out at the dark estate.

* * *

Oliver never retired early, at least not alone. But he could not remain in Arabella's company a minute longer. Not if she insisted on discussing her plans for finding a lover. That was more than any man should be expected to endure. It was a form of torture that could rival the medieval rack.

He reached the foot of the stairs and stopped. After undergoing such torture the likelihood of him being able to sleep was extremely remote. He turned and headed along the corridor, down the back stairs, through the kitchen.

As he passed through the servants' area, he waved his hands, palm down, to signal that they should remain seated and ignore his presence.

Once outside he breathed in deeply to relieve the constriction in his chest and began walking, briskly. This was another first. When had he ever been forced to take exercise to rid himself of his reaction to a woman? Never. But his pent-up energy had to be expended somehow and, for once, it would not be in a bed with a willing lover.

He walked along the dark avenue of trees, shimmering in the light evening breeze. This situation really was impossible. It would be funny if it wasn't so damn tragic. He wanted to bed his wife. Under normal circumstances that was a perfectly acceptable thing to want to do—more than acceptable, it was expected, it was part of the marriage contract. But these were not normal circumstances. He had known his bride for a few short weeks. They had married against their will. And she deserved so much more than to lose her virginity to a man like him, a man who was incapable of commitment. She did not deserve to live the life that his mother had been forced to live, sharing a man with a multitude of other women. He would not subject any woman to such a life, particularly Arabella.

Not to mention that bedding her would break two of his cardinal rules.

He increased his walking pace, heading into the woodland area. But that was something he did not want to think about. The sooner Arabella left Somerfeld Manor and returned to her life in London the better. Then he wouldn't be tormented by that bewitching face, that gorgeous body, or that silky skin, and the memory of those creamy breasts rising and falling above the bodice of her beautiful yellow gown.

Crashing through the thick undergrowth, Oliver knew that he most definitely had to get all thoughts of Arabella out of his mind.

He spotted the dark form of a tenant, hiding behind a tree, a shotgun under his arm. The man was presumably out poaching. Well, good luck to him. He presumably had a family to feed and was using some initiative. Oliver tipped his hand to his head in a gesture of greeting as he quickly passed. He smiled at the thought of the man's surprise. He must make a ludicrous sight, the lord of the manor, dressed in formal evening wear, all but running around his estate in the middle of the night.

He slowed down and headed back towards the house, physical exhaustion starting to overcome him. Hopefully this would not be a regular occurrence. Hopefully he wouldn't have to spend every night running around his estate like a mad man. As soon as

Arabella found employment as an actress she would be out of his house, out of his life. That would make her happy and her absence, while perhaps not making him happy, precisely, would most certainly be the best for both of them.

He entered the house and headed up the stairs to his bedroom. After such exercise he could only hope that he would now be able to sleep, that he would not lie in bed, awake, thinking of the woman lying in bed in the room next to his, with only an adjoining door between them.

Instead of calling for his valet, he undressed alone, drew on his robe and paced the room, his body still agitated. It seemed sleep wasn't going to come. He walked over to the window and stared out at the estate, lying in quiet darkness. The sooner she left Somerfeld Manor the better. Until then he was going to have to learn to endure this torture.

What was it that someone said, in one of Oscar Wilde's plays? That they could resist anything except temptation. Much to Oliver's annoyance, that applied equally to him. Resisting temptation was something he had such little practice at.

A creaking noise behind him interrupted his thoughts. He turned and saw his wife standing in the doorway. Wearing a white nightgown, her long black hair flowing freely, she was temptation itself. One Oliver knew it would take a man much stronger than him to resist.

Chapter Fifteen

It had taken every ounce of self-confidence Arabella possessed to turn the door handle to the adjoining room. And now here she was, standing in his bedroom, staring up at him, and it was taking even more strength to stay and not flee back to her own room.

When she had seen the light from his lamp appear under the door, she knew she did not want to spend another night staring at that light and wondering. She did not want to lie in bed thinking about him, wishing and wanting. So, she had got out of bed and opened his door. But she hadn't thought about what she would do once she was in his room.

He continued to stare at her, not moving from the window. He was dressed in a loosely tied maroon robe and her gaze was drawn to his muscular chest, visible at the robe's opening. He was naked underneath. She gulped, her startled gaze moving back up to his face.

Surely he would take some action. Do something. Not just stand there. Surely he knew why she was here. Was that all he was going to do? Just stay exactly where he was, staring at her? It seemed it was.

Her heart thumping loudly against her chest, she gasped in a series of breaths to give herself courage. If he wasn't going to do anything, then she would have to. She placed her hands at her neckline, closed her eyes and pulled at the laces holding the front of her nightgown together.

'What are you doing, Arabella?' he asked, his voice thick and constricted.

Instead of answering she continued to fumble at her laces with clumsy fingers.

He crossed the room, took hold of her hands and stilled the action. 'Arabella, I've told you. I don't seduce virgins.'

She pulled in another deep breath and spoke as clearly as she possibly could. 'In case you haven't noticed, you're not seducing me. I'm seducing you.' Well, that was what she was trying to do, but it was a bit difficult when she couldn't even unlace her nightgown.

She looked up at him, praying she would not see him laughing at her. Instead there was an unmistakable look of passion burning in his eyes. Passion for her. She had not been wrong. The way he had spoken to her over dinner, the things he had said to her, the way he had behaved had all led her to think he wanted her. And the look in his eyes confirmed that. It was the same as she had seen before he kissed her, the same as when he'd stared at her with such hunger earlier today.

'Arabella, are you sure?'

She nodded. Of course she was sure. She had never been more sure of anything in her life. 'Yes,' she said, her voice little more than a whisper.

He lifted her fingers to his lips. 'You know what sort of man I am. I can't offer you commitment, I can't offer you fidelity.'

She shook her head. 'I'm not asking you for either of those things.'

He lowered her hands and held them close against his chest, so close she could feel his heart pounding, could sense the tension in his body. His eyes never left hers and the intent of that look was undeniable. He most certainly wasn't laughing at her. He was looking at her as if he wanted to devour her. And that was exactly what Arabella wanted him to do.

That look in his eye making her bold, she smiled up at him, teasingly. 'I'm just a married woman who wants some fun.'

His lips slowly curled into that mischievous smile she loved so much. 'Well, in that case, my dear, let's have some fun.'

His hands slid around her waist, pulling her towards him. His kiss was gentle, but that was not what she wanted. She wanted him to kiss her the way he had when he'd burst into her dressing room. That kiss had possessed her, taken her over, caused her to lose herself, to forget everything and everyone around her until she'd kissed him back in front of everyone. And she wanted him to more than just kiss her now. Did he still require permission? Then she would give it to him. She wrapped her hands around his neck, running her hands through his thick blond hair and holding him tightly against her.

Parting her lips, she kissed him back, her body hard up against him, the touch of his naked skin against her breasts, her legs against his, letting him know she wanted him to deepen the kiss.

His grip on her waist tightened and he pulled her possessively towards him, his fierce kiss crashing over her, hard, demanding, potent.

Yes, this was what she wanted. She released a quiet moan of pleasure as his tongue entered her mouth, plundering, probing. Her body melted into his. Oh, yes, this was most definitely what she wanted. This was why she had risked everything and entered his room.

His hand slid down from her waist, cupping her buttocks. Every inch of her body pulsated for him, ached for him. Her mind going blank, she clasped him tighter, her swelling breasts rubbing against his muscular chest, wanting to feel his skin against hers, his body surrounding her, his hands caressing her.

He stepped back from her and desperation gripped her. No. He could not be stopping now. She would not let him. She looked up at him, her confused mind trying to formulate the words that would make him kiss her again.

'Raise your arms above your head,' he said, his voice a low growl.

Arabella followed his command and in one swift movement he lifted up her nightgown, pulled it off her body and tossed it to the side of the room. She was now standing naked in front of him.

Any fleeting embarrassment was swept away when his lips found hers again, kissing her, devouring her.

Still kissing her, he lifted her up in one smooth movement and carried her over to his bed. Placing her carefully in the middle, he stood back, looked down at her and smiled.

'You really are beautiful, Arabella. The most beautiful woman I've ever seen. And this is how I imagined seeing you from the very first time I laid eyes on you.'

Lying naked in front of him, Arabella knew she should be feeling embarrassed. But she didn't. *He had wanted her in his bed from the moment he had first seen her.* That admission sent a heady wave tingling through her body and any residual shyness evaporated. He desired her, had always desired her. And right now, with him looking at her with such fierce passion, that was exactly how she felt—desirable.

His robe dropped to the ground and it was now her turn to admire his body. And it was a body worthy of admiration. Her gaze took in the firm, strong muscles of his chest and his flat hard stomach, with a scattering of dark hairs drawing her gaze down his body. And if she had any remaining doubt of his desire for her, she no longer did. His desire was standing, firm and hard in front of her.

Her eyes returned to his and she saw that devilish smile on his lips. He had seen where her gaze had travelled.

Arabella bit the edge of her lip and smiled back at him. 'So, are you going to show me some of that fun you promised?'

He laughed lightly and joined her on the bed. 'Happy to oblige.'

Arabella arched towards him and wrapped her arms around his neck, longing to feel his touch. He smiled down at her and watched her reaction as his hands moved slowly over her sensitive skin. His fingers lightly ran over her stomach and up her ribcage. A low groan escaped her lips and she closed her eyes, surrendering herself to the sensation of his touch.

His hand reached her breasts. He cupped each one in turn and his thumb moved over the now achingly tight buds. She writhed on the bed as his hands tormented her nipples. A pounding deep within her core possessed her body and her moans came louder, faster, her mind and body consumed by his caresses. When he leant down and took one nipple in his mouth it felt as if she was about to die from pleasure. His tongue rasped over the stiff nub, licking, sucking. Her moans became cries of ecstasy. Louder and louder, in time to the rhythm of his tongue.

His hand slid down her body and moved between her legs. She felt his fingers gently stroke along her folds and enter her most intimate of places. His palm pressed between her legs, intensifying the throbbing that was engulfing her, while his lips continued to tease and torment her nipples. Surrendering herself to the experience, she rubbed herself against him, her back instinctively arched, matching his rhythm, increasing the pleasure, a pleasure that kept mounting, growing, intensifying until a forceful, ecstatic wave crashed over her. She released a loud, shuddering cry and collapsed back on the bed.

When she opened her eyes, he was smiling down at her. She blinked away a few tears that had sprung to her eyes and smiled back at him. 'That was…that was…' She couldn't think of the words.

'So, do you want some more of that?' he asked gently.

'Oh, yes,' she replied. 'Yes, yes, yes.'

He kissed her again and she melted into his kiss. His tongue entered her mouth and she once again savoured the masculine taste of him, inhaling that wonderful musky scent she loved so much. Her hands wrapped around his shoulders, moving down his strong back, loving the feel of his hard muscles under her fingers, then down to those firm tight buttocks.

But she wanted more than his kisses, more than his caresses.

She withdrew from his lips and lifted herself up towards him. 'Make love to me, Oliver,' she urged.

He hugged her closer, his chest hard against hers. 'I don't want to cause you any pain, Bella.'

'You won't. I want this, Oliver.' She rubbed the inside of her thigh against his leg and smiled at his quick intake of breath. Unable to stop herself, even if she wanted to, Arabella parted her legs and arched her body towards him.

'Make love to me, now, Oliver.'

He did not need to be asked again. He wrapped her in his arms, his strong thighs moving between hers. As if under their own command, her legs wrapped themselves around his waist. She felt the tip of him at the edge of her feminine folds, but still he hesitated.

'Stop me at any time, Bella,' he murmured.

But Arabella knew she would not stop him, could not stop him. He pushed himself slowly into her. She gasped out loudly, but in pleasure, not pain. Slowly he withdrew and even more slowly he entered her again, watching her carefully as he did so. She cried out in pleasure and clasped his buttocks tightly, pushing him towards her, letting him know this was what she wanted.

She looked up into his eyes. Concern was now gone, replaced by a look of primal hunger, a hunger that only intensified her need for him. He entered her more deeply and she cried out his name, urging him on. He responded immediately, pushing into her again and again, deeper, harder.

With each stroke her cries became louder, her body moving against his, in time to his thrusting rhythm.

Her eyes closed, she lost herself to the sensations swelling up inside her, taking her higher and higher, until they reached a pitch of intensity that was almost more than she could bear and a convulsive shudder whipped through her, causing her to dig her fingers into his buttocks and cry out, before collapsing back on to the bed. Just as her body went limp, she felt his heart suddenly pound harder against her sweat-slickened breasts. He muttered her name on a soft moan and pulled out from her just before he released himself.

Wrapped in each other's arms, they held each other tightly while their panting breaths slowed down and Arabella could hardly believe that such a feeling of fulfilment was possible.

When his breath returned to normal, Oliver lifted himself up on to one arm, smiled down at her and brushed a stray lock of hair from her face. 'Well, I don't know about you, Duchess, but personally I feel thoroughly seduced.'

Arabella laughed, wrapping her arms tightly around him as he kissed her once again.

Chapter Sixteen

Oliver gazed down at his sleeping wife, at her long black eyelashes resting on her soft, porcelain-cream skin, at her full red lips, swollen from his repeated kisses. She looked so angelic in repose, but last night there had been nothing angelic about her behaviour. He smiled at the memory of her standing in the doorway, dressed only in her nightgown. The light from behind her had made the gown almost translucent and he had been able to see the outline of her beautiful body, those luscious curves and long, shapely legs.

It had taken a level of iron willpower he didn't know he possessed to not move, to not cross the room and rip off that nightgown so he could feast on her beauty. Like a mantra he had kept reciting to himself, again and again, *You do not seduce virgins, you do not seduce virgins* in order to keep himself fixed to the spot.

But even iron can bend if exposed to a high enough temperature. And his iron willpower had been unable to withstand the fury of the heat generated when she

had whispered those words in his ear, 'You're not seducing me, I'm seducing you'.

He ran his finger gently down the side of her face
and curled a strand of her long black hair around his
finger. She had made it clear to him that he was not
taking advantage of her innocence. She had given
him permission to stop fighting his attraction to her
and to give vent to the surging passion that had been
building up inside him like a volcano.

And he had discovered his initial assessment of
her had been correct. When he had kissed her on the
night they had first met he had suspected there was a
well of untapped passion simmering within her, just
waiting to be ignited.

And last night he had definitely stoked those fires.
They had made love repeatedly. Each time she had become more adventurous, continually surprising him,
and her appetite had been as ravenous as his own.

Last night had been unlike anything he had experienced with a woman. The intensity, the passion, the
intimacy, it had been utterly intoxicating. And like a
drug that had entered his bloodstream and taken him
over, he had craved more, much more.

Why he should have experienced such a strength
of feeling he had no idea. He couldn't be that cliché,
a man who became puffed up with masculine pride
because he was a woman's first lover. Could he?

Oliver knew it wasn't that. Was it because Arabella was so different from any other woman he had
known?

He continued to gaze at her lovely face. She had a
delicate beauty, but that disguised a strength of character that was admirable.

Her determination to succeed on the stage, to carve out a life of her own, despite being the daughter of an extremely wealthy man, made her unique in his world. He knew no other woman, or man for that matter, who was prepared to forgo all that wealth could give them, to risk it all so they could achieve their dream.

And last night, by coming into his room, she had shown that strength in a different way. She had been so nervous, her hands shaking as she'd tried to free herself from her nightgown, yet she had forced herself to continue. He smiled with warm pleasure. She had been willing to take a risk and expose her vulnerability to him.

He really was a lucky man to have a woman like Arabella in his bed, not just because making love to her had been so magical, but because she was so special, unique.

His smile turned to a loud, exasperated sigh. But he would have to enjoy it while it lasted. They would soon be returning to their own lives. Their time together was just an interlude, a very enjoyable, very satisfying interlude, but an interlude all the same.

He rolled over on to his back, put his hands behind his head and stared up at the ceiling. Last night he had told her he couldn't offer her commitment and fidelity and she had accepted that. He only hoped she meant it and they weren't idle words. It was true, he had never committed to a woman. Experience had taught him he was incapable of doing so.

But he could not subject Arabella to the life his mother had led with his father, waiting dutifully at home while her husband moved from woman to woman without a backward glance. That was not the life that she should be leading. But it was also a life he knew a woman like Arabella would never accept. His jaw tensing, he knew that one day she would find someone who could offer her what he couldn't— commitment, fidelity, love. When that happened, he would have to accept it.

He rolled back to his side and gazed down at her. But that was all in the future. Right now, they were here together and he should be just enjoying the moment, not worrying about what would one day happen. Right now, she was with him, here, in his bed. And right now, he had no interest in any other woman. He was exactly where he wanted to be and with the woman he wanted to be with.

But how long would that last?

A leopard never changed his spots. He was not a one-woman man.

Eventually he would revert to type. He just had to ensure that he had set Arabella free before that happened.

He pushed away that thought. He did not need to think of it now. He ran his fingers down the soft, creamy skin of her shoulder and arm. She moved sensually in the bed. Her eyes opened and she smiled at him. Soon they would be parting and life would return to normal, but one more taste would do no harm. He leant down and kissed his wife's waiting lips, then took her in his arms to make love to her one more time.

Making love to Oliver…it had to be the perfect way to start the day. Arabella smiled and stretched lazily in the four-poster bed, her body tired and sated. She was so happy. Last night and this morning had been more thrilling than she could possibly have imagined. Now all she had to do was ignore the little voice in the back of her head that was asking, *What happens now?*

She did not know how this was going to work. Last night, she had promised Oliver that she would not interfere in the way he lived his life and she would abide by that promise. There would be other women in his life and that was something she was going to have to accept. She would just have to learn to control the pain that clenched her heart whenever she thought of him with someone else.

That was the deal. He had promised he would do nothing to interfere with her career on the stage and he had abided by that. More than abided by it, he was actually helping her achieve her goals. And Arabella would do the same for him.

Well, she wouldn't actually help him pursue other women. She wasn't a complete martyr and he hardly needed any help in that area anyway.

But she would at least do nothing to stop him. No matter how much heartache it caused her.

In the meantime, she would enjoy this moment while it lasted. Feasting her eyes on her husband's gorgeous body, she moved them slowly over every inch of him, as if committing each sculpted muscle to memory. Her fingers then followed the same path as her eyes, moving up those strong arms, across his wide shoulders, down the rock-hard chest to that flat, firm stomach. She smiled wickedly, her hand slowly moving lower.

It was amazing how last night had changed her. Those initial nerves had soon disappeared. She had felt so safe in Oliver's arms, safe enough to release a delicious wantonness she had not known she possessed, a wantonness she had thoroughly enjoyed exploring.

He grinned when her teasing fingers reached their destination. 'Again? Already? You will be the death of me.'

She laughed as his arms surrounded her.

'But this would definitely be something worth dying for,' he said, his lips finding hers and stifling her laughter.

They spent the day in bed together, never moving except to eat. When each discreet knock came at the door, Oliver would retrieve the tray left by the servants and they would picnic among the bedclothes, feeding each other an array of delicious treats prepared by the cook. Then they would make love again. Each time, when she fell back on to the bed, wondrously replete, Arabella was sure her hunger for him had finally been satisfied. They would remain in bed, talking and laughing, but before long that ache would start again, an ache that only he could soothe.

And so they passed another day and night together.

On the third day, the ever-thoughtful Nellie left a note to say she had prepared a bath in Arabella's dressing room. Leaving the tangled knot of sheets and blankets, Arabella led a naked Oliver by the hand through to her rooms, stepped into the bath and lay back as the warm water wrapped around her.

'Allow me,' Oliver said, picking up a sponge and slowly lathering her body.

Bliss, was all Arabella could think as she closed her eyes and surrendered herself to the touch of the sponge, the warmth of the water and the scent of lily of the valley from the soap.

But there was something that would make this experience even more blissful. She opened her eyes and smiled invitingly at Oliver. 'Join me.'

He frowned slightly. 'There's hardly room.'

'Then we'll make room.' She sat up straighter and curled in her legs.

His frown turned into a mischievous smile and he climbed into the bath. The water level rose, lapping at the rim. His large frame filled the other end of the bath and he wrapped his long legs around her.

'Right, now it's my turn.' She picked up the sponge, pulled herself into a kneeling position and rubbed the sponge along his shoulders, chest and slowly down his stomach.

Her attempts were thwarted when he grabbed her round the waist and kissed her, sending a tidal wave of water sloshing over the side on to the carpeted floor.

They both peered over the side at the mess they had made, then back at each other. 'This is not going to work, is it?' he said.

Laughing, she shook her head.

'In that case…' He scooped her up, dripping from the bath, and lowered her to her feet, her wet skin gliding against his glistening body. Taking one of the fluffy white towels left on a nearby wooden chair, he wrapped her in it and dried her slowly, then quickly ran the towel over himself.

'Right, now that we're clean, there appears to be a bed we haven't christened yet,' he murmured, scooping her up again and carrying her into her bedroom.

'So how many bedrooms does Somerfeld Manor have?' she asked as he lowered her on to her bed.

'I've never counted them, but I believe there's around forty.'

Arabella smiled, her toes curling in excitement. 'It looks as though we've got a lot of christening ahead of us.'

Oliver laughed, joining her on the bed. 'Then I'd better get busy, hadn't I, and get this one ticked off our list.'

Another rapturous day and night had passed. It was as if the outside world hardly existed. There was only this room, this bed and this man. And that was just how Arabella wanted it to remain.

Another discreet knock at the door alerted them to the arrival of more food. Arabella was famished. She had never felt more in need of sustenance, but then she had been indulging in some rather strenuous exercise recently.

Oliver disentangled himself from the sheets and strode across the room. She hummed with satisfaction as she surveyed his naked form from behind, all taut, powerful muscles. Was there anything more attractive than his firm round buttocks? Arabella doubted that very much.

He opened the door and retrieved the tray. She sat up, anxious to see what tasty food had been prepared for them. She had lost count of the time, did not know which meal it would be, but was sure that Cook would have once again prepared something delicious. It was funny how food tasted so much better when it was eaten in bed with your lover.

Removing the lid from the serving dish, she saw it was a selection of cold meats, cheeses, pâtés and bread. It must be lunch time, perfect.

Then she spotted a letter, standing upright between the silver salt and pepper shakers. She picked it up and turned it over. It was from the Limelight Theatre and addressed to Oliver.

Suddenly struggling to breathe, she handed it to him. 'This is for you,' she whispered.

He put down his plate and took the letter from her outstretched hand, read the address and handed it back to her. 'It might be addressed to me, but it will be about your future. You should be the one to read it.'

With trembling fingers, she picked up the ivory letter opener that had been placed on the tray and slit open the envelope. She quickly scanned the contents, then re-read them again, more slowly, her stomach clenching as she absorbed each word. She handed the letter to Oliver and watched him carefully as he read it.

When he had finished, he looked up at her. They held each other's gazes, his solemn expression reflecting exactly how she was feeling.

Chapter Seventeen

It was good news. Of course it was good news and Oliver would be selfish to think otherwise. But he *was* selfish. He wished they could continue to stay in bed together, let the world pass them by and forget everything and everyone else.

But for once in his life he would not be selfish. Arabella deserved more than that.

'That's excellent. Exactly what you wanted,' he said, jumping out of bed and grabbing his robe. 'You must return to London immediately.' He pulled the bell cord to call for a servant and forced himself to smile at her with as much excitement as he could summon.

Arabella remained in bed, still clutching the letter in her hand. She didn't look particularly pleased, Oliver mused. Perhaps it was because it was unexpected. Or maybe she was nervous about the part she had been offered in the new play, which, while not one of the leads, was more substantial than her previous role.

She smiled tentatively at him, slowly climbed out

of bed and looked around for her discarded night-gown. After four days of being continuously naked, she suddenly appeared uncomfortable and self-consciously crossed her arms, covering her breasts. He picked up her nightgown and handed it to her. She took it from his outstretched hand and quickly pulled it over her head. Her body disappeared from his gaze. Oliver hoped and prayed he had not seen it for the last time.

She once again looked around the room, as if un-certain what to do next.

'You *are* happy, aren't you, Bella? This is what you want, isn't it? You're not worried about anything, are you?'

She nodded. 'Oh, no, I'm not worried, and yes, yes, of course I'm happy. I'm just a bit taken aback that the reply came so quickly. That's all. But, yes, of course I'm happy.'

It wasn't how happy usually looked. Happy didn't normally appear so confused or pensive.

A quiet knock at the door stopped him from ques-tioning her reaction. He opened the door and told his valet to arrange for her trunks to be packed and for the carriage to be prepared so they could return to London on the next train.

Arabella tilted her head. 'Will you be returning to London as well?'

Oliver nodded. 'Yes, I have business to attend to there, so I might as well join you. Plus, it will give you a chance to get settled in at my town house.'

Business? What business?

Oliver was unsure. All he knew was that he did not want to leave Arabella. Not yet.

She remained standing in the middle of his room, staring up at him.

'Perhaps you should summon your lady's maid so you can prepare for the journey,' he suggested.

Her gaze moved to their unmade bed, at the tray of now-abandoned lunch. 'Oh, yes, of course.'

She exited through to the adjoining room and closed the door behind her. Another quiet knock came at his door and he opened it to admit his valet, carrying his shaving equipment and a bowl of hot water.

Oliver always preferred to shave himself, so while he lathered his face his valet prepared his clothing for the journey.

He would be returning to London. Back to his old life.

He paused and stared at his reflection in the shaving mirror, his razor poised at the edge of his soaped cheek.

Wasn't that what he wanted? To go back to the constant round of parties, the gambling dens and the other delights London had to offer?

Of course it was. Why wouldn't it be? That's who he was, after all. He ran the razor along his cheek, then washed the soap off the razor in the hot water. It was a good outcome for both of them, *wasn't it*? The last few days had certainly been enjoyable, but it was time for things to get back to normal. And Arabella being offered a part in a new play was certainly all for the best. While he returned to his old life, she would be busy forging a career on the stage.

It had all worked out perfectly. So why wasn't he more pleased? He tilted back his head and ran the razor up his neck, scraping off several days' stubble.

The answer to that question was obvious. Because he was selfish. He wanted to spend more time in bed with Arabella. He had not yet completely satisfied his need for her.

He rinsed the razor again and stared down at the bowl. When had that ever happened before? Never. He had never had to move on from a woman before he was ready. But it looked as though this time he was going to have to. And if he was to avoid acting like a petulant child who'd had his favourite toy taken away from him, he would have to keep his feelings to himself.

He finished off his shaving and rubbed a warm towel over his face.

This was a brilliant opportunity for Arabella and she did not need a husband who was thinking only of his own carnal needs holding her back.

He pulled on his shirt and his valet buttoned on the stiff white collar, then helped him into his waist-coat and jacket. All was not yet lost, Oliver reminded his reflection in the full-length mirror while his valet brushed down his jacket. They would be together at his London town house and maybe there, with any luck, he would have ample opportunity to satisfy his need for his wife and finally get her out of his system.

Arabella was meant to be happy. After all, how could she not be? This was wonderful news. So why did she feel as if she had suffered a defeat, not a victory? Until a few days ago the only thing that really gave her pleasure was the thought of being back on stage. Now she had experienced another source of exquisite pleasure, in the arms of her husband. And it was a pleasure she wasn't ready to give up, not yet.

She sat in silence in front of her dressing table mirror as Nellie styled her hair. Like it or not, she was going to have to give up that pleasure. She was returning to London, back to where she had first met Oliver, back to his world, a world inhabited by an array of beautiful women like Lady Bufford and Lucy Baker. Here, at Somerfeld Manor, she'd had him all to herself, but now she would have to share him.

Getting a part at the Limelight was a victory, but losing Oliver to his real life was most definitely a defeat.

But she had told him she would accept him the way he was and put up no objections to the way he lived. It was now time to keep that promise.

She stood up so Nellie could help her into her travelling dress. There was no reason why she should feel sorry for herself. Didn't she have everything she wanted? She was to resume work as an actress and had just experienced a few days of pleasure, the level of which she previously didn't know existed. No, she had nothing to feel sorry about. So she wouldn't. She would celebrate the victory and ignore the defeat.

Because when it came down to it, she had no other option. It was a defeat of her own making. Hadn't she promised she'd make no demands on him? Hadn't that been the only reason he had made love to her, gone against his rules of not seducing virgins?

She nodded decisively at her reflection. No, she had absolutely no right to feel sorry for herself. And there was no question about whether she would abide by her promise. Of course she would.

She forced herself to smile as Nellie brushed down her dress. She *would* be happy. She would return to London, her old life, her real life, the life that she loved.

She joined Oliver, waiting for her outside the house beside the carriage already loaded with their trunks. With as much enthusiasm as she could summon, she smiled at him as he helped her into the carriage which would take them to the train station.

Forcing herself to maintain a façade of gaiety, she made polite conversation throughout the trip. As the Surrey countryside passed them by, outside the train window, she worked hard to ignore that annoying voice reminding her that this was indeed the end of their journey together.

Arriving in London, they took a cab from the station to his Mayfair town house. The quiet of the neighbourhood was a stark contrast to the bustle of the railway station and the busy, chaotic streets they had travelled through, with horses, carts, carriages, omnibuses and pedestrians all jostling for position on the teeming roads. It was hard to believe that they were in the centre of a busy city. It was so tranquil, the only sound being the twittering of birds, singing in the large trees that lined the pavement, and the subdued chatter of two passing nannies, pushing their large, black perambulators.

'Rather pleasant, isn't it?' Nellie whispered to her, her hand on her hat as she looked up at the three-storey brick façade. 'I'm going to enjoy living here.'

'Don't get too comfortable, Nellie. We're not staying here. We'll be moving into the boarding house along with the rest of the cast.'

Nellie rolled her eyes, but followed Arabella through the columned entranceway and into the house. Servants were rushing up and down the staircases, still making the house ready for their sudden arrival. Arabella looked up at the ornate carved ceiling, soaring above them three storeys high, each storey with a carved wooden balcony overlooking the entrance.

Yes, Arabella had to admit it was quite an improvement on the boarding house where the actors stayed. But she was committed to returning to her old life. Now that her father had left the country, she did not have to stay at the Savoy. While the cast and crew always treated her as if she was no different, Arabella was always aware that she came from a privileged background and, unlike them, was not dependent on the paltry wage that acting brought in.

So to prove to them that she would not be adopting any airs, now that she was a duchess, she would organise to join them at their humble boarding house. And it would prove to Oliver that she was really committed to returning to her real life.

'Let me show you to your rooms,' Oliver said, leading her up the stairs. She caught Nellie's eye, who gave her an encouraging smile and nod. But Nellie would have to accept disappointment. They would not be staying at this house, and she would soon be explaining this situation to Oliver.

He opened the door to her room and smiled at her. 'I hope this is satisfactory.' If she was actually staying, it would be more than satisfactory. The spacious room, with floor-to-ceiling windows overlooking the garden courtyard, had a light and airy feel. It was a delightfully feminine room, with delicate red and cream wallpaper with a Japanese blossom motif, Persian rugs on the wooden floor and a large four-poster bed. Nellie was right, this would be a very comfortable place to stay. And, once again, her rooms would be adjoining Oliver's with only an interconnecting door between them.

That was another very good reason for her to not stay at his town house. How many other women was Oliver going to entertain in the room next door to hers? She had promised him freedom, but it did not mean she wanted to be present to witness him exercise it. She shuddered, despite the warmth of the summer's day. No, that would be asking too much of her. She would have to get used to the thought of him with another woman, but she wanted it all to happen out of sight, then hopefully, it might just be out of her mind as well.

'Well, I think I'll go straight to the theatre.'

Oliver moved to one side as she barged past him. 'But surely you want to get settled in first,' he said to her retreating back.

She headed towards the stairs. 'No, the letter said they're starting rehearsals immediately, so I don't want to miss a single day.'

'Then I'll accompany you.'

'There's no need.' Arabella quickly rushed down the stairs. She did not want Oliver at the theatre. She most definitely did not want to risk some other actress capturing his eye. 'Honestly, there really isn't,' she called back to him.

He caught up with her at the bottom of the stairs. 'I'd like to accompany you. I love watching you perform and I've never seen a play in rehearsal before.'

Arabella paused at the entrance, trying to think of an excuse as he asked a footman to arrange for his carriage to be brought to the front of the house. She could hardly tell him the real reason she did not want him to accompany her. She had already told the other actresses that their marriage was to be one in name only and she knew there were several who more than adequately fitted Oliver's requirements of wanting to have fun with no commitments. If he was going to have other women in his life, she would rather it not be any she knew.

It looked as though her resolve was about to be sorely tested. With the greatest reluctance she nodded and tried to ignore his obvious smile of delight.

Chapter Eighteen

Arabella's father had been true to his word. He had promised to inject much-needed funds into the Limelight Theatre and, looking up at the once crumbling façade Oliver could see the transformation. The flaking plaster had been removed, the exterior freshly painted and the broken brown and cream tiles in the entranceway replaced. It now looked like a professional theatre ready to welcome its eager patrons.

The interior was as much a revelation. The previously shabby chairs in the auditorium had been re-upholstered in plush red velvet, a gold-ruched curtain was suspended above the stage and a new, thick purple and gold carpet had been laid to replace the old, threadbare floor coverings.

He looked around the walls and could see modern electric lighting had also been installed. Arabella's father must have had men working round the clock to complete the renovations before he left for America. It was an impressive sight. The Limelight now rivalled any theatre in the city in terms of opulence.

The cast were assembled on stage and Arabella

rushed forward to join them, as if she couldn't get away from him fast enough. He took a seat in the auditorium to watch his wife embrace her new life, one that didn't include him.

As soon as she appeared on stage, she was surrounded by excited actresses, all eager to see the rings on her finger and from Arabella's awkward stance they were also presumably asking her about married life. Her taciturn answers told Oliver just how reluctant she was to share any information and how uncomfortable she was with their questioning. The director hushed the chatter and Oliver saw a look of relief pass over his wife's face.

But what else should he expect? Neither of them had wanted to be married. It was hardly a love match or a whirlwind romance. It had all been arranged against her will. She was unlikely to be acting like a love-struck newlywed, all girlish blushes and coquettish simpering.

Their marriage was simply a convenient way for Mr van Haven to get the title he wanted and for Arabella to continue to live the independent life she wanted, unrestricted by the demands of either her father or a husband. Oliver had been true to his word by marrying her. Now it was time for him to step out of her life.

He settled down more comfortably into the plush chair. It would hardly matter if he watched just one rehearsal first.

The cast began a read through of their lines. After a few tentative glances out into the auditorium Arabella seemed to forget about him and he watched as his wife transformed herself before his eyes. She became completely lost in her part, taking on the appearance and the mannerisms of her character, that of a poverty-stricken young woman trying to protect her family from an evil landlord.

Oliver felt himself swell with pride as he watched her performance. There was no denying his wife was extremely talented. He was also pleased he had played a small part in ensuring that she was able to continue doing what she loved and that the world would be able to share her talent, too.

But he wasn't *completely* invisible to her. Each time the director interrupted with instructions, she looked out into the auditorium. He sent her what he hoped was an encouraging smile, although he doubted she could see him in the darkened theatre.

When the rehearsal came to an end the cast all gathered around, talking and laughing, excited by the progress they had already made.

Oliver joined them on stage and everyone except his wife appeared pleased to see him. She was standing alone, staring down at the script clasped in her hands. He would have assumed she was still engrossed in learning her lines, if it wasn't for the quick, furtive glances she kept sending in his direction.

Slowly the hubbub died down and people started taking their leave, with much kissing of cheeks and theatrical waving of hands.

'Right, your carriage awaits, m'lady,' Oliver said with a low bow, getting caught up in the theatrics surrounding him. 'Shall we return home?' He extended his arm for her to take.

'Um…actually, I've decided I'll stay at the boarding house with the other actors.'

Oliver's extended arm dropped to his side. 'You'll *what*?'

'It's just that I don't want the others to treat me any differently,' she said, her words coming out in an embarrassed rush.

She had nothing to be embarrassed about, just as he had no right to feel disappointed. It was her choice how she decided to live her life. But that didn't make it any easier. They would not be spending any more time together. She would not be sharing his bed each night.

'As you wish,' he said, trying hard to disguise his disappointment. 'But allow me to escort you to your new accommodation.'

She shook her head. 'No. If I'm to try to act like one of the crew, arriving in a carriage with your crest on the door would hardly be appropriate.'

Oliver laughed. 'I very much doubt if it will be the first time a carriage bearing a duke's crest has delivered an actress home.'

Her mouth drew into a tight line and she scowled. He had said the wrong thing.

'If it will make you feel any better, I can offer other members of the cast a ride as well.' He looked around and gestured towards the group of actresses watching them with interest from the wings.

'That won't be necessary,' she said hurriedly, frowning in their direction. She inhaled deeply. 'I'm sorry. Yes, thank you, Oliver, I would like you to give me a ride to my lodgings and if you could please arrange for my trunk to be delivered as well, I would be grateful.'

The boarding house was even shabbier than Oliver had expected. He accompanied her into her room and tried to hide his shock. With bare wooden floorboards, it was much smaller than her bedchamber at his town house, but contained four single beds. It seemed she would be sharing with three others. The one window, which let in minimal light, looked out on to the brick wall of the neighbouring building, and from the musty smell he suspected the dark paint on the bedroom walls was disguising damp and possibly mould.

And she chose to live here, rather than with him at his town house. Unbelievable.

'Are you sure about this, Bella?' He patted a mattress, feeling how thin it was and causing the rusty springs to creak.

'Yes, of course I am.'

There was a hesitation in her voice. It was clearly his opportunity to convince her of her mistake.

'You don't have to stay here. You can always come home to my town house. No one will think any less of you. I'm sure if any of the other actresses had the opportunity to exchange this…' he gestured around the room '…for their own suite of rooms in Mayfair they'd jump at the chance.'

She pulled back her shoulders and glared at him. 'I don't care what any other actress would or would not jump at. This is where I want to be.'

He shook his head in disbelief and stared at her.

She held his gaze for a moment, then turned and looked out of the window at the non-existent view. He was tempted to argue with her, to insist she come home with him, but he knew it would fall on deaf ears. And who was he to tell her what she could and couldn't do? She was an independent woman who could make her own choices.

She turned from the window. 'Now, if you don't mind, I'd like to get settled in. Will you please arrange for my trunk to be delivered?'

He stood helplessly in the middle of the room, unwilling to leave, even though she was making it clear that his presence was no longer required or wanted.

But leave he must. 'As you wish.' He remained standing, unable to move. Once again she looked out of the window at the brick wall.

He gave a slight bow, even though with her back turned she couldn't see it, and headed down the narrow wooden stairs to his waiting carriage.

It was ridiculous. She was being ridiculous. He climbed into the carriage and looked up at the shabby exterior. She really was determined to do things the hard way. If she didn't want to stay at his town house, the allowance he had allocated to her meant she had enough money to stay in any of the best hotels in London if she wanted to. Was she also reluctant to take his money? It would seem so. It was obvious she wanted nothing more from him.

Oliver returned to his town house alone. He was now, once again, a free man. He could do anything he wanted.

He looked around the drawing room. It appeared different somehow, as if something was missing, but it was exactly how he had left it just a few weeks ago. He quickly poured himself a glass of brandy, the crystal decanter clinking against the glass. He knew exactly what was missing. Arabella was missing. He had expected them to spend some more time together, had wanted to spend more time with her. He had not tired of making love to her, far from it. He had expected to have her in his bed tonight and for many nights to come. He had hoped to continue what they had started at his Surrey estate. Instead he would have to find other ways to entertain himself. He poured another glass of brandy, tossed it back and wondered how he would spend his evening.

Perhaps he should ask his wife to dine with him.

She didn't want to live in his house, but that didn't mean she didn't want to spend time with him. And once they had finished dining, maybe she would like to come back to the town house for a nightcap, and then, perhaps, he could encourage her to stay the night. After all, what harm would one more night together do?

He dismissed that idea. It was ludicrous.

That was not what she wanted. She had made it clear they were now to live as if their marriage had never happened.

And if that was what she wanted, then there was one thing he was certain about. He could not remain at home alone. He had never been a man to ruminate or agonise over what might or might not have been and he wasn't about to start now.

He grabbed his hat and gloves and asked the footman to hail a cab. He would start at his club and then let the night unfold the way countless other nights had in the past. He might be a married man, but Arabella was getting on with her own life, so it was time he did the same.

Nellie stood at the entrance of the bedroom, looking just as disapproving as Oliver had earlier that evening.

She placed her suitcase on one of the beds, turned to face Arabella and tilted her head, waiting for an explanation.

'I know, I know, Nellie, it's a bit grim, but I had to let Oliver know that I expect nothing from him. And that meant I wouldn't be living at his town house, nor would I be taking his allowance. I want to do this on my own, to prove to everyone I'm capable of making my way in the world as an actress.'

Nellie sat on the bed, grimaced as it emitted a pained creak, and stood up again.

'An actress with her own lady's maid? That's a bit unusual, though, don't you think?' Nellie ran her finger along the dusty mantelpiece and frowned.

'Yes, about that. I hope you don't mind, Nellie, but I've arranged for you to work at the theatre doing hair, make-up and helping with the costumes.'

Nellie brushed her hands together to rid herself of the dust and smiled. 'No, of course I don't mind. It will be fun. And I suppose this won't be too bad once we've got used to it.'

She looked around the room and Arabella could see Nellie was trying to put on a brave face.

'And after all it's only temporary,' Nellie continued. 'You'll soon be a famous actress living it up in your own luxurious home and then I'll have my own hairdressing salon and beauty parlour and be making all those frumpy old toffs look more gorgeous than they thought possible.'

Arabella smiled at her. Nellie was always so supportive and optimistic.

'Thank you, Nellie,' she said and began helping her lady's maid unpack their bags.

Laughter suddenly filled the room as Flora and Harriet, the two other actresses they would be sharing with, burst through the door.

When they saw Arabella, their laughter died and they stared at her as if she was a green-skinned monster.

'You're *staying* here?' Flora said. They looked at each other, then back at Arabella, their mouths open.

Arabella had expected their reaction. It was the same reaction she had got when she had told the theatre manager that she wanted to stay at the boarding house, but it didn't make it any easier to bear.

'Why aren't you staying with the Duke?' Flora asked. 'What's gone wrong? He hasn't chucked you over already, has he?'

Arabella bristled, but forced herself to continue hanging dresses in the small wardrobe. 'No, he *hasn't* chucked me over.' She forced herself to continue in a calm manner. 'In case you haven't heard, the Duke and I merely married because my father was determined that I would marry a man with a title. Neither of us wanted the marriage and we have both agreed that we will be man and wife in name only.'

The two wide-eyed actresses looked at each other, then back at Arabella. 'Well, I had heard something like that, but I didn't really believe it. If I was you, I wouldn't care if it was in name only,' Flora said. 'I'd be taking advantage of being his wife. I'd be living at his town house and doing my best to keep that one on a short leash.'

Flora looked over at Harriet, who nodded enthusiastically.

Arabella shrugged, moved the coat hangers along the rack, then back again, and wished they would change the subject.

Flora approached her and placed her hand gently on Arabella's arm. 'You do know what sort of man the Duke of Somerfeld is, don't you, Arabella? He's a bit of a one for the ladies.'

Yes, Arabella knew that already. Knew it very well indeed. 'What he does is his own business.'

Flora dropped her hand from Arabella's arm and narrowed her eyes. 'So, what are you saying? The Duke can carry on living in exactly the same way as he did before he was married? Seeing who he wants, doing whatever he wants, and you won't care?'

Arabella's jaw clenched tightly and her hands gripped the fabric of the nearest dress. She breathed deeply and exhaled slowly to try to free her constricted chest. 'That's exactly what I'm saying.'

She could not ignore the gaze that passed between the two pretty actresses. It was obvious what they were thinking. The Duke of Somerfeld was available for the taking, that any woman after some fun with a fabulously wealthy man just had to bat her eyelashes in his direction and she could have everything the Duke had to offer, even if it was just for a short time.

Arabella swallowed to relieve the burning in her throat. That was a reaction from women she was going to have to learn to deal with. She might have shared a few wonderful days with the Duke of Somerfeld, as had many other women before her, but he was not hers. Never had been. Never would be. And she needed to put aside any unwanted feelings of jealousy, to concentrate on her career, to move on and leave the Duke of Somerfeld in the past.

Chapter Nineteen

Oliver rose uncharacteristically early the next morning and arrived at the Limelight Theatre just as rehearsals were commencing. He crept into the auditorium and took a seat upstairs near the back, where he would not be noticed. Then he settled down to watch his wife perform. It wasn't long before he became absorbed in watching Arabella act, just as she became absorbed in her own performance.

It was so obvious she was doing what she loved and her determination to be just one of the cast was obviously working. No one was deferring to her. No one was treating her like a duchess or an heiress.

This was definitely her home, where she wanted to be, where she belonged.

It might not fit in with what he wanted, but he would do nothing to stop her achieving her dream, even if it meant stepping back from her life.

As he watched, hour after hour, he could see the play coming together, the performances becoming more polished. Even though the actors had gone over their lines again and again, the more they repeated them the more spontaneous they appeared. It was a pleasure to watch.

And his greatest pleasure came from watching Arabella. He was biased, of course he was, but he could tell that Arabella's performance was particularly stunning. His eyes were constantly drawn to her when she was on stage, whether she was speaking or not.

She definitely had something special and he was sure he wasn't just thinking that because she was his wife, or even because they had spent four incredible days and nights in bed together exploring each other's bodies.

The longer he watched, the less he noticed the other actors and actresses, until he barely registered when they were speaking. He could only see Arabella. Watch her performance grow, her confidence increase.

She was a superb actress and acting was what she was born to do.

Her father might have dominated her off the stage, structured her whole life, even forced her into an unwanted marriage, but on stage she was a different woman. She commanded the stage and became the part she was playing. The director would give her instructions and like a chameleon she would instantly assume the form he required. It was brilliant and impressive to watch.

When the rehearsal drew to a close, he quietly slipped out of the theatre before anyone noticed. It was already early evening. The entire day had passed without his noticing. He summoned a cab to take him home so he could make ready for the evening's entertainment. He had no idea how he would spend it, but he knew exactly where he would be the next day, and the days after that. Seated right at the back of the Limelight Theatre, watching his beautiful, talented wife.

Arabella was being foolish. She knew she was. But at every rehearsal it was as if she was performing only for Oliver. She wanted him to be proud of her, to think highly of her acting abilities, so she gave it her all and imagined him saying how impressed he was.

Yes, it was ridiculous, but thinking that Oliver was watching her as she worked was certainly doing wonders for her performance. She was receiving so much praise from the director and the other cast members that it was almost going to her head. But it was one man's praise she really wanted and that was something she would not be getting. She had cut him from her life, had let him know she wanted her independence more than she wanted him. And he had given her exactly what she wanted. What she'd *thought* she wanted.

And when she was in rehearsals, she could almost convince herself that she did indeed have exactly what she wanted. But as soon as rehearsals were over that empty void was waiting, threatening to swallow her up, and she had to work hard to keep it at bay. She had to force herself to keep smiling, to pretend that everything in her life was exactly as she wanted it to be.

Now, after a week of intense rehearsals, opening night was looming large.

The final dress rehearsal had gone well and tomorrow night they would be performing before the live audience. The entire cast was tired from working hard all day, but they were still bubbling with enthusiasm as they returned to the boarding house, confident they would have a stunning opening night.

Arabella had tried hard to join in with their enthusiasm. And she *was* enthusiastic, but part of her still felt as though something was missing. As much as she tried to ignore it, she knew that she was missing Oliver. She was missing him so much that some days she could hardly bear it. But bear it she must.

She had exactly what she wanted, didn't she? She might be married, but to a man who had given her complete freedom. Her father was back in America and leaving her alone to live her life the way she wanted to. She had a major part in a play. She was surrounded by the cast and crew of a tight-knit theatre group. Everything she had ever dreamed of had come true. She had no right to feel miserable. And she wouldn't be feeling miserable. If she had never met Oliver Huntsbury, she would be unaware of any other life, would not know what true happiness felt like.

As usual the actresses were getting ready for a night out. They went out most evenings, either to parties or to dine with their various admirers, and tonight, with opening night just one night away, everyone was in a party mood. No one would be staying home at the boarding house. No one, that is, except Arabella.

Nellie, too, had gone out for the evening with her latest conquest. She had offered to stay home and keep her company, but Arabella had insisted that she was perfectly happy on her own and that she would prefer it if Nellie went out.

But she wasn't happy. Far from it.

Oliver had said she was a free woman. She was free to do anything she wanted. If she wanted to go to parties, she could. If a man showed interest in her, there was nothing to stop her from taking him as her lover. But that was the last thing she felt like doing. There was only one man she wanted as her lover and he was out of bounds. Instead, while the other actresses were out enjoying themselves, she had stayed at the boarding house, until she was starting to go mad with boredom.

And once again she was facing a night alone. As the other actresses preened in front of the mirror and chatted about the night to come, Arabella could feel that empty void starting to surround her and drag her under.

This had to change. She had to take action.

'Going anywhere special tonight?' she asked Flora with as much nonchalance as she could summon.

'To a party in Mayfair. Nicholas de Valle has been showing rather a lot of interest of late and has invited all of us. You can come, too, if you like. It should be fun. He's a duke, you know, and is rather partial to actresses,' Flora laughed. 'Aren't they all, these posh gents? You should come. It'll get you out of yourself.'

Arabella kept smiling as she cringed inside. Yes, weren't they all like that. And one duke in particular. No, she did not feel like going to a party where *posh gents* would be chasing after actresses. But nor did she want to be alone. Alone with her thoughts. Alone with the dark void.

She very much doubted that Oliver would be alone tonight. She couldn't picture him moping around in his town house. So, what was sauce for the goose should be sauce for the gander, or in this case the other way around.

'All right. I will.'

She reached into her wardrobe and removed her most stylish gown, then put it back and selected something a bit less fashionable. She did not want to stand out from the other actresses.

With Nellie off pursuing her own dreams, Arabella did her best to fix her own hair, until Flora took pity on her and helped.

They ordered a carriage, which Flora assured her the party's host would be paying for, and six of the actresses set off, laughing and talking loudly, all looking forward to the night's fun.

Arabella forced herself to join in, to laugh and jest along with them. She *would* enjoy herself tonight. She would push aside all her sadness and have fun. She would replace the dark void with lightness, happiness and laughter.

The carriage pulled up in front of a brightly lit town house and the sound of laughter, loud talking and music spilled out on to the pavement.

The actresses pushed their way through the crowds milling at the entranceway and joined the noisy, jostling throng. Arabella could see that the guests came from all walks of life. Well, the women did. There were wealthy women, dressed in the latest fashions, women like her actress friends who did not have money for expensive gowns and jewellery, and other women dressed in a manner that suggested they worked in somewhat more disreputable professions.

But there was one thing that all these women had in common: they were all young and good looking. The men, however, were of all ages and all bore the signs of privilege and wealth. Another thing the men had in common was the way they were looking at the women. As Arabella and her friends made their way through the crowd, they were being stared at as if they were fresh delicacies being served up for the men's appreciation.

Arabella paused at the entrance to the drawing room, which was packed wall-to-wall with a boisterous crowd. Did she really want to be part of this world?

But what was her option? Return alone to the boarding house? Alone with those unhappy thoughts that kept churning through her head.

She forced herself to enter the room and took the glass of champagne that was thrust into her hand. It was obvious from the loudness of the crowd, the array of florid complexions and the raucous laughter that a lot of champagne had already been consumed.

Arabella looked around for a familiar face. Flora had already disappeared, presumably with the host, and the other actresses had instantly been swallowed up by the party. Unlike Arabella, they had no problem entering into the spirit of the occasion, flirting and laughing with circles of adoring men.

Arabella tried hard to smile, but it just wouldn't happen. Her lips just wouldn't move.

This was a mistake.

She did not want to be here. She might not want to be back at the boarding house, alone with her thoughts. But she was no less alone in this crowd. If anything, this boisterous party was making her feel even more lonely.

She placed her untouched glass of champagne on a table and looked around for a footman who could summon her a cab.

Then she saw him.

Oliver entered the room, laughing, surrounded by a group of attractive women. They were all smiling up at him as if he was the most amusing man they had ever met. And they were all sending him undeniably provocative looks.

He looked as though he didn't have a care in the world. Let alone a wife.

Now she most definitely wanted to leave. She turned quickly. A servant stepped into her path. She bumped into him, sending his tray of champagne flutes crashing to the floor.

A wild cheer of enthusiasm went up from the partygoers, as if she had done something amusing and entertaining, rather than a clumsy act brought on by her panic.

She looked around the room, her face contorted into a rictus of a smile. Everyone was laughing and applauding.

Everyone except Oliver.

He was staring straight at her, his cold eyes boring into her, his lips a thin line of disapproval.

Her strained smile froze as their gazes locked across the room. The cheering crowd merged into a swirling mass. The raucous sound of their laughter disappeared. All she could focus on was the scowling man across the room, glaring at her.

Chapter Twenty

He had no right to look at her like that. He had absolutely no right to condemn her for attending this party. She had as much right to be here as he did. Weren't they both free to do as they pleased? And Oliver certainly was doing something that pleased him very much, if the coterie of admiring young women surrounding him was anything to go by.

As if she were emerging from a trance, the noise of the crowd exploded into Arabella's consciousness, even louder than before.

No, she would not be cowed by his disapproval. Using all her skills as an actress, she sent the room her most radiant smile, made a theatrical curtsy, took a glass of champagne from another servant's tray and raised it in a toast to the cheering crowd. Much to the partygoers' enthusiastic response.

Only one man was not cheering. The man she was married to.

Arabella forced her smile not to quiver as she saw him excuse himself from his group of adoring women, push his way through the jostling partygoers and cross the room towards her.

She would not show any sign of nerves. Would not let him know how much seeing him had unsettled her.

'Hello, Your Grace, fancy meeting you here.' With false joviality she made another deep curtsy.

'And I'm equally surprised to see you here, Arabella,' he responded, no hint of a smile on his face. 'This is not the sort of party I would expect you to attend.'

She shrugged. 'But it is obviously the sort of party *you* attend, judging by how well known you are here.'

She nodded in the direction of the group of attractive young women, who were still watching them from across the room with undisguised interest. 'I assume they are a few more of your good friends. So how many good friends of yours are actually here tonight?'

She looked around the room, as if taking an inventory, her false smile still frozen on her face.

Her sweeping gaze returned to him. He glared down at her. That mischievous smile was nowhere in sight. There was no laughter in his cold, dark eyes.

She cringed. Had she let a hint of jealousy enter her voice? She did not want to sound jealous. After all, she had no right to be. And she most certainly did not want him to think she was.

Yes, they had made love, but that had been under her instigation. He owed her nothing. Yet here she was, feeling jealous because he was doing exactly what she told him he could do.

'This is no place for you. You need to leave. Immediately.'

She gave an incredulous laugh. That was exactly what she had intended to do until he had seen her. Now she was determined to stand her ground. 'Surely you're not telling me what to do? Wasn't freedom to do as we pleased part of our agreement?'

He inhaled deeply through clenched teeth. 'Listen to me. You do not want to stay here. If you think this party is loud and raucous now, it is nothing compared to how it will soon become. It's time you left.'

Still smiling, Arabella looked around the room and noticed several couples involved in decidedly amorous encounters, encounters that should only be conducted in private. She was unable to suppress a gasp when a man ran his hand up the inside of a woman's leg, under her gown. Surely the woman would object. Surely someone would stop them. But no one noticed. The drinking and carousing continued around them.

He was right.

This was most definitely not the sort of party she wanted to attend. But the same could *not* be said for Oliver. This was his world. A world where she did not belong. A world in which she did not want to belong. A world full of women who wanted to have fun with no commitments. His sort of women.

Her scan of the room moved to a woman staring at her from across the room. Lady Bufford. With eyes narrowed, like an assassin assessing her target, she sauntered over to join them.

'Ollie, darling, I see you've brought your wife to tonight's entertainment,' she said, her voice dripping with derision. 'Delightful. If you're not otherwise occupied, perhaps the two of you would like to join me upstairs. Your wife can show me what techniques she used to get a man like you to the altar. She must be able to do something for you that I can't do and lord knows I've tried every trick in the book.'

Arabella gasped and her face exploded in a fiery blush while Lady Bufford laughed at her obvious discomfort.

'Hold your tongue, Violet. You go too far,' Oliver said, taking hold of Arabella's arm. 'We were just leaving.'

'Oh, I am sorry. Do I take it from her blushes that it wasn't her experience that attracted you? Oh, you men, you're all the same. You can't resist a virgin.'

He turned his back on Lady Bufford, ignoring her, his grip tightening on Arabella's arm. 'I don't care what we agreed. You are leaving this place and you are leaving it now.'

Shaken by Lady Bufford's words Arabella lost the will to protest. Deflated and embarrassed, she allowed Oliver to bustle her out through the crowd. He flagged down a passing cab and all but lifted her inside, then gave the driver the address of his town house before climbing in beside her.

After the noise of the party, the silence inside the cab almost had a physical presence, with the clip-clopping of the horse's hooves the only sound as they drove through Mayfair's quiet streets.

'I'm so sorry, Arabella. Violet Bufford has a cruel tongue,' Oliver said quietly, breaking the heavy silence. 'You should not have been subjected to that.'

'It's of no matter.' She blinked away the tears that had embarrassingly sprung to her eyes and shivered. The summer's evening must have been chillier than Arabella had expected as she suddenly felt very cold.

'And you didn't have to leave on my account. You can return me to the boarding house and go back to your party.'

Oliver took off his jacket and draped it round her shoulders. 'You've had a shock, Arabella. You should not be alone. I'll take you back to our town house until you recover and then return you to your lodgings.'

Arabella wanted to protest, but she did not want to be alone. He was right. She'd had a shock. The party, all the women flirting with Oliver, and then Lady Bufford's acid comments had left her shaken. And Oliver's coat around her shoulders, still containing the warmth of his body, went some way towards assuaging that shock. She closed her eyes, breathed in deeply and inhaled the masculine scent of him.

That scent was both comforting and arousing. It reminded her of how it had felt to be held in his arms, to be made love to by this strong, attractive man. But those thoughts battled with images of the women at the party. They, including Lady Bufford, also knew what it was like to be made love to by Oliver. And if she hadn't unexpectedly arrived at the party, he would have been making love to one or more of them tonight.

She shrugged off his jacket from her shoulders and handed it back to him. 'Thank you, but I'm perfectly fine. You can ask your driver to return me to my lodgings now.'

He shook his head, but took his jacket from her outstretched hand. 'I will do no such thing.'

They slipped back into silence and Arabella couldn't stop herself from replaying everything that had happened during the short time she was at the party. The riotous noise, the inappropriately amorous behaviour between the guests, the women giving Oliver looks that could only be described as lustful. Despite the shivers still running through her body, her cheeks once again exploded with burning heat. That was Oliver's world and it could never include her.

The carriage drew up outside his town house.

'I said I want to go home. This is not my home. I want to return to where I really live, where I belong.'

He opened the carriage door as if she hadn't spoken and held out his hand to help her descend.

'I said I want to go home.'

He exhaled loudly. 'Arabella, please, just come inside for a while. I can see how upset you are and, despite what you think of me, I will not let any woman, even my wife, go home by herself in such a distressed state. Once you have settled down, I'll order my driver to take you back to your boarding house, but for now I insist that you come inside.'

She stared straight ahead. He remained standing at the door, his hand outstretched. She knew she was being petulant, but she felt petulant. She was angry. Angry with him and angry with herself. But he was right, she did not want to be on her own.

Reluctantly she accepted his hand and allowed him to lead her up the stairs and through the entrance to his house. He asked the footman to prepare coffee and they entered the drawing room.

Arabella sat on the *chaise longue*, feeling like a chastised child. But she had done nothing wrong. All she had done was go to a party that he was also attending. But she *did* feel she had done something wrong. He was right, that party was not the sort of place she would usually frequent. She should have known that Flora would take her somewhere wild. But even if she *had* made a mistake, he still had no right to judge her.

Leaning on the marble mantelpiece, he looked down at her. 'So, are you going to explain what you were doing at that party?'

Arabella pulled herself up, squared her shoulders and lifted her chin, determined to give him a defiant answer. She would not let him know how out of her depth she had been. Nor would she let him know that she had already intended to escape before he had seen her. 'My roommate, Flora, had been invited so I decided to join her. I thought it might be a bit of fun.'

'And was it?'

She shrugged. 'But why should it matter to you? You have no more right to question why I was at that party than I have to question you. That wasn't in our agreement.'

He stared at her, then frowned. 'Yes, I suppose you are right. But we didn't agree that we wouldn't offer each other advice. I know that world, Arabella. It's not for you. If you want to have fun, find it somewhere else, not at parties hosted by men like Nicholas de Valle. The man's a notorious rake and his parties are legendary.'

Arabella shrugged again. 'And he's a friend of yours?'

Oliver gave a quick nod.

'So, it's all right for you to go to such parties, but not me?'

'I'm a man, Arabella. So, yes, it is all right for me, but not for you.'

Arabella felt her eyes grow wide and her mouth almost fell open. *Had he really said that?* Had he really told her what she could or couldn't do? Had he really said it was all right for him, but not her? Was he worried what people might think if his wife went to such parties? Or was it that he did not want to be seen consorting with other women in front of his wife? Or did he think it might put off some of his conquests if his wife was present? Although it certainly wouldn't put off women like Lady Bufford.

Well, he was soon going to discover that if he wanted an obedient wife, he had married the wrong woman. Standing up, she put her hands on her hips and stared him straight in the eye. 'How dare you? How dare you say I can't go to such parties because I'm a woman? Next you'll be saying that as my husband you forbid it.'

'Sit down, Arabella,' he said firmly. 'You know you're being ridiculous. Why don't you just admit it? You made a mistake and went somewhere you didn't belong.'

'Oh, so I didn't belong there, did I? But you did. And Lady Bufford did. And all those other simpering women hanging on your every word as if you were some sort of god, did, but not me. Not your wife.'

She had intended to shame him, but he remained standing at the mantelpiece, unmoved by her outburst. 'Yes, it was a party for women like Lady Bufford and those so-called simpering women, but not for you.'

'And what makes me so special? Is it because I'm your wife that you don't want me seen at such places? Or are you worried that I might just find myself another lover and people might think that the famous rake Oliver Huntsbury can't satisfy his own wife?'

Her words had hit their intended target. Oliver's skin darkened, his jaw clenched and he stared back at her, his brown eyes unflinching.

'Is that what you want? To find another lover?' he asked, his voice dangerously quiet.

'Perhaps.' She glared back at him with more defiance than she felt. 'Isn't that what you were there for? To find another one of your sort of women? Well, perhaps I'm starting to become just that sort of woman as well.'

He gripped the edge of the marble mantelpiece, his back rigid, his eyes granite hard. 'You are not that sort of woman. You never have been and you never will be.'

Arabella bristled at his curt dismissal. 'And how could you possibly know what sort of woman I might be, or the sort of woman I might become? Things have changed for me, haven't they? A few weeks ago, I was a single woman and I was a…a…' She paused.

'A virgin.'

Heat exploded on her cheeks. 'Yes, a virgin. I'm neither of those things now. So perhaps I'm changing.'

'You can't change who you are, Arabella. And why would you want to?'

So I can become the sort of woman you would be attracted to.

'Why not? Why shouldn't I change? Why shouldn't I find a lover as well? Why shouldn't I have some fun?'

'If it's a lover you want, you don't have to go to parties to find one.' He quickly crossed the room.

Before Arabella had time to fully register what was happening, she was in his arms. His lips were on hers. Hot, hungry lips, devouring her. She kissed him back, unable to halt the reckless desire that the touch of his body had ignited deep within her. Her body aflame, she moulded herself into his strong arms and chest, her lips and tongue tasting him. Her fingers moved through his hair, wanting to hold him close, wanting to never let him go.

'Is this what you want, Arabella? Do you want a man to make love to you?' he ground out harshly, before kissing a line down her neck.

She tilted back her head and gasped in a breath. 'Yes,' she whispered, her heart pounding so hard she could feel blood pumping through every inch of her body.

Yes. This was exactly what she wanted. This was what she needed to fill that aching void caused by being apart from him, what she needed to quench the fire that raged within her. She needed him. She wanted him.

Breaking from her, he took her by the hand and led her up the stairs to his bedroom.

Chapter Twenty-One

It was not how Oliver had expected the evening to end, but he couldn't have wished for a better conclusion. To have his wife back in his bed—it was what he had hoped for, but had never thought would happen.

She rolled over and gazed up at him, her long black hair falling over her creamy shoulder and curling round her full breasts. His gaze followed the line of that tress, then continued along her body, across her small waist, to her rounded hips, down her long, slim legs, then back up to her blue eyes.

'Good morning, Husband.' She smiled at him. 'So it seems we both got what we went to the party for. I found a lover and you took a married woman who wants to have fun to your bed.'

Her smile grew wider to let him know it was a joke, but Oliver still cringed. Was that what she thought of him, like a tomcat always on the prowl? It might have been true once, but was it any longer?

He ran his hand gently along her cheek. 'Going to the party was as much a mistake for me as it was for you, Bella. I had hoped it would provide me with a diversion, but it failed. Just as it has failed every night since you left.'

She propped herself up on her elbow and stared at him, her brow furrowed. 'What do you mean?'

He sighed and fell back on to the pillows. 'I forced myself to go, just as I have every night since we returned to London, but when I got there I wondered why. Nothing about the party interested me. In fact, it all seemed a bit desperate. I felt surrounded by people who were trying to drown their unhappiness in noise, drink and other people's bodies.'

'So, you didn't want to be there? You weren't interested in any of those other women?'

An urgency had entered her voice and he smiled up at her. 'There's only one woman I'm interested in. I was actually about to leave when you arrived. You thought you saw me surrounded by a group of simpering women, but what you actually saw was me saying my goodbyes.'

She bit the edge of her bottom lip. 'So, you weren't interested in any them? Truly?'

He smiled. It seemed she needed even more reassurance. 'No, Bella, the only woman I'm interested in is the one I've been watching in rehearsals every day.'

Her blue eyes grew wide. 'You've been attending my rehearsals every day?'

'Yes, I've been watching you from up in the gallery, where you wouldn't see me.'

Her smile grew tentative. 'So, what do you think of the play?'

He laughed, wrapped his arms round her waist, and rolled her beneath him. 'The play is wonderful.

You're wonderful. I have no doubts that the play is going to be a big hit and you're going to be famous.'

She wrapped her arms around his neck and joined in his laughter.

'So, before you become famous and throw me over for some backstage Johnny, I'd like to make love to my wife one more time.'

'Just the once?' She laughed, wrapping her legs around his waist. 'Surely you've got more stamina than that, Your Grace.'

Stifling her laughter, he kissed her, determined to prove his stamina was more than up to the challenge.

Arabella lay on her side, Oliver's arms wrapped around her, his breath warm on her neck. She could stay like this for ever. Could spend the rest of her life making love to this wonderful, virile man. Her husband.

But she couldn't. Tonight was opening night. She had to go to the theatre.

Opening night.

Tonight was opening night.

She should be at the Limelight getting ready for tonight's performance. She sat up quickly and looked frantically around the room. 'What's the time?'

Oliver stretched out a lazy arm and grabbed his waistcoat, abandoned beside the bed. He pulled out his fob watch and, still lying on his back, opened the clasp. 'It's five o'clock.'

Arabella threw back the covers, jumped out of bed and grabbed her gown. 'I need to get home. I need to get changed. I have to get to the theatre.'

How could she have forgotten? In the past it would

have been the only thing she'd have been able to think about from the moment she woke up. But she had been completely distracted.

And it was no surprise. Being in Oliver's arms—how could that not be a distraction of the most wonderful kind? But she had to get dressed and get to the theatre. Now. It was almost unbelievable that she had forgotten, even for a moment, that tonight was opening night.

'Oliver. I have to leave,' she reiterated to the man still stretched out on the bed like a contented cat. 'Tonight's opening night.'

She scanned the room for her clothes, strewn chaotically around the room from when Oliver had all but ripped them from her body last night. She picked up her corset and one shoe, and searched the room for its companion.

Oliver rose from the bed and she paused in her anxious search to take a quick scan of his taut, muscular body, then went back to gathering up her clothes.

'Well, I'd hate to interfere with your panicking,' he said as he picked up her silk stockings and handed them to her. 'But if you slow down, I can arrange for some clothes to be collected from your boarding house while you're at your toilette. Then we can take my carriage to the theatre and we'll get there in plenty of time.'

She took the stockings from his outstretched hands. His calmness helped her tense body relax and her churning stomach to settle down. He was going to take care of everything. He was going to arrange everything for her, so she didn't have to panic. She smiled at him. It was so nice to be looked after.

* * *

In a much calmer frame of mind, she had got ready and was soon travelling with Oliver to the theatre. As they rode through the busy streets, he took her hands in his and murmured gentle words of encouragement and support in her ear, helping to keep those nerves at bay. Oh, yes, it was very nice to be looked after like this by a strong, supportive man.

When they arrived at the Limelight Theatre, she left him to join the cast in the dressing rooms. Backstage, without Oliver by her side, her pre-performance nerves started to bubble up within her. And she wasn't the only one. Everyone was tense, going through their own calming routine to get themselves ready for tonight's performance and working hard to not let their own anxiety affect anyone else.

Some had their little superstitious rituals they performed, others were doing breathing exercises and some were staring at their reflections and giving themselves silent pep talks. In among this Nellie was running around, making sure everyone's makeup, hair and costumes were perfect.

A stagehand called through the door that there was five minutes to show time and the cast whispered break a leg to each other, as a final good luck wish, and made their way to the wings.

As Arabella would be appearing in the first scene, she entered the stage along with the leading actors and waited anxiously for the curtain to be raised. Tonight she would not only be performing for an audience, but she would be performing for Oliver as well. He would be sitting in the auditorium, watching her, just as he had done every day during rehearsals. She prayed she would make him proud and not get struck by the dreaded curse of stage fright.

The curtain started to rise. The cast all breathed in, deeply and audibly, then the leading actor confidently projected his first line out to the darkened auditorium, capturing the audience's attention.

From that moment Arabella's nervousness dissolved. She forgot about everything except the play in which she was acting. Her absorption into her part became complete as each actor gave it their all, the energy on stage becoming almost palpable.

When the entire cast assembled on stage at the end of the performance, took each other's hands and made their final bow, Arabella could tell it had been a resounding success. The audience stood as one, clapping and stamping their feet. Arabella lost count of how many curtain calls they had made as they returned again and again to ever-rapturous applause. She also couldn't fail to notice how loud the applause grew each time she took a solo bow.

The performance had exceeded the cast's most optimistic expectations and they were united in their sense of euphoria, as they finally gathered in an excited huddle at the edge of the stage, laughing, talking loudly and slapping each other on the back.

Arabella's happiness was complete when Oliver joined them, wrapped his arms around her waist, lifted her off her feet and kissed her. 'What can I say? That was magnificent. You were magnificent. I have never felt more proud of you.'

She smiled down at him, certain she was about to burst with happiness.

Rosie and her husband joined them. They had come up to London especially for the opening night and Arabella was so happy to see her best friend again. 'Oh, Bella, you were at your very best,' Rosie said. 'That truly was a virtuoso performance.'

Even the smiling director joined their group and kissed her on both cheeks. 'Arabella, you were marvellous, simply marvellous. You shone tonight. Whatever you did last night it certainly put that extra spark in you, so please keep doing it. You were superb.'

Oliver winked at her as the director wandered off to congratulate another actor. 'You heard what the man said,' he whispered in her ear, his arm around her waist. 'You're under strict instructions to keep doing what you did last night.'

Arabella giggled, reached up and kissed him. 'Oh, well, if I'm going to keep that spark, I'll have to do that every night of the play's run. And then there will be more plays after that. I'm going to need that spark for a long time to come.'

Oliver laughed, picked her up and whirled her around. 'Happy to oblige.' Lowering her to her feet, he turned to the assembled crowd. 'The champagne is on me,' he called out to a roar of approval. 'The Savoy is booked and the champagne is already on ice.'

The jubilant crowd tumbled into waiting cabs and, with much banter being shouted between the racing cabs, they made their way to the hotel.

The champagne immediately started to flow freely and the exuberant cast and crew took advantage of the food and drink on offer. The entire patronage of the Savoy seemed to get caught up in their excitement and soon everyone in the restaurant was joining in with the celebration.

Arabella was so pleased she could share this occasion with Oliver, who looked as triumphant as she felt.

The celebrations continued well into the small hours of the morning. It wasn't until the stagehands arrived with the early editions of the morning papers that a hush descended.

A suddenly anxious cast and crew crowded round the director as he opened the first newspaper on the top of the pile. The reviews could make or break a play. They could determine whether they played to a season of full houses or to rows of empty seats. Arabella held her breath as the director began reading.

The first newspaper had a rave review, then the second, the third. With each review the volume of the happy voices grew until the director was having to shout to be heard above the high-spirited noise.

The champagne started to flow again, even more freely. The hugging and cheek kissing resumed, and people began dancing and singing, unable to contain their excitement.

'It seems I'm married to a woman who shines, a woman who captures the audiences' hearts and is destined for greatness,' Oliver said, repeating some of the flattering comments made by the reviewers about her.

Arabella smiled at him. 'Oh, Oliver. I couldn't have asked for more. The play will be a success now. The theatre is saved. I doubt if it will ever need money from my father again.'

'And I like to think I played a small part in your

success.' Oliver laughed. 'So, if you've had enough of the celebrations, let's get you home so I can put some more of that spark in you.' Oliver sent her that mischievous smile she loved so much. 'After all, you have been given strict instructions from your director to keep doing what you did last night and there's another performance tomorrow.'

Arabella nodded her head enthusiastically. She could think of no more perfect way to end this perfect evening than in Oliver's bed, making love to that magnificent man. 'While you order a cab, I'll just freshen up in the powder room.'

He nodded and turned to leave. She grabbed hold of his arm to halt his progress. 'And make sure you order a cab with fresh horses. I want to get home as quickly as possible. I can already feel that spark starting to fade. You need to renew it urgently.'

With a playful salute Oliver headed towards the door and Arabella retired to the powder room, determined to make herself as attractive as she could for the rest of the night's entertainment.

Arabella smiled at her reflection as the attendant helped her to fix her hair. Happiness had definitely improved her appearance, her eyes sparkled and her skin was glowing.

She did a little twirl in front of the mirror and thanked the attendant for her help. She headed towards the door, but her exit was halted when Lady Bufford entered.

Arabella's smile faltered before returning as large as before. She would not let that toxic woman ruin her evening.

'Good evening, Lady Bufford,' she said in her sweetest voice.

'Good evening, Your Grace. And congratulations on tonight's performance. I didn't manage to catch the play, but I hear you performed rather well.'

'Thank you.' Arabella nodded and turned to leave.

'A better performance than the one I hear you gave on your wedding night.'

Arabella froze, her body suddenly turning cold, as her legs weakened beneath her.

'I suppose that was why Oliver didn't stay in your bed but came to mine instead.'

Arabella turned slowly. She saw her reflection in the mirror, standing behind a preening Lady Bufford, her pink cheeks now white, her eyes dull and lifeless, her shoulders slumped.

'I thought it a bit strange for a man to be with another woman on his wedding night,' Lady Bufford continued in a sing-song voice. 'But I suppose after he'd deflowered you, he wanted a bit of real satisfaction so he decided to join me in my bed.'

'You are a cruel, nasty woman,' Arabella said, her voice strained and shaking.

Lady Bufford shrugged, smiled at Arabella and left the room.

Arabella groped her way to the nearest chair and collapsed on to it, her shaking legs no longer able to hold her up. The attendant passed her a hand towel to wipe away the tears Arabella had been unaware were coursing down her cheeks.

While she had been lying awake on her wedding night, wishing that Oliver would join her, he was in another woman's bed. How could he have done that? On her wedding night? Yes, they had agreed to give each other freedom. But her wedding night? Could he not have slept alone for one night? Did he not know how much that would shame her? Did he not realise how humiliating that was? Did he not care? He might say he cared about her now, and she did not doubt that was true, but they were lovers now. On the night of their wedding they were not. On that night he didn't care how much he hurt her, how much he humiliated her. How could he be so selfish?

The door opened again, and Arabella attempted to rise. She would not let Lady Bufford see her in this condition, would not let her know how much her cruel words had pierced her heart.

But it wasn't Lady Bufford, it was Rosie, who instantly rushed to her side, knelt down beside her chair and took her hands in hers.

'Bella, what is it? What's wrong? Why are you crying?'

Arabella shook her head. 'Rosie, can I stay with you this evening? Can you take me away from here without Oliver seeing? I'll explain everything when we get back to your town house. But I want to leave, now.'

'Of course I will. I'll tell my husband to get us a cab and I'll be back soon.' Rosie rushed out and Arabella put her head in her hands and dissolved into tears of pain and humiliation.

Once again, she had misjudged a man, had seen only what she wanted to see. She had thought Arnold Emerson loved her, that he wanted to marry her and cared nothing for her money. It was only her father's cruel action of offering him money so he wouldn't marry her that had proven what that man was really like. And the cruel words of Lady Bufford had proven once again that when it came to men, she was completely naive.

Oliver pushed his way through the partying crowd, looking for Arabella. She was nowhere in sight. He had expected her to be ready and waiting by the door, wanting to get back to their town house and to their bed as anxiously as he did. Could she still be in the powder room? If she was still fixing her hair and making herself attractive for him, she was wasting her time. He would soon be dishevelling her carefully styled hair and she could not possibly make herself any more beautiful to his eyes than she already was.

He spotted Arabella's lady's maid, dancing with one of the actors, and cut in between them.

'Nellie. Can you please go into the rest room and tell Arabella her carriage awaits?'

Nellie nodded and Oliver diverted himself by watching the cheerful crowd while he waited for his wife. They were still in high spirits and he doubted they would be retiring soon. While the party was certainly fun, he was looking forward to having much more fun when he got home.

Nellie returned; her face surprisingly sombre. 'She's not in there and the attendant said she left with the Duke and Duchess of Knightsbrook.'

He shook his head. 'No, there's some mistake, Nellie. Arabella asked me to order a cab to take us back to our town house. Perhaps she's waiting somewhere else.' He looked around the room.

'No, you're the one who's made the mistake. The attendant told me all about it. You ought to be ashamed of yourself.'

He looked down at the scowling Nellie. 'What? Who told you what? What are you talking about?'

The lady's maid's nostrils flared in disgust and she looked him up and down. 'She's gone. That's all you need to know.' With that, she turned her back on him and joined the partygoers.

He looked at Nellie, then around the gathering, as if somewhere in this crowded room he would find the answer to his confusion. What on earth was going on? He scanned the room again, hoping to see Arabella smiling at the trick she had played on him. But she was still nowhere to be seen. And neither were the Duke and Duchess of Knightsbrook. Perhaps Arabella *had* left with them. But why would she do that without telling him? And what was all that nonsense about the powder-room attendant? This was all very peculiar. But there was only one way to find out what had gone wrong. He would have to ask his wife.

He pushed his way back through the crowd, jumped into the waiting hansom cab and gave the driver the address of the Duke of Knightsbrook's town house.

The sooner he put this ridiculous confusion to rights the better.

When he arrived, the house was in darkness, except for one upstairs light. Despite the unsociable hour Oliver pounded on the door, which was almost immediately opened by the footman, followed by the Duke still in his evening clothes.

'I believe Arabella is here. I need to speak to her. Now.'

The Duke's stern expression suggested he had no interest in seeing Oliver and even less inclination to let him into his house. 'My wife is upstairs comforting your wife. Neither of them wishes to see you so I suggest you leave, immediately.'

Oliver shook his head. This was getting more and more confusing. 'What's going on? Why would Arabella need to be comforted? And why did she leave the party so suddenly?'

'Don't push your luck,' the Duke said through clenched teeth. 'If it was left to me, I'd give you a good thrashing for causing that lovely young woman such distress, but out of respect for my wife's wishes all I'll do is bar your entrance.' With that the Duke shut the door in Oliver's face. He stared at the closed door, inches from his nose, momentarily stunned.

This really was ridiculous. And getting more ridiculous with every passing minute. Something had obviously happened while he had been ordering a cab, but whatever it was he couldn't do anything about it until his wife spoke to him and explained her actions.

But what was he supposed to do? She didn't want to see him and unless he broke down the door there was no way he was going to get access to this town house.

He looked up and down the outside of the three-storey house. There was no easy way of scaling the outside and getting up to the only room which still had a light. The room where Arabella was presumably being comforted by her friend over the distress caused by some crime he had no knowledge of committing. And even if he could find a way up to the second storey, hanging tentatively outside a closed window would hardly be the easiest way to have a serious conversation with his wife about what had upset her.

This was something that was going to have to be left until the morning. With reluctance, he turned from the door, climbed back into the cab and made his way home through the quiet early-morning streets.

Oliver rose early after a sleepless night and took pen to paper. If he couldn't see Arabella in person, then he would write to her. They could solve whatever the problem was through correspondence. He scribbled a quick letter asking her why she had left and if it was due to anything he had done, or not done, said, or not said. Then he asked her to give him an opportunity to explain himself. Surely that was only fair.

Instead of getting his footman to deliver the letter he carried it round in person. When the footman opened the door he took the letter, but was obviously under strict instructions not to let Oliver in as he immediately closed the door in his face.

With no other choice Oliver returned home and waited for a reply to arrive. Several hours passed. No letter arrived. He took another piece of paper from his writing desk and dipped his pen into the ink well.

This time he took his time composing the letter. He apologised for whatever transgression he was being accused of and begged Arabella to return. It was hard to believe. He had never apologised for his behaviour before and had certainly never begged a woman for anything. But he had no reservations about doing it now. Whatever had upset Arabella he wanted to put it right. If he had said or done something to upset her, then he *was* profoundly sorry and he had no hesitation in apologising.

There was no point delivering the letter himself. He could all but guarantee he would not be allowed entrance, so he sent it with his footman. Then he waited. And waited. The first post arrived. There was no letter. It was the same with the second post. But finally, with the third post, there it was. The letter he was waiting for.

He grabbed it off the footman's silver tray, immediately ripped it open and scanned the contents.

It wasn't from Arabella. It was from his mother, informing him that a woman had arrived at Somerfeld Manor, claiming that her child had been fathered by the previous Duke.

This was a disaster. Another disaster.

The two women who meant the most to him in the world demanded his attention at the same time. He could not allow his mother to deal with this situation on her own, but he had to set things straight with Arabella and he had to stay in London if he was to do that.

He read the letter again. A shock like this would have a devastating effect on his mother. He could not leave her to cope alone. He had to return to his Surrey estate.

In haste, he penned another letter to Arabella, told her how reluctant he was to leave London until they had sorted out their problems, but that his mother needed his immediate help. Then he asked his valet to pack his bags. He would have to get the next train back to Surrey.

But the last thing he did before he left was to remind all the servants that if any mail arrived for him, it had to be forwarded on to his estate— immediately.

The stack of unopened letters was mounting up. Arabella just couldn't bring herself to read them. She didn't want to hear any of his excuses, any of his explanations. She had married a man with an insatiable sexual appetite. She had always known that; she just hadn't allowed herself to fully accept what that implied.

And it wouldn't have mattered quite so much if she hadn't been so foolish as to go and fall in love with him. But the reality was she had. And this time it was even worse than when she had fallen in love with Arnold Emerson. That time she had not known what the man was really like. She had not realised that he loved money more than her. But with Oliver she knew exactly what sort of man he was, a man who was incapable of fidelity, and she had fallen in love with him anyway.

Unlike Arnold, he had not lied to her. He had let her know from the moment they met exactly what he was like. But her heart had chosen to ignore the facts. Ignore them until Lady Bufford had forced her to face cold, hard reality.

As angry and as upset as she was, she had no right to condemn Oliver for being the man he was. She could only condemn herself for falling in love with him.

And that had never been part of the arrangement.

If their marriage *had* remained one in name only, perhaps she could have forgiven him going to Lady Bufford's bed on their wedding night. Perhaps.

Although the thought that any man could humiliate his wife in such a way was more than she could countenance. It was only one night, for goodness sake. Could he not sleep alone for one night to avoid humiliating his new wife? It would seem not.

She picked up the pile of letters and looked at the embossed envelopes bearing Oliver's family crest, two rampant stags holding a shield.

She threw them back on the desk, causing the pile to scatter. A rampant stag—how appropriate. She shook her head and gave a humourless laugh. That stag was so rampant he couldn't go one night without finding a woman to satisfy his need to rut.

No, she would not read his letters. If she was to protect her heart, she would have nothing to do with him, ever again.

Forcing herself to ignore Oliver's scattered letters she picked up the other pile, the letters she had actually opened, the ones from well-wishers who had seen the play. That was what she should be focusing on. She should be celebrating her success, not dwelling on her humiliation.

Among the letters were invitations from leading theatres inviting her to audition and several offers of parts in forthcoming productions. And, most prized of all, were letters of congratulations from Oscar Wilde and Arthur Sullivan of the famous duo Gilbert and Sullivan.

Yes, that was what she should be focusing on, not those other letters. She cast a disparaging glance at the disordered pile. His latest letters bore the post office stamps from Surrey.

Good. If he was now living in the country, he would not be turning up at the Limelight Theatre. She would not have to see him again. And she never wanted to see him again. Ever.

She continued to stare at the pile. If she was to never see Oliver again, then there was only one solution. She was going to have to formally end their marriage. There was no other way. While they remained married, they were still tied to each other. He would still be part of her life, whether she saw him or not. There was only one solution available. They would have to end this marriage. They would have to divorce.

She sat down in the nearest chair and took in the ramification of this decision.

It was not impossible. People did divorce, after all. It didn't happen very often, and when it did it certainly caused a scandal and was the subject of gossip for many years. People were still talking about the divorce of Lady Mordaunt and Sir Charles Mordaunt and that had happened twenty years ago. But then, that divorce had involved the Prince of Wales, and his letters to Harriet Mordaunt had been published in the *New York Times* in all their titillating detail. Arabella's divorce would not involve such notable people, but it would still be hard to divorce Oliver discreetly.

But what choice did she have? She could not stay married to Oliver. And their marriage had served its intended purpose. It had saved him from getting his just desserts from Lord Bufford and saved the Limelight Theatre from financial ruin.

The success of the play meant the theatre was safe. Even if her father withdrew all his funding or sold off the Limelight it would still survive. No one would lose their jobs.

Yes, it was time to put an end to her marriage.

She picked up a pen and pulled a sheet of paper from the desk drawer. Divorce was the only answer. The ensuing scandal would horrify her father and he quite possibly would never forgive her, but if she did not break completely with Oliver she would never move on. A clean break was essential if she was to put this marriage firmly behind her.

With new determination she dipped her pen in the ink bottle and, before she could debate the matter further she composed a straightforward letter to Oliver, informing him that she would be divorcing him, that their marriage had never been more than one of convenience and it had served its purpose. She also informed him she wanted nothing from him. Would make no claims on his estate, that she would enter into no further communication with him and would appreciate it if he did the same, and she would be consulting with a lawyer immediately.

When she had finished, she ran the blotter over the ink and read what she had written.

It was blunt, to the point, and that was all that was required.

That done, she picked up his letters, took them over to the empty fireplace, struck a match and watched them burn. She should have felt some satisfaction as the pages curled up, turned brown at the edges, then burst into flame, but she didn't.

It was the end. The end of her marriage. The end

of her time with Oliver. There was no denying how happy she had been when she was with him. But there was also no denying how much sorrow she had felt.

No, now that the blinkers were off her eyes and she could see him for who he truly was, she knew that if they remained married all she would feel from now onwards would be sorrow. And that was not something she could tolerate.

Rosie and Nellie had both argued that she should give Oliver a chance to explain. As much as she respected her friends' opinions, she knew she wouldn't do that. She could not trust herself. As soon as she saw him her resolve was certain to falter. One look at that handsome face would cause her to forget her pain, her humiliation, just so she could have him back in her life again.

She turned her back on the still-smouldering letters, pushed the bell for the footman and handed him the letter.

She had made the right decision. There was no going back now.

Chapter Twenty-Two

The lawyer listened politely while Arabella detailed her reasons for wanting to divorce Oliver, then drew in a long, deep breath and stared at her from behind his large mahogany desk stacked with thick legal books and piles of paper.

'I'm afraid, my dear, it's not as simple as that. While your husband could divorce you for adultery, the law does not make the same provisions for the wife. If you're to divorce your husband, then you'll have to prove he's not only committed adultery, but also subjected you to unbearable levels of cruelty.'

Arabella fought to hold back her tears. Surely spending your wedding night in your mistress's bed constituted cruelty, but it seemed the law did not see things this way.

'Another option is an annulment.'

She blinked to clear her eyes and sat up straighter. 'Yes, let's do that then.' That way they could also hopefully avoid a scandal while still putting an end to this farce of a marriage.

'Of course, you'd have to prove that the marriage

was never consummated.' He waited for Arabella to answer.

'Oh, I see,' he said, presumably reacting to the fierce blushing that erupted on Arabella's cheeks. 'And while no one would have trouble believing that Oliver Huntsbury had committed adultery, I doubt that any court would believe he had not consummated his marriage.' He gave a small chuckle before his face resumed its serious, professional look.

'Another option is you could return to your homeland. I believe in some States a divorce is much easier to procure than it is in England.' He chuckled again. 'I've even heard that some of them are making quite a business out of it. South Dakota is getting a reputation for people moving there to get a divorce they wouldn't be able to get anywhere else and the hotels are doing a roaring trade.'

Once again his face resumed its serious countenance. 'If you're determined to divorce, then going back to America might be your best option. But really, my dear, I think you should think long and hard about getting a divorce. It rarely goes well for the woman. Consider what happened to Lady Mordaunt. She was sent to an asylum, the courts taking a dim view of women having relations with men other than their husband, particularly as she had done so in daylight hours. I believe the poor woman is still locked away and other women have been shunned by society, even when they're the aggrieved party. Perhaps you should consider doing what so many others have done before you—live as if you're divorced even though on paper you're still married.'

Arabella pulled herself out of the leather chair and

shook hands with the lawyer. He hadn't been much help, but that wasn't his fault, it was these unfair laws that made life so hard for women. But she would not give up. As she walked down the stairs and out on to the busy streets her determination increased with every step she took.

She would do anything that was required to end this marriage. If it meant she had to return to America to get her divorce, then that was exactly what she would do.

But she needed to put all that aside for now. She had a matinee performance to prepare for.

Returning to her dressing room, she went through her deep breathing routine to try to clear her mind and still her nerves. She had to put everything the lawyer had said out of her mind. She had to forget all about Oliver and get in character, something that was becoming harder and harder to do.

The continuing stress was making her nerves so bad that it was affecting her health. She wasn't sleeping properly, was hardly eating and was constantly restless. No wonder she felt so unwell.

And she could not afford to be ill. Now that she was to be a fully independent woman, with no financial support from either a father or a husband, she would need to remain fit and strong if she was to earn her own income.

She continued with her breathing exercises, but they seemed to be having the opposite effect to the one intended. Instead of stilling her nerves, those pesky butterflies in her stomach were becoming more agitated. Her stomach clenched. She felt clammy and nausea swept through her.

This was the worst case of nerves she had ever experienced. She rose quickly from her seat, upsetting her make-up kit, rushed out of the dressing room and ran down the corridor to the bathroom.

Flora was waiting for her when she emerged, carrying a wash bowl and jug of warm water.

'I'm sorry about that,' Arabella said, wiping her mouth. 'I'm not usually this bad, but…you know…'

Flora smiled and handed her a flannel. While Arabella was washing her face Flora gently ran her hand up and down her spine.

'Never mind, Arabella,' she said in a conciliatory voice. 'You're not the first actress who has been with child while on stage and your costume is loose enough to hide your growing belly.'

Arabella stopped, then slowly lowered the flannel from the back of her neck. She stared at Flora and shook her head. 'No, I'm not…it's just… I'm just…'

Flora raised her eyebrows and tilted her head.

Could she be? She had put her mood swings, her fatigue and her tiredness down to the situation with Oliver. She had even decided her courses had stopped because she was so upset and worried about her plans to divorce him. And being sick, well, that was just nerves, wasn't it?

She could not be pregnant, not now.

The flannel dropped to the floor as her hands shot to her face to cover her mouth. This was a disaster. Of course she was pregnant. Pregnant by a man she didn't want to be with, a man she was going to divorce. A man she knew that, despite his faults, would insist on supporting her, would insist on being a father to his child.

She wanted to be free of him, but now she never would be.

It was worse than Oliver had expected. Not only had one of his father's mistresses arrived unannounced at Somerfeld Manor with her child in tow, a child that bore an uncanny similarity to the late Duke, but she had also informed his mother about all the other illegitimate children the errant Duke had fathered.

His mother had been totally bereft. Her illusions about her husband had been well and truly shattered, and Oliver was at a loss as to how he could repair the damage.

All he could do was to stay with his mother, to comfort her, to try to remind her of all the good times they had had as a family, all the things about her husband she had loved.

And his mother's crisis meant he could not leave her. He could not return to London and solve the crisis in his own marriage. He had continued to write to Arabella, to beg her to explain why she had left him, to let him know what he had done wrong and how he could repair any damage he had done.

But she had not replied. When a letter finally did arrive, its contents were most definitely not what he had expected.

Although he had been anxious to read the letter, he had forced himself to remain calm, to not snatch the letter off the footman's tray and rip it open to get at the contents. Instead he had walked to his desk, sat down and, with a calm bearing he had not felt, opened the letter.

But when he had read the contents his feigned calmness had evaporated. He had screwed up the letter, thrown it across the room, had paced up and down, desperately trying to release the explosive energy coursing through his body. In his mind he had argued with her, told her how wrong she was, how she should give him a second chance, until he had finally calmed down and realised that she was right.

It *had* only ever been a marriage of convenience, to get her out of a difficult situation and to save Lady Bufford's reputation, in danger of being destroyed by her bellicose husband.

And hadn't he always told himself that Arabella deserved someone better than him? Well, with their marriage over she had a chance to find that someone.

He had unscrewed the letter and read it again, then written to his own lawyer informing him of the planned divorce and telling him that he would accept whatever blame Arabella's lawyer wanted to throw at him.

He had also urged his lawyer to do everything he could to keep the divorce out of the papers, to protect Arabella's reputation and to make the guilt solely his own, no matter what the cost. He could withstand any scandal a divorce might bring—it wasn't as if he had a good reputation to tarnish. His reputation had lost any lustre it might have had many years ago and society tended to be forgiving of a man, particularly a duke, no matter how he transgressed.

His short-term marriage was to come to an end. He should be grateful to his wife for granting him his freedom, but it was not a sense of gratitude and freedom that filled Oliver's mind as the days passed by. Instead the world seemed to have turned a dull shade of grey.

But there was one ray of hope in an otherwise desolate landscape. During the weeks he had spent at Somerfeld Manor his mother had slowly started to get over the shock of knowing her husband wasn't the man she thought he was. He wouldn't tell her of the forthcoming divorce. She did not need to hear anything that might cause her to suffer a setback. But he knew he would have to eventually. She had asked repeatedly about Arabella and told him how much she was looking forward to seeing her delightful daughter-in-law again. All he could tell her was that Arabella was very busy with the play so was unable to get away—not entirely a lie.

As his mother's strength came back, she had even started to ask questions about the children her husband had fathered. She wanted to know their names, where they lived, what provisions had been made for them and what sort of people they were.

It seemed his mother had more inner strength than he had ever given her credit for.

She also approved of the fact that Oliver was ensuring they were all well looked after and eventually suggested that perhaps they could be invited to the Somerfeld estate, which was their family home after all.

Once this idea had entered her head, she became quite invigorated by the prospect of filling the Somerfeld estate with the sound of children's voices. It was obvious his mother was well on the way to recovery.

He wished he could say the same about himself. His lawyer had received no correspondence about the divorce, so all Oliver could do was wait. In the meantime he had decided to keep himself secreted away at his estate. During the day he took long walks with his mother, around the estate, and in the evenings, instead of partying, he could be found seated in his study, reading through the books that had not been touched for many years. He had no interest in seeing anyone else, no interest in entertaining or being entertained. It would be hard to believe if it wasn't actually happening, but the Duke of Somerfeld was becoming a hermit.

He doubted if he would leave the estate again until he had to go to London for the divorce. He just wished he was able to protect Arabella from any adverse publicity. His lawyer had informed him he would be unable to keep it a secret and there would be nothing he could do once it went to court and was in the public domain.

Oliver knew the newspapers would eat up such scandal, knowing that coverage of a divorce between a duke and an American actress would sell scores of newspapers and keep the readership entertained for many weeks. But as long as he kept a low profile, he would do nothing to add to the scandal and the upset that it might cause Arabella.

Returning from another long walk, he saw a carriage parked in front of the house. No one had been invited and his heart sank as he approached and saw Lord Bufford's crest on the carriage door.

It was the last thing he wanted right now, to deal with that buffoon.

Entering the house, the footman told him that Lady Bufford had arrived and had been seated in the blue drawing room.

Oliver was unsure whether that was better or worse news. Violet's company was also something he could do without right now.

As soon as he entered, she stood up and rushed towards him. 'You cannot, will not, involve me in this divorce,' she said in a garbled rush. 'There's already gossip about what your wife plans to do and I cannot get caught up in such a scandal. My husband would disown me. I'd be ruined. You cannot do this to me, Oliver. I beseech you, please, keep my name out of this.'

Oliver took her arm and gently led her to the nearest chair. 'My divorce has nothing to do with you, Violet. You won't be involved. Why would you even think that you might be?'

She sat down, but her hands continued to clasp and unclasp in an agitated manner. 'Well, I was your lover once, or have you forgotten?'

Oliver took a seat opposite her. 'That was before I was married, adultery has to occur after the marriage. You have nothing to worry about, Violet. Your name won't be mentioned.'

She stood again and paced the room. 'Well, you say that, but can you be so sure your wife won't say that you committed adultery with me?'

Oliver walked over to the mantelpiece. She was being ridiculous. She would not be involved in his divorce, but it was also obvious she needed reassurance. 'Arabella is not like that. And in the unlikely event that her lawyer did try to say we were having an affair, which I'm sure he won't, he would need to produce proof and no such proof exists.'

She turned and faced him, her hands clenched, her lips pinched. 'Well, your wife could say that I told her we were having an affair.' Her clenched hands tightened their grip and she resumed pacing. 'And then there's that stupid powder-room attendant. She heard it all. They could call her as a witness. I'd be ruined.' She sank down into a chair and gripped the sides of her head. 'If this was all made public, my husband would divorce *me*. I'd have nothing. I'd be shunned by society. You have to make sure she doesn't say anything.'

'What are you saying?' Oliver asked, his teeth clenched together. 'What did you say to Arabella? What did the attendant hear?'

'What?' Looking up at him, she saw his expression and gave a small laugh. 'Oh, don't look at me like that. It was just a bit of fun. On the night you were all celebrating at the Savoy. She was looking so smug, and you and her were so cosy, I decided to play a little trick on her. It was all a bit of foolishness at the time, but it's come back to bite me and I have to put it right. You have to put it right. I can't be dragged through the divorce courts.'

'What...did...you...say...to... Arabella?' Oliver asked, slowly enunciating each word.

'Oh, I told her that on your wedding night after you'd deflowered her you came to my bed. I saw her walking in the garden early in the morning after your wedding night and I heard through the servants that you and she had awoken in separate beds, so I knew something had gone wrong and I thought I'd wipe that smug look off her face. But please, Oliver, promise me that nothing that I said to her will come out in court.'

Without answering, Oliver left the room, jumped into Lady Bufford's carriage and ordered the driver to take him to the train station.

Chapter Twenty-Three

Oliver wasted no time. The moment the train pulled into the station, he leapt out, ran down the platform to the waiting cabs and ordered the driver to take him straight to the Limelight Theatre. He knew there was no need to hurry. Arabella would still be on stage and he wouldn't be able to speak to her until after her performance, but still he urged the driver to make haste. His heart was pumping so hard and his body was coiled tight like a spring. He was incapable of keeping still, incapable of slowing down. It was as if by constant motion he could speed up time.

He arrived at the Limelight Theatre and rushed down the alleyway and through the backstage entrance. Then he was forced to wait. He had no choice. But he was finding it impossible to stay still. For what felt like an interminable amount of time he paced backwards and forward, and repeatedly looked at his fob watch, the hands of which seemed to be moving unnaturally slowly.

Once again, he rehearsed what he was going to say. He didn't know if informing her of what Violet

Bufford had told him would make a difference. There might be other reasons why she wanted to divorce him—after all, he was hardly the sort of man a sensible woman would want to remain married to—but he had to try. He had to let her know he would not treat her in such a disrespectful manner.

When he heard the thunderous sound of the audience's final applause, he quickly walked through the backstage area to wait in the wings. To his mounting frustration, he had to endure a seemingly endless round of curtain calls. Once he would have been so proud of the ongoing accolades his wife was receiving, and he was still proud, he just wished the audience would hurry up and finish expressing their appreciation.

Finally, the cast came off stage, all chattering excitedly, all, that is, except his wife, her face inexplicably forlorn. She saw him and stopped in her tracks, her eyes wide, her body rigid, as if a wild animal was cutting off her path.

'Bella,' he said gently, 'I need to talk to you. Please, can you just give me a few minutes of your time?'

She gave him a wary, sideways glance. 'I don't believe we have anything to discuss. And anything you want to say to me can be said through our lawyers.'

'We do need to talk, Bella,' he pleaded. 'I've heard something that changes everything.'

Her shoulders slumped and she released a sigh of exasperation. 'I suppose you were bound to find out eventually, but it makes no difference. I still want a divorce. We'll work out the details later.'

He stepped towards her. 'Please, Bella, hear me

out. If you hear what I have to say, it might change things between us.'

She shook her head. 'No, Oliver. I still want a divorce. But I'm sure you'll want to be involved in our child's life. I won't stop that, but I don't want you involved in my life.'

Oliver stared at his wife as if she was speaking a foreign language. 'Child? What child?'

She tilted her head and stared at him; her gaze still wary. 'Isn't that why you're here, because you've heard that I'm with child?'

He struggled to breathe as he stared at her, trying to take in the implication of what she had just said. She was with child. He was going to be a father, something he had vowed would never happen. It was one of the two vows he had made to himself as a young man, so he could be sure of never hurting anyone the way his father had hurt so many. He had also promised that he would never marry. He'd already broken that vow when he'd married Arabella. Now he had broken the second vow. He was no better than his father after all. But he had tried to be careful, hadn't he? Hadn't he always withdrawn when they made love so that this would not happen?

He closed his eyes and drew in a strained breath. No, he hadn't. Not every time. Selfishly there had been times he had thought only of his own pleasure and had let his desire to be as close as possible to her override any thought of the consequences.

He opened his eyes. And now she was pregnant, pregnant with his child. He was going to be a father. Oliver smiled at the thought.

He was going to be a father.

His smile grew wider. Arabella was having his child. This beautiful, talented woman was going to be the mother of his child.

This was not bad news. Not bad news at all. It was the best news he had ever heard. 'Bella, that's wonderful. You're going to be a wonderful mother and don't worry about your acting career. After all, Lillie Langtry and Sarah Bernhardt both continued acting after they had children. If they can do it, then the fabulously talented Arabella Huntsbury can do it as well.' He knew he was babbling, but he couldn't stop. 'And my mother is going to love being a grandmother. This is the best news.'

She continued to look at him sideways, her expression still wary. 'You didn't know about the child?'

'No, but I couldn't be happier. You've made me a very happy man.'

'So why are you here?'

He tried to stop smiling, but couldn't. They were going to have a child together. He wanted to shout it out so all the world could hear. But that wasn't why he was here. He needed to concentrate. He forced his smiling face to take on a more serious demeanour. 'Violet Bufford visited me at Somerfeld Manor. She was worried that she might get caught up in the divorce proceedings.'

'Oh, I see.' She pushed past him and walked quickly down the corridor, her body rigid.

He rushed after her. 'Bella, we must talk. You must listen to me.'

She increased her walking pace. 'I don't have to listen to you and I certainly don't have to discuss your mistress's worries.'

He gently took her arms to halt her progress. 'Bella, please listen to me.'

She looked down at his hand, her face tight with disapproval. He was about to release her, but changed his mind. He would not let her flee before he had a chance to explain. 'I'm sorry, this is not coming out the way I meant. I rehearsed what I was going to say all the way here, but now I've made a mess of things.'

'Yes, you have,' she said, pulling against his grip.

'Violet Bufford lied to you,' he blurted out before she could pull away. 'She made up that story to hurt you. Of course I *didn't* spend our wedding night in her bed. I spent it lying in my own bed, staring at the door to your room. I didn't sleep. I just tossed and turned all night. All I could think about was you, so close but so unattainable.'

'Lady Bufford lied?' She stopped pulling against his grip and looked up at him.

'Yes, she lied. I most certainly wasn't thinking about her on our wedding night, or any other woman. In fact, I haven't thought of any other woman since I first kissed you in this very building.'

He released her arm and stared at her, the implication of his words hitting him. 'That's also true,' he said, hardly able to believe it himself. 'I haven't thought of another woman since I first saw you. Unbelievable.' He smiled in amazed joy. 'You're the only woman I ever think about. The only woman I want. The only woman I will ever want.' He looked down at her and shook his head. 'Bella, it seems I've fallen in love with you.'

She stared up at him, his own astonishment reflected in her face.

'Of course I've fallen in love with you.' He laughed with relief. 'That explains everything. It explains why I think about you the moment I wake up in the morning and continue to think about you until I fall asleep at night. Why I dream about you every night. It's because I love you.'

'You love me?' She whispered her question, staring up at him wide eyed.

'Yes, I love you,' he repeated, certain that he would never tire of saying those three words. 'When we said our wedding vows, I promised to forsake all others and that's exactly what I've done. I've forsaken all women not just in act, but in thought as well. Bella, you've done what I had once thought would be impossible. You have changed me, reformed me, made me the man I've always wanted to be, but thought I couldn't. Bella, I love you and I want to marry you. Will you marry me?'

'You…what…will I what?'

'I love you and I want to marry you. Bella, will you marry me?'

Her blue eyes still enormous, she shook her head. 'What? What are you talking about? We're already married. It was our divorce we were discussing.'

'But I don't want to divorce you. I want to marry you.'

'But…but…'

He pulled himself together. With the announcement of the baby and the realisation that he was in love he had lost track of what he was meant to be saying and he knew he was rambling. 'Why do you want to divorce me? Is it because you don't trust me? Is it because of Violet Bufford's lies? Because that's all they are, Bella, lies. Violet Bufford is an unhappy woman in an unhappy marriage. She wanted to ruin our happiness and she almost succeeded.'

She stared at him. 'But she said…she was so convincing… I thought—'

'And I can understand why you believed her. I can see why you thought a man like me would do something like that. I can see why you thought I could be so cruel and so selfish.' It was true. Violet Bufford had indeed lied, but Arabella had believed her lies because she knew he was capable of such despicable behaviour. That spoke volumes about the sort of man he was, a man who was certainly not worthy of her love. Perhaps he *was* a fool to think a woman like Arabella could ever love a man like him, even if he did love her entirely, with his mind, body and soul.

She placed her hand gently on his arm. 'You're not a cruel man, or a selfish one, Oliver,' she said quietly. 'You care about people. You're a loving son to your mother. And there's all those women and children you support. You even married me to get me out of a difficult situation with my father. A bad man would not have done that.'

She looked up at him with those soft blue eyes. 'And I realise now that of course Lady Bufford was lying. You would never do anything that cruel. You would never humiliate anyone in the way I thought you had humiliated me. I judged you harshly because I misjudged a man once before, a man I thought I loved, and I had been hurt as a result. I didn't want to be hurt again so I chose to believe Lady Bufford's lies.'

Hope blossomed inside him. 'Does that mean you

are willing to give me another chance, to give us another chance?' He clasped her hand in both of his. 'If you will, then I promise you, I will do everything in my power to be worthy of you. I have enough love for you to make it work and I already love our child, and perhaps if I prove myself you will come to love me the way I love you.'

She bit the edge of her lip. 'You *are* a worthy man, Oliver, you always have been. And, well… I suppose I love you as well,' she said in a quiet voice.

Hope flourished in Oliver's heart, making him feel light and buoyant. He put his hand to his ear as if he was hard of hearing. 'What was that? What did you say? Something about love?'

Her smile grew wider. 'Oh, all right. It's true. Yes, I'm in love with you as well. I think I started falling in love with you the first time you kissed me and that love has continued to grow. Yes, I love you, Oliver Huntsbury.'

It was exactly what Oliver wanted to hear. He picked her up, twirled her around before kissing her. 'And I love you, Arabella, with my heart and soul. I love being with you, laughing with you, talking with you and, of course, making love to you.'

A group of giggling actresses pushed past them and he lowered her slowly to the ground, his hands still around her waist.

'But if you're going to give me a second chance, then let me do this properly.' He dropped to one knee and took her hand in his. 'Arabella, would you do me the honour of becoming my wife? My real wife. I want to marry you, to cherish you and love you until death do us part.'

Arabella giggled. 'Well, I *do* want to marry you, but I'm already married, and I've already promised to stay with *him* until death do us part.'

'Oh, *him*, that man was never good enough for you, but I promise you I will be.'

'You already are, Oliver,' she laughed, pulling him to his feet.

With that he lifted her up and kissed her again, to the resounding applause of the cast who had emerged from their dressing rooms, all eager to see the real-life drama being played out before them.

Epilogue

Arabella took her bow, revelling in the applause of the ecstatic audience. When her run at the Limelight Theatre had finished, she'd taken up the offer to appear in the latest Gilbert and Sullivan production.

Flora had been right, she had been able to act through her confinement, although she doubted that would have happened without the support of her loving husband. Oliver had told her there was no reason why she couldn't have it all, motherhood and an acting career. And when their daughter, Olivia, was born he had been true to his word.

He had not only acted as her theatrical agent, but had also been a doting father, not to mention a wonderful husband and lover.

Arabella bowed again. As much as she was enjoying the success of the play, she was anxious to get back to her family. A family that not only included her husband and child, but stretched the length of the country. Now that Oliver's mother had discovered just how many children her husband had fathered she had been determined to include them all. It meant baby

Olivia was now part of a large extended family, with a multitude of doting uncles and aunts.

Even Arabella's father had joined the family, rather than continuing to seclude himself away in New York, buried in the world of finance.

As soon as Arabella had sent word that she was with child Mr van Haven had left New York and returned to England.

His reaction to her pregnancy had taken her by surprise. She had seen real fear on his face and throughout her pregnancy he had been constantly concerned about her well-being, wanting to call the doctor on an almost daily basis in reaction to a raft of imagined ailments.

Eventually she had asked him what was wrong, why he was behaving so out of character. After much prodding he had told her how her mother's death, as a result of complications following childbirth, had devastated him. Arabella's pregnancy had brought back all those emotions that his wife's death had caused, emotions that he had buried for the last twenty-one years. With tears in his eyes he apologised for the way he had closed down, had never been a true father to her, but he had been so scared of ever exposing himself to love again, and the pain it could cause, that he couldn't even show love to his only daughter. Instead he had focused solely on making more and more money, trying to fill the void left by his wife's death, but all that had done was make him more dead inside, had meant he had missed out on so much.

But he was making up for it now. Just like Oliver's mother, he too had become a doting grandparent. The two grandparents were spending so much time together Oliver and Arabella were beginning to wonder whether wedding bells might be chiming again in the near future.

A stagehand presented Arabella with a large bouquet of flowers as she took her final bow and departed the stage.

If they did marry, it would be the third marriage in the family. Oliver had insisted that they hold another marriage service, one that was a celebration rather than a mere contract. They had held it at the estate, with only his mother and the Duke and Duchess of Knightsbrook in attendance. It might not have been a real wedding, like the official wedding they had held in the church, but it had felt more real and had been the happiest day of Arabella's life. Up until the day she'd given birth, that is. Then she'd had the joy of becoming a mother and, since then, every day had become even more of a joy than the day before.

* * * * *